New Arabian Nights

Yours ever affectionately
R. L. Stevenson

New Arabian Nights

Robert Louis Stevenson

Shambhala
Boston & London
1986

SHAMBHALA PUBLICATIONS, INC.
314 DARTMOUTH STREET
BOSTON, MASSACHUSETTS 02116

9 8 7 6 5 4 3 2 1

First Shambhala edition
Printed in the United States of America
Distributed in the United States by Random House
and in Canada by Random House of Canada Ltd.

Cover art © 1986 by William Gilkerson

Library of Congress Cataloging-in-Publication Data
Stevenson, Robert Louis, 1850–1894.
  New Arabian nights.
  1. Adventure stories, Scottish. I. Title.
PR5484.N5 1986 823'.8 86-12291
ISBN 0-87773-382-1 (pbk.)

CONTENTS

THE SUICIDE CLUB:

STORY OF THE YOUNG MAN WITH THE CREAM
TARTS . . . . . . 11 *PAGE*

THE STORY OF THE PHYSICIAN AND THE SARATOGA
TRUNK 45

THE ADVENTURE OF THE HANSOM CABS . . 74

THE RAJAH'S DIAMOND:

STORY OF THE BANDBOX 97

STORY OF THE YOUNG MAN IN HOLY ORDERS . 124

THE STORY OF THE HOUSE WITH THE GREEN
BLINDS 142

THE ADVENTURE OF PRINCE FLORIZEL AND A
DETECTIVE 176

THE PAVILION ON THE LINKS:

I. TELLS HOW I CAMPED IN GRADEN SEA-WOOD,
AND BEHELD A LIGHT IN THE PAVILION . 184

II. TELLS OF THE NOCTURNAL LANDING FROM THE
YACHT 191

III. TELLS HOW I BECAME ACQUAINTED WITH MY
WIFE 198

IV. TELLS IN WHAT A STARTLING MANNER I
LEARNED THAT I WAS NOT ALONE IN
GRADEN SEA-WOOD 208

V. TELLS OF AN INTERVIEW BETWEEN NORTH-
MOUR, CLARA, AND MYSELF . . . 216

VI. TELLS OF MY INTRODUCTION TO THE TALL
MAN 222

VII. TELLS HOW A WORD WAS CRIED THROUGH THE
PAVILION WINDOW 228

CONTENTS

		PAGE
VIII.	TELLS THE LAST OF THE TALL MAN	235
IX.	TELLS HOW NORTHMOUR CARRIED OUT HIS THREAT	242
A LODGING FOR THE NIGHT		249
THE SIRE DE MALÉTROIT'S DOOR		274
PROVIDENCE AND THE GUITAR		299

New Arabian Nights

THE SUICIDE CLUB

STORY OF THE YOUNG MAN WITH THE CREAM TARTS

DURING his residence in London, the accomplished Prince Florizel of Bohemia gained the affection of all classes by the seduction of his manner and by a well-considered generosity. He was a remarkable man even by what was known of him ; and that was but a small part of what he actually did. Although of a placid temper in ordinary circumstances, and accustomed to take the world with as much philosophy as any ploughman, the Prince of Bohemia was not without a taste for ways of life more adventurous and eccentric than that to which he was destined by his birth. Now and then, when he fell into a low humour, when there was no laughable play to witness in any of the London theatres, and when the season of the year was unsuitable to those field sports in which he excelled all competitors, he would summon his confidant and Master of the Horse, Colonel Geraldine, and bid him prepare himself against an evening ramble. The Master of the Horse was a young officer of a brave and even temerarious disposition. He greeted the news with delight, and hastened to make ready. Long practice and a varied acquaintance of life had given him a singular facility in disguise ; he could adapt, not only his face and bearing, but his voice and almost his thoughts, to those of any rank, character, or nation ; and in this way he diverted attention from the Prince, and sometimes gained admission for the pair into strange societies. The civil authorities were never taken into the secret of these adventures ; the imperturbable courage of the one and the ready invention and chivalrous devotion of the other had brought them through a score of dangerous passes ; and they grew in confidence as time went on.

One evening in March they were driven by a sharp fall of sleet into an Oyster Bar in the immediate neighbourhood of Leicester Square. Colonel Geraldine was dressed and painted to represent a person connected with the Press in reduced circumstances ; while the Prince had, as usual, travestied his appearance by the addition of false whiskers and a pair of large adhesive eyebrows. These lent him a shaggy and weather-beaten air, which, for one of his urbanity, formed the most impenetrable disguise. Thus equipped, the commander and his satellite sipped their brandy and soda in security.

The bar was full of guests, male and female; but though more than one of these offered to fall into talk with our adventurers, none of them promised to grow interesting upon a nearer acquaintance. There was nothing present but the lees of London and the commonplace of disrespectability ; and the Prince had already fallen to yawning, and was beginning to grow weary of the whole excursion, when the swing doors were pushed violently open, and a young man, followed by a couple of commissionaires, entered the bar. Each of the commissionaires carried a large dish of cream tarts under a cover, which they at once removed ; and the young man made the round of the company, and pressed these confections upon every one's acceptance with an exaggerated courtesy. Sometimes his offer was laughingly accepted ; sometimes it was firmly, or even harshly, rejected. In these latter cases the new-comer always ate the tart himself, with some more or less humorous commentary.

At last he accosted Prince Florizel.

"Sir," said he, with a profound obeisance, proffering the tart at the same time between his thumb and forefinger, "will you so far honour an entire stranger? I can answer for the quality of the pastry, having eaten two dozen and three of them myself since five o'clock."

"I am in the habit," replied the Prince, "of looking not so much to the nature of a gift as to the spirit in which it is offered."

"The spirit, sir," returned the young man, with another bow, "is one of mockery."

"Mockery!" repeated Florizel. "And whom do you propose to mock?"

"I am not here to expound my philosophy," replied the other, "but to distribute these cream tarts. If I mention that I heartily include myself in the ridicule of the transaction, I hope you will consider honour satisfied and condescend. If not, you will constrain me to eat my twenty-eighth, and I own to being weary of the exercise."

"You touch me," said the Prince, "and I have all the will in the world to rescue you from this dilemma, but upon one condition. If my friend and I eat your cakes—for which we have neither of us any natural inclination—we shall expect you to join us at supper by way of recompense."

The young man seemed to reflect.

"I have still several dozen upon hand," he said at last; "and that will make it necessary for me to visit several more bars before my great affair is concluded. This will take some time; and if you are hungry——"

The Prince interrupted him with a polite gesture.

"My friend and I will accompany you," he said; "for we have already a deep interest in your very agreeable mode of passing an evening. And now that the preliminaries of peace are settled, allow me to sign the treaty for both."

And the Prince swallowed the tart with the best grace imaginable.

"It is delicious," said he.

"I perceive you are a connoisseur," replied the young man.

Colonel Geraldine likewise did honour to the pastry ; and every one in that bar having now either accepted or refused his delicacies, the young man with the cream tarts led the way to another and similar establishment. The two commissionaires, who seemed to have grown accustomed to their absurd employment, followed immediately after ; and the Prince and the Colonel brought up the rear, arm in arm, and smiling to each other as they went. In this order the company visited two other taverns, where scenes were enacted of a like nature to that already described—some refusing, some accepting, the favours of this vagabond hospitality, and the young man himself eating each rejected tart.

On leaving the third saloon the young man counted his store. There were but nine remaining, three in one tray and six in the other.

"Gentlemen," said he, addressing himself to his two new followers, "I am unwilling to delay your supper. I am positively sure you must be hungry. I feel that I owe you a special consideration. And on this great day for me, when I am closing a career of folly by my most conspicuously silly action, I wish to behave handsomely to all who give me countenance. Gentlemen, you shall wait no longer. Although my constitution is shattered by previous excesses, at the risk of my life I liquidate the suspensory condition."

With these words he crushed the nine remaining tarts into his mouth, and swallowed them at a single movement each. Then, turning to the commissionaires, he gave them a couple of sovereigns.

"I have to thank you," said he, "for your extra-ordinary patience."

And he dismissed them with a bow apiece. For some seconds he stood looking at the purse from which he had just paid his assistants, then, with a laugh, he tossed it into the middle of the street, and signified his readiness for supper.

In a small French restaurant in Soho, which had enjoyed an exaggerated reputation for some little while, but had already begun to be forgotten, and in a private room up two pair of stairs, the three companions made a very elegant supper, and drank three or four bottles of champagne, talking the while upon indifferent subjects. The young man was fluent and gay, but he laughed louder than was natural in a person of polite breeding ; his hands trembled violently, and his voice took sudden and surprising inflections, which seemed to be independent of his will. The dessert had been cleared away, and all three had lighted their cigars, when the Prince addressed him in these words :—

"You will, I am sure, pardon my curiosity. What I have seen of you has greatly pleased but even more puzzled me. And though I should be loth to seem indiscreet, I must tell you that my friend and I are persons very well worthy to be entrusted with a secret. We have many of our own, which we are continually revealing to improper ears. And if, as I suppose, your story is a silly one, you need have no delicacy with us, who are two of the silliest men in England. My name is Godall, Theophilus Godall ; my friend is Major Alfred Hammersmith—or at least, such is the name by which he chooses to be known. We pass our lives entirely in the search for extravagant adventures ; and there is no extravagance with which we are not capable of sympathy."

"I like you, Mr. Godall," returned the young man ; "you inspire me with a natural confidence ; and I have

not the slightest objection to your friend the Major, whom
I take to be a nobleman in masquerade. At least, I am
sure he is no soldier."

The Colonel smiled at this compliment to the perfection of his art ; and the young man went on in a more
animated manner.

" There is every reason why I should not tell you my
story. Perhaps that is just the reason why I am going to
do so. At least, you seem so well prepared to hear a tale
of silliness that I cannot find it in my heart to disappoint
you. My name, in spite of your example, I shall keep to
myself. My age is not essential to the narrative. I am
descended from my ancestors by ordinary generation, and
from them I inherited the very eligible human tenement
which I still occupy and a fortune of three hundred
pounds a year. I suppose they also handed on to me a
harebrain humour, which it has been my chief delight to indulge. I received a good education. I can play the violin
nearly well enough to earn money in the orchestra of a
penny gaff, but not quite. The same remark applies to the
flute and the French horn. I learned enough of whist to
lose about a hundred a year at that scientific game. My
acquaintance with French was sufficient to enable me to
squander money in Paris with almost the same facility as
in London. In short, I am a person full of manly accomplishments. I have had every sort of adventure, including
a duel about nothing. Only two months ago I met a
young lady exactly suited to my taste in mind and body ;
I found my heart melt ; I saw that I had come upon my
fate at last, and was in the way to fall in love. But when
I came to reckon up what remained to me of my capital,
I found it amounted to something less than four hundred
pounds ! I ask you fairly—can a man who respects himself fall in love on four hundred pounds ? I concluded,
certainly not ; left the presence of my charmer, and
slightly accelerating my usual rate of expenditure, came

this morning to my last eighty pounds. This I divided into two equal parts; forty I reserved for a particular purpose; the remaining forty I was to dissipate before the night. I have passed a very entertaining day, and played many farces besides that of the cream tarts which procured me the advantage of your acquaintance; for I was determined, as I told you, to bring a foolish career to a still more foolish conclusion; and when you saw me throw my purse into the street the forty pounds were at an end. Now you know me as well as I know myself: a fool, but consistent in his folly; and, as I will ask you to believe, neither a whimperer nor a coward."

From the whole tone of the young man's statement it was plain that he harboured very bitter and contemptuous thoughts about himself. His auditors were led to imagine that his love affair was nearer his heart than he admitted, and that he had a design on his own life. The farce of the cream tarts began to have very much the air of a tragedy in disguise.

"Why, is this not odd," broke out Geraldine, giving a look to Prince Florizel, "that we three fellows should have met by the merest accident in so large a wilderness as London, and should be so nearly in the same condition?"

"How?" cried the young man. "Are you, too, ruined? Is this supper a folly like my cream tarts? Has the devil brought three of his own together for a last carouse?"

"The devil, depend upon it, can sometimes do a very gentlemanly thing," returned Prince Florizel; "and I am so much touched by this coincidence that, although we are not entirely in the same case, I am going to put an end to the disparity. Let your heroic treatment of the last cream tarts be my example."

So saying, the Prince drew out his purse and took from it a small bundle of bank-notes.

4—C

"You see, I was a week or so behind you, but I mean to catch you up and come neck-and-neck into the winning-post," he continued. " This," laying one of the notes upon the table, "will suffice for the bill. As for the rest——"

He tossed them into the fire, and they went up the chimney in a single blaze.

The young man tried to catch his arm, but as the table was between them his interference came too late.

"Unhappy man," he cried, "you should not have burned them all ! You should have kept forty pounds."

"Forty pounds ! " repeated the Prince. "Why, in heaven's name, forty pounds ? "

"Why not eighty ? " cried the Colonel; "for to my certain knowledge there must have been a hundred in the bundle."

" It was only forty pounds he needed," said the young man gloomily. "But without them there is no admission. The rule is strict. Forty pounds for each. Accursed life, where a man cannot even die without money ! "

The Prince and the Colonel exchanged glances.

"Explain yourself," said the latter. " I have still a pocket-book tolerably well lined, and I need not say how readily I should share my wealth with Godall. But I must know to what end : you must certainly tell us what you mean."

The young man seemed to awaken : he looked uneasily from one to the other, and his face flushed deeply.

"You are not fooling me ? " he asked. " You are indeed ruined men like me ? "

" Indeed, I am for my part," replied the Colonel.

" And for mine," said the Prince, " I have given you proof. Who but a ruined man would throw his notes into the fire ? The action speaks for itself."

" A ruined man—yes," returned the other suspiciously, "or else a millionaire."

"Enough, sir," said the Prince; "I have said so, and
I am not accustomed to have my word remain in doubt."

"Ruined?" said the young man. "Are you ruined,
like me? Are you, after a life of indulgence, come to such
a pass that you can only indulge yourself in one thing
more? Are you"—he kept lowering his voice as he went
on—"are you going to give yourselves that last indulgence? Are you going to avoid the consequences of your
folly by the one infallible and easy path? Are you going
to give the slip to the sheriff's officers of conscience by
the one open door?"

Suddenly he broke off and attempted to laugh.

"Here is your health!" he cried, emptying his glass,
"and good night to you, my merry ruined men."

Colonel Geraldine caught him by the arm as he was
about to rise.

"You lack confidence in us," he said, "and you are
wrong. To all your questions I make answer in the
affirmative. But I am not so timid, and can speak the
Queen's English plainly. We too, like yourself, have had
enough of life, and are determined to die. Sooner or
later, alone or together, we meant to seek out death and
beard him where he lies ready. Since we have met you,
and your case is more pressing, let it be to-night—and at
once—and, if you will, all three together. Such a penniless trio," he cried, "should go arm in arm into the halls
of Pluto, and give each other some countenance among
the shades!"

Geraldine had hit exactly on the manners and intona-
tions that became the part he was playing. The Prince
himself was disturbed, and looked over at his confidant
with a shade of doubt. As for the young man, the flush
came back darkly into his cheek, and his eyes threw
out a spark of light.

"You are the men for me!" he cried, with an almost
terrible gaiety. "Shake hands upon the bargain!" (his

hand was cold and wet). "You little know in what a company you will begin the march! You little know in what a happy moment for yourselves you partook of my cream tarts! I am only a unit, but I am a unit in an army. I know Death's private door. I am one of his familiars, and can show you into eternity without cere- mony and yet without scandal."

They called upon him eagerly to explain his meaning.

"Can you muster eighty pounds between you?" he demanded.

Geraldine ostentatiously consulted his pocket-book, and replied in the affirmative.

"Fortunate beings!" cried the young man. "Forty pounds is the entry-money of the Suicide Club."

"The Suicide Club," said the Prince, "why, what the devil is that?"

"Listen," said the young man; "this is the age of conveniences, and I have to tell you of the last perfection of the sort. We have affairs in different places; and hence railways were invented. Railways separated us infallibly from our friends; and so telegraphs were made that we might communicate speedily at great distances. Even in hotels we have lifts to spare us a climb of some hundred steps. Now, we know that life is only a stage to play the fool upon as long as the part amuses us. There was one more convenience lacking to modern com- fort: a decent, easy way to quit that stage; the back stairs to liberty; or, as I said this moment, Death's private door. This, my two fellow-rebels, is supplied by the Suicide Club. Do not suppose that you and I are alone, or even exceptional, in the highly reasonable desire that we profess. A large number of our fellowmen, who have grown heartily sick of the performance in which they are expected to join daily, and all their lives long, are only kept from flight by one or two considerations. Some have families who would be shocked, or even blamed, if the matter became public ; others have a weakness at heart and recoil from the circumstances of death. That is, to some extent, my own experience. I cannot put a pistol to my head and draw the trigger ; for something stronger than myself withholds the act ; and although I loathe life, I have not strength enough in my body to take hold of death and be done with it. For such as I, and for all who desire to be out of the coil without posthumous scandal, the Suicide Club has been inaugurated. How this has been managed, what is its history, or what may be its ramifications in other lands, I am myself uninformed ; and what I know of its constitution, I am not at liberty to communicate to you. To this extent, however, I am at your service. If you are truly tired of life, I will introduce you to-night to a meeting ; and if not to-night, at least some time within the week, you will be easily relieved of your existences. It is now (consulting his watch) eleven ; by half-past, at latest, we must leave this place ; so that you have half an hour before you to consider my proposal. It is more serious than a cream tart," he added, with a smile ; "and I suspect more palatable."

"More serious, certainly," returned Colonel Geraldine ; "and as it is so much more so, will you allow me five minutes' speech in private with my friend Mr. Godall ? "

"It is only fair," answered the young man. "If you will permit, I will retire."

"You will be very obliging," said the Colonel.

As soon as the two were alone—"What," said Prince Florizel, "is the use of this confabulation, Geraldine ? I see you are flurried, whereas my mind is very tranquilly made up. I will see the end of this."

"Your Highness," said the Colonel, turning pale ; "let me ask you to consider the importance of your life, not only to your friends, but to the public interest. 'If not to-night,' said this madman ; but supposing that to-night some irreparable disaster were to overtake your Highness's person, what, let me ask you, what would be my despair, and what the concern and disaster of a great nation ? "

" I will see the end of this," repeated the Prince in his most deliberate tones ; " and have the kindness, Colonel Geraldine, to remember and respect your word of honour as a gentleman.   Under no circumstances, recollect, nor without my special authority, are you to betray the incognito under which I choose to go abroad.   These were my commands, which I now reiterate.   And now," he added, " let me ask you to call for the bill."

Colonel Geraldine bowed in submission ; but he had a very white face as he summoned the young man of the cream tarts, and issued his directions to the waiter. The Prince preserved his undisturbed demeanour, and described a Palais-Royal farce to the young suicide with great humour and gusto.   He avoided the Colonel's appealing looks without ostentation, and selected another cheroot with more than usual care.   Indeed, he was now the only man of the party who kept any command over his nerves.

The bill was discharged, the Prince giving the whole change of the note to the astonished waiter ; and the three drove off in a four-wheeler.   They were not long upon the way before the cab stopped at the entrance to a rather dark court.   Here all descended.

After Geraldine had paid the fare, the young man turned, and addressed Prince Florizel as follows :—

" It is still time, Mr. Godall, to make good your escape into thraldom.   And for you too, Major Hammersmith.   Reflect well before you take another step ; and if your hearts say no—here are the cross-roads."

" Lead on, sir," said the Prince, " I am not the man to go back from a thing once said."

" Your coolness does me good," replied their guide. " I have never seen any one so unmoved at this conjuncture; and yet you are not the first whom I have escorted to this door. More than one of my friends has preceded me, where I knew I must shortly follow. But this is of no interest to you. Wait me here for only a few moments; I shall return as soon as I have arranged the preliminaries of your introduction."

And with that the young man, waving his hand to his companions, turned into the court, entered a doorway and disappeared.

"Of all our follies," said Colonel Geraldine in a low voice, "this is the wildest and most dangerous."

"I perfectly believe so," returned the Prince.

"We have still," pursued the Colonel, "a moment to ourselves. Let me beseech your Highness to profit by the opportunity and retire. The consequences of this step are so dark, and may be so grave, that I feel myself justified in pushing a little further than usual the liberty which your Highness is so condescending as to allow me in private."

"Am I to understand that Colonel Geraldine is afraid?" asked his Highness, taking his cheroot from his lips, and looking keenly into the other's face.

"My fear is certainly not personal," replied the other proudly; "of that your Highness may rest well assured."

"I had supposed as much," returned the Prince, with undisturbed good-humour; "but I was unwilling to remind you of the difference in our stations. No more—no more," he added, seeing Geraldine about to apologise; "you stand excused."

And he smoked placidly, leaning against a railing, until the young man returned.

"Well," he asked, "has our reception been arranged?"

"Follow me," was the reply. "The President will see you in the cabinet. And let me warn you to be frank in your answers. I have stood your guarantee ; but the club requires a searching inquiry before admission ; for the indiscretion of a single member would lead to the dispersion of the whole society for ever."

The Prince and Geraldine put their heads together for a moment. " Bear me out in this," said the one ; and " bear me out in that," said the other ; and by boldly taking up the characters of men with whom both were acquainted, they had come to an agreement in a twinkling, and were ready to follow their guide into the President's cabinet.

There were no formidable obstacles to pass. The outer door stood open ; the door of the cabinet was ajar ; and there, in a small but very high apartment, the young man left them once more.

" He will be here immediately," he said with a nod, as he disappeared.

Voices were audible in the cabinet through the folding-doors which formed one end ; and now and then the noise of a champagne cork, followed by a burst of laughter, intervened among the sounds of conversation. A single tall window looked out upon the river and the embankment ; and by the disposition of the lights they judged themselves not far from Charing Cross station. The furniture was scanty, and the coverings worn to the thread ; and there was nothing movable except a hand-bell in the centre of a round table, and the hats and coats of a considerable party hung round the wall on pegs.

"What sort of a den is this ? " said Geraldine.

" That is what I have come to see," replied the Prince. "If they keep live devils on the premises, the thing may grow amusing."

Just then the folding door was opened no more than was necessary for the passage of a human body ; and there entered at the same moment a louder buzz of talk, and the redoubtable President of the Suicide Club. The President was a man of fifty or upwards; large and rambling in his gait, with shaggy side whiskers, a bald top to his head, and a veiled grey eye, which now and then emitted a twinkle. His mouth, which embraced a large cigar, he kept continually screwing round and round and from side to side, as he looked sagaciously and coldly at the strangers. He was dressed in light tweeds, with his neck very open in a striped shirt collar; and carried a minute-book under one arm.

"Good-evening," said he, after he had closed the door behind him. "I am told you wish to speak with me."

"We have a desire, sir, to join the Suicide Club," replied the Colonel.

The President rolled his cigar about in his mouth.

"What is that?" he said abruptly.

"Pardon me," returned the Colonel, "but I believe you are the person best qualified to give us information on that point."

"I?" cried the President. "A Suicide Club? Come, come! this is a frolic for All Fools' Day. I can make allowances for gentlemen who get merry in their liquor; but let there be an end to this."

"Call your club what you will," said the Colonel; "you have some company behind these doors, and we insist on joining it."

"Sir," returned the President curtly, "you have made a mistake. This is a private house, and you must leave it instantly."

The Prince had remained quietly in his seat throughout this little colloquy; but now, when the Colonel looked over to him, as much as to say, "Take your answer and come away, for God's sake!" he drew his cheroot from his mouth, and spoke—

"I have come here," said he, "upon the invitation

of a friend of yours. He has doubtless informed you of my intention in thus intruding on your party. Let me remind you that a person in my circumstances has exceedingly little to bind him, and is not at all likely to tolerate much rudeness. I am a very quiet man, as a usual thing; but, my dear sir, you are either going to oblige me in the little matter of which you are aware, or you shall very bitterly repent that you ever admitted me to your ante-chamber."

The President laughed aloud.

"That is the way to speak," said he. " You are a man who is a man. You know the way to my heart, and can do what you like with me. Will you," he continued, addressing Geraldine, " will you step aside for a few minutes ? I shall finish first with your companion, and some of the club's formalities require to be fulfilled in private."

With the words he opened the door of a small closet, into which he shut the Colonel.

"I believe in you," he said to Florizel, as soon as they were alone; "but are you sure of your friend ? "

" Not so sure as I am of myself, though he has more cogent reasons," answered Florizel, " but sure enough to bring him here without alarm. He has had enough to cure the most tenacious man of life. He was cashiered the other day for cheating at cards."

"A good reason, I daresay," replied the President ; " at least, we have another in the same case, and I feel sure of him. Have you also been in the Service, may I ask ? "

" I have," was the reply ; "·but I was too lazy—I left it early."

" What is your reason for being tired of life ? " pursued the President.

" The same, as near as I can make out," answered the Prince : "unadulterated laziness."

The President started. " D—n it," said he, " you must have something better than that."

"I have no more money," added Florizel. "That is also a vexation, without doubt. It brings my sense of idleness to an acute point."

The President rolled his cigar round in his mouth for some seconds, directing his gaze straight into the eyes of this unusual neophyte ; but the Prince supported his scrutiny with unabashed good temper.

"If I had not a deal of experience," said the President at last, "I should turn you off. But I know the world ; and this much any way, that the most frivolous excuses for a suicide are often the toughest to stand by. And when I downright like a man, as I do you, sir, I would rather strain the regulation than deny him."

The Prince and the Colonel, one after the other, were subjected to a long and particular interrogatory : the Prince alone ; but Geraldine in the presence of the Prince, so that the President might observe the countenance of the one while the other was being warmly cross-examined. The result was satisfactory ; and the President, after having booked a few details of each case, produced a form of oath to be accepted. Nothing could be conceived more passive than the obedience promised, or more stringent than the terms by which the juror bound himself. The man who forfeited a pledge so awful could scarcely have a rag of honour or any of the consolations of religion left to him. Florizel signed the document, but not without a shudder ; the Colonel followed his example with an air of great depression. Then the President received the entry money ; and without more ado, introduced the two friends into the smoking-room of the Suicide Club.

The smoking-room of the Suicide Club was the same height as the cabinet into which it opened, but much larger, and papered from top to bottom with an imitation of oak wainscot. A large and cheerful fire and a number

of gas-jets illuminated the company. The Prince and his
follower made the number up to eighteen. Most of the
party were smoking, and drinking champagne ; a feverish
hilarity reigned, with sudden and rather ghastly pauses.

"Is this a full meeting ? " asked the Prince.

" Middling," said the President.—" By the way," he
added, " if you have any money, it is usual to offer some
champagne. It keeps up a good spirit, and is one of my
own little perquisites."

" Hammersmith," said Florizel, " I may leave the
champagne to you."

And with that he turned away and began to go round
among the guests. Accustomed to play the host in the
highest circles, he charmed and dominated all whom he
approached ; there was something at once winning and
authoritative in his address ; and his extraordinary coolness gave him yet another distinction in this half-maniacal
society. As he went from one to another he kept both his
eyes and ears open, and soon began to gain a general idea
of the people among whom he found himself. As in all
other places of resort, one type predominated : people in
the prime of youth, with every show of intelligence and
sensibility in their appearance, but with little promise of
strength or the quality that makes success. Few were
much above thirty, and not a few were still in their teens.
They stood, leaning on tables and shifting on their feet ;
sometimes they smoked extraordinarily fast, and sometimes they let their cigars go out ; some talked well, but
the conversation of others was plainly the result of nervous
tension, and was equally without wit or purport. As each
new bottle of champagne was opened, there was a mani-
fest improvement in gaiety. Only two were seated—one
in a chair in the recess of the window, with his head
hanging and his hands plunged deep into his trousers
pockets, pale, visibly moist with perspiration, saying never
a word, a very wreck of soul and body ; the other sat on

the divan close by the chimney, and attracted notice by
a trenchant dissimilarity from all the rest. He was probably upwards of forty, but he looked fully ten years
older; and Florizel thought he had never seen a man
more naturally hideous, nor one more ravaged by disease
and ruinous excitements. He was no more than skin
and bone, was partly paralysed, and wore spectacles of
such unusual power that his eyes appeared through the
glasses greatly magnified and distorted in shape. Except
the Prince and the President, he was the only person in
the room who preserved the composure of ordinary life.

There was little decency among the members of the
club. Some boasted of the disgraceful actions, the consequences of which had reduced them to seek refuge
in death; and the others listened without disapproval.
There was a tacit understanding against moral judg-
ments; and whoever passed the club doors enjoyed
already some of the immunities of the tomb. They
drank to each other's memories, and to those of notable
suicides in the past. They compared and developed
their different views of death—some declaring that it
was no more than blackness and cessation; others full
of a hope that that very night they should be scaling
the stars and commercing with the mighty dead.

"To the eternal memory of Baron Trenck, the type of
suicides!" cried one. "He went out of a small cell into
a smaller, that he might come forth again to freedom."

"For my part," said a second, " I wish no more than a
bandage for my eyes and cotton for my ears. Only they
have no cotton thick enough in this world."

A third was for reading the mysteries of life in a future
state; and a fourth professed that he would never have
joined the club if he had not been induced to believe in
Mr. Darwin.

"I could not bear," said this remarkable suicide, "to
be descended from an ape."

Altogether, the Prince was disappointed by the bearing and conversation of the members.

"It does not seem to me," he thought, "a matter for so much disturbance. If a man has made up his mind to kill himself, let him do it, in God's name, like a gentleman. This flutter and big talk is out of place."

In the meanwhile Colonel Geraldine was a prey to the blackest apprehensions; the club and its rules were still a mystery, and he looked round the room for some one who should be able to set his mind at rest. In this survey his eye lighted on the paralytic person with the strong spectacles; and seeing him so exceedingly tranquil, he besought the President, who was going in and out of the room under a pressure of business, to present him to the gentleman on the divan.

The functionary explained the needlessness of all such formalities within the club, but nevertheless presented Mr. Hammersmith to Mr. Malthus.

Mr. Malthus looked at the Colonel curiously, and then requested him to take a seat upon his right.

"You are a new-comer," he said, "and wish information? You have come to the proper source. It is two years since I first visited this charming club."

The Colonel breathed again. If Mr. Malthus had frequented the place for two years there could be little danger for the Prince in a single evening. But Geraldine was none the less astonished, and began to suspect a mystification.

"What!" cried he, "two years! I thought—but indeed I see I have been made the subject of a pleasantry."

"By no means," replied Mr. Malthus mildly. "My case is peculiar. I am not, properly speaking, a suicide at all; but, as it were, an honorary member. I rarely visit the club twice in two months. My infirmity and the kindness of the President have procured me these little immunities, for which besides I pay at an advanced rate. Even as it is, my luck has been extraordinary."

" I am afraid," said the Colonel, " that I must ask you to be more explicit. You must remember that I am still most imperfectly acquainted with the rules of the club."

" An ordinary member who comes here in search of death, like yourself," replied the paralytic, " returns every evening until fortune favours him. He can even, if he is penniless, get board and lodging from the President : very fair, I believe, and clean, although, of course, not luxurious ; that could hardly be, considering the exiguity (if I may so express myself) of the subscription. And then the President's company is a delicacy in itself."

" Indeed ! " cried Geraldine, " he had not greatly prepossessed me."

" Ah ! " said Mr. Malthus, " you do not know the man : the drollest fellow ! What stories ! What cynicism ! He knows life to admiration, and, between ourselves, is probably the most corrupt rogue in Christendom."

" And he also," asked the Colonel, " is a permanency— like yourself, if I may say so without offence ? "

" Indeed, he is a permanency in a very different sense from me," replied Mr. Malthus. " I have been graciously spared, but I must go at last. Now he never plays. He shuffles and deals for the club, and makes the necessary arrangements. That man, my dear Mr. Hammersmith, is the very soul of ingenuity. For three years he has pursued in London his useful and, I think I may add, his artistic calling ; and not so much as a whisper of suspicion has been once aroused. I believe himself to be inspired. You doubtless remember the celebrated case, six months ago, of the gentleman who was accidentally poisoned in a chemist's shop ? That was one of the least rich, one of the least racy, of his notions ; but then, how simple ! and how safe ! "

"You astound me," said the Colonel. "Was that unfortunate gentleman one of the——" He was about to say "victims"; but bethinking himself in time, he substituted—"members of the club?"

In the same flash of thought it occurred to him that Mr. Malthus himself had not at all spoken in the tone of one who is in love with death; and he added hurriedly—

"But I perceive I am still in the dark. You speak of shuffling and dealing; pray, for what end? And since you seem rather unwilling to die than otherwise, I must own that I cannot conceive what brings you here at all."

"You say truly that you are in the dark," replied Mr. Malthus with more animation. "Why, my dear sir, this club is the temple of intoxication. If my enfeebled health could support the excitement more often, you may depend upon it I should be more often here. It requires all the sense of duty engendered by a long habit of ill-health and careful regimen, to keep me from excess in this, which is, I may say, my last dissipation. I have tried them all, sir," he went on, laying his hand on Geraldine's arm, "all, without exception, and I declare to you, upon my honour, there is not one of them that has not been grossly and untruthfully overrated. People trifle with love. Now, I deny that love is a strong passion. Fear is the strong passion; it is with fear that you must trifle if you wish to taste the intensest joys of living. Envy me—envy me, sir," he added with a chuckle, "I am a coward!"

Geraldine could scarcely repress a movement of repulsion for this deplorable wretch; but he commanded himself with an effort, and continued his inquiries.

"How, sir," he asked, "is the excitement so artfully prolonged? and where is there any element of uncertainty?"

"I must tell you how the victim for every evening is selected," returned Mr. Malthus; "and not only the victim, but another member, who is to be the instrument in the club's hands, and death's high priest for that occasion."

"Good God!" said the Colonel, "do they then kill each other?"

"The trouble of suicide is removed in that way," returned Malthus with a nod.

"Merciful heavens!" ejaculated the Colonel, "and may you—may I—may the—my friend, I mean—may any of us be pitched upon this evening as the slayer of another man's body and immortal spirit? Can such things be possible among men born of women? Oh! infamy of infamies!"

He was about to rise in his horror, when he caught the Prince's eye. It was fixed upon him from across the room with a frowning and angry stare. And in a moment Geraldine recovered his composure.

"After all," he added, "why not? and since you say the game is interesting, *vogue la galère*—I follow the club!"

Mr. Malthus had keenly enjoyed the Colonel's amazement and disgust. He had the vanity of wickedness; and it pleased him to see another man give way to a generous movement, while he felt himself, in his entire corruption, superior to such emotions.

"You now, after your first moment of surprise," said he, "are in a position to appreciate the delights of our society. You can see how it combines the excitement of a gaming-table, a duel, and a Roman amphitheatre. The Pagans did well enough; I cordially admire the refinement of their minds; but it has been reserved for a Christian country to attain this extreme, this quintessence, this absolute of poignancy. You will understand how vapid are all amusements to a man who has acquired a taste for this one. The game we play," he continued, "is one of extreme simplicity. A full pack—but I perceive you are about to see the thing in progress. Will

4—D

you lend me the help of your arm? I am unfortunately paralysed."

Indeed, just as Mr. Malthus was beginning his description, another pair of folding-doors was thrown open, and the whole club began to pass, not without some hurry, into the adjoining room. It was similar in every respect to the one from which it was entered, but somewhat differently furnished. The centre was occupied by a long green table, at which the President sat shuffling a pack of cards with great particularity. Even with the stick and the Colonel's arm, Mr. Malthus walked with so much difficulty that every one was seated before this pair and the Prince, who had waited for them, entered the apartment; and, in consequence, the three took seats close together at the lower end of the board.

"It is a pack of fifty-two," whispered Mr. Malthus. "Watch for the ace of spades, which is the sign of death, and the ace of clubs, which designates the official of the night. Happy, happy young men!" he added. "You have good eyes, and can follow the game. Alas! I cannot tell an ace from a deuce across the table."

And he proceeded to equip himself with a second pair of spectacles.

"I must at least watch the faces," he explained.

The Colonel rapidly informed his friend of all that he had learned from the honorary member, and of the horrible alternative that lay before them. The Prince was conscious of a deadly chill and a contraction about his heart; he swallowed with difficulty, and looked from side to side like a man in a maze.

"One bold stroke," whispered the Colonel, "and we may still escape."

But the suggestion recalled the Prince's spirits.

"Silence!" said he. "Let me see that you can play like a gentleman for any stake, however serious."

And he looked about him, once more to all appearance at his ease, although his heart beat thickly, and he was conscious of an unpleasant heat in his bosom. The members were all very quiet and intent ; every one was pale, but none so pale as Mr. Malthus. His eyes protruded ; his head kept nodding involuntarily upon his spine ; his hands found their way, one after the other, to his mouth, where they made clutches at his tremulous and ashen lips. It was plain that the honorary member enjoyed his membership on very startling terms.

" Attention, gentlemen ! " said the President.

And he began slowly dealing the cards about the table in the reverse direction, pausing until each man had shown his card. Nearly every one hesitated ; and sometimes you would see a player's fingers stumble more than once before he could turn over the momentous slip of pasteboard. As the Prince's turn drew nearer, he was conscious of a growing and almost suffocating excitement ; but he had somewhat of the gambler's nature, and recognised almost with astonishment that there was a degree of pleasure in his sensations. The nine of clubs fell to his lot ; the three of spades was dealt to Geraldine ; and the queen of hearts to Mr. Malthus, who was unable to suppress a sob of relief. The young man of the cream tarts almost immediately afterwards turned over the ace of clubs, and remained frozen with horror, the card still resting on his finger ; he had not come there to kill, but to be killed ; and the Prince in his generous sympathy with his position almost forgot the peril that still hung over himself and his friend.

The deal was coming round again, and still Death's card had not come out. The players held their respiration, and only breathed by gasps. The Prince received another club ; Geraldine had a diamond ; but when Mr. Malthus turned up his card a horrible noise, like that of something breaking, issued from his mouth ; and he rose from his seat and sat down again, with no sign of his paralysis. It was the ace of spades. The honorary member had trifled once too often with his terrors.

Conversation broke out again almost at once. The players relaxed their rigid attitudes, and began to rise from the table and stroll back by twos and threes into the smoking-room. The President stretched his arms and yawned, like a man who has finished his day's work. But Mr. Malthus sat in his place, with his head in his hands, and his hands upon the table, drunk and motionless—a thing stricken down.

The Prince and Geraldine made their escape at once. In the cold night air their horror of what they had witnessed was redoubled.

"Alas !" cried the Prince, "to be bound by an oath in such a matter ! to allow this wholesale trade in murder to be continued with profit and impunity ! If I but dared to forfeit my pledge !"

"That is impossible for your Highness," replied the Colonel, "whose honour is the honour of Bohemia. But I dare, and may with propriety, forfeit mine."

"Geraldine," said the Prince, "if your honour suffers in any of the adventures into which you follow me, not only will I never pardon you, but—what I believe will much more sensibly affect you—I should never forgive myself."

"I receive your Highness's commands," replied the Colonel. "Shall we go from this accursed spot ?"

"Yes," said the Prince. "Call a cab in Heaven's name, and let me try to forget in slumber the memory of this night's disgrace."

But it was notable that he carefully read the name of the court before he left it.

The next morning, as soon as the Prince was stirring, Colonel Geraldine brought him a daily newspaper, with the following paragraph marked :—

"MELANCHOLY ACCIDENT.—This morning, about two

o'clock, Mr. Bartholomew Malthus, of 16 Chepstow Place, Westbourne Grove, on his way home from a party at a friend's house, fell over the upper parapet in Trafalgar Square, fracturing his skull and breaking a leg and an arm. Death was instantaneous. Mr. Malthus, accompanied by a friend, was engaged in looking for a cab at the time of the unfortunate occurrence. As Mr. Malthus was paralytic, it is thought that his fall may have been occasioned by another seizure. The unhappy gentleman was well known in the most respectable circles, and his loss will be widely and deeply deplored."

"If ever a soul went straight to Hell," said Geraldine solemnly, "it was that paralytic man's."

The Prince buried his face in his hands, and remained silent.

"I am almost rejoiced," continued the Colonel, "to know that he is dead. But for our young man of the cream tarts I confess my heart bleeds."

"Geraldine," said the Prince, raising his face, "that unhappy lad was last night as innocent as you and I ; and this morning the guilt of blood is on his soul. When I think of the President, my heart grows sick within me. I do not know how it shall be done, but I shall have that scoundrel at my mercy as there is a God in heaven. What an experience, what a lesson, was that game of cards !"

"One," said the Colonel, "never to be repeated."

The Prince remained so long without replying that Geraldine grew alarmed.

"You cannot mean to return," he said. "You have suffered too much and seen too much horror already. The duties of your high position forbid the repetition of the hazard."

"There is much in what you say," replied Prince Florizel, "and I am not altogether pleased with my own determination. Alas ! in the clothes of the greatest potentate what is there but a man? I never felt my weakness more acutely than now, Geraldine, but it is stronger than I. Can I cease to interest myself in the fortunes of the unhappy young man who supped with us some hours ago? Can I leave the President to follow his nefarious career unwatched? Can I begin an adventure so entrancing, and not follow it to an end? No, Geraldine, you ask of the Prince more than the man is able to perform. To-night, once more, we take our places at the table of the Suicide Club."

Colonel Geraldine fell upon his knees.

"Will your Highness take my life?" he cried. "It is his—his freely; but do not, O do not! let him ask me to countenance so terrible a risk."

"Colonel Geraldine," replied the Prince, with some haughtiness of manner, "your life is absolutely your own. I only looked for obedience; and when that is unwillingly rendered, I shall look for that no longer. I add one word: your importunity in this affair has been sufficient."

The Master of the Horse regained his feet at once.

"Your Highness," he said, "may I be excused in my attendance this afternoon? I dare not, as an honourable man, venture a second time into that fatal house until I have perfectly ordered my affairs. Your Highness shall meet, I promise him, with no more opposition from the most devoted and grateful of his servants."

"My dear Geraldine," returned Prince Florizel, "I always regret when you oblige me to remember my rank. Dispose of your day as you think fit, but be here before eleven in the same disguise."

The club, on this second evening, was not so fully attended; and when Geraldine and the Prince arrived there were not above half a dozen persons in the smoking-room. His Highness took the President aside and congratulated him warmly on the demise of Mr. Malthus.

"I like," he said, "to meet with capacity, and certainly

find much of it in you. Your profession is of a very delicate nature, but I see you are well qualified to conduct it with success and secrecy."

The President was somewhat affected by these compliments from one of his Highness's superior bearing. He acknowledged them almost with humility.

"Poor Malthy!" he added, "I shall hardly know the club without him. The most of my patrons are boys, sir, and poetical boys, who are not much company for me. Not but what Malthy had some poetry too; but it was of a kind that I could understand."

"I can readily imagine you should find yourself in sympathy with Mr. Malthus," returned the Prince. "He struck me as a man of a very original disposition."

The young man of the cream tarts was in the room, but painfully depressed and silent. His late companions sought in vain to lead him into conversation.

"How bitterly I wish," he cried, "that I had never brought you to this infamous abode! Begone, while you are clean-handed. If you could have heard the old man scream as he fell, and the noise of his bones upon the pavement! Wish me, if you have any kindness to so fallen a being—wish the ace of spades for me to-night!"

A few more members dropped in as the evening went on, but the club did not muster more than the devil's dozen when they took their places at the table. The Prince was again conscious of a certain joy in his alarms; but he was astonished to see Geraldine so much more self-possessed than on the night before.

"It is extraordinary," thought the Prince, "that a will, made or unmade, should so greatly influence a young man's spirit."

"Attention, gentlemen!" said the President, and he began to deal.

Three times the cards went all round the table, and neither of the marked cards had yet fallen from his hand.

The excitement as he began the fourth distribution was overwhelming. There were just cards enough to go once more entirely round. The Prince, who sat second from the dealer's left, would receive, in the reverse mode of dealing practised at the club, the second last card. The third player turned up a black ace—it was the ace of clubs. The next received a diamond, the next a heart, and so on; but the ace of spades was still undelivered. At last Geraldine, who sat upon the Prince's left, turned his card; it was an ace, but the ace of hearts.

When Prince Florizel saw his fate upon the table in front of him, his heart stood still. He was a brave man, but the sweat poured off his face. There were exactly fifty chances out of a hundred that he was doomed. He reversed the card; it was the ace of spades. A loud roaring filled his brain, and the table swam before his eyes. He heard the player on his right break into a fit of laughter that sounded between mirth and disappointment; he saw the company rapidly dispersing, but his mind was full of other thoughts. He recognised how foolish, how criminal, had been his conduct. In perfect health, in the prime of his years, the heir to a throne, he had gambled away his future and that of a brave and loyal country. "God," he cried, "God forgive me!" And with that the confusion of his senses passed away, and he regained his self-possession in a moment.

To his surprise Geraldine had disappeared. There was no one in the card-room but his destined butcher consulting with the President, and the young man of the cream tarts, who slipped up to the Prince and whispered in his ear—

"I would give a million, if I had it, for your luck."

His Highness could not help reflecting, as the young man departed, that he would have sold his opportunity for a much more moderate sum.

The whispered conference now came to an end. The

holder of the ace of clubs left the room with a look of intelligence, and the President, approaching the unfortunate Prince, proffered him his hand.

"I am pleased to have met you, sir," said he, "and pleased to have been in a position to do you this trifling service. At least, you cannot complain of delay. On the second evening—what a stroke of luck!"

The Prince endeavoured in vain to articulate something in response, but his mouth was dry and his tongue seemed paralysed.

"You feel a little sickish?" asked the President, with some show of solicitude. "Most gentlemen do. Will you take a little brandy?"

The Prince signified in the affirmative, and the other immediately filled some of the spirit into a tumbler.

"Poor old Malthy!" ejaculated the President, as the Prince drained the glass. "He drank near upon a pint, and little enough good it seemed to do him!"

"I am more amenable to treatment," said the Prince, a good deal revived. "I am my own man again at once, as you perceive. And so, let me ask you, what are my directions?"

"You will proceed along the Strand in the direction of the City, and on the left-hand pavement, until you meet the gentleman who has just left the room. He will continue your instructions, and him you will have the kindness to obey; the authority of the club is vested in his person for the night. And now," added the President, "I wish you a pleasant walk."

Florizel acknowledged the salutation rather awkwardly, and took his leave. He passed through the smoking-room, where the bulk of the players were still consuming champagne, some of which he had himself ordered and paid for; and he was surprised to find himself cursing them in his heart. He put on his hat and greatcoat in the cabinet, and selected his umbrella from a corner. The familiarity of these acts, and the thought that he was about them for the last time, betrayed him into a fit of laughter which sounded unpleasantly in his own ears. He conceived a reluctance to leave the cabinet, and turned instead to the window. The sight of the lamps and the darkness recalled him to himself.

"Come, come, I must be a man," he thought, "and tear myself away."

At the corner of Box Court three men fell upon Prince Florizel, and he was unceremoniously thrust into a carriage, which at once drove rapidly away. There was already an occupant.

"Will your Highness pardon my zeal?" said a well-known voice.

The Prince threw himself upon the Colonel's neck in a passion of relief.

"How can I ever thank you?" he cried. "And how was this effected?"

Although he had been willing to march upon his doom, he was overjoyed to yield to friendly violence, and return once more to life and hope.

"You can thank me effectually enough," replied the Colonel, "by avoiding all such dangers in the future. And as for your second question, all has been managed by the simplest means. I arranged this afternoon with a celebrated detective. Secrecy has been promised and paid for. Your own servants have been principally engaged in the affair. The house in Box Court has been surrounded since nightfall, and this, which is one of your own carriages, has been awaiting you for nearly an hour."

"And the miserable creature who was to have slain me—what of him?" inquired the Prince.

"He was pinioned as he left the club," replied the Colonel, "and now awaits your sentence at the Palace, where he will soon be joined by his accomplices."

"Geraldine," said the Prince, " you have saved me

against my explicit orders, and you have done well. I owe you not only my life, but a lesson; and I should be unworthy of my rank if I did not show myself grateful to my teacher. Let it be yours to choose the manner."

There was a pause, during which the carriage continued to speed through the streets, and the two men were each buried in his own reflections. The silence was broken by Colonel Geraldine.

"Your Highness," said he, "has by this time a considerable body of prisoners. There is at least one criminal among the number to whom justice should be dealt. Our oath forbids us all recourse to law; and discretion would forbid it equally if the oath were loosened. May I inquire your Highness's intention?"

"It is decided," answered Florizel; "the President must fall in duel. It only remains to choose his adversary."

"Your Highness has permitted me to name my own recompense," said the Colonel. "Will he permit me to ask the appointment of my brother? It is an honourable post, but I dare assure your Highness that the lad will acquit himself with credit."

"You ask me an ungracious favour," said the Prince, "but I must refuse you nothing."

The Colonel kissed his hand with the greatest affection; and at that moment the carriage rolled under the archway of the Prince's splendid residence.

An hour after, Florizel in his official robes, and covered with all the orders of Bohemia, received the members of the Suicide Club.

"Foolish and wicked men," said he, "as many of you as have been driven into this strait by the lack of fortune shall receive employment and remuneration from my officers. Those who suffer under a sense of guilt must have recourse to a higher and more generous Potentate than I. I feel pity for all of you, deeper than you can imagine ; to-morrow you shall tell me your stories ; and as you answer more frankly, I shall be the more able to remedy your misfortunes. As for you," he added, turning to the President, " I should only offend a person of your parts by any offer of assistance ; but I have instead a piece of diversion to propose to you. Here," laying his hand on the shoulder of Colonel Geraldine's young brother, " is an officer of mine who desires to make a little tour upon the Continent ; and I ask you, as a favour, to accompany him on this excursion. Do you," he went on, changing his tone, "do you shoot well with the pistol? Because you may have need of that accomplishment. When two men go travelling together, it is best to be prepared for all. Let me add that, if by any chance you should lose young Mr. Geraldine upon the way, I shall always have another member of my household to place at your disposal ; and I am known, Mr. President, to have long eyesight, and as long an arm."

With these words, said with much sternness, the Prince concluded his address. Next morning the members of the club were suitably provided for by his munificence, and the President set forth upon his travels, under the supervision of Mr. Geraldine, and a pair of faithful and adroit lackeys, well trained in the Prince's household. Not content with this, discreet agents were put in possession of the house in Box Court, and all letters or visitors for the Suicide Club or its officials were to be examined by Prince Florizel in person.

Here (says my Arabian author) *ends* THE STORY OF THE YOUNG MAN WITH THE CREAM TARTS, *who is now a comfortable householder in Wigmore Street, Cavendish Square. The number, for obvious reasons, I suppress. Those who care to pursue the adventures of Prince Florizel and the President of the Suicide Club, may read*

THE STORY OF THE PHYSICIAN AND THE
SARATOGA TRUNK

MR. SILAS Q. SCUDDAMORE was a young American of a simple and harmless disposition, which was the more to his credit as he came from New England—a quarter of the New World not precisely famous for those qualities. Although he was exceedingly rich, he kept a note of all his expenses in a little paper pocket-book ; and he had chosen to study the attractions of Paris from the seventh story of what is called a furnished hotel in the Latin Quarter. There was a great deal of habit in his penuriousness ; and his virtue, which was very remarkable among his associates, was principally founded upon diffidence and youth.

The next room to his was inhabited by a lady, very attractive in her air and very elegant in toilette, whom, on his first arrival, he had taken for a Countess. In course of time he had learned that she was known by the name of Madame Zéphyrine, and that whatever station she occupied in life it was not that of a person of title. Madame Zéphyrine, probably in the hope of enchanting the young American, used to flaunt by him on the stairs with a civil inclination, a word of course, and a knock-down look out of her black eyes, and disappear in a rustle of silk, and with the revelation of an admirable foot and ankle. But these advances, so far from encouraging Mr. Scuddamore, plunged him into the depths of depression and bashfulness. She had come to him several times for a light, or to apologise for the imaginary depredations of her poodle ; but his mouth was closed in the presence of so superior a being, his French promptly left him, and he could only stare and stammer until she was gone. The slenderness of their intercourse did not prevent him from throwing out insinuations of a very glorious order when he was safely alone with a few males.

The room on the other side of the American's—for there were three rooms on a floor in the hotel—was tenanted by an old English physician of rather doubtful reputation. Dr. Noel, for that was his name, had been forced to leave London, where he enjoyed a large and increasing practice ; and it was hinted that the police had been the instigators of this change of scene. At least he, who had made something of a figure in earlier life, now dwelt in the Latin Quarter in great simplicity and solitude, and devoted much of his time to study. Mr. Scuddamore had made his acquaintance, and the pair would now and then dine together frugally in a restaurant across the street.

Silas Q. Scuddamore had many little vices of the more respectable order, and was not restrained by delicacy from indulging them in many rather doubtful ways. Chief among his foibles stood curiosity. He was a born gossip; and life, and especially those parts of it in which he had no experience, interested him to the degree of passion. He was a pert, invincible questioner, pushing his inquiries with equal pertinacity and indiscretion ; he had been observed, when he took a letter to the post, to weigh it in his hand, to turn it over and over, and to study the address with care ; and when he found a flaw in the partition between his room and Madame Zéphyrine's, instead of filling it up, he enlarged and improved the opening, and made use of it as a spy-hole on his neighbour's affairs.

One day, in the end of March, his curiosity growing as it was indulged, he enlarged the hole a little further, so that he might command another corner of the room. That evening, when he went as usual to inspect Madame Zéphyrine's movements, he was astonished to find the aperture obscured in an odd manner on the other side, and still more abashed when the obstacle was suddenly withdrawn and a titter of laughter reached his ears. Some of the plaster had evidently betrayed the secret of his spy-hole, and his neighbour had been returning the compliment in kind. Mr. Scuddamore was moved to a very acute feeling of annoyance ; he condemned Madame Zéphyrine unmercifully : he even blamed himself ; but when he found, next day, that she had taken no means to baulk him of his favourite pastime, he continued to profit by her carelessness, and gratify his idle curiosity.

That next day Madame Zéphyrine received a long visit from a tall, loosely-built man of fifty or upwards, whom Silas had not hitherto seen. His tweed suit and coloured shirt, no less than his shaggy side-whiskers, identified him as a Britisher, and his dull grey eye affected Silas with a sense of cold. He kept screwing his mouth from side to side and round and round during the whole colloquy, which was carried on in whispers. More than once it seemed to the young New Englander as if their gestures indicated his own apartment ; but the only thing definite he could gather by the most scrupulous attention was this remark, made by the Englishman in a somewhat higher key, as if in answer to some reluctance or opposition—

" I have studied his taste to a nicety, and I tell you again and again you are the only woman of the sort that I can lay my hands on."

In answer to this, Madame Zéphyrine sighed, and appeared by a gesture to resign herself, like one yielding to unqualified authority.

That afternoon the observatory was finally blinded, a wardrobe having been drawn in front of it upon the other side ; and while Silas was still lamenting over this misfortune, which he attributed to the Britisher's malign suggestion, the *concierge* brought him up a letter in a female handwriting. It was conceived in French of no very rigorous orthography, bore no signature, and in the most encouraging terms invited the young

American to be present in a certain part of the Bullier
Ball at eleven o'clock that night. Curiosity and timidity
fought a long battle in his heart; sometimes he was all
virtue, sometimes all fire and daring; and the result of
it was that, long before ten, Mr. Silas Q. Scuddamore
presented himself in unimpeachable attire at the door
of the Bullier Ball Rooms, and paid his entry money
with a sense of reckless devilry that was not without its
charm.

It was Carnival time, and the Ball was very full and
noisy. The lights and the crowd at first rather abashed our
young adventurer, and then, mounting to his brain with
a sort of intoxication, put him in possession of more
than his own share of manhood. He felt ready to face
the devil, and strutted in the ball-room with the swagger
of a cavalier. While he was thus parading, he became
aware of Madame Zéphyrine and her Britisher in conference behind a pillar. The cat-like spirit of eaves-
dropping overcame him at once. He stole nearer and
nearer on the couple from behind, until he was within
earshot.

"That is the man," the Britisher was saying;
"there—with the long blond hair—speaking to a girl in
green."

Silas identified a very handsome young fellow of
small stature, who was plainly the object of this designation.

"It is well," said Madame Zéphyrine. "I shall do
my utmost. But, remember, the best of us may fail
in such a matter."

"Tut!" returned her companion; "I answer for
the result. Have I not chosen you from thirty? Go;
but be wary of the Prince. I cannot think what
cursed accident has brought him here to-night. As if
there were not a dozen balls in Paris better worth his
notice than this riot of students and counter-jumpers!

See him where he sits, more like a reigning Emperor at home than a Prince upon his holidays!"

Silas was again lucky. He observed a person of rather a full build, strikingly handsome, and of a very stately and courteous demeanour, seated at table with another handsome young man, several years his junior, who addressed him with conspicuous deference. The name of Prince struck gratefully on Silas's Republican hearing, and the aspect of the person to whom that name was applied exercised its usual charm upon his mind. He left Madame Zéphyrine and her Englishman to take care of each other, and threading his way through the assembly, approached the table which the Prince and his confidant had honoured with their choice.

"I tell you, Geraldine," the former was saying, "the action is madness. Yourself (I am glad to remember it) chose your brother for this perilous service, and you are bound in duty to have a guard upon his conduct. He has consented to delay so many days in Paris; that was already an imprudence, considering the character of the man he has to deal with; but now, when he is within eight-and-forty hours of his departure, when he is within two or three days of the decisive trial, I ask you, is this a place for him to spend his time? He should be in a gallery at practice; he should be sleeping long hours and taking moderate exercise on foot; he should be on a rigorous diet, without white wines or brandy. Does the dog imagine we are all playing comedy? The thing is deadly earnest, Geraldine."

"I know the lad too well to interfere," replied Colonel Geraldine, "and well enough not to be alarmed. He is more cautious than you fancy, and of an indomitable spirit. If it had been a woman I should not say so much, but I trust the President to him and the two valets without an instant's apprehension."

4—E

" I am gratified to hear you say so," replied the Prince ; "but my mind is not at rest. These servants are well-trained spies, and already has not this miscreant succeeded three times in eluding their observation and spending several hours on each in private, and most likely dangerous, affairs ? An amateur might have lost him by accident, but if Rudolph and Jérome were thrown off the scent, it must have been done on purpose, and by a man who had a cogent reason and exceptional resources."

" I believe the question is now one between my brother and myself," replied Geraldine, with a shade of offence in his tone.

"I permit it to be so, Colonel Geraldine," returned Prince Florizel. "Perhaps, for that very reason, you should be all the more ready to accept my counsels. But enough. That girl in yellow dances well."

And the talk veered into the ordinary topics of a Paris ball-room in the Carnival.

Silas remembered where he was, and that the hour was already near at hand when he ought to be upon the scene of his assignation. The more he reflected the less he liked the prospect, and as at that moment an eddy in the crowd began to draw him in the direction of the door, he suffered it to carry him away without resistance. The eddy stranded him in a corner under the gallery, where his ear was immediately struck with the voice of Madame Zéphyrine. She was speaking in French with the young man of the blond locks who had been pointed out by the strange Britisher not half an hour before.

"I have a character at stake," she said, "or I would put no other condition than my heart recommends. But you have only to say so much to the porter, and he will let you go by without a word."

"But why this talk of debt ? " objected her companion.

" Heavens ! " said she, "do you think I do not understand my own hotel ? "

And she went by, clinging affectionately to her companion's arm.

This put Silas in mind of his billet.

"Ten minutes hence," thought he, "and I may be walking with as beautiful a woman as that, and even better dressed—perhaps a real lady, possibly a woman of title."

And then he remembered the spelling, and was a little downcast.

"But it may have been written by her maid," he imagined.

The clock was only a few minutes from the hour, and this immediate proximity set his heart beating at a curious and rather disagreeable speed. He reflected with relief that he was in no way bound to put in an appearance. Virtue and cowardice were together, and he made once more for the door, but this time of his own accord, and battling against the stream of people which was now moving in a contrary direction. Perhaps this prolonged resistance wearied him, or perhaps he was in that frame of mind when merely to continue in the same determination for a certain number of minutes produces a reaction and a different purpose. Certainly, at least, he wheeled about for a third time, and did not stop until he had found a place of concealment within a few yards of the appointed place.

Here he went through an agony of spirit, in which he several times prayed to God for help, for Silas had been devoutly educated. He had now not the least inclination for the meeting; nothing kept him from flight but a silly fear lest he should be thought unmanly; but this was so powerful that it kept head against all other motives; and although it could not decide him to advance, prevented him from definitely running away. At last the clock indicated ten minutes past the hour. Young Scuddamore's spirit began to rise; he peered round the corner and saw no one at the place of meeting; doubtless

his unknown correspondent had wearied and gone away.
He became as bold as he had formerly been timid. It
seemed to him that if he came at all to the appointment,
however late, he was clear from the charge of cowardice.
Nay, now he began to suspect a hoax, and actually
complimented himself on his shrewdness in having suspected and out-manœuvred his mystifiers. So very idle
a thing is a boy's mind !

Armed with these reflections, he advanced boldly from
his corner ; but he had not taken above a couple of steps
before a hand was laid upon his arm. He turned and
beheld a lady cast in a very large mould and with somewhat stately features, but bearing no mark of severity
in her looks.

" I see that you are a very self-confident lady-killer,"
said she ; " for you make yourself expected. But I was
determined to meet you. When a woman has once so
far forgotten herself as to make the first advance, she has
long ago left behind her all considerations of petty pride."

Silas was overwhelmed by the size and attractions of
his correspondent and the suddenness with which she had
fallen upon him. But she soon set him at his ease. She
was very towardly and lenient in her behaviour ; she led
him on to make pleasantries, and then applauded him to
the echo ; and in a very short time, between blandish-
ments and a liberal exhibition of warm brandy, she had
not only induced him to fancy himself in love, but to
declare his passion with the greatest vehemence.

" Alas ! " she said ; " I do not know whether I ought
not to deplore this moment, great as is the pleasure you
give me by your words. Hitherto I was alone to suffer ;
now, poor boy, there will be two. I am not my own
mistress. I dare not ask you to visit me at my own
house, for I am watched by jealous eyes. Let me
see," she added ; " I am older than you, although so
much weaker ; and while I trust in your courage and

determination, I must employ my own knowledge of the world for our mutual benefit. Where do you live?"

He told her that he lodged in a furnished hotel, and named the street and number.

She seemed to reflect for some minutes, with an effort of mind.

"I see," she said at last. "You will be faithful and obedient, will you not?"

Silas assured her eagerly of his fidelity.

"To-morrow night, then," she continued, with an encouraging smile, "you must remain at home all the evening; and if any friends should visit you, dismiss them at once on any pretext that most readily presents itself. Your door is probably shut by ten?" she asked.

"By eleven," answered Silas.

"At a quarter past eleven," pursued the lady, "leave the house. Merely cry for the door to be opened, and be sure you fall into no talk with the porter, as that might ruin everything. Go straight to the corner where the Luxembourg Gardens join the Boulevard; there you will find me waiting you. I trust you to follow my advice from point to point: and remember, if you fail me in only one particular, you will bring the sharpest trouble on a woman whose only fault is to have seen and loved you."

"I cannot see the use of all these instructions," said Silas.

"I believe you are already beginning to treat me as a master," she cried, tapping him with her fan upon the arm. "Patience, patience! that should come in time. A woman loves to be obeyed at first, although afterwards she finds her pleasure in obeying. Do as I ask you, for Heaven's sake, or I will answer for nothing. Indeed, now I think of it," she added, with a manner of one who has just seen further into a difficulty, "I find a better plan of keeping importunate visitors away. Tell the porter to admit no one for you, except a person who may come that night to claim a debt; and speak with some feeling, as though you feared the interview, so that he may take your words in earnest."

"I think you may trust me to protect myself against intruders," he said, not without a little pique.

"That is how I should prefer the thing arranged," she answered coldly. "I know you men; you think nothing of a woman's reputation."

Silas blushed and somewhat hung his head; for the scheme he had in view had involved a little vain-glorying before his acquaintances.

"Above all," she added, "do not speak to the porter as you come out."

"And why?" said he. "Of all your instructions, that seems to me the least important."

"You at first doubted the wisdom of some of the others, which you now see to be very necessary," she replied. "Believe me, this also has its uses; in time you will see them; and what am I to think of your affection, if you refuse me such trifles at our first interview?"

Silas confounded himself in explanations and apologies; in the middle of these she looked up at the clock and clapped her hands together with a suppressed scream.

"Heavens!" she cried, "is it so late? I have not an instant to lose. Alas, we poor women, what slaves we are! What have I not risked for you already?"

And after repeating her directions, which she artfully combined with caresses and the most abandoned looks, she bade him farewell and disappeared among the crowd.

The whole of the next day Silas was filled with a sense of great importance; he was now sure she was a countess; and when evening came he minutely obeyed her orders and was at the corner of the Luxembourg Gardens by the hour appointed. No one was there. He waited nearly half an hour, looking in the face of every one who passed or loitered near the spot; he even visited the neighbouring corners of the Boulevard and made a complete circuit of the garden railings; but there was no beautiful countess to throw herself into his arms. At last, and most reluctantly, he began to retrace his steps towards his hotel. On the way he remembered the words he had heard pass between Madame Zéphyrine and the blond young man, and they gave him an indefinite uneasiness.

" It appears," he reflected, "that every one has to tell lies to our porter."

He rang the bell, the door opened before him, and the porter in his bed-clothes came to offer him a light.

" Has he gone ? " inquired the porter.

" He ? Whom do you mean ? " asked Silas, somewhat sharply, for he was irritated by his disappointment.

" I did not notice him go out," continued the porter, " but I trust you paid him. We do not care, in this house, to have lodgers who cannot meet their liabilities."

"What the devil do you mean ? " demanded Silas, rudely. " I cannot understand a word of this farrago."

" The short, blond young man who came for his debt," returned the other. " Him it is I mean. Who else should it be, when I had your orders to admit no one else ? "

" Why, good God ! of course he never came," retorted Silas.

" I believe what I believe," returned the porter, putting his tongue into his cheek with a most roguish air.

" You are an insolent scoundrel," cried Silas, and, feeling that he had made a ridiculous exhibition of asperity, and at the same time bewildered by a dozen alarms, he turned and began to run upstairs.

" Do you not want a light, then ? " cried the porter.

But Silas only hurried the faster, and did not pause until he had reached the seventh landing and stood in front of his own door. There he waited a moment to recover his breath, assailed by the worst forebodings, and almost dreading to enter the room.

When at last he did so he was relieved to find it dark, and to all appearance untenanted. He drew a long breath. Here he was, home again in safety, and this should be his last folly as certainly as it had been his first. The matches stood on a little table by the bed, and he began to grope his way in that direction. As he moved, his apprehensions grew upon him once more, and he was pleased, when his foot encountered an obstacle, to find it nothing more alarming than a chair. At last he touched curtains. From the position of the window, which was faintly visible, he knew he must be at the foot of the bed, and had only to feel his way along it in order to reach the table in question.

He lowered his hand, but what it touched was not simply a counterpane—it was a counterpane with something underneath it like the outline of a human leg. Silas withdrew his arm and stood a moment petrified.

"What, what," he thought, "can this betoken?"

He listened intently, but there was no sound of breathing. Once more, with a great effort, he reached out the end of his finger to the spot he had already touched; but this time he leaped back half a yard, and stood shivering and fixed with terror. There was something in his bed. What it was he knew not, but there was something there.

It was some seconds before he could move. Then, guided by an instinct, he fell straight upon the matches, and, keeping his back towards the bed, lighted a candle. As soon as the flame had kindled, he turned slowly round and looked for what he feared to see. Sure enough, there was the worst of his imaginations realised. The coverlid was drawn carefully up over the pillow, but it moulded the outline of a human body lying motionless; and when he dashed forward and flung aside the sheets, he beheld the blond young man whom he had seen in the Bullier Ball the night before, his eyes open and without speculation, his face swollen and blackened, and a thin stream of blood trickling from his nostrils.

Silas uttered a long, tremulous wail, dropped the candle and fell on his knees beside the bed.

Silas was awakened from the stupor into which his terrible discovery had plunged him, by a prolonged but discreet tapping at the door. It took him some seconds to remember his position ; and when he hastened to prevent any one from entering it was already too late. Dr. Noel, in a tall nightcap, carrying a lamp which lighted up his long white countenance, sidling in his gait, and peering and cocking his head like some sort of bird, pushed the door slowly open, and advanced into the middle of the room.

"I thought I heard a cry," began the Doctor, "and fearing you might be unwell I did not hesitate to offer this intrusion."

Silas, with a flushed face and a fearful beating heart, kept between the Doctor and the bed ; but he found no voice to answer.

"You are in the dark," pursued the Doctor ; "and yet you have not even begun to prepare for rest. You will not easily persuade me against my own eyesight ; and your face declares most eloquently that you require either a friend or a physician—which is it to be ? Let me feel your pulse, for that is often a just reporter of the heart."

He advanced to Silas, who still retreated before him backwards, and sought to take him by the wrist ; but the strain on the young American's nerves had become too great for endurance. He avoided the Doctor with a febrile movement, and, throwing himself upon the floor, burst into a flood of weeping.

As soon as Dr. Noel perceived the dead man in the bed his face darkened ; and hurrying back to the door, which he had left ajar, he hastily closed and double-locked it.

"Up!" he cried, addressing Silas in strident tones; "this is no time for weeping. What have you done? How came this body in your room? Speak freely to one who may be helpful. Do you imagine I would ruin you? Do you think this piece of dead flesh on your pillow can alter in any degree the sympathy with which you have inspired me? Credulous youth, the horror with which blind and unjust law regards an action never attaches to the doer in the eyes of those who love him; and if I saw the friend of my heart return to me out of seas of blood he would be in no way changed in my affection. Raise yourself," he said; "good and ill are a chimera; there is nought in life except destiny, and however you may be circumstanced there is one at your side who will help you to the last."

Thus encouraged, Silas gathered himself together, and in a broken voice, and helped out by the Doctor's interrogations, contrived at last to put him in possession of the facts. But the conversation between the Prince and Geraldine he altogether omitted, as he had understood little of its purport, and had no idea that it was in any way related to his own misadventure.

"Alas!" cried Dr. Noel, "I am much abused, or you have fallen innocently into the most dangerous hands in Europe. Poor boy, what a pit has been dug for your simplicity! into what a deadly peril have your unwary feet been conducted! This man," he said, "this Englishman, whom you twice saw, and whom I suspect to be the soul of the contrivance, can you describe him? Was he young or old? tall or short?"

But Silas, who, for all his curiosity, had not a seeing eye in his head, was able to supply nothing but meagre generalities, which it was impossible to recognise.

"I would have it a piece of education in all schools!"

cried the Doctor angrily. " Where is the use of eyesight
and articulate speech if a man cannot observe and recollect
the features of his enemy ? I, who know all the gangs
of Europe, might have identified him, and gained new
weapons for your defence. Cultivate this art in future,
my poor boy ; you may find it of momentous service."

" The future ! " repeated Silas. " What future is there
left for me except the gallows ? "

" Youth is but a cowardly season," returned the
Doctor ; " and a man's own troubles look blacker than
they are. I am old, and yet I never despair."

" Can I tell such a story to the police ? " demanded
Silas.

" Assuredly not," replied the Doctor. " From what
I see already of the machination in which you have
been involved, your case is desperate upon that side ;
and for the narrow eye of the authorities you are infallibly the guilty person. And remember that we only
know a portion of the plot ; and the same infamous
contrivers have doubtless arranged many other circumstances which would be elicited by a police inquiry, and
help to fix the guilt more certainly upon your innocence."

" I am then lost, indeed ! " cried Silas.

" I have not said so," answered Dr. Noel, " for I am
a cautious man."

" But look at this ! " objected Silas, pointing to the
body. " Here is this object in my bed : not to be explained, not to be disposed of, not to be regarded
without horror."

" Horror ? " replied the Doctor. " No. When this
sort of clock has run down, it is no more to me than
an ingenious piece of mechanism, to be investigated
with the bistoury. When blood is once cold and stagnant, it is no longer human blood ; when flesh is once
dead, it is no longer that flesh which we desire in
our lovers and respect in our friends. The grace, the

attraction, the terror, have all gone from it with the animating spirit. Accustom yourself to look upon it with composure; for if my scheme is practicable you will have to live some days in constant proximity to that which now so greatly horrifies you."

"Your scheme?" cried Silas. "What is that? Tell me speedily, Doctor; for I have scarcely courage enough to continue to exist."

Without replying, Dr. Noel turned towards the bed, and proceeded to examine the corpse.

"Quite dead," he murmured. "Yes, as I had supposed, the pockets empty. Yes, and the name cut off the shirt. Their work has been done thoroughly and well. Fortunately, he is of small stature."

Silas followed these words with an extreme anxiety. At last the Doctor, his autopsy completed, took a chair and addressed the young American with a smile.

"Since I came into your room," said he, "although my ears and my tongue have been so busy, I have not suffered my eyes to remain idle. I noted a little while ago that you have there, in the corner, one of those monstrous constructions which your fellow-countrymen carry with them into all quarters of the globe—in a word, a Saratoga trunk. Until this moment I have never been able to conceive the utility of these erections; but then I began to have a glimmer. Whether it was for convenience in the slave-trade, or to obviate the results of too ready an employment of the bowie-knife, I cannot bring myself to decide. But one thing I see plainly — the object of such a box is to contain a human body."

"Surely," cried Silas, "surely this is not a time for jesting."

"Although I may express myself with some degree of pleasantry," replied the Doctor, "the purport of my words is entirely serious. And the first thing we have to do, my young friend, is to empty your coffer of all that it contains."

Silas, obeying the authority of Dr. Noel, put himself at his disposition. The Saratoga trunk was soon gutted of its contents, which made a considerable litter on the floor ; and then—Silas taking the heels and the Doctor supporting the shoulders—the body of the murdered man was carried from the bed, and, after some difficulty, doubled up and inserted whole into the empty box. With an effort on the part of both, the lid was forced down upon this unusual baggage, and the trunk was locked and corded by the Doctor's own hand, while Silas disposed of what had been taken out between the closet and a chest of drawers.

"Now," said the Doctor, "the first step has been taken on the way to your deliverance. To-morrow, or rather to-day, it must be your task to allay the suspicions of your porter, paying him all that you owe ; while you may trust me to make the arrangements necessary to a safe conclusion. Meantime, follow me to my room, where I shall give you a safe and powerful opiate ; for, whatever you do, you must have rest."

The next day was the longest in Silas's memory ; it seemed as if it would never be done. He denied himself to his friends, and sat in a corner with his eyes fixed upon the Saratoga trunk in dismal contemplation. His own former indiscretions were now returned upon him in kind ; for the observatory had been once more opened, and he was conscious of an almost continual study from Madame Zéphyrine's apartment. So distressing did this become that he was at last obliged to block up the spy-hole from his own side ; and when he was thus secured from observation he spent a considerable portion of his time in contrite tears and prayer.

Late in the evening Dr. Noel entered the room carrying in his hand a pair of sealed envelopes without address,

one somewhat bulky, and the other so slim as to seem
without enclosure.

"Silas," he said, seating himself at the table, " the
time has now come for me to explain my plan for your
salvation. To-morrow morning, at an early hour, Prince
Florizel of Bohemia returns to London, after having
diverted himself for a few days with the Parisian Carnival. It was my fortune, a good while ago, to do Colonel
Geraldine, his Master of the Horse, one of those services,
so common in my profession, which are never forgotten
upon either side. I have no need to explain to you the
nature of the obligation under which he was laid ; suffice
it to say that I knew him ready to serve me in any
practicable manner. Now, it was necessary for you to
gain London with your trunk unopened. To this the
Custom House seemed to oppose a fatal difficulty ; but
I bethought me that the baggage of so considerable a
person as the Prince is, as a matter of courtesy, passed
without examination by the officers of Custom. I applied
to Colonel Geraldine, and succeeded in obtaining a favourable answer. To-morrow, if you go before six to the
hotel where the Prince lodges, your baggage will be
passed over as a part of his, and you yourself will make
the journey as a member of his suite."

"It seems to me, as you speak, that I have already
seen both the Prince and Colonel Geraldine ; I even overheard some of their conversation the other evening at the
Bullier Ball."

"It is probable enough ; for the Prince loves to mix
with all societies," replied the Doctor. " Once arrived in
London," he pursued, " your task is nearly ended. In
this more bulky envelope I have given you a letter which
I dare not address ; but in the other you will find the
designation of the house to which you must carry it along
with your box, which will there be taken from you and
not trouble you any more."

" Alas ! " said Silas, " I have every wish to believe you ;
but how is it possible ? You open up to me a bright
prospect, but, I ask you, is my mind capable of receiving so unlikely a solution ?   Be more generous, and let
me further understand your meaning."

The Doctor seemed painfully impressed.

" Boy," he answered, " you do not know how hard
a thing you ask of me. But be it so. I am now inured
to humiliation ; and it would be strange if I refused you
this, after having granted you so much. Know, then,
that although I now make so quiet an appearance—
frugal, solitary, addicted to study—when I was younger,
my name was once a rallying-cry among the most astute
and dangerous spirits of London ; and while I was out-
wardly an object for respect and consideration, my true
power resided in the most secret, terrible, and criminal
relations. It is to one of the persons who then obeyed
me that I now address myself to deliver you from your
burden. They were men of many different nations and
dexterities, all bound together by a formidable oath, and
working to the same purposes ; the trade of the association was in murder ; and I who speak to you, innocent as
I appear, was the chieftain of this redoubtable crew."

" What ? " cried Silas. " A murderer ? And one with
whom murder was a trade ? Can I take your hand ?
Ought I so much as to accept your services ? Dark and
criminal old man, would you make an accomplice of my
youth and my distress ? "

The Doctor bitterly laughed.

" You are difficult to please, Mr. Scuddamore," said
he ; " but I now offer you your choice of company
between the murdered man and the murderer. If your
conscience is too nice to accept my aid, say so, and I will
immediately leave you. Thenceforward you can deal
with your trunk and its belongings as best suits your
upright conscience."

" I own myself wrong," replied Silas. " I should have remembered how generously you offered to shield me, even before I had convinced you of my innocence, and I continue to listen to your counsels with gratitude."

" That is well," returned the Doctor ; " and I perceive you are beginning to learn some of the lessons of experience."

" At the same time," resumed the New-Englander, " as you confess yourself accustomed to this tragical business, and the people to whom you recommend me are your own former associates and friends, could you not yourself undertake the transport of the box, and rid me at once of its detested presence ? "

" Upon my word," replied the Doctor, " I admire you cordially. If you do not think I have already meddled sufficiently in your concerns, believe me, from my heart I think the contrary. Take or leave my services as I offer them ; and trouble me with no more words of gratitude, for I value your consideration even more lightly than I do your intellect. A time will come, if you should be spared to see a number of years in health of mind, when you will think differently of all this, and blush for your to-night's behaviour."

So saying, the Doctor arose from his chair, repeated his directions briefly and clearly, and departed from the room without permitting Silas any time to answer.

The next morning Silas presented himself at the hotel, where he was politely received by Colonel Geraldine, and relieved, from that moment, of all immediate alarm about his trunk and its grisly contents. The journey passed over without much incident, although the young man was horrified to overhear the sailors and railway porters complaining among themselves about the unusual weight of the Prince's baggage. Silas travelled in a carriage with the valets, for Prince Florizel chose to be alone with his Master of the Horse. On board the steamer, however,

Silas attracted his Highness's attention by the melancholy of his air and attitude as he stood gazing at the pile of baggage; for he was still full of disquietude about the future.

"There is a young man," observed the Prince, "who must have some cause for sorrow."

"That," replied Geraldine, "is the American for whom I obtained permission to travel with your suite."

"You remind me that I have been remiss in courtesy," said Prince Florizel, and advancing to Silas, he addressed him with the most exquisite condescension in these words :—

"I was charmed, young sir, to be able to gratify the desire you made known to me through Colonel Geraldine. Remember, if you please, that I shall be glad at any future time to lay you under a more serious obligation."

And he then put some questions as to the political condition of America, which Silas answered with sense and propriety.

"You are still a young man," said the Prince ; "but I observe you to be very serious for your years. Perhaps you allow your attention to be too much occupied with grave studies. But, perhaps, on the other hand, I am myself indiscreet and touch upon a painful subject."

"I have certainly cause to be the most miserable of men," said Silas ; "never has a more innocent person been more dismally abused."

"I will not ask you for your confidence," returned Prince Florizel. "But do not forget that Colonel Geraldine's recommendation is an unfailing passport ; and that I am not only willing, but possibly more able than many others, to do you a service."

Silas was delighted with the amiability of this great personage ; but his mind soon returned upon its gloomy preoccupations ; for not even the favour of a Prince to a Republican can discharge a brooding spirit of its cares.

4—F

The train arrived at Charing Cross, where the officers of the Revenue respected the baggage of Prince Florizel in the usual manner. The most elegant equipages were in waiting ; and Silas was driven, along with the rest, to the Prince's residence. There Colonel Geraldine sought him out, and expressed himself pleased to have been of any service to a friend of the physician's, for whom he professed a great consideration.

"I hope," he added, "that you will find none of your porcelain injured. Special orders were given along the line to deal tenderly with the Prince's effects."

And then, directing the servants to place one of the carriages at the young gentleman's disposal, and at once to charge the Saratoga trunk upon the dickey, the Colonel shook hands and excused himself on account of his occupations in the princely household.

Silas now broke the seal of the envelope containing the address, and directed the stately footman to drive him to Box Court, opening off the Strand. It seemed as if the place were not at all unknown to the man, for he looked startled and begged a repetition of the order. It was with a heart full of alarms that Silas mounted into the luxurious vehicle, and was driven to his destination. The entrance to Box Court was too narrow for the passage of a coach ; it was a mere footway between railings, with a post at either end. On one of these posts was seated a man, who at once jumped down and exchanged a friendly sign with the driver, while the footman opened the door and inquired of Silas whether he should take down the Saratoga trunk, and to what number it should be carried.

"If you please," said Silas. "To number three."

The footman and the man who had been sitting on the post, even with the aid of Silas himself, had hard work to carry in the trunk ; and before it was deposited at the door of the house in question, the young American was horrified to find a score of loiterers looking on. But he knocked with as good a countenance as he could muster up, and presented the other envelope to him who opened.

"He is not at home," said he, "but if you will leave your letter and return to-morrow early, I shall be able to inform you whether and when he can receive your visit. Would you like to leave your box?" he added.

"Dearly," cried Silas; and the next moment he repented his precipitation, and declared, with equal emphasis, that he would rather carry the box along with him to the hotel.

The crowd jeered at his indecision, and followed him to the carriage with insulting remarks; and Silas, covered with shame and terror, implored the servants to conduct him to some quiet and comfortable house of entertainment in the immediate neighbourhood.

The Prince's equipage deposited Silas at the Craven Hotel in Craven Street, and immediately drove away, leaving him alone with the servants of the inn. The only vacant room, it appeared, was a little den up four pairs of stairs, and looking towards the back. To this hermitage, with infinite trouble and complaint, a pair of stout porters carried the Saratoga trunk. It is needless to mention that Silas kept closely at their heels throughout the ascent, and had his heart in his mouth at every corner. A single false step, he reflected, and the box might go over the banisters and land its fatal contents, plainly discovered, on the pavement of the hall.

Arrived in the room, he sat down on the edge of his bed to recover from the agony that he had just endured; but he had hardly taken his position when he was recalled to a sense of his peril by the action of the boots, who had knelt beside the trunk, and was proceeding officiously to undo its elaborate fastenings.

"Let it be!" cried Silas. "I shall want nothing from it while I stay here."

"You might have let it lie in the hall, then," growled

the man ; "a thing as big and heavy as a church.   What
you have inside I cannot fancy.   If it is all money, you
are a richer man than me."

"Money ? " repeated Silas, in a sudden perturbation.
"What do you mean by money ?   I have no money, and
you are speaking like a fool."

"All right, captain," retorted the boots with a wink.
"There's nobody will touch your lordship's money.   I'm
as safe as the bank," he added ; "but as the box is heavy,
I shouldn't mind drinking something to your lordship's
health."

Silas pressed two Napoleons upon his acceptance,
apologising, at the same time, for being obliged to trouble
him with foreign money, and pleading his recent arrival
for excuse.   And the man, grumbling with even greater
fervour, and looking contemptuously from the money in
his hand to the Saratoga trunk, and back again from the
one to the other, at last consented to withdraw.

For nearly two days the dead body had been packed
into Silas's box ; and as soon as he was alone the unfortunate New-Englander nosed all the cracks and openings
with the most passionate attention.   But the weather was
cool, and the trunk still managed to contain his shocking
secret.

He took a chair beside it, and buried his face in his
hands, and his mind in the most profound reflection.
If he were not speedily relieved, no question but
he must be speedily discovered.   Alone in a strange
city, without friends or accomplices, if the Doctor's
introduction failed him, he was indubitably a lost
New - Englander.   He reflected pathetically over his
ambitious designs for the future ; he should not now
become the hero and spokesman of his native place
of Bangor, Maine ; he should not, as he had fondly
anticipated, move on from office to office, from honour to honour ; he might as well divest himself at

once of all hope of being acclaimed President of the United States, and leaving behind him a statue, in the worst possible style of art, to adorn the Capitol at Washington. Here he was, chained to a dead Englishman doubled up inside a Saratoga trunk; whom he must get rid of, or perish from the rolls of national glory!

I should be afraid to chronicle the language employed by this young man to the Doctor, to the murdered man, to Madame Zéphyrine, to the boots of the hotel, to the Prince's servants, and, in a word, to all who had been ever so remotely connected with his horrible misfortune.

He slunk down to dinner about seven at night; but the yellow coffee-room appalled him, the eyes of the other diners seemed to rest on his with suspicion, and his mind remained upstairs with the Saratoga trunk. When the waiter came to offer him cheese, his nerves were already so much on edge that he leaped half-way out of his chair and upset the remainder of a pint of ale upon the table-cloth.

The fellow offered to show him to the smoking-room when he had done; and although he would have much preferred to return at once to his perilous treasure, he had not the courage to refuse, and was shown downstairs to the black, gas-lit cellar, which formed, and possibly still forms, the divan of the Craven Hotel.

Two very sad betting men were playing billiards, attended by a moist, consumptive marker; and for the moment Silas imagined that these were the only occupants of the apartment. But at the next glance his eye fell upon a person smoking in the farthest corner, with lowered eyes and a most respectable and modest aspect. He knew at once that he had seen the face before; and, in spite of the entire change of clothes,

recognised the man whom he had found seated on a post at the entrance to Box Court, and who had helped him to carry the trunk to and from the carriage. The New - Englander simply turned and ran, nor did he pause until he had locked and bolted himself into his bedroom.

There, all night long, a prey to the most terrible imaginations, he watched beside the fatal boxful of dead flesh. The suggestion of the boots that his trunk was full of gold inspired him with all manner of new terrors, if he so much as dared to close an eye; and the presence in the smoking-room, and under an obvious disguise, of the loiterer from Box Court convinced him that he was once more the centre of obscure machinations.

Midnight had sounded some time, when, impelled by uneasy suspicions, Silas opened his bedroom door and peered into the passage. It was dimly illuminated by a single jet of gas; and some distance off he perceived a man sleeping on the floor in the costume of an hotel under-servant. Silas drew near the man on tiptoe. He lay partly on his back, partly on his side, and his right fore-arm concealed his face from recognition. Suddenly, while the American was still bending over him, the sleeper removed his arm and opened his eyes, and Silas found himself once more face to face with the loiterer of Box Court.

"Good night, sir," said the man pleasantly.

But Silas was too profoundly moved to find an answer, and regained his room in silence.

Towards morning, worn out by apprehension, he fell asleep on his chair, with his head forward on the trunk. In spite of so constrained an attitude and such a grisly pillow, his slumber was sound and prolonged, and he was only awakened at a late hour and by a sharp tapping at the door.

He hurried to open, and found the boots without.

"You are the gentleman who called yesterday at Box Court?" he asked.

Silas, with a quaver, admitted that he had done so.

"Then this note is for you," added the servant, proffering a sealed envelope.

Silas tore it open, and found inside the words: "Twelve o'clock."

He was punctual to the hour; the trunk was carried before him by several stout servants; and he was himself ushered into a room, where a man sat warming himself before the fire with his back towards the door. The sound of so many persons entering and leaving, and the scraping of the trunk as it was deposited upon the bare boards, were alike unable to attract the notice of the occupant; and Silas stood waiting, in an agony of fear, until he should deign to recognise his presence.

Perhaps five minutes had elapsed before the man turned leisurely about, and disclosed the features of Prince Florizel of Bohemia.

"So, sir," he said, with great severity, "this is the manner in which you abuse my politeness. You join yourself to persons of condition, I perceive, for no other purpose than to escape the consequences of your crimes; and I can readily understand your embarrassment when I addressed myself to you yesterday."

"Indeed," cried Silas, "I am innocent of everything except misfortune."

And in a hurried voice, and with the greatest ingenuousness, he recounted to the Prince the whole history of his calamity.

"I see I have been mistaken," said his Highness, when he had heard him to an end. "You are no other than a victim, and since I am not to punish you may be sure I shall do my utmost to help.—And now," he continued, "to business. Open your box at once, and let me see what it contains."

Silas changed colour.

"I almost fear to look upon it," he exclaimed.

"Nay," replied the Prince, "have you not looked at it already? This is a form of sentimentality to be resisted. The sight of a sick man, whom we can still help, should appeal more directly to the feelings than that of a dead man who is equally beyond help or harm, love or hatred. Nerve yourself, Mr. Scuddamore,"—and then, seeing that Silas still hesitated, "I do not desire to give another name to my request," he added.

The young American awoke as if out of a dream, and with a shiver of repugnance addressed himself to loose the straps and open the lock of the Saratoga trunk. The Prince stood by, watching with a composed countenance and his hands behind his back. The body was quite stiff, and it cost Silas a great effort, both moral and physical, to dislodge it from its position, and discover the face.

Prince Florizel started back with an exclamation of painful surprise.

"Alas!" he cried, "you little know, Mr. Scuddamore, what a cruel gift you have brought me. This is a young man of my own suite, the brother of my trusted friend; and it was upon matters of my own service that he has thus perished at the hands of violent and treacherous men. Poor Geraldine," he went on, as if to himself, "in what words am I to tell you of your brother's fate? How can I excuse myself in your eyes, or in the eyes of God, for the presumptuous schemes that led him to this bloody and unnatural death? Ah, Florizel! Florizel! when will you learn the discretion that suits mortal life, and be no longer dazzled with the image of power at your disposal? Power!" he cried; "who is more powerless? I look upon this young man whom I have sacrificed, Mr. Scuddamore, and feel how small a thing it is to be a Prince."

Silas was moved at the sight of his emotion. He tried to murmur some consolatory words, and burst into tears.

The Prince, touched by his obvious intention, came up to him and took him by the hand.

"Command yourself," said he. "We have both much to learn, and we shall both be better men for to-day's meeting."

Silas thanked him in silence with an affectionate look.

"Write me the address of Doctor Noel on this piece of paper," continued the Prince, leading him towards the table; "and let me recommend you, when you are again in Paris, to avoid the society of that dangerous man. He has acted in this matter on a generous inspiration; that I must believe; had he been privy to young Geraldine's death he would never have despatched the body to the care of the actual criminal."

"The actual criminal!" repeated Silas in astonishment.

"Even so," returned the Prince. "This letter, which the disposition of Almighty Providence has so strangely delivered into my hands, was addressed to no less a person than the criminal himself, the infamous President of the Suicide Club. Seek to pry no further in these perilous affairs, but content yourself with your own miraculous escape, and leave this house at once. I have pressing affairs, and must arrange at once about this poor clay, which was so lately a gallant and handsome youth."

Silas took a grateful and submissive leave of Prince Florizel, but he lingered in Box Court until he saw him depart in a splendid carriage on a visit to Colonel Henderson of the police. Republican as he was, the young American took off his hat with almost a sentiment of devotion to the retreating carriage. And the same night he started by rail on his return to Paris.

Here (observes my Arabian author) *is the end of* THE HISTORY OF THE PHYSICIAN AND THE SARATOGA TRUNK. *Omitting some reflections on the power of*

Providence, highly pertinent in the original, but little suited to our Occidental taste, I shall only add that Mr. Scuddamore has already begun to mount the ladder of political fame, and by last advices was the Sheriff of his native town.

THE ADVENTURE OF THE HANSOM CABS

LIEUTENANT BRACKENBURY RICH had greatly distinguished himself in one of the lesser Indian hill wars. He it was who took the chieftain prisoner with his own hand ; his gallantry was universally applauded ; and when he came home, prostrated by an ugly sabre-cut and a protracted jungle-fever, society was prepared to welcome the Lieutenant as a celebrity of minor lustre. But his was a character remarkable for unaffected modesty ; adventure was dear to his heart, but he cared little for adulation ; and he waited at foreign watering-places and in Algiers until the fame of his exploits had run through its nine days' vitality and begun to be forgotten. He arrived in London at last, in the early season, with as little observation as he could desire ; and as he was an orphan and had none but distant relatives who lived in the provinces, it was almost as a foreigner that he installed himself in the capital of the country for which he had shed his blood.

On the day following his arrival he dined alone at a military club. He shook hands with a few old comrades, and received their warm congratulations ; but as one and all had some engagement for the evening, he found himself left entirely to his own resources. He was in dress, for he had entertained the notion of visiting a theatre. But the great city was new to him ; he had gone from a provincial school to a military college, and thence direct to the Eastern Empire ; and he promised himself a variety of delights in this world for exploration. Swinging his cane, he took his way westward. It was a mild evening, already dark, and now and then threatening rain. The succession of faces in the lamplight stirred the Lieutenant's imagination ; and it seemed to him as if he could walk for ever in that stimulating city atmosphere and surrounded by the mystery of four million private lives. He glanced at the houses, and marvelled what was passing behind those warmly-lighted windows ; he looked into face after face, and saw them each intent upon some unknown interest, criminal or kindly.

" They talk of war," he thought, " but this is the great battlefield of mankind."

And then he began to wonder that he should walk so long in this complicated scene, and not chance upon so much as the shadow of an adventure for himself.

"All in good time," he reflected. " I am still a stranger, and perhaps wear a strange air. But I must be drawn into the eddy before long."

The night was already well advanced when a plump of cold rain fell suddenly out of the darkness. Brackenbury paused under some trees, and as he did so he caught sight of a hansom cabman making him a sign that he was disengaged. The circumstance fell in so happily to the occasion that he at once raised his cane in answer, and had soon ensconced himself in the London gondola.

" Where to, sir ? " asked the driver.

"Where you please," said Brackenbury.

And immediately, at a pace of surprising swiftness, the hansom drove off through the rain into a maze of villas. One villa was so like another, each with its front garden, and there was so little to distinguish the deserted lamp-lit streets and crescents through which the flying hansom took its way, that Brackenbury soon lost all idea of direction. He would have been tempted to believe that the cabman was amusing himself by driving him round and round and in and out about a small quarter, but there was something business-like in the speed which convinced him of the contrary. The man had an object in view, he was hastening towards a definite end ; and Brackenbury was at once astonished at the fellow's skill in picking a way through such a labyrinth, and a little concerned to imagine what was the occasion of his hurry. He had heard tales of strangers falling ill in London. Did the driver belong to some bloody and treacherous association ? and was he himself being whirled to a murderous death ?

The thought had scarcely presented itself, when the cab swung sharply round a corner and pulled up before the garden gate of a villa in a long and wide road. The house was brilliantly lighted up. Another hansom had just driven away, and Brackenbury could see a gentleman being admitted at the front door and received by several liveried servants. He was surprised that the cabman should have stopped so immediately in front of a house where a reception was being held ; but he did not doubt it was the result of accident, and sat placidly smoking where he was, until he heard the trap thrown open over his head.

" Here we are, sir," said the driver.

" Here ! " repeated Brackenbury. " Where ? "

" You told me to take you where I pleased, sir," returned the man with a chuckle, " and here we are."

It struck Brackenbury that the voice was wonderfully smooth and courteous for a man in so inferior a position ; he remembered the speed at which he had been driven ; and now it occurred to him that the hansom was more luxuriously appointed than the common run of public conveyances.

" I must ask you to explain," said he. " Do you mean to turn me out into the rain ? My good man, I suspect the choice is mine."

" The choice is certainly yours," replied the driver ; " but when I tell you all, I believe I know how a gentleman of your figure will decide. There is a gentleman's party in this house. I do not know whether the master be a stranger to London and without acquaintances of his own ; or whether he is a man of odd notions. But certainly I was hired to kidnap single gentlemen in evening dress, as many as I pleased, but military officers by preference. You have simply to go in and say that Mr. Morris invited you."

"Are you Mr. Morris ? " inquired the Lieutenant.

" Oh, no," replied the cabman. " Mr. Morris is the person of the house."

" It is not a common way of collecting guests," said Brackenbury : " but an eccentric man might very well indulge the whim without any intention to offend. And suppose that I refuse Mr. Morris's invitation," he went on, " what then ? "

" My orders are to drive you back where I took you from," replied the man, " and set out to look for others up to midnight. Those who have no fancy for such an adventure, Mr. Morris said, were not the guests for him."

These words decided the Lieutenant on the spot.

" After all," he reflected, as he descended from the hansom, " I have not had long to wait for my adventure."

He had hardly found footing on the side-walk, and was still feeling in his pocket for the fare, when the cab swung about and drove off by the way it came at the former break-neck velocity. Brackenbury shouted after the man, who paid no heed, and continued to drive away ; but the sound of his voice was overheard in the house, the door was again thrown open, emitting a flood of light upon the garden, and a servant ran down to meet him holding an umbrella.

" The cabman has been paid," observed the servant in a very civil tone ; and he proceeded to escort Brackenbury along the path and up the steps. In the hall several other attendants relieved him of his hat, cane, and

paletot, gave him a ticket with a number in return, and
politely hurried him up a stair adorned with tropical
flowers, to the door of an apartment on the first story.
Here a grave butler inquired his name, and announcing,
"Lieutenant Brackenbury Rich," ushered him into the
drawing-room of the house.

A young man, slender and singularly handsome, came
forward and greeted him with an air at once courtly and
affectionate. Hundreds of candles, of the finest wax, lit
up a room that was perfumed, like the staircase, with a
profusion of rare and beautiful flowering shrubs. A side-
table was loaded with tempting viands. Several servants
went to and fro with fruits and goblets of champagne.
The company was perhaps sixteen in number, all men,
few beyond the prime of life, and, with hardly an exception, of a dashing and capable exterior. They were
divided into two groups, one about a roulette-board,
and the other surrounding a table at which one of their
number held a bank of baccarat.

"I see," thought Brackenbury, "I am in a private
gambling saloon, and the cabman was a tout."

His eye had embraced the details, and his mind formed
the conclusion, while his host was still holding him by
the hand ; and to him his looks returned from this rapid
survey. At a second view Mr. Morris surprised him still
more than on the first. The easy elegance of his manners,
the distinction, amiability, and courage that appeared upon
his features, fitted very ill with the Lieutenant's pre-
conceptions on the subject of the proprietor of a hell ; and
the tone of his conversation seemed to mark him out
for a man of position and merit. Brackenbury found he
had an instinctive liking for his entertainer ; and though
he chid himself for the weakness, he was unable to resist
a sort of friendly attraction for Mr. Morris's person and
character.

"I have heard of you, Lieutenant Rich," said Mr.

Morris, lowering his tone ; " and believe me I am gratified to make your acquaintance. Your looks accord with the reputation that has preceded you from India. And if you will forget for a while the irregularity of your presentation in my house, I shall feel it not only an honour, but a genuine pleasure besides. A man who makes a mouthful of barbarian cavaliers," he added with a laugh, "should not be appalled by a breach of etiquette, however serious."

And he led him towards the sideboard and pressed him to partake of some refreshment.

"Upon my word," the Lieutenant reflected, "this is one of the pleasantest fellows and, I do not doubt, one of the most agreeable societies in London."

He partook of some champagne, which he found excellent ; and observing that many of the company were already smoking, he lit one of his own Manillas, and strolled up to the roulette-board, where he sometimes made a stake and sometimes looked on smilingly on the fortune of others. It was while he was thus idling that he became aware of a sharp scrutiny to which the whole of the guests were subjected. Mr. Morris went here and there, ostensibly busied on hospitable concerns ; but he had ever a shrewd glance at disposal ; not a man of the party escaped his sudden, searching looks ; he took stock of the bearing of heavy losers, he valued the amount of the stakes, he paused behind couples who were deep in conversation ; and, in a word, there was hardly a characteristic of any one present but he seemed to catch and make a note of it. Brackenbury began to wonder if this were indeed a gambling-hell : it had so much the air of a private inquisition. He followed Mr. Morris in all his movements ; and although the man had a ready smile, he seemed to perceive, as it were under a mask, a haggard, careworn, and preoccupied spirit. The fellows around him laughed and made their game ; but Brackenbury had lost interest in the guests.

"This Morris," thought he, "is no idler in the room. Some deep purpose inspires him; let it be mine to fathom it."

Now and then Mr. Morris would call one of his visitors aside ; and after a brief colloquy in an ante-room, he would return alone, and the visitors in question reappeared no more. After a certain number of repetitions, this performance excited Brackenbury's curiosity to a high degree. He determined to be at the bottom of this minor mystery at once ; and strolling into the ante-room, found a deep window recess concealed by curtains of the fashionable green. Here he hurriedly ensconced himself; nor had he to wait long before the sound of steps and voices drew near him from the principal apartment. Peering through the division, he saw Mr. Morris escorting a fat and ruddy personage, with somewhat the look of a commercial traveller, whom Brackenbury had already remarked for his coarse laugh and under-bred behaviour at the table. The pair halted immediately before the window, so that Brackenbury lost not a word of the following discourse :—

"I beg you a thousand pardons !" began Mr. Morris, with the most conciliatory manner ; "and, if I appear rude, I am sure you will readily forgive me. In a place so great as London accidents must continually happen ; and the best that we can hope is to remedy them with as small delay as possible. I will not deny that I fear you have made a mistake and honoured my poor house by inadvertence ; for, to speak openly, I cannot at all remember your appearance. Let me put the question without unnecessary circumlocution—between gentlemen of honour a word will suffice—Under whose roof do you suppose yourself to be ? "

"That of Mr. Morris," replied the other, with a prodigious display of confusion, which had been visibly growing upon him throughout the last few words.

" Mr. John or Mr. James Morris ? " inquired the host.

" I really cannot tell you," returned the unfortunate guest. " I am not personally acquainted with the gentleman, any more than I am with yourself."

" I see," said Mr. Morris. " There is another person of the same name farther down the street ; and I have no doubt the policeman will be able to supply you with his number. Believe me, I felicitate myself on the misunderstanding which has procured me the pleasure of your company for so long ; and let me express a hope that we may meet again upon a more regular footing. Meantime, I would not for the world detain you longer from your friends. John," he added, raising his voice, " will you see that this gentleman finds his great-coat ? "

And with the most agreeable air Mr. Morris escorted his visitor as far as the ante-room door, where he left him under conduct of the butler. As he passed the window, on his return to the drawing-room, Brackenbury could hear him utter a profound sigh, as though his mind was loaded with a great anxiety, and his nerves already fatigued with the task on which he was engaged.

For perhaps an hour the hansoms kept arriving with such frequency that Mr. Morris had to receive a new guest for every old one that he sent away, and the company preserved its number undiminished. But towards the end of that time the arrivals grew few and far between, and at length ceased entirely, while the process ot elimination was continued with unimpaired activity. The drawing-room began to look empty : the baccarat was discontinued for lack of a banker ; more than one person said good-night of his own accord, and was suffered to depart without expostulation ; and in the meanwhile Mr. Morris redoubled in agreeable attentions to those who stayed behind. He went from group to group and from person to person with looks of the readiest sympathy and

4—G

the most pertinent and pleasing talk ; he was not so much like a host as like a hostess, and there was a feminine coquetry and condescension in his manner which charmed the hearts of all.

As the guests grew thinner, Lieutenant Rich strolled for a moment out of the drawing-room into the hall in quest of fresher air. But he had no sooner passed the threshold of the ante-chamber than he was brought to a dead halt by a discovery of the most surprising nature. The flowering shrubs had disappeared from the staircase ; three large furniture-waggons stood before the garden gate ; the servants were busy dismantling the house upon all sides ; and some of them had already donned their great-coats and were preparing to depart.   It was like the end of a country ball, where everything has been supplied by contract.   Brackenbury had indeed some matter for reflection.   First, the guests, who were no real guests, after all, had been dismissed ; and now the servants, who could hardly be genuine servants, were actively dispersing.

"Was the whole establishment a sham ? " he asked himself. "The mushroom of a single night which should disappear before morning ? "

Watching a favourable opportunity, Brackenbury dashed upstairs to the higher regions of the house. It was as he had expected. He ran from room to room, and saw not a stick of furniture nor so much as a picture on the walls. Although the house had been painted and papered, it was not only uninhabited at present, but plainly had never been inhabited at all. The young officer remembered with astonishment its specious, settled, and hospitable air on his arrival. It was only at a prodigious cost that the imposture could have been carried out upon so great a scale.

Who, then, was Mr. Morris ?   What was his intention in thus playing the householder for a single night in the remote west of London? And why did he collect his visitors at hazard from the streets?

Brackenbury remembered that he had already delayed too long, and hastened to join the company. Many had left during his absence; and, counting the Lieutenant and his host, there were not more than five persons in the drawing-room—recently so thronged. Mr. Morris greeted him, as he re-entered the apartment, with a smile, and immediately rose to his feet.

"It is now time, gentlemen," said he, "to explain my purpose in decoying you from your amusements. I trust you did not find the evening hang very dully on your hands; but my object, I will confess it, was not to entertain your leisure, but to help myself in an unfortunate necessity. You are all gentlemen," he continued, "your appearance does you that much justice, and I ask for no better security. Hence, I speak it without concealment, I ask you to render me a dangerous and delicate service; dangerous because you may run the hazard of your lives, and delicate because I must ask an absolute discretion upon all that you shall see or hear. From an utter stranger the request is almost comically extravagant; I am well aware of this; and I would add at once, if there be any one present who has heard enough, if there be one among the party who recoils from a dangerous confidence and a piece of Quixotic devotion to he knows not whom— here is my hand ready, and I shall wish him good-night and God-speed with all the sincerity in the world."

A very tall, black man, with a heavy stoop, immediately responded to this appeal.

"I commend your frankness, Sir," said he; "and, for my part, I go. I make no reflections; but I cannot deny that you fill me with suspicious thoughts. I go myself, as I say; and perhaps you will think I have no right to add words to my example."

"On the contrary," replied Mr. Morris, "I am obliged to you for all you say. It would be impossible to exaggerate the gravity of my proposal."

"Well, gentlemen, what do you say?" said the tall man, addressing the others. "We have had our evening's frolic; shall we all go homeward peaceably in a body? You will think well of my suggestion in the morning, when you see the sun again in innocence and safety."

The speaker pronounced the last words with an intonation which added to their force; and his face wore a singular expression, full of gravity and significance. Another of the company rose hastily, and, with some appearance of alarm, prepared to take his leave. There were only two who held their ground, Brackenbury and an old red-nosed cavalry Major; but these two preserved a nonchalant demeanour, and, beyond a look of intelligence which they rapidly exchanged, appeared entirely foreign to the discussion that had just been terminated.

Mr. Morris conducted the deserters as far as the door, which he closed upon their heels; then he turned round, disclosing a countenance of mingled relief and animation, and addressed the two officers as follows.

"I have chosen my men like Joshua in the Bible," said Mr. Morris, "and I now believe I have the pick of London. Your appearance pleased my hansom cabmen; then it delighted me; I have watched your behaviour in a strange company, and under the most unusual circumstances: I have studied how you played and how you bore your losses; lastly, I have put you to the test of a staggering announcement, and you received it like an invitation to dinner. It is not for nothing," he cried, "that I have been for years the companion and the pupil of the bravest and wisest potentate in Europe."

"At the affair of Bunderchang," observed the Major, "I asked for twelve volunteers, and every trooper in the ranks replied to my appeal. But a gaming party is not the same thing as a regiment under fire. You may be pleased, I suppose, to have found two, and two who will not fail you at a push. As for the pair who ran away, I count them among the most pitiful hounds I ever met with.—Lieutenant Rich," he added, addressing Brackenbury, "I have heard much of you of late ; and I cannot doubt but you have also heard of me. I am Major O'Rooke."

And the veteran tendered his hand, which was red and tremulous, to the young Lieutenant.

"Who has not ?" answered Brackenbury.

"When this little matter is settled," said Mr. Morris, "you will think I have sufficiently rewarded you ; for I could offer neither a more valuable service than to make him acquainted with the other."

"And now," said Major O'Rooke, "is it a duel ?"

"A duel after a fashion," replied Mr. Morris, "a duel with unknown and dangerous enemies, and, as I gravely fear, a duel to the death. I must ask you," he continued, "to call me Morris no longer ; call me, if you please, Hammersmith ; my real name, as well as that of another person to whom I hope to present you before long, you will gratify me by not asking, and not seeking to discover for yourselves. Three days ago the person of whom I speak disappeared suddenly from home ; and, until this morning, I received no hint of his situation. You will fancy my alarm when I tell you that he is engaged upon a work of private justice. Bound by an unhappy oath, too lightly sworn, he finds it necessary, without the help of law, to rid the earth of an insidious and bloody villain. Already two of our friends, and one of them my own born brother, have perished in the enterprise. He himself, or I am much deceived, is taken in the same fatal toils. But at least he still lives and still hopes, as this billet sufficiently proves."

And the speaker, no other than Colonel Geraldine, proffered a letter, thus conceived :—

"MAJOR HAMMERSMITH,—On Wednesday, at 3 A.M., you will be admitted by the small door to the gardens of Rochester House, Regent's Park, by a man who is entirely in my interest. I must request you not to fail me by a second. Pray bring my case of swords, and, if you can find them, one or two gentlemen of conduct and discretion to whom my person is unknown. My name must not be used in this affair.　"T. GODALL."

"From his wisdom alone, if he had no other title," pursued Colonel Geraldine, when the others had each satisfied his curiosity, "my friend is a man whose directions should implicitly be followed. I need not tell you, therefore, that I have not so much as visited the neighbourhood of Rochester House ; and that I am still as wholly in the dark as either of yourselves as to the nature of my friend's dilemma. I betook myself, as soon as I had received this order, to a furnishing contractor, and, in a few hours, the house in which we now are had assumed its late air of festival. My scheme was at least original ; and I am far from regretting an action which has procured me the services of Major O'Rooke and Lieutenant Brackenbury Rich. But the servants in the street will have a strange awakening. The house which this evening was full of lights and visitors they will find uninhabited and for sale to-morrow morning. Thus even the most serious concerns," added the Colonel, "have a merry side."

"And let us add a merry ending," said Brackenbury.

The Colonel consulted his watch.

"It is now hard on two," he said. "We have an hour before us, and a swift cab is at the door. Tell me if I may count upon your help."

"During a long life," replied Major O'Rooke, "I never took back my hand from anything, nor so much as hedged a bet."

Brackenbury signified his readiness in the most becoming terms ; and after they had drunk a glass or two of wine, the Colonel gave each of them a loaded revolver, and the three mounted into the cab and drove off for the address in question.

Rochester House was a magnificent residence on the banks of the canal. The large extent of the garden isolated it in an unusual degree from the annoyances of neighbourhood. It seemed the *parc aux cerfs* of some great nobleman or millionaire. As far as could be seen from the street, there was not a glimmer of light in any of the numerous windows of the mansion ; and the place had a look of neglect, as though the master had been long from home.

The cab was discharged, and the three gentlemen were not long in discovering the small door, which was a sort of postern in a lane between two garden walls. It still wanted ten or fifteen minutes of the appointed time ; the rain fell heavily, and the adventurers sheltered themselves below some pendent ivy, and spoke in low tones of the approaching trial.

Suddenly Geraldine raised his finger to command silence, and all three bent their hearing to the utmost. Through the continuous noise of the rain, the steps and voices of two men became audible from the other side of the wall ; and, as they drew nearer, Brackenbury, whose sense of hearing was remarkably acute, could even distinguish some fragments of their talk.

" Is the grave dug ? " asked one.

" It is," replied the other ; " behind the laurel hedge. When the job is done, we can cover it with a pile of stakes."

The first speaker laughed, and the sound of his merriment was shocking to the listeners on the other side.

" In an hour from now," he said.

And by the sound of the steps it was obvious that the pair had separated, and were proceeding in contrary directions.

Almost immediately after the postern door was cautiously opened, a white face was protruded into the lane, and a hand was seen beckoning to the watchers. In dead silence the three passed the door, which was immediately locked behind them, and followed their guide through several garden alleys to the kitchen entrance of the house. A single candle burned in the great paved kitchen, which was destitute of the customary furniture ; and as the party proceeded to ascend from thence by a flight of winding stairs, a prodigious noise of rats testified still more plainly to the dilapidation of the house.

Their conductor preceded them, carrying the candle. He was a lean man, much bent, but still agile ; and he turned from time to time and admonished silence and caution by his gestures. Colonel Geraldine followed on his heels, the case of swords under one arm, and a pistol ready in the other. Brackenbury's heart beat thickly. He perceived that they were still in time ; but he judged from the alacrity of the old man that the hour of action must be near at hand ; and the circumstances of this adventure were so obscure and menacing, the place seemed so well chosen for the darkest acts, that an older man than Brackenbury might have been pardoned a measure of emotion as he closed the procession up the winding stair.

At the top the guide threw open a door and ushered the three officers before him into a small apartment, lighted by a smoky lamp and the glow of a modest fire. At the chimney corner sat a man in the early prime of life, and of a stout but courtly and commanding appearance. His attitude and expression were those of the most unmoved composure ; he was smoking a cheroot with much enjoyment and deliberation, and on a table by his elbow stood a long glass of some effervescing beverage which diffused an agreeable odour through the room.

"Welcome," said he, extending his hand to Colonel Geraldine. "I knew I might count on your exactitude."

"On my devotion," replied the Colonel, with a bow.

"Present me to your friends," continued the first; and, when that ceremony had been performed, "I wish, gentlemen," he added, with the most exquisite affability, "that I could offer you a more cheerful programme; it is ungracious to inaugurate an acquaintance upon serious affairs; but the compulsion of events is stronger than the obligations of good-fellowship. I hope and believe you will be able to forgive me this unpleasant evening; and for men of your stamp it will be enough to know that you are conferring a considerable favour."

"Your Highness," said the Major, "must pardon my bluntness. I am unable to hide what I know. For some time back I have suspected Major Hammersmith, but Mr. Godall is unmistakable. To seek two men in London unacquainted with Prince Florizel of Bohemia was to ask too much at Fortune's hands."

"Prince Florizel!" cried Brackenbury in amazement.

And he gazed with the deepest interest on the features of the celebrated personage before him.

"I shall not lament the loss of my incognito," remarked the Prince, "for it enables me to thank you with the more authority. You would have done as much for Mr. Godall, I feel sure, as for the Prince of Bohemia; but the latter can perhaps do more for you. The gain is mine," he added, with a courteous gesture.

And the next moment he was conversing with the two officers about the Indian army and the native troops, a subject on which, as on all others, he had a remarkable fund of information and the soundest views.

There was something so striking in this man's

attitude at a moment of deadly peril that Brackenbury was overcome with respectful admiration ; nor was he less sensible to the charm of his conversation or the surprising amenity of his address. Every gesture, every intonation, was not only noble in itself, but seemed to ennoble the fortunate mortal for whom it was intended ; and Brackenbury confessed to himself with enthusiasm that this was a sovereign for whom a brave man might thankfully lay down his life.

Many minutes had thus passed, when the person who had introduced them into the house, and who had sat ever since in a corner, and with his watch in his hand, arose and whispered a word into the Prince's ear.

"It is well, Dr. Noel," replied Florizel aloud ; and then addressing the others, " You will excuse me, gentlemen," he added, "if I have to leave you in the dark. The moment now approaches."

Dr. Noel extinguished the lamp. A faint, grey light, premonitory of the dawn, illuminated the window, but was not sufficient to illuminate the room ; and when the Prince rose to his feet, it was impossible to distinguish his features or to make a guess at the nature of the emotion which obviously affected him as he spoke. He moved towards the door, and placed himself at one side of it in an attitude of the wariest attention.

" You will have the kindness," he said, " to maintain the strictest silence, and to conceal yourselves in the densest of the shadow."

The three officers and the physician hastened to obey, and for nearly ten minutes the only sound in Rochester House was occasioned by the excursions of the rats behind the woodwork. At the end of that period, a loud creak of a hinge broke in with surprising distinctness on the silence ; and shortly after, the watchers could distinguish a slow and cautious tread approaching up the kitchen stair. At every second step the intruder seemed to pause and lend an ear, and during these intervals, which seemed of an incalculable duration, a profound disquiet possessed the spirit of the listeners. Dr. Noel, accustomed as he was to dangerous emotions, suffered an almost pitiful physical prostration ; his breath whistled in his lungs, his teeth grated one upon another, and his joints cracked aloud as he nervously shifted his position.

At last a hand was laid upon the door, and the bolt shot back with a slight report. There followed another pause, during which Brackenbury could see the Prince draw himself together noiselessly as if for some unusual exertion. Then the door opened, letting in a little more of the light of the morning ; and the figure of a man appeared upon the threshold and stood motionless. He was tall, and carried a knife in his hand. Even in the twilight they could see his upper teeth bare and glistening, for his mouth was open like that of a hound about to leap. The man had evidently been over the head in water but a minute or two before ; and even while he stood there the drops kept falling from his wet clothes and pattered on the floor.

The next moment he crossed the threshold. There was a leap, a stifled cry, an instantaneous struggle ; and before Colonel Geraldine could spring to his aid, the Prince held the man, disarmed and helpless, by the shoulders.

" Dr. Noel," he said, " you will be so good as to re-light the lamp."

And relinquishing the charge of his prisoner to Geraldine and Brackenbury, he crossed the room and set his back against the chimney-piece. As soon as the lamp had kindled, the party beheld an unaccustomed sternness on the Prince's features. It was no longer Florizel, the careless gentleman ; it was the Prince of Bohemia, justly incensed and full of deadly purpose, who now raised his head and addressed the captive President of the Suicide Club.

"President," he said, "you have laid your last snare, and your own feet are taken in it. The day is beginning; it is your last morning. You have just swum the Regent's Canal; it is your last bathe in this world. Your old accomplice, Dr. Noel, so far from betraying me, has delivered you into my hands for judgment. And the grave you had dug for me this afternoon shall serve, in God's almighty providence, to hide your own just doom from the curiosity of mankind. Kneel and pray, sir, if you have a mind that way; for your time is short, and God is weary of your iniquities."

The President made no answer either by word or sign; but continued to hang his head and gaze sullenly on the floor, as though he were conscious of the Prince's prolonged and unsparing regard.

" Gentlemen," continued Florizel, resuming the ordinary tone of his conversation, " this is a fellow who has long eluded me, but whom, thanks to Dr. Noel, I now have tightly by the heels. To tell the story of his misdeeds would occupy more time than we can now afford; but if the canal had contained nothing but the blood of his victims, I believe the wretch would have been no drier than you see him. Even in an affair of this sort I desire to preserve the forms of honour. But I make you the judges, gentlemen—this is more an execution than a duel; and to give the rogue his choice of weapons would be to push too far a point of etiquette. I cannot afford to lose my life in such a business," he continued, unlocking the case of swords; "and as a pistol-bullet travels so often on the wings of chance, and skill and courage may fall by the most trembling marksman, I have decided, and I feel sure you will approve my determination, to put this question to the touch of swords."

When Brackenbury and Major O'Rooke, to whom these remarks were particularly addressed, had each intimated his approval, " Quick, sir," added Prince Florizel to the President, "choose a blade and do not keep me waiting; I have an impatience to be done with you for ever."

For the first time since he was captured and disarmed the President raised his head, and it was plain that he began instantly to pluck up courage. "Is it to be stand up?" he asked eagerly, "and between you and me?"

"I mean so far to honour you," replied the Prince.

"Oh, come!" cried the President. "With a fair field, who knows how things may happen? I must add that I consider it handsome behaviour on your Highness's part; and if the worst comes to the worst I shall die by one of the most gallant gentlemen in Europe."

And the President, liberated by those who had detained him, stepped up to the table and began, with minute attention, to select a sword. He was highly elated, and seemed to feel no doubt that he should issue victorious from the contest. The spectators grew alarmed in the face of so entire a confidence, and adjured Prince Florizel to reconsider his intention.

"It is but a farce," he answered; "and I think I can promise you, gentlemen, that it will not be long a-playing."

"Your Highness will be careful not to overreach," said Colonel Geraldine.

"Geraldine," returned the Prince, "did you ever know me fail in a debt of honour? I owe you this man's death, and you shall have it."

The President at last satisfied himself with one of the rapiers, and signified his readiness by a gesture that was not devoid of a rude nobility. The nearness of peril, and the sense of courage, even to this obnoxious villain, lent an air of manhood and a certain grace.

The Prince helped himself at random to a sword.

"Colonel Geraldine and Doctor Noel," he said, "will have the goodness to await me in this room. I wish no personal friend of mine to be involved in this transaction. Major O'Rooke, you are a man of some years and a settled reputation—let me recommend the President to your good graces. Lieutenant Rich will be so good as lend me his attentions : a young man cannot have too much experience in such affairs."

" Your Highness," replied Brackenbury, " it is an honour I shall prize extremely."

" It is well," returned Prince Florizel; " I shall hope to stand your friend in more important circumstances."

And so saying he led the way out of the apartment and down the kitchen stairs.

The two men who were thus left alone threw open the window and leaned out, straining every sense to catch an indication of the tragical events that were about to follow. The rain was now over ; day had almost come, and the birds were piping in the shrubbery and on the forest-trees of the garden. The Prince and his companions were visible for a moment as they followed an alley between two flowering thickets ; but at the first corner a clump of foliage intervened, and they were again concealed from view. This was all that the Colonel and the Physician had an opportunity to see, and the garden was so vast, and the place of combat evidently so remote from the house, that not even the noise of sword-play reached their ears.

" He has taken him towards the grave," said Dr. Noel, with a shudder.

" God," cried the Colonel, " God defend the right ! "

And they awaited the event in silence, the Doctor shaking with fear, the Colonel in an agony of sweat. Many minutes must have elapsed, the day was sensibly broader, and the birds were singing more heartily in the garden before a sound of returning footsteps recalled their glances towards the door. It was the Prince and the two Indian officers who entered. God had defended the right.

"I am ashamed of my emotion," said Prince Florizel; "I feel it is a weakness unworthy of my station, but the continued existence of that hound of hell had begun to prey upon me like a disease, and his death has more refreshed me than a night of slumber. Look, Geraldine," he continued, throwing his sword upon the floor, "there is the blood of the man who killed your brother. It should be a welcome sight. And yet," he added, "see how strangely we men are made! my revenge is not yet five minutes old, and already I am beginning to ask myself if even revenge be attainable on this precarious stage of life. The ill he did, who can undo it? The career in which he amassed a huge fortune (for the house itself in which we stand belonged to him)—that career is now a part of the destiny of mankind for ever; and I might weary myself making thrusts in carte until the crack of judgment, and Geraldine's brother would be none the less dead, and a thousand other innocent persons would be none the less dishonoured and debauched! The existence of a man is so small a thing to take, so mighty a thing to employ! Alas!" he cried, "is there anything in life so disenchanting as attainment?"

"God's justice has been done," replied the Doctor. "So much I behold. The lesson, your Highness, has been a cruel one for me; and I await my own turn with deadly apprehension."

"What was I saying?" cried the Prince. "I have punished, and here is the man beside us who can help me to undo. Ah, Dr. Noel! you and I have before us many a day of hard and honourable toil; and perhaps, before we have done, you may have more than redeemed your early errors."

"And in the meantime," said the Doctor, "let me go and bury my oldest friend."

And this (observes the erudite Arabian) *is the fortunate conclusion of the tale. The Prince, it is superfluous to mention, forgot none of those who served him in this great exploit; and to this day his authority and influence help them forward in their public career, while his condescending friendship adds a charm to their private life.* To collect, continues my author, *all the strange events in which this Prince has played the part of Providence were to fill the habitable globe with books.* But the stories which relate to the fortunes of THE RAJAH'S DIAMOND *are of too entertaining a description,* says he, *to be omitted.* Following prudently in the footsteps of this Oriental, we shall now begin the series to which he refers with the STORY OF THE BANDBOX.

THE RAJAH'S DIAMOND

STORY OF THE BANDBOX

Up to the age of sixteen, at a private school and afterwards at one of those great institutions for which England is justly famous, Mr. Harry Hartley had received the ordinary education of a gentleman. At that period he manifested a remarkable distaste for study; and his only surviving parent being both weak and ignorant, he was permitted thenceforward to spend his time in the attainment of petty and purely elegant accomplishments. Two years later, he was left an orphan and almost a beggar. For all active and industrious pursuits, Harry was unfitted alike by nature and training. He could sing romantic ditties, and accompany himself with discretion on the piano; he was a graceful although a timid cavalier; he had a pronounced taste for chess; and nature had sent him into the world with one of the most engaging exteriors that can well be fancied. Blond and pink, with dove's eyes and a gentle smile, he had an air of agreeable tenderness and melancholy and the most submissive and caressing manners. But when all is said, he was not the man to lead armaments of war or direct the councils of a State.

A fortunate chance and some influence obtained for Harry, at the time of his bereavement, the position of private secretary to Major - General Sir Thomas Vandeleur, C.B. Sir Thomas was a man of sixty, loud-spoken, boisterous, and domineering. For some reason, some service the nature of which had been often whispered and repeatedly denied, the Rajah of Kashgar had presented this officer with the sixth known diamond of the world. The gift transformed General Vandeleur from a poor into a wealthy man, from an obscure and unpopular soldier into one of the lions of London society; the possessor of the Rajah's Diamond was welcome in the most exclusive circles; and he had found a lady, young, beautiful, and well-born, who was willing to call the diamond hers even at the price of marriage with Sir Thomas Vandeleur. It was commonly said at the time that, as like draws to like, one jewel had attracted another; certainly Lady Vandeleur was not only a gem of the finest water in her own person, but she showed herself to the world in a very costly setting; and she was considered by many respectable authorities as one among the three or four best-dressed women in England.

Harry's duty as secretary was not particularly onerous; but he had a dislike for all prolonged work; it gave him pain to ink his fingers; and the charms of Lady Vandeleur and her toilettes drew him often from the library to the boudoir. He had the prettiest ways among women, could talk fashions with enjoyment, and was never more happy than when criticising a shade of ribbon or running on an errand to the milliner's. In short, Sir Thomas's correspondence fell into pitiful arrears, and my Lady had another lady's maid.

At last the General, who was one of the least patient of military commanders, arose from his place in a violent access of passion, and indicated to his secretary that he had no further need for his services, with one of those explanatory gestures which are most rarely employed between gentlemen. The door being unfortunately open, Mr. Hartley fell downstairs head-foremost.

He arose somewhat hurt and very deeply aggrieved. The life in the General's house precisely suited him; he moved, on a more or less doubtful footing, in very genteel company, he did little, he ate of the best, and he had a lukewarm satisfaction in the presence of Lady Vandeleur, which, in his own heart, he dubbed by a more emphatic name.

Immediately after he had been outraged by the military foot, he hurried to the boudoir and recounted his sorrows.

"You know very well, my dear Harry," replied Lady Vandeleur, for she called him by name like a child or a domestic servant, "that you never by any chance do what the General tells you. No more do I, you may say. But that is different. A woman can earn her pardon for a good year of disobedience by a single adroit submission ; and, besides, no one is married to his private secretary. I shall be sorry to lose you ; but since you cannot stay longer in a house where you have been insulted, I shall wish you good-bye, and I promise you to make the General smart for his behaviour."

Harry's countenance fell ; tears came into his eyes, and he gazed on Lady Vandeleur with a tender reproach.

"My Lady," said he, "what is an insult ? I should think little indeed of any one who could not forgive them by the score. But to leave one's friends ; to tear up the bonds of affection——"

He was unable to continue, for his emotion choked him, and he began to weep.

Lady Vandeleur looked at him with a curious expression.

"This little fool," she thought, "imagines himself to be in love with me. Why should he not become my servant instead of the General's ? He is good-natured, obliging, and understands dress ; and besides, it will keep him out of mischief. He is positively too pretty to be unattached."

That night she talked over the General, who was already somewhat ashamed of his vivacity ; and Harry was transferred to the feminine department, where his life was little short of heavenly. He was always dressed with uncommon nicety, wore delicate flowers in his button-hole, and could entertain a visitor with tact and pleasantry. He took a pride in servility to a beautiful woman; received Lady Vandeleur's commands as so many marks of favour; and was pleased to exhibit himself before other men, who derided and despised him, in his character of male lady's-maid and man-milliner. Nor could he think enough of his existence from a moral point of view. Wickedness seemed to him an essentially male attribute, and to pass one's days with a delicate woman, and principally occupied about trimmings, was to inhabit an enchanted isle among the storms of life.

One fine morning he came into the drawing-room and began to arrange some music on the top of the piano. Lady Vandeleur, at the other end of the apartment, was speaking somewhat eagerly with her brother, Charlie Pendragon, an elderly young man, much broken with dissipation, and very lame of one foot. The private secretary, to whose entrance they paid no regard, could not avoid overhearing a part of their conversation.

"To-day or never," said the lady. "Once and for all, it shall be done to-day."

"To-day, if it must be," replied the brother, with a sigh. "But it is a false step, a ruinous step, Clara; and we shall live to repent it dismally."

Lady Vandeleur looked her brother steadily and somewhat strangely in the face.

"You forget," she said; "the man must die at last."

"Upon my word, Clara," said Pendragon, "I believe you are the most heartless rascal in England."

"You men," she returned, "are so coarsely built, that you can never appreciate a shade of meaning. You are yourselves rapacious, violent, immodest, careless of distinction; and yet the least thought for the future shocks

you in a woman. I have no patience with such stuff.
You would despise in a common banker the imbecility
that you expect to find in us."

" You are very likely right," replied her brother ;
"you were always cleverer than I. And, anyway, you
know my motto : The family before all."

" Yes, Charlie," she returned, taking his hand in hers,
" I know your motto better than you know it yourself.
' And Clara before the family ! ' Is not that the second
part of it ? Indeed, you are the best of brothers, and I
love you dearly."

Mr. Pendragon got up, looking a little confused by
these family endearments.

" I had better not be seen," said he. " I understand my
part to a miracle, and I'll keep an eye on the Tame Cat."

" Do," she replied. " He is an abject creature, and
might ruin all."

She kissed the tips of her fingers to him daintily ; and
the brother withdrew by the boudoir and the back stair.

" Harry," said Lady Vandeleur turning towards the
secretary as soon as they were alone, " I have a commission for you this morning. But you shall take a cab ;
I cannot have my secretary freckled."

She spoke the last words with emphasis and a look
of half-motherly pride that caused great contentment to
poor Harry ; and he professed himself charmed to find
an opportunity of serving her.

" It is another of our great secrets," she went on
archly, "and no one must know of it but my secretary
and me. Sir Thomas would make the saddest disturbance ; and if you only knew how weary I am of these
scenes ! O Harry, Harry, can you explain to me what
makes you men so violent and unjust ? But, indeed, I
know you cannot ; you are the only man in the world
who knows nothing of these shameful passions ; you are
so good, Harry, and so kind ; you, at least, can be a

woman's friend ; and, do you know ? I think you make
the others more ugly by comparison."

"It is you," said Harry gallantly, "who are so kind
to me. You treat me like——"

"Like a mother," interposed Lady Vandeleur ; "I try
to be a mother to you. Or, at least," she corrected herself with a smile, "almost a mother. I am afraid I am
too young to be your mother really. Let us say a friend
—a dear friend."

She paused long enough to let her words take effect
in Harry's sentimental quarters, but not long enough to
allow him a reply.

"But all this is beside our purpose," she resumed.
"You will find a bandbox in the left-hand side of the
oak wardrobe ; it is underneath the pink slip that I wore
on Wednesday with my Mechlin. You will take it immediately to this address," and she gave him a paper,
"but do not, on any account, let it out of your hands
until you have received a receipt written by myself. Do
you understand ? Answer, if you please—answer ! This
is extremely important, and I must ask you to pay some
attention."

Harry pacified her by repeating her instructions perfectly ; and she was just going to tell him more when
General Vandeleur flung into the apartment, scarlet with
anger, and holding a long and elaborate milliner's bill in
his hand.

"Will you look at this, madam ? " cried he. "Will
you have the goodness to look at this document ? I
know well enough you married me for my money, and
I hope I can make as great allowances as any other man
in the service ; but, as sure as God made me, I mean to
put a period to this disreputable prodigality."

"Mr. Hartley," said Lady Vandeleur, "I think you
understand what you have to do. May I ask you to see
to it at once ? "

"Stop," said the General, addressing Harry, "one word before you go." And then, turning again to Lady Vandeleur, "What is this precious fellow's errand?" he demanded. "I trust him no further than I do yourself, let me tell you. If he had as much as the rudiments of honesty, he would scorn to stay in this house; and what he does for his wages is a mystery to all the world. What is his errand, madam? and why are you hurrying him away?"

"I supposed you had something to say to me in private," replied the lady.

"You spoke about an errand," insisted the General. "Do not attempt to deceive me in my present state of temper. You certainly spoke about an errand."

"If you insist on making your servants privy to our humiliating dissensions," replied Lady Vandeleur, "perhaps I had better ask Mr. Hartley to sit down. No?" she continued; "then you may go, Mr. Hartley. I trust you may remember all that you have heard in this room; it may be useful to you."

Harry at once made his escape from the drawing-room; and as he ran upstairs he could hear the General's voice upraised in declamation, and the thin tones of Lady Vandeleur planting icy repartees at every opening. How cordially he admired the wife! How skilfully she could evade an awkward question! with what secure effrontery she repeated her instructions under the very guns of the enemy! and on the other hand, how he detested the husband!

There had been nothing unfamiliar in the morning's events, for he was continually in the habit of serving Lady Vandeleur on secret missions, principally connected with millinery. There was a skeleton in the house, as he well knew. The bottomless extravagance and the unknown liabilities of the wife had long since swallowed her own fortune, and threatened day by day to engulf that of the husband. Once or twice in every year exposure and ruin seemed imminent, and Harry kept trotting round to all sorts of furnishers' shops, telling small fibs, and paying small advances on the gross amount, until another term was tided over, and the lady and her faithful secretary breathed again. For Harry, in a double capacity, was heart and soul upon that side of the war; not only did he adore Lady Vandeleur and fear and dislike her husband, but he naturally sympathised with the love of finery, and his own single extravagance was at the tailor's.

He found the bandbox where it had been described, arranged his toilette with care, and left the house. The sun shone brightly; the distance he had to travel was considerable, and he remembered with dismay that the General's sudden irruption had prevented Lady Vandeleur from giving him money for a cab. On this sultry day there was every chance that his complexion would suffer severely; and to walk through so much of London with a bandbox on his arm was a humiliation almost insupportable to a youth of his character. He paused, and took counsel with himself. The Vandeleurs lived in Eaton Place; his destination was near Notting Hill; plainly, he might cross the Park by keeping well in the open and avoiding populous alleys; and he thanked his stars when he reflected that it was still comparatively early in the day.

Anxious to be rid of his incubus, he walked somewhat faster than his ordinary, and he was already some way through Kensington Gardens when, in a solitary spot among trees, he found himself confronted by the General.

"I beg your pardon, Sir Thomas," observed Harry, politely falling on one side; for the other stood directly in his path.

"Where are you going, sir?" asked the General.

"I am taking a little walk among the trees," replied the lad.

The General struck the bandbox with his cane.

"With that thing?" he cried; "you lie, sir, and you know you lie!"

"Indeed, Sir Thomas," returned Harry, "I am not accustomed to be questioned in so high a key."

"You do not understand your position," said the General. "You are my servant, and a servant of whom I have conceived the most serious suspicions. How do I know but that your box is full of tea-spoons?"

"It contains a silk hat belonging to a friend," said Harry.

"Very well," replied General Vandeleur. "Then I want to see your friend's silk hat. I have," he added grimly, "a singular curiosity for hats; and I believe you know me to be somewhat positive."

"I beg your pardon, Sir Thomas; I am exceedingly grieved," Harry apologised; "but indeed this is a private affair."

The General caught him roughly by the shoulder with one hand, while he raised his cane in the most menacing manner with the other. Harry gave himself up for lost; but at the same moment Heaven vouchsafed him an unexpected defender in the person of Charlie Pendragon, who now strode forward from behind the trees.

"Come, come, General, hold your hand," said he; "this is neither courteous nor manly."

"Aha!" cried the General, wheeling round upon his new antagonist, "Mr. Pendragon! And do you suppose, Mr. Pendragon, that because I have had the misfortune to marry your sister, I shall suffer myself to be dogged and thwarted by a discredited and bankrupt libertine like you? My acquaintance with Lady Vandeleur, sir, has taken away all my appetite for the other members of her family."

"And do you fancy, General Vandeleur," retorted
Charlie, "that because my sister has had the misfortune
to marry you, she there and then forfeited her rights and
privileges as a lady? I own, sir, that by that action she
did as much as anybody could to derogate from her position; but to me she is still a Pendragon. I make it
my business to protect her from ungentlemanly outrage,
and if you were ten times her husband I would not permit
her liberty to be restrained, nor her private messengers to
be violently arrested."

"How is that, Mr. Hartley?" interrogated the General.
"Mr. Pendragon is of my opinion, it appears. He too
suspects that Lady Vandeleur has something to do with
your friend's silk hat."

Charlie saw that he had committed an unpardonable
blunder, which he hastened to repair.

"How, sir?" he cried; "I suspect, do you say? I
suspect nothing. Only where I find strength abused and
a man brutalising his inferiors, I take the liberty to interfere."

As he said these words he made a sign to Harry, which
the latter was too dull or too much troubled to understand.

"In what way am I to construe your attitude, sir?"
demanded Vandeleur.

"Why, sir, as you please," returned Pendragon.

The General once more raised his cane, and made a
cut for Charlie's head; but the latter, lame foot and all,
evaded the blow with his umbrella, ran in, and immediately closed with his formidable adversary.

"Run, Harry, run!" he cried; "run, you dolt!"

Harry stood petrified for a moment, watching the two
men sway together in this fierce embrace; then he turned
and took to his heels. When he cast a glance over his
shoulder he saw the General prostrate under Charlie's
knee, but still making desperate efforts to reverse the

situation; and the Gardens seemed to have filled with people, who were running from all directions towards the scene of fight. This spectacle lent the secretary wings; and he did not relax his pace until he had gained the Bayswater Road, and plunged at random into an unfrequented by-street.

To see two gentlemen of his acquaintance thus brutally mauling each other was deeply shocking to Harry. He desired to forget the sight; he desired, above all, to put as great a distance as possible between himself and General Vandeleur; and in his eagerness for this he forgot everything about his destination, and hurried before him headlong and trembling. When he remembered that Lady Vandeleur was the wife of one and the sister of the other of these gladiators, his heart was touched with sympathy for a woman so distressingly misplaced in life. Even his own situation in the General's household looked hardly so pleasing as usual in the light of these violent transactions.

He had walked some little distance, busied with these meditations, before a slight collision with another passenger reminded him of the bandbox on his arm.

"Heavens!" cried he, "where was my head? and whither have I wandered?"

Thereupon he consulted the envelope which Lady Vandeleur had given him. The address was there, but without a name. Harry was simply directed to ask for "the gentleman who expected a parcel from Lady Vandeleur," and if he were not at home to await his return. The gentleman, added the note, should present a receipt in the handwriting of the lady herself. All this seemed mightily mysterious, and Harry was above all astonished at the omission of the name and the formality of the receipt. He had thought little of this last when he heard it dropped in conversation; but reading it in cold blood, and taking it in connection with the other strange particulars, he became convinced that he was engaged in perilous affairs. For half a moment he had a doubt of Lady Vandeleur herself; for he found these obscure proceedings somewhat unworthy of so high a lady, and became more critical when her secrets were preserved against himself. But her empire over his spirit was too complete, he dismissed his suspicions, and blamed himself roundly for having so much as entertained them.

In one thing, however, his duty and interest, his generosity and his terrors, coincided—to get rid of the bandbox with the greatest possible despatch.

He accosted the first policeman and courteously inquired his way. It turned out that he was already not far from his destination, and a walk of a few minutes brought him to a small house in a lane, freshly painted, and kept with the most scrupulous attention. The knocker and bell-pull were highly polished : flowering pot-herbs garnished the sills of the different windows ; and curtains of some rich material concealed the interior from the eyes of curious passengers. The place had an air of repose and secrecy ; and Harry was so far caught with this spirit that he knocked with more than usual discretion, and was more than usually careful to remove all impurity from his boots.

A servant-maid of some personal attractions immediately opened the door, and seemed to regard the secretary with no unkind eyes.

"This is the parcel from Lady Vandeleur," said Harry.

" I know," replied the maid, with a nod. " But the gentleman is from home. Will you leave it with me ? "

" I cannot," answered Harry. " I am directed not to part with it but upon a certain condition, and I must ask you, I am afraid, to let me wait."

" Well," said she, " I suppose I may let you wait. I am lonely enough, I can tell you, and you do not look as though you would eat a girl. But be sure and do not ask the gentleman's name, for that I am not to tell you."

"Do you say so?" cried Harry. "Why, how strange! But indeed for some time back I walk among surprises. One question I think I may surely ask without indiscretion : Is he the master of this house?"

"He is a lodger, and not eight days old at that," returned the maid. "And now a question for a question : Do you know Lady Vandeleur?"

"I am her private secretary," replied Harry, with a glow of modest pride.

"She is pretty, is she not?" pursued the servant.

"Oh, beautiful!" cried Harry; "wonderfully lovely, and not less good and kind!"

"You look kind enough yourself," she retorted; "and I wager you are worth a dozen Lady Vandeleurs."

Harry was properly scandalised.

"I!" he cried. "I am only a secretary!"

"Do you mean that for me?" said the girl. "Because I am only a housemaid, if you please." And then, relenting at the sight of Harry's obvious confusion, "I know you mean nothing of the sort," she added; "and I like your looks; but I think nothing of your Lady Vandeleur. Oh, these mistresses!" she cried. "To send out a real gentleman like you—with a bandbox—in broad day!"

During this talk they had remained in their original positions—she on the doorstep, he on the side-walk, bareheaded for the sake of coolness, and with the bandbox on his arm. But upon this last speech Harry, who was unable to support such point-blank compliments to his appearance, nor the encouraging look with which they were accompanied, began to change his attitude, and glance from left to right in perturbation. In so doing he turned his face towards the lower end of the lane, and there, to his indescribable dismay, his eyes encountered those of General Vandeleur. The General, in a prodigious fluster of heat, hurry, and indignation, had been scouring the streets in chase of his brother-in-law ; but so soon as he caught a glimpse of the delinquent secretary, his purpose changed, his anger flowed into a new channel, and he turned on his heel and came tearing up the lane with truculent gestures and vociferations.

Harry made but one bolt of it into the house, driving the maid before him ; and the door was slammed in his pursuer's countenance.

"Is there a bar ? Will it lock ? " asked Harry, while a salvo on the knocker made the house echo from wall to wall.

"Why, what is wrong with you ? " asked the maid. "Is it this old gentleman ? "

"If he gets hold of me," whispered Harry, "I am as good as dead. He has been pursuing me all day, carries a sword-stick, and is an Indian military officer."

"These are fine manners," cried the maid. "And what, if you please, may be his name ? "

"It is the General, my master," answered Harry. "He is after this bandbox."

"Did not I tell you ? " cried the maid in triumph. "I told you I thought worse than nothing of your Lady Vandeleur ; and if you had an eye in your head you might see what she is for yourself. An ungrateful minx, I will be bound for that ! "

The General renewed his attack upon the knocker, and his passion growing with delay, began to kick and beat upon the panels of the door.

"It is lucky," observed the girl, "that I am alone in the house ; your General may hammer until he is weary, and there is none to open for him. Follow me ! "

So saying she led Harry into the kitchen, where she made him sit down, and stood by him herself in an affectionate attitude, with a hand upon his shoulder. The din at the door, so far from abating, continued to increase in volume, and at each blow the unhappy secretary was shaken to the heart.

" What is your name ? " asked the girl.

" Harry Hartley," he replied.

" Mine," she went on, " is Prudence. Do you like it ? "

" Very much," said Harry. " But hear for a moment how the General beats upon the door. He will certainly break it in, and then, in heaven's name, what have I to look for but death ? "

" You put yourself very much about with no occasion," answered Prudence. " Let your General knock, he will do no more than blister his hands. Do you think I would keep you here if I were not sure to save you ? Oh, no, I am a good friend to those that please me ! and we have a back door upon another lane. But," she added, checking him, for he had got upon his feet immediately on this welcome news, " But I will not show where it is unless you kiss me. Will you, Harry ? "

" That I will," he cried, remembering his gallantry, " not for your back door, but because you are good and pretty."

And he administered two or three cordial salutes, which were returned to him in kind.

Then Prudence led him to the back gate, and put her hand upon the key.

" Will you come and see me ? " she asked.

" I will indeed," said Harry. " Do not I owe you my life ?

" And now," she added, opening the door, " run as hard as you can, for I shall let in the General."

Harry scarcely required this advice ; fear had him by the forelock ; and he addressed himself diligently to flight. A few steps, and he believed he would escape from his trials, and return to Lady Vandeleur in honour and safety. But these few steps had not been taken before he heard a man's voice hailing him by name with many execrations, and, looking over his shoulder, he beheld Charlie Pendragon waving him with both arms to return. The shock of this new incident was so sudden and profound, and Harry was already worked into so high a state of nervous tension, that he could think of nothing better than to accelerate his pace and continue running. He should certainly have remembered the scene in Kensington Gardens; he should certainly have concluded that, where the General was his enemy, Charlie Pendragon could be no other than a friend. But such was the fever and perturbation of his mind that he was struck by none of these considerations, and only continued to run the faster up the lane.

Charlie, by the sound of his voice and the vile terms that he hurled after the secretary, was obviously beside himself with rage. He, too, ran his very best; but, try as he might, the physical advantages were not upon his side, and his outcries and the fall of his lame foot on the macadam began to fall farther and farther into the wake.

Harry's hopes began once more to arise. The lane was both steep and narrow, but it was exceedingly solitary, bordered on either hand by garden walls, overhung with foliage ; and, for as far as the fugitive could see in front of him, there was neither a creature moving nor an open door. Providence, weary of persecution, was now offering him an open field for his escape.

Alas ! as he came abreast of a garden door under a tuft of chestnuts, it was suddenly drawn back, and he could see inside, upon a garden path, the figure of a butcher's boy with his tray upon his arm. He had hardly recognised the fact before he was some steps beyond upon the other side. But the fellow had had time to observe him ; he was evidently much surprised to see a gentleman go by at so unusual a pace ; and he came out into the lane and began to call after Harry with shouts of ironical encouragement.

His appearance gave a new idea to Charlie Pendragon, who, although he was now sadly out of breath, once more upraised his voice.

"Stop, thief!" he cried.

And immediately the butcher's boy had taken up the cry and joined in the pursuit.

This was a bitter moment for the hunted secretary. It is true that his terror enabled him once more to improve his pace, and gain with every step on his pursuers; but he was well aware that he was near the end of his resources, and should he meet any one coming the other way, his predicament in the narrow lane would be desperate indeed.

"I must find a place of concealment," he thought, "and that within the next few seconds, or all is over with me in this world."

Scarcely had the thought crossed his mind than the lane took a sudden turning, and he found himself hidden from his enemies. There are circumstances in which even the least energetic of mankind learn to behave with vigour and decision, and the most cautious forget their prudence and embrace foolhardy resolutions. This was one of those occasions for Harry Hartley; and those who knew him best would have been the most astonished at the lad's audacity. He stopped dead, flung the bandbox over a garden wall, and leaping upward with incredible agility, and seizing the copestone with his hands, he tumbled headlong after it into the garden.

He came to himself a moment afterwards, seated in a border of small rose-bushes. His hands and knees were cut and bleeding, for the wall had been protected against such an escalade by a liberal provision of old bottles; and he was conscious of a general dislocation and a painful swimming in the head. Facing him across the garden, which was in admirable order, and set with flowers of the most delicious perfume, he beheld the back of a house. It was of considerable extent, and plainly habitable; but, in odd contrast to the grounds, it was crazy, ill-kept, and of a mean appearance. On all other sides the circuit of the garden wall appeared unbroken.

He took in these features of the scene with mechanical glances, but his mind was still unable to piece together or draw a rational conclusion from what he saw. And when he heard footsteps advancing on the gravel, although he turned his eyes in that direction, it was with no thought either for defence or flight.

The new-comer was a large, coarse, and very sordid personage, in gardening clothes, and with a watering-pot in his left hand. One less confused would have been affected with some alarm at the sight of this man's huge proportions and black and lowering eyes. But Harry was too gravely shaken by his fall to be so much as terrified; and if he was unable to divert his glances from the gardener, he remained absolutely passive, and suffered him to draw near, to take him by the shoulder, and to plant him roughly on his feet, without a motion of resistance.

For a moment the two stared into each other's eyes, Harry fascinated, the man filled with wrath and a cruel, sneering humour.

"Who are you?" he demanded at last. "Who are you to come flying over my wall and break my *Gloire de Dijons*? What is your name?" he added, shaking him; "and what may be your business here?"

Harry could not as much as proffer a word in explanation.

But just at that moment Pendragon and the butcher's boy went clumping past, and the sound of their feet and their hoarse cries echoed loudly in the narrow lane. The gardener had received his answer; and he looked down into Harry's face with an obnoxious smile.

"A thief!" he said. "Upon my word, and a very good thing you must make of it; for I see you dressed like a gentleman from top to toe. Are you not ashamed to go about the world in such a trim, with honest folk, I daresay, glad to buy your cast-off finery second-hand? Speak up, you dog," the man went on; "you can understand English, I suppose; and I mean to have a bit of talk with you before I march you to the station."

"Indeed, sir," said Harry, "this is all a dreadful misconception; and if you will go with me to Sir Thomas Vandeleur's in Eaton Place, I can promise that all will be made plain. The most upright person, as I now perceive, can be led into suspicious positions."

"My little man," replied the gardener, "I will go with you no farther than the station-house in the next street. The inspector, no doubt, will be glad to take a stroll with you as far as Eaton Place, and have a bit of afternoon tea with your great acquaintances. Or would you prefer to go direct to the Home Secretary? Sir Thomas Vandeleur, indeed! Perhaps you think I don't know a gentleman when I see one, from a common run-the-hedge like you? Clothes or no clothes, I can read you like a book. Here is a shirt that maybe cost as much as my Sunday hat; and that coat, I take it, has never seen the inside of Rag-fair, and then your boots——"

The man, whose eyes had fallen upon the ground, stopped short in his insulting commentary, and remained for a moment looking intently upon something at his feet. When he spoke his voice was strangely altered.

"What, in God's name," said he, "is all this?"

Harry, following the direction of the man's eyes, beheld a spectacle that struck him dumb with terror and amazement. In his fall he had descended vertically upon the bandbox, and burst it open from end to end; thence a great treasure of diamonds had poured forth, and now lay abroad, part trodden in the soil, part scattered on the surface in regal and glittering profusion. There was a magnificent coronet which he had often admired on Lady Vandeleur; there were rings and brooches, ear-drops and bracelets, and even unset brilliants rolling here and there among the rose-bushes like drops of morning dew. A princely fortune lay between the two men upon the ground—a fortune in the most inviting, solid, and durable form, capable of being carried in an apron, beautiful in itself, and scattering the sunlight in a million rainbow flashes.

"Good God!" said Harry, "I am lost!"

His mind racked backwards into the past with the incalculable velocity of thought, and he began to comprehend his day's adventures, to conceive them as a whole, and to recognise the sad imbroglio in which his own character and fortunes had become involved. He looked round him as if for help, but he was alone in the garden, with his scattered diamonds and his redoubtable interlocutor; and when he gave ear, there was no sound but the rustle of the leaves and the hurried pulsation of his heart. It was little wonder if the young man felt himself deserted by his spirits, and with a broken voice repeated his last ejaculation—

"I am lost!"

The gardener peered in all directions with an air of guilt; but there was no face at any of the windows, and he seemed to breathe again.

"Pick up a heart," he said, "you fool! The worst of it is done. Why could you not say at first there was enough for two? Two?" he repeated, "ay, and for two hundred! But come away from here, where we may be observed; and, for the love of wisdom, straighten out your hat and brush your clothes. You could not travel two steps the figure of fun you look just now."

While Harry mechanically adopted these suggestions, the gardener, getting upon his knees, hastily drew together the scattered jewels and returned them to the bandbox. The touch of these costly crystals sent a shiver of emotion through the man's stalwart frame; his face was transfigured, and his eyes shone with concupiscence; indeed, it seemed as if he luxuriously prolonged his occupation, and dallied with every diamond that he handled. At last, however, it was done; and concealing the bandbox in his smock, the gardener beckoned to Harry and preceded him in the direction of the house.

Near the door they were met by a young man, evidently in holy orders, dark and strikingly handsome, with a look of mingled weakness and resolution, and very neatly attired after the manner of his caste. The gardener was plainly annoyed by this encounter; but he put as good a face upon it as he could, and accosted the clergyman with an obsequious and smiling air.

"Here is a fine afternoon, Mr. Rolles," said he: "a fine afternoon, as sure as God made it! And here is a young friend of mine who had a fancy to look at my roses. I took the liberty to bring him in, for I thought none of the lodgers would object."

"Speaking for myself," replied the Reverend Mr. Rolles, "I do not; nor do I fancy any of the rest of us would be more difficult upon so small a matter. The garden is your own, Mr. Raeburn; we must none of us forget that; and because you give us liberty to walk there we should be indeed ungracious if we so far presumed upon your politeness as to interfere with the convenience of your friends. But, on second thoughts," he added, "I believe that this gentleman and I have met before. Mr. Hartley, I think. I regret to observe that you have had a fall."

And he offered his hand.

A sort of maiden dignity, and a desire to delay as

long as possible the necessity for explanation, moved
Harry to refuse this chance of help, and to deny his
own identity. He chose the tender mercies of the gardener, who was at least unknown to him, rather than
the curiosity and perhaps the doubts of an acquaintance.

"I fear there is some mistake," said he. "My name
is Thomlinson and I am a friend of Mr. Raeburn's."

"Indeed?" said Mr. Rolles. "The likeness is amazing."

Mr. Raeburn, who had been upon thorns throughout this colloquy, now felt it high time to bring it to
a period.

"I wish you a pleasant saunter, sir," said he.

And with that he dragged Harry after him into the
house, and then into a chamber on the garden. His first
care was to draw down the blind, for Mr. Rolles still
remained where they had left him, in an attitude of
perplexity and thought. Then he emptied the broken
bandbox on the table, and stood before the treasure,
thus fully displayed, with an expression of rapturous
greed, and rubbing his hands upon his thighs. For
Harry, the sight of the man's face under the influence
of this base emotion added another pang to those he
was already suffering. It seemed incredible that, from
his life of pure and delicate trifling, he should be plunged
in a breath among sordid and criminal relations. He
could reproach his conscience with no sinful act ; and
yet he was now suffering the punishment of sin in its
most acute and cruel forms—the dread of punishment,
the suspicions of the good, and the companionship and
contamination of vile and brutal natures. He felt he
could lay his life down with gladness to escape from
the room and the society of Mr. Raeburn.

"And now," said the latter, after he had separated
the jewels into two nearly equal parts, and drawn one
of them nearer to himself; "and now," said he, "every-

thing in this world has to be paid for, and some things sweetly. You must know, Mr. Hartley, if such be your name, that I am a man of a very easy temper, and good-nature has been my stumbling-block from first to last. I could pocket the whole of these pretty pebbles, if I chose, and I should like to see you dare to say a word; but I think I must have taken a liking to you; for I declare I have not the heart to shave you so close. So, do you see, in pure kind feeling, I propose that we divide; and these," indicating the two heaps, "are the proportions that seem to me just and friendly. Do you see any objection, Mr. Hartley, may I ask? I am not the man to stick upon a brooch."

"But, sir," cried Harry, "what you propose to me is impossible. The jewels are not mine, and I cannot share what is another's, no matter with whom, nor in what proportions."

"They are not yours, are they not?" returned Raeburn. "And you could not share them with anybody, couldn't you? Well, now, that is what I call a pity; for here am I obliged to take you to the station. The police—think of that," he continued; "think of the disgrace for your respectable parents; think," he went on, taking Harry by the wrist; "think of the Colonies and the Day of Judgment."

"I cannot help it," wailed Harry. "It is not my fault. You will not come with me to Eaton Place."

"No," replied the man; "I will not, that is certain. And I mean to divide these playthings with you here."

And so saying he applied a sudden and severe torsion to the lad's wrist.

Harry could not suppress a scream, and the perspiration burst forth upon his face. Perhaps pain and terror quickened his intelligence, but certainly at that moment the whole business flashed across him in another light; and he saw that there was nothing for it but to accede to the ruffian's proposal, and trust to find the house and force him to disgorge, under more favourable circumstances, and when he himself was clear from all suspicion.

"I agree," he said.

"There is a lamb," sneered the gardener. "I thought you would recognise your interests at last. This bandbox," he continued, "I shall burn with my rubbish; it is a thing that curious folk might recognise; and as for you, scrape up your gaieties and put them in your pocket."

Harry proceeded to obey, Raeburn watching him, and every now and again, his greed rekindled by some bright scintillation, abstracting another jewel from the secretary's share, and adding it to his own.

When this was finished, both proceeded to the front door, which Raeburn cautiously opened to observe the street. This was apparently clear of passengers; for he suddenly seized Harry by the nape of the neck, and holding his face downward so that he could see nothing but the roadway and the doorsteps of the houses, pushed him violently before him down one street and up another for the space of perhaps a minute and a half. Harry had counted three corners before the bully relaxed his grasp, and crying, "Now be off with you!" sent the lad flying head-foremost with a well-directed and athletic kick.

When Harry gathered himself up, half-stunned and bleeding freely at the nose, Mr. Raeburn had entirely disappeared. For the first time, anger and pain so completely overcame the lad's spirits that he burst into a fit of tears and remained sobbing in the middle of the road.

After he had thus somewhat assuaged his emotion, he began to look about him and read the names of the streets at whose intersection he had been deserted by the gardener. ↑ He was still in an unfrequented portion of West London, among villas and large gardens; but he could see some persons at a window who had evidently witnessed his misfortune ; and almost immediately after a servant came running from the house and offered him a glass of water. At the same time, a dirty rogue, who had been slouching somewhere in the neighbourhood, drew near him from the other side.

"Poor fellow," said the maid, "how vilely you have been handled, to be sure ! Why, your knees are all cut, and your clothes ruined ! Do you know the wretch who used you so ? "

"That I do !" cried Harry, who was somewhat refreshed by the water ; "and shall run him home in spite of his precautions. He shall pay dearly for this day's work, I promise you."

"You had better come into the house and have yourself washed and brushed," continued the maid. "My mistress will make you welcome, never fear. And see, I will pick up your hat. Why, love of mercy !" she screamed, "if you have not dropped diamonds all over the street !"

Such was the case ; a good half of what remained to him after the depredations of Mr. Raeburn had been shaken out of his pockets by the summersault, and once more lay glittering on the ground. He blessed his fortune that the maid had been so quick of eye; "there is nothing so bad but it might be worse," thought he ; and the recovery of these few seemed to him almost as great an affair as the loss of all the rest. But, alas ! as he stooped to pick up his treasures, the loiterer made a rapid onslaught, overset both Harry and the maid with a movement of his arms, swept up a double-handful of the diamonds, and made off along the street with an amazing swiftness.

Harry, as soon as he could get upon his feet, gave chase to the miscreant with many cries, but the latter was too fleet of foot, and probably too well acquainted with the locality ; for turn where the pursuer would he could find no traces of the fugitive.

In the deepest despondency, Harry revisited the scene of his mishap, where the maid, who was still waiting, very honestly returned him his hat and the remainder of the fallen diamonds. Harry thanked her from his heart, and being now in no humour for economy, made his way to the nearest cabstand and set off for Eaton Place by coach.

The house, on his arrival, seemed in some confusion, as if a catastrophe had happened in the family ; and the servants clustered together in the hall, and were unable, or perhaps not altogether anxious, to suppress their merriment at the tatterdemalion figure of the secretary. He passed them with as good an air of dignity as he could assume, and made directly for the boudoir. When he opened the door an astonishing and even menacing spectacle presented itself to his eyes ; for he beheld the General and his wife and, of all people, Charlie Pendragon, closeted together and speaking with earnestness and gravity on some important subject. Harry saw at once that there was little left for him to explain—plenary confession had plainly been made to the General of the intended fraud upon his pocket, and the unfortunate miscarriage of the scheme ; and they had all made common cause against a common danger.

"Thank Heaven !" cried Lady Vandeleur, "here he is ! The bandbox, Harry—the bandbox !"

But Harry stood before them silent and downcast.

"Speak !" she cried. "Speak ! Where is the bandbox ?"

And the men, with threatening gestures, repeated the demand.

Harry drew a handful of jewels from his pocket. He was very white.

"This is all that remains," said he. "I declare before

Heaven it was through no fault of mine ; and if you will
have patience, although some are lost, I am afraid, for
ever, others, I am sure, may be still recovered."

"Alas !" cried Lady Vandeleur, "all our diamonds
are gone, and I owe ninety thousand pounds for dress !"

"Madam," said the General, "you might have paved
the gutter with your own trash ; you might have made
debts to fifty times the sum you mention ; you might
have robbed me of my mother's coronet and ring ; and
Nature might have still so far prevailed that I could have
forgiven you at last. But, madam, you have taken the
Rajah's Diamond—the Eye of Light, as the Orientals
poetically termed it—the Pride of Kashgar! You have
taken from me the Rajah's Diamond," he cried, raising
his hands, "and all, madam, all is at an end between
us !"

"Believe me, General Vandeleur," she replied, "that
is one of the most agreeable speeches that ever I heard
from your lips ; and since we are to be ruined, I could
almost welcome the change, if it delivers me from you.
You have told me often enough that I married you for
your money ; let me tell you now that I always bitterly
repented the bargain ; and if you were still marriageable,
and had a diamond bigger than your head, I should
counsel even my maid against a union so uninviting and
disastrous.—As for you, Mr. Hartley," she continued,
turning on the secretary, "you have sufficiently exhibited
your valuable qualities in this house ; we are now persuaded that you equally lack manhood, sense, and self-
respect ; and I can see only one course open for you—
to withdraw instanter, and, if possible, return no more.
For your wages you may rank as a creditor in my late
husband's bankruptcy."

Harry had scarcely comprehended this insulting address
before the General was down upon him with another.

"And in the meantime," said that personage, "follow

me before the nearest Inspector of Police. You may
impose upon a simple-minded soldier, sir, but the eye of
the law will read your disreputable secret. If I must
spend my old age in poverty through your underhand
intriguing with my wife, I mean at least that you shall
not remain unpunished for your pains; and God, sir, will
deny me a very considerable satisfaction if you do not
pick oakum from now until your dying day."

With that, the General dragged Harry from the apartment, and hurried him down-stairs and along the street
to the police-station of the district.

Here (says my Arabian author) *ended this deplorable
business of the bandbox. But to the unfortunate secretary
the whole affair was the beginning of a new and manlier
life. The police were easily persuaded of his innocence;
and, after he had given what help he could in the subse-
quent investigations, he was even complimented by one of
the chiefs of the detective department on the probity and
simplicity of his behaviour. Several persons interested
themselves in one so unfortunate; and soon after he
inherited a sum of money from a maiden aunt in Wor-
cestershire. With this he married Prudence, and set sail
for Bendigo, or, according to another account, for Trinco-
malee, exceedingly content, and with the best of prospects.*

STORY OF THE YOUNG MAN IN HOLY ORDERS

THE Reverend Mr. Simon Rolles had distinguished himself in the Moral Sciences, and was more than usually
proficient in the study of Divinity. His essay "On the
Christian Doctrine of the Social Obligations" obtained
for him, at the moment of its production, a certain celebrity in the University of Oxford; and it was understood
in clerical and learned circles that young Mr. Rolles had
in contemplation a considerable work—a folio, it was said

—on the authority of the Fathers of the Church. These attainments, these ambitious designs, however, were far from helping him to any preferment; and he was still in quest of his first curacy when a chance ramble in that part of London, the peaceful and rich aspect of the garden, a desire for solitude and study, and the cheapness of the lodging, led him to take up his abode with Mr. Raeburn, the nurseryman of Stockdove Lane.

It was his habit every afternoon, after he had worked seven or eight hours on St. Ambrose or St. Chrysostom, to walk for a while in meditation among the roses. And this was usually one of the most productive moments of his day. But even a sincere appetite for thought, and the excitement of grave problems awaiting solution, are not always sufficient to preserve the mind of the philosopher against the petty shocks and contacts of the world. And when Mr. Rolles found General Vandeleur's secretary, ragged and bleeding, in the company of his landlord; when he saw both change colour and seek to avoid his questions; and, above all, when the former denied his own identity with the most unmoved assurance, he speedily forgot the Saints and Fathers in the vulgar interest of curiosity.

"I cannot be mistaken," thought he. "That is Mr. Hartley beyond a doubt. How comes he in such a pickle? why does he deny his name? and what can be his business with that black-looking ruffian, my landlord?"

As he was thus reflecting, another peculiar circumstance attracted his attention. The face of Mr. Raeburn appeared at a low window next the door; and, as chance directed, his eyes met those of Mr. Rolles. The nurseryman seemed disconcerted, and even alarmed; and immediately after the blind of the apartment was pulled sharply down.

"This may all be very well," reflected Mr. Rolles; "it

may be all excellently well; but I confess freely that I do not think so. Suspicious, underhand, untruthful, fearful of observation—I believe upon my soul," he thought, "the pair are plotting some disgraceful action."

The detective that there is in all of us awoke and became clamant in the bosom of Mr. Rolles; and with a brisk, eager step, that bore no resemblance to his usual gait, he proceeded to make the circuit of the garden. When he came to the scene of Harry's escalade, his eye was at once arrested by a broken rose-bush and marks of trampling on the mould. He looked up, and saw scratches on the brick, and a rag of trouser floating from a broken bottle. This, then, was the mode of entrance chosen by Mr. Raeburn's particular friend! It was thus that General Vandeleur's secretary came to admire a flower-garden! The young clergyman whistled softly to himself as he stooped to examine the ground. He could make out where Harry had landed from his perilous leap; he recognised the flat foot of Mr. Raeburn where it had sunk deeply in the soil as he pulled up the secretary by the collar; nay, on a closer inspection, he seemed to distinguish the marks of groping fingers, as though something had been spilt abroad and eagerly collected.

"Upon my word," he thought, "the thing grows vastly interesting."

And just then he caught sight of something almost entirely buried in the earth. In an instant he had disinterred a dainty morocco case, ornamented and clasped in gilt. It had been trodden heavily underfoot, and thus escaped the hurried search of Mr. Raeburn. Mr. Rolles opened the case, and drew a long breath of almost horrified astonishment; for there lay before him, in a cradle of green velvet, a diamond of prodigious magnitude and of the finest water. It was of the bigness of a duck's egg; beautifully shaped, and without a flaw; and as the sun shone upon it, it gave forth a lustre like that of electricity, and seemed to burn in his hand with a thousand internal fires.

He knew little of precious stones ; but the Rajah's Diamond was a wonder that explained itself ; a village child, if he found it, would run screaming for the nearest cottage ; and a savage would prostrate himself in adoration before so imposing a fetich. The beauty of the stone flattered the young clergyman's eyes ; the thought of its incalculable value overpowered his intellect. He knew that what he held in his hand was worth more than many years' purchase of an archiepiscopal see ; that it would build cathedrals more stately than Ely or Cologne ; that he who possessed it was set free for ever from the primal curse, and might follow his own inclinations without concern or hurry, without let or hindrance. And as he suddenly turned it, the rays leaped forth again with renewed brilliancy, and seemed to pierce his very heart.

Decisive actions are often taken in a moment and without any conscious deliverance from the rational parts of man. So it was now with Mr. Rolles. He glanced hurriedly round ; beheld, like Mr. Raeburn before him, nothing but the sunlit flower-garden, the tall tree-tops, and the house with blinded windows ; and in a trice he had shut the case, thrust it into his pocket, and was hastening to his study with the speed of guilt.

The Reverend Simon Rolles had stolen the Rajah's Diamond.

Early in the afternoon the police arrived with Harry Hartley. The nurseryman, who was beside himself with terror, readily discovered his hoard ; and the jewels were identified and inventoried in the presence of the secretary. As for Mr. Rolles, he showed himself in a most obliging temper, communicated what he knew with freedom, and professed regret that he could do no more to help the officers in their duty.

"Still," he added, " I suppose your business is nearly
at an end."

" By no means," replied the man from Scotland Yard ;
and he narrated the second robbery of which Harry had
been the immediate victim, and gave the young clergyman
a description of the more important jewels that were still
not found, dilating particularly on the Rajah's Diamond.

" It must be worth a fortune," observed Mr. Rolles.

" Ten fortunes—twenty fortunes," cried the officer.

"The more it is worth," remarked Simon shrewdly,
" the more difficult it must be to sell. Such a thing has
a physiognomy not to be disguised, and I should fancy a
man might as easily negotiate St. Paul's Cathedral."

" Oh, truly ! " said the officer ; "but if the thief be a
man of any intelligence, he will cut it into three or four,
and there will be still enough to make him rich."

" Thank you," said the clergyman. " You cannot
imagine how much your conversation interests me."

Whereupon the functionary admitted that they knew
many strange things in his profession, and immediately
after took his leave.

Mr. Rolles regained his apartment. It seemed smaller
and barer than usual ; the materials for his great work
had never presented so little interest ; and he looked upon
his library with the eye of scorn. He took down, volume
by volume, several Fathers of the Church, and glanced
them through ; but they contained nothing to his purpose.

" These old gentlemen," thought he, " are no doubt
very valuable writers, but they seem to me conspicuously
ignorant of life. Here am I, with learning enough to be
a Bishop, and I positively do not know how to dispose
of a stolen diamond. I glean a hint from a common
policeman, and, with all my folios, I cannot so much as
put it into execution. This inspires me with very low
ideas of University training."

Herewith he kicked over his book-shelf and, putting on his hat, hastened from the house to the club of which he was a member. In such a place of mundane resort he hoped to find some man of good counsel and a shrewd experience in life. In the reading-room he saw many of the country clergy and an Archdeacon ; there were three journalists and a writer upon the Higher Metaphysic, playing pool ; and at dinner only the raff of ordinary club frequenters showed their commonplace and obliterated countenances. None of these, thought Mr. Rolles, would know more on dangerous topics than he knew himself ; none of them were fit to give him guidance in his present strait. At length, in the smoking-room, up many weary stairs, he hit upon a gentleman of somewhat portly build and dressed with conspicuous plainness. He was smoking a cigar and reading the *Fortnightly Review ;* his face was singularly free from all sign of preoccupation or fatigue ; and there was something in his air which seemed to invite confidence and to expect submission. The more the young clergyman scrutinised his features, the more he was convinced that he had fallen on one capable of giving pertinent advice.

" Sir," said he, "you will excuse my abruptness ; but I judge you from your appearance to be pre-eminently a man of the world."

" I have indeed considerable claims to that distinction," replied the stranger, laying aside his magazine with a look of mingled amusement and surprise.

" I, sir," continued the curate, " am a recluse, a student, a creature of ink-bottles and patristic folios. A recent event has brought my folly vividly before my eyes, and I desire to instruct myself in life. By life," he added, " I do not mean Thackeray's novels ; but the crimes and secret possibilities of our society, and the principles of wise conduct among exceptional events.

4—J

I am a patient reader ; can the thing be learnt in books ? "

" You put me in a difficulty," said the stranger. " I confess I have no great notion of the use of books, except to amuse a railway journey ; although, I believe, there are some very exact treatises on astronomy, the use of the globes, agriculture, and the art of making paper-flowers. Upon the less apparent provinces of life I fear you will find nothing truthful. Yet stay," he added, " have you read Gaboriau ? "

Mr. Rolles admitted that he had never even heard the name.

" You may gather some notions from Gaboriau," resumed the stranger. " He is at least suggestive ; and as he is an author much studied by Prince Bismarck, you will, at the worst, lose your time in good society."

" Sir," said the curate, " I am infinitely obliged by your politeness."

" You have already more than repaid me," returned the other.

" How ? " inquired Simon.

" By the novelty of your request," replied the gentleman ; and with a polite gesture, as though to ask permission, he resumed the study of the *Fortnightly Review*.

On his way home Mr. Rolles purchased a work on precious stones and several of Gaboriau's novels. These last he eagerly skimmed until an advanced hour in the morning ; but although they introduced him to many new ideas, he could nowhere discover what to do with a stolen diamond. He was annoyed, moreover, to find the information scattered amongst romantic story-telling, instead of soberly set forth after the manner of a manual ; and he concluded that, even if the writer had thought much upon these subjects, he was totally lacking in educational method. For the character and attainments of Lecoq, however, he was unable to contain his admiration.

"He was truly a great creature," ruminated Mr. Rolles. "He knew the world as I know Paley's Evidences. There was nothing that he could not carry to a termination with his own hand, and against the largest odds. Heavens!" he broke out suddenly, "is not this the lesson? Must I not learn to cut diamonds for myself?"

It seemed to him as if he had sailed at once out of his perplexities; he remembered that he knew a jeweller, one B. Macculloch, in Edinburgh, who would be glad to put him in the way of the necessary training; a few months, perhaps a few years, of sordid toil, and he would be sufficiently expert to divide and sufficiently cunning to dispose with advantage of the Rajah's Diamond. That done, he might return to pursue his researches at leisure, a wealthy and luxurious student, envied and respected by all. Golden visions attended him through his slumber, and he awoke refreshed and light-hearted with the morning sun.

Mr. Raeburn's house was on that day to be closed by the police, and this afforded a pretext for his departure. He cheerfully prepared his baggage, transported it to King's Cross, where he left it in the cloak-room, and returned to the club to while away the afternoon and dine.

"If you dine here to-day, Rolles," observed an acquaintance, "you may see two of the most remarkable men in England—Prince Florizel of Bohemia, and old Jack Vandeleur."

"I have heard of the Prince," replied Mr. Rolles; "and General Vandeleur I have even met in society."

"General Vandeleur is an ass!" returned the other. "This is his brother John, the biggest adventurer, the best judge of precious stones, and one of the most acute diplomatists in Europe. Have you never heard of his duel

with the Duc de Val d'Orge ? of his exploits and atrocities
when he was Dictator of Paraguay ? of his dexterity in
recovering Sir Samuel Levi's jewellery ? nor of his services
in the Indian Mutiny—services by which the Government
profited, but which the Government dared not recognise ?
You make me wonder what we mean by fame, or even by
infamy ; for Jack Vandeleur has prodigious claims to both.
Run down stairs," he continued, " take a table near them,
and keep your ears open. You will hear some strange
talk, or I am much misled."

" But how shall I know them ? " inquired the clergyman.

" Know them ! " cried his friend ; " why, the Prince is
the finest gentleman in Europe, the only living creature
who looks like a king ; and as for Jack Vandeleur, if you
can imagine Ulysses at seventy years of age, and with
a sabre-cut across his face, you have the man before you !
Know them, indeed ! Why, you could pick either of
them out of a Derby day ! "

Rolles eagerly hurried to the dining-room. It was as
his friend had asserted ; it was impossible to mistake the
pair in question. Old John Vandeleur was of a remarkable force of body, and obviously broken to the most
difficult exercises. He had neither the carriage of a
swordsman, nor of a sailor, nor yet of one much inured to
the saddle ; but something made up of all these, and the
result and expression of many different habits and dexterities. His features were bold and aquiline ; his expression arrogant and predatory ; his whole appearance that
of a swift, violent, unscrupulous man of action ; and his
copious white hair and the deep sabre-cut that traversed
his nose and temple added a note of savagery to a head
already remarkable and menacing in itself.

In his companion, the Prince of Bohemia, Mr. Rolles
was astonished to recognise the gentleman who had
recommended him the study of Gaboriau. Doubtless

Prince Florizel, who rarely visited the club, of which, as of most others, he was an honorary member, had been waiting for John Vandeleur when Simon accosted him on the previous evening.

The other diners had modestly retired into the angles of the room, and left the distinguished pair in a certain isolation, but the young clergyman was unrestrained by any sentiment of awe, and, marching boldly up, took his place at the nearest table.

The conversation was, indeed, new to the student's ears. The ex-Dictator of Paraguay stated many extraordinary experiences in different quarters of the world ; and the Prince supplied a commentary which, to a man of thought, was even more interesting than the events themselves. Two forms of experience were thus brought together and laid before the young clergyman ; and he did not know which to admire the most—the desperate actor or the skilled expert in life ; the man who spoke boldly of his own deeds and perils, or the man who seemed, like a god, to know all things and to have suffered nothing. The manner of each aptly fitted with his part in the discourse. The Dictator indulged in brutalities alike of speech and gesture ; his hand opened and shut and fell roughly on the table ; and his voice was loud and heady. The Prince, on the other hand, seemed the very type of urbane docility and quiet ; the least movement, the least inflection, had with him a weightier significance than all the shouts and pantomime of his companion ; and if ever, as must frequently have been the case, he described some experience personal to himself, it was so aptly dissimulated as to pass unnoticed with the rest.

At length the talk wandered on to the late robberies and the Rajah's Diamond.

" That diamond would be better in the sea," observed Prince Florizel.

"As a Vandeleur," replied the Dictator, "your Highness may imagine my dissent."

"I speak on grounds of public policy," pursued the
Prince. "Jewels so valuable should be reserved for the
collection of a Prince or the treasury of a great nation.
To hand them about among the common sort of men is
to set a price on Virtue's head; and if the Rajah of
Kashgar—a Prince, I understand, of great enlightenment
—desired vengeance upon the men of Europe, he could
hardly have gone more efficaciously about his purpose
than by sending us this apple of discord. There is no
honesty too robust for such a trial. I myself, who have
many duties and many privileges of my own—I myself,
Mr. Vandeleur, could scarce handle the intoxicating crystal and be safe. As for you, who are a diamond-hunter
by taste and profession, I do not believe there is a crime
in the calendar you would not perpetrate—I do not
believe you have a friend in the world whom you would
not eagerly betray—I do not know if you have a family,
but if you have I declare you would sacrifice your children
—and all this for what? Not to be richer, nor to have
more comforts or more respect, but simply to call this
diamond yours for a year or two until you die, and now
and again to open a safe and look at it as one looks at
a picture."

"It is true," replied Vandeleur. "I have hunted most
things, from men and women down to mosquitos; I have
dived for coral; I have followed both whales and tigers;
and a diamond is the tallest quarry of the lot. It has
beauty and worth; it alone can properly reward the
ardours of the chase. At this moment, as your Highness
may fancy, I am upon the trail; I have a sure knack,
a wide experience; I know every stone of price in my
brother's collection as a shepherd knows his sheep;
and I wish I may die if I do not recover them every
one."

"Sir Thomas Vandeleur will have great cause to thank you," said the Prince.

"I am not so sure," returned the Dictator, with a laugh. "One of the Vandeleurs will. Thomas or John—Peter or Paul—we are all apostles."

"I did not catch your observation," said the Prince, with some disgust.

And at the same moment the waiter informed Mr. Vandeleur that his cab was at the door.

Mr. Rolles glanced at the clock, and saw that he also must be moving; and the coincidence struck him sharply and unpleasantly, for he desired to see no more of the diamond-hunter.

Much study having somewhat shaken the young man's nerves, he was in the habit of travelling in the most luxurious manner; and for the present journey he had taken a sofa in the sleeping carriage.

"You will be very comfortable," said the guard; "there is no one in your compartment, and only one old gentleman in the other end."

It was close upon the hour, and the tickets were being examined, when Mr. Rolles beheld this other fellow-passenger ushered by several porters into his place; certainly, there was not another man in the world whom he would not have preferred—for it was old John Vandeleur, the ex-Dictator.

The sleeping carriages on the Great Northern line were divided into three compartments — one at each end for travellers, and one in the centre fitted with the conveniences of a lavatory. A door running in grooves separated each of the others from the lavatory; but as there were neither bolts nor locks, the whole suite was practically common ground.

When Mr. Rolles had studied his position, he perceived himself without defence. If the Dictator chose to pay him a visit in the course of the night, he could do no less than receive it; he had no means of fortification, and lay open to attack as if he had been lying in the fields. This situation caused him some agony of mind. He recalled with alarm the boastful statements of his fellow-traveller across the dining-table, and the professions of immorality which he had heard him offering to the disgusted Prince. Some persons, he remembered to have read, are endowed with a singular quickness of perception for the neighbourhood of precious metals; through walls and even at considerable distances they are said to divine the presence of gold. Might it not be the same with diamonds? he wondered; and if so, who was more likely to enjoy this transcendental sense than the person who gloried in the appellation of the Diamond Hunter? From such a man he recognised that he had everything to fear, and longed eagerly for the arrival of the day.

In the meantime he neglected no precaution, concealed his diamond in the most internal pocket of a system of greatcoats, and devoutly recommended himself to the care of Providence.

The train pursued its usual even and rapid course; and nearly half the journey had been accomplished before slumber began to triumph over uneasiness in the breast of Mr. Rolles. For some time he resisted its influence; but it grew upon him more and more, and a little before York he was fain to stretch himself upon one of the couches and suffer his eyes to close; and almost at the same instant consciousness deserted the young clergyman. His last thought was of his terrifying neighbour.

When he awoke it was still pitch dark, except for the flicker of the veiled lamp; and the continual roaring and oscillation testified to the unrelaxed velocity of the train. He sat upright in a panic, for he had been tormented by the most uneasy dreams; it was some seconds before he recovered his self-command; and even after he had resumed a recumbent attitude sleep continued to flee him, and he lay awake with his brain in a state of violent agitation, and his eyes fixed upon the lavatory door. He pulled his clerical felt hat over his brow still further to shield him from the light ; and he adopted the usual expedients, such as counting a thousand or banishing thought, by which experienced invalids are accustomed to woo the approach of sleep. In the case of Mr. Rolles they proved one and all vain ; he was harassed by a dozen different anxieties—the old man in the other end of the carriage haunted him in the most alarming shapes ; and in whatever attitude he chose to lie, the diamond in his pocket occasioned him a sensible physical distress. It burned, it was too large ; it bruised his ribs ; and there were infinitesimal fractions of a second in which he had half a mind to throw it from the window.

While he was thus lying, a strange incident took place.

The sliding-door into the lavatory stirred a little, and then a little more, and was finally drawn back for the space of about twenty inches. The lamp in the lavatory was unshaded, and in the lighted aperture thus disclosed Mr. Rolles could see the head of Mr. Vandeleur in an attitude of deep attention. He was conscious that the gaze of the Dictator rested intently on his own face ; and the instinct of self-preservation moved him to hold his breath, to refrain from the least movement, and, keeping his eyes lowered, to watch his visitor from underneath the lashes. After about a moment, the head was withdrawn and the door of the lavatory replaced.

The Dictator had not come to attack, but to observe ; his action was not that of a man threatening another, but that of a man who was himself threatened ; if Mr. Rolles was afraid of him, it appeared that he, in his turn, was not quite easy on the score of Mr. Rolles. He had come, it would seem, to make sure that his only fellow-traveller was asleep ; and, when satisfied on that point, he had at once withdrawn.

The clergyman leaped to his feet. The extreme of terror had given place to a reaction of foolhardy daring. He reflected that the rattle of the flying train concealed all other sounds, and determined, come what might, to return the visit he had just received. Divesting himself of his cloak, which might have interfered with the freedom of his action, he entered the lavatory and paused to listen. As he had expected, there was nothing to be heard above the roar of the train's progress ; and laying his hand on the door at the farther side, he proceeded cautiously to draw it back for about six inches. Then he stopped, and could not contain an ejaculation of surprise.

John Vandeleur wore a fur travelling-cap with lappets to protect his ears ; and this may have combined with the sound of the express to keep him in ignorance of what was going forward. It is certain, at least, that he did not raise his head, but continued without interruption to pursue his strange employment. Between his feet stood an open hat-box ; in one hand he held the sleeve of his sealskin greatcoat ; in the other a formidable knife, with which he had just slit up the lining of the sleeve. Mr. Rolles had read of persons carrying money in a belt ; and as he had no acquaintance with any but cricket-belts, he had never been able rightly to conceive how this was managed. But here was a stranger thing before his eyes ; for John Vandeleur, it appeared, carried diamonds in the lining of his sleeve ; and even as the young clergyman gazed, he could see one glittering brilliant drop after another into the hat-box.

He stood rivetted to the spot, following this unusual business with his eyes. The diamonds were, for the most part, small, and not easily distinguishable either in shape or fire. Suddenly the Dictator appeared to find a difficulty ; he employed both hands and stooped over his task ; but it was not until after considerable manœuvring that he extricated a large tiara of diamonds from the

lining, and held it up for some seconds' examination before
he placed it with the others in the hat-box. The tiara
was a ray of light to Mr. Rolles; he immediately recognised it for a part of the treasure stolen from Harry Hartley
by the loiterer. There was no room for mistake; it was
exactly as the detective had described it; there were the
ruby stars, with a great emerald in the centre; there were
the interlacing crescents; and there were the pear-shaped
pendants, each a single stone, which gave a special value
to Lady Vandeleur's tiara.

Mr. Rolles was hugely relieved. The Dictator was as
deeply in the affair as he was; neither could tell tales
upon the other. In the first glow of happiness, the
clergyman suffered a deep sigh to escape him; and as
his bosom had become choked and his throat dry during
his previous suspense, the sigh was followed by a cough.

Mr. Vandeleur looked up; his face contracted with
the blackest and most deadly passion; his eyes opened
widely, and his under jaw dropped in an astonishment
that was upon the brink of fury. By an instinctive movement he had covered the hat-box with the coat. For
half a minute the two men stared upon each other in
silence. It was not a long interval, but it sufficed for
Mr. Rolles; he was one of those who think swiftly on
dangerous occasions; he decided on a course of action
of a singularly daring nature; and although he felt he
was setting his life upon the hazard, he was the first to
break silence.

"I beg your pardon," said he.

The Dictator shivered slightly, and when he spoke
his voice was hoarse.

"What do you want here?" he asked.

"I take a particular interest in diamonds," replied Mr.
Rolles, with an air of perfect self-possession. "Two con-
noisseurs should be acquainted. I have here a trifle of
my own which may perhaps serve for an introduction."

And so saying, he quietly took the case from his pocket, showed the Rajah's Diamond to the Dictator for an instant, and replaced it in security.

"It was once your brother's," he added.

John Vandeleur continued to regard him with a look of almost painful amazement; but he neither spoke nor moved.

"I was pleased to observe," resumed the young man, "that we have gems from the same collection."

The Dictator's surprise overpowered him.

"I beg your pardon," he said; "I begin to perceive that I am growing old! I am positively not prepared for little incidents like this. But set my mind at rest upon one point: do my eyes deceive me, or are you indeed a parson?"

"I am in holy orders," answered Mr. Rolles.

"Well," cried the other, "as long as I live I will never hear another word against the cloth!"

"You flatter me," said Mr. Rolles.

"Pardon me," replied Vandeleur; "pardon me, young man. You are no coward, but it still remains to be seen whether you are not the worst of fools. Perhaps," he continued, leaning back upon his seat, "perhaps you would oblige me with a few particulars. I must suppose you had some object in the stupefying impudence of your proceedings, and I confess I have a curiosity to know it."

"It is very simple," replied the clergyman; "it proceeds from my great inexperience of life."

"I shall be glad to be persuaded," answered Vandeleur.

Whereupon Mr. Rolles told him the whole story of his connection with the Rajah's Diamond, from the time he found it in Raeburn's garden to the time when he left London in the Flying Scotchman. He added a brief sketch of his feelings and thoughts during the journey, and concluded in these words:—

"When I recognised the tiara I knew we were in the

same attitude towards Society, and this inspired me with a
hope, which I trust you will not say was ill-founded, that
you might become in some sense my partner in the diffi-
culties and, of course, the profits of my situation. To one
of your special knowledge and obviously great experience
the negotiation of the diamond would give but little
trouble, while to me it was a matter of impossibility. On
the other part, I judged that I might lose nearly as much
by cutting the diamond, and that not improbably with
an unskilful hand, as might enable me to pay you with
proper generosity for your assistance. The subject was
a delicate one to broach ; and perhaps I fell short in
delicacy. But I must ask you to remember that for me
the situation was a new one, and I was entirely unacquainted with the etiquette in use. I believe without
vanity that I could have married or baptised you in a very
acceptable manner ; but every man has his own aptitudes,
and this sort of bargain was not among the lists of my
accomplishments."

"I do not wish to flatter you," replied Vandeleur ;
"but upon my word, you have an unusual disposition for
a life of crime. You have more accomplishments than
you imagine ; and though I have encountered a number of
rogues in different quarters of the world, I never met with
one so unblushing as yourself. Cheer up, Mr. Rolles, you
are in the right profession at last ! As for helping you,
you may command me as you will. I have only a day's
business in Edinburgh on a little matter for my brother ;
and once that is concluded, I return to Paris, where I
usually reside. If you please, you may accompany me
thither. And before the end of a month I believe I shall
have brought your little business to a satisfactory conclusion."

*At this point, contrary to all the canons of his art,
our Arabian Author breaks off the* STORY OF THE

YOUNG MAN IN HOLY ORDERS. *I regret and condemn such practices ; but I must follow my original, and refer the reader for the conclusion of Mr. Rolles' adventures to the next number of the cycle,*

THE STORY OF THE HOUSE WITH THE GREEN BLINDS

FRANCIS SCRYMGEOUR, a clerk in the Bank of Scotland at Edinburgh, had attained the age of twenty-five in a sphere of quiet, creditable, and domestic life. His mother died while he was young ; but his father, a man of sense and probity, had given him an excellent education at school, and brought him up at home to orderly and frugal habits. Francis, who was of a docile and affectionate disposition, profited by these advantages with zeal, and devoted himself heart and soul to his employment. A walk upon Saturday afternoon, an occasional dinner with members of his family, and a yearly tour of a fortnight in the Highlands or even on the continent of Europe were his principal distractions, and he grew rapidly in favour with his superiors, and enjoyed already a salary of nearly two hundred pounds a year, with the prospect of an ultimate advance to almost double that amount. Few young men were more contented, few more willing and laborious, than Francis Scrymgeour. Sometimes at night, when he had read the daily paper, he would play upon the flute to amuse his father, for whose qualities he entertained a great respect.

One day he received a note from a well-known firm of Writers to the Signet, requesting the favour of an immediate interview with him. The letter was marked " Private and Confidential," and had been addressed to him at the bank, instead of at home—two unusual circumstances which made him obey the summons with the more alacrity. The senior member of the firm, a man of much austerity of manner, made him gravely welcome, requested him to take a seat, and proceeded to explain the matter in hand in the picked expressions of a veteran man of business. A person, who must remain nameless, but of whom the lawyer had every reason to think well—a man, in short, of some station in the country, — desired to make Francis an annual allowance of five hundred pounds. The capital was to be placed under the control of the lawyer's firm and two trustees who must also remain anonymous. There were conditions annexed to this liberality, but he was of opinion that his new client would find nothing either excessive or dishonourable in the terms ; and he repeated these two words with emphasis, as though he desired to commit himself to nothing more.

Francis asked their nature.

"The conditions," said the Writer to the Signet, "are, as I have twice remarked, neither dishonourable nor excessive. At the same time I cannot conceal from you that they are most unusual. Indeed, the whole case is very much out of our way ; and I should certainly have refused it had it not been for the reputation of the gentleman who entrusted it to my care, and, let me add, Mr. Scrymgeour, the interest I have been led to take in yourself by many complimentary and, I have no doubt, well-deserved reports."

Francis entreated him to be more specific.

"You cannot picture my uneasiness as to these conditions," he said.

"They are two," replied the lawyer, "only two ; and the sum, as you will remember, is five hundred a year—and unburdened, I forgot to add, unburdened."

And the lawyer raised his eyebrows at him with solemn gusto.

"The first," he resumed, "is of remarkable simplicity.

You must be in Paris by the afternoon of Sunday, the 15th ; there you will find, at the box-office of the Comédie Française, a ticket for admission taken in your name and waiting you. You are requested to sit out the whole performance in the seat provided, and that is all."

" I should certainly have preferred a week - day," replied Francis. "But, after all, once in a way——"

"And in Paris, my dear sir," added the lawyer soothingly. " I believe I am something of a precisian myself, but upon such a consideration, and in Paris, I should not hesitate an instant."

And the pair laughed pleasantly together.

" The other is of more importance," continued the Writer to the Signet. "It regards your marriage. My client, taking a deep interest in your welfare, desires to advise you absolutely in the choice of a wife. Absolutely, you understand," he repeated.

"Let us be more explicit, if you please," returned Francis. "Am I to marry any one, maid or widow, black or white, whom this invisible person chooses to propose ? "

" I was to assure you that suitability of age and position should be a principle with your benefactor," replied the lawyer. "As to race, I confess the difficulty had not occurred to me, and I failed to inquire ; but if you like I will make a note of it at once, and advise you on the earliest opportunity."

" Sir," said Francis, " it remains to be seen whether this whole affair is not a most unworthy fraud. The circumstances are inexplicable—I had almost said incredible ; and until I see a little more daylight, and some plausible motive, I confess I should be very sorry to put a hand to the transaction. I appeal to you in this difficulty for information. I must learn what is at the bottom of it all. If you do not know, cannot guess, or are not at liberty to tell me, I shall take my hat and go back to my bank as I came."

"I do not know," answered the lawyer, "but I have an excellent guess. Your father, and no one else, is at the root of this apparently unnatural business."

"My father!" cried Francis, in extreme disdain. "Worthy man, I know every thought of his mind, every penny of his fortune!"

"You misinterpret my words," said the lawyer. "I do not refer to Mr. Scrymgeour, senior ; for he is not your father. When he and his wife came to Edinburgh, you were already nearly one year old, and you had not yet been three months in their care. The secret has been well kept ; but such is the fact. Your father is un-known, and I say again that I believe him to be the original of the offers I am charged at present to transmit to you."

It would be impossible to exaggerate the astonishment of Francis Scrymgeour at this unexpected information. He pled this confusion to the lawyer.

"Sir," said he, "after a piece of news so startling, you must grant me some hours for thought. You shall know this evening what conclusion I have reached."

The lawyer commended his prudence ; and Francis, excusing himself upon some pretext at the bank, took a long walk into the country, and fully considered the different steps and aspects of the case. A pleasant sense of his own importance rendered him the more deliberate : but the issue was from the first not doubtful. His whole carnal man leaned irresistibly towards the five hundred a year, and the strange conditions with which it was burdened ; he discovered in his heart an invincible repug-nance to the name of Scrymgeour, which he had never hitherto disliked ; he began to despise the narrow and unromantic interests of his former life ; and when once his mind was fairly made up, he walked with a new

4—K

feeling of strength and freedom, and nourished himself with the gayest anticipations.

He said but a word to the lawyer, and immediately received a cheque for two quarters' arrears ; for the allowance was ante-dated from the first of January. With this in his pocket, he walked home. The flat in Scotland Street looked mean in his eyes ; his nostrils, for the first time, rebelled against the odour of broth ; and he observed little defects of manner in his adoptive father which filled him with surprise, and almost with disgust. The next day, he determined, should see him on his way to Paris.

In that city, where he arrived long before the appointed date, he put up at a modest hotel frequented by English and Italians, and devoted himself to improvement in the French tongue. For this purpose he had a master twice a week, entered into conversation with loiterers in the Champs Elysées, and nightly frequented the theatre. He had his whole toilette fashionably renewed ; and was shaved and had his hair dressed every morning by a barber in a neighbouring street. This gave him something of a foreign air, and seemed to wipe off the reproach of his past years.

At length, on the Saturday afternoon, he betook himself to the box-office of the theatre in the Rue Richelieu. No sooner had he mentioned his name than the clerk produced the order in an envelope of which the address was scarcely dry.

" It has been taken this moment," said the clerk.

" Indeed ! " said Francis. " May I ask what the gentleman was like ? "

" Your friend is easy to describe," replied the official. " He is old and strong and beautiful, with white hair and a sabre-cut across his face. You cannot fail to recognise so marked a person."

" No, indeed," returned Francis ; " and I thank you for your politeness."

"He cannot yet be far distant," added the clerk. "If you make haste you might still overtake him."

Francis did not wait to be twice told; he ran precipitately from the theatre into the middle of the street and looked in all directions. More than one white-haired man was within sight; but though he overtook each of them in succession, all wanted the sabre-cut. For nearly half an hour he tried one street after another in the neighbourhood, until at length, recognising the folly of continued search, he started on a walk to compose his agitated feelings; for this proximity of an encounter with him to whom he could not doubt he owed the day had profoundly moved the young man.

It chanced that his way lay up the Rue Drouot and thence up the Rue des Martyrs; and chance, in this case, served him better than all the forethought in the world. For on the outer boulevard he saw two men in earnest colloquy upon a seat. One was dark, young, and handsome, secularly dressed, but with an indelible clerical stamp; the other answered in every particular to the description given him by the clerk. Francis felt his heart beat high in his bosom; he knew he was now about to hear the voice of his father; and making a wide circuit, he noiselessly took his place behind the couple in question, who were too much interested in their talk to observe much else. As Francis had expected, the conversation was conducted in the English language.

"Your suspicions begin to annoy me, Rolles," said the older man. "I tell you I am doing my utmost; a man cannot lay his hand on millions in a moment. Have I not taken you up, a mere stranger, out of pure goodwill? Are you not living largely on my bounty?"

"On your advances, Mr. Vandeleur," corrected the other.

"Advances, if you choose; and interest instead of good-will, if you prefer it," returned Vandeleur angrily.

" I am not here to pick expressions.   Business is business; and your business, let me remind you, is too muddy for such airs.   Trust me, or leave me alone and find someone else ; but let us have an end, for God's sake, of your jeremiads."

" I am beginning to learn the world," replied the other, " and I see that you have every reason to play me false, and not one to deal honestly.   I am not here to pick expressions either ; you wish the diamond for yourself ; you know you do—you dare not deny it. Have you not already forged my name, and searched my lodging in my absence ?   I understand the cause of your delays ; you are lying in wait ; you are the diamond-hunter, forsooth ; and sooner or later, by fair means or foul, you'll lay your hands upon it. I tell you, it must stop ; push me much further and I promise you a surprise."

" It does not become you to use threats," returned Vandeleur.   " Two can play at that.   My brother is here in Paris ; the police are on the alert ; and if you persist in wearying me with your caterwauling, I will arrange a little astonishment for you, Mr. Rolles.   But mine shall be once and for all.   Do you understand, or would you prefer me to tell it you in Hebrew ?   There is an end to all things, and you have come to the end of my patience.   Tuesday, at seven ; not a day, not an hour sooner, not the least part of a second, if it were to save your life.   And if you do not choose to wait, you may go to the bottomless pit for me, and welcome."

And so saying, the Dictator arose from the bench, and marched off in the direction of Montmartre, shaking his head and swinging his cane with a most furious air ; while his companion remained where he was, in an attitude of great dejection.

Francis was at the pitch of surprise and horror ; his sentiments had been shocked to the last degree ; the hopeful tenderness with which he had taken his place upon the bench was transformed into repulsion and despair; old Mr. Scrymgeour, he reflected, was a far more kindly and creditable parent than this dangerous and violent intriguer; but he retained his presence of mind, and suffered not a moment to elapse before he was on the trail of the Dictator.

That gentleman's fury carried him forward at a brisk pace, and he was so completely occupied in his angry thoughts that he never so much as cast a look behind him till he reached his own door.

His house stood high up in the Rue Lepic, commanding a view of all Paris, and enjoying the pure air of the heights. It was two stories high, with green blinds and shutters; and all the windows looking on the street were hermetically closed. Tops of trees showed over the high garden wall, and the wall was protected by *chevaux-de-frise*. The Dictator paused a moment while he searched his pocket for a key; and then, opening a gate, disappeared within the enclosure.

Francis looked about him; the neighbourhood was very lonely, the house isolated in its garden. It seemed as if his observation must here come to an abrupt end. A second glance, however, showed him a tall house next door presenting a gable to the garden, and in this gable a single window. He passed to the front and saw a ticket offering unfurnished lodgings by the month; and, on inquiry, the room which commanded the Dictator's garden proved to be one of those to let. Francis did not hesitate a moment; he took the room, paid an advance upon the rent, and returned to his hotel to seek his baggage.

The old man with the sabre-cut might or might not be his father; he might or he might not be upon the true scent; but he was certainly on the edge of an exciting mystery, and he promised himself that he would not relax his observation until he had got to the bottom of the secret.

From the window of his new apartment Francis Scrymgeour commanded a complete view into the garden of the house with the green blinds. Immediately below him a very comely chestnut with wide boughs sheltered a pair of rustic tables where people might dine in the height of summer. On all sides save one a dense vegetation concealed the soil ; but there, between the tables and the house, he saw a patch of gravel walk leading from the verandah to the garden gate. Studying the place from between the boards of the Venetian shutters, which he durst not open for fear of attracting attention, Francis observed but little to indicate the manners of the inhabitants, and that little argued no more than a close reserve and a taste for solitude. The garden was conventual, the house had the air of a prison. The green blinds were all drawn down upon the outside ; the door into the verandah was closed ; the garden, as far as he could see it, was left entirely to itself in the evening sunshine. A modest curl of smoke from a single chimney alone testified to the presence of living people.

In order that he might not be entirely idle, and to give a certain colour to his way of life, Francis had purchased Euclid's Geometry in French, which he set himself to copy and translate on the top of his portmanteau and seated on the floor against the wall ; for he was equally without chair or table. From time to time he would rise and cast a glance into the enclosure of the house with the green blinds ; but the windows remained obstinately closed and the garden empty.

Only late in the evening did anything occur to reward his continued attention. Between nine and ten the sharp tinkle of a bell aroused him from a fit of dozing ; and he sprang to his observatory in time to hear an important noise of locks being opened and bars removed, and to see Mr. Vandeleur, carrying a lantern and clothed in a flowing robe of black velvet with a skull-cap to match, issue from under the verandah and proceed leisurely towards the garden gate. The sound of bolts and bars was then repeated; and a moment after, Francis perceived the Dictator escorting into the house, in the mobile light of the lantern, an individual of the lowest and most despicable appearance.

Half an hour afterwards the visitor was reconducted to the street; and Mr. Vandeleur, setting his light upon one of the rustic tables, finished a cigar with great deliberation under the foliage of the chestnut. Francis, peering through a clear space among the leaves, was able to follow his gestures as he threw away the ash or enjoyed a copious inhalation; and beheld a cloud upon the old man's brow and a forcible action of the lips, which testified to some deep and probably painful train of thought. The cigar was already almost at an end, when the voice of a young girl was heard suddenly crying the hour from the interior of the house.

"In a moment," replied John Vandeleur.

And, with that, he threw away the stump, and, taking up the lantern, sailed away under the verandah for the night. As soon as the door was closed, absolute darkness fell upon the house; Francis might try his eyesight as much as he pleased, he could not detect so much as a single chink of light below a blind; and he concluded, with great good sense, that the bed-chambers were all upon the other side.

Early the next morning (for he was early awake after an uncomfortable night upon the floor) he saw cause to adopt a different explanation. The blinds rose, one after another, by means of a spring in the interior, and disclosed steel shutters such as we see on the front of shops; these in their turn were rolled up by a similar contrivance; and for the space of about an hour the chambers were left open to the morning air. At the end of that time Mr. Vandeleur, with his own hand, once

more closed the shutters and replaced the blinds from
within.

While Francis was still marvelling at these precautions, the door opened and a young girl came forth to
look about her in the garden. It was not two minutes
before she re-entered the house, but even in that short
time he saw enough to convince him that she possessed
the most unusual attractions. His curiosity was not only
highly excited by this incident, but his spirits were improved to a still more notable degree. The alarming
manners and more than equivocal life of his father ceased
from that moment to prey upon his mind; from that
moment he embraced his new family with ardour; and
whether the young lady should prove his sister or his
wife, he felt convinced she was an angel in disguise. So
much was this the case that he was seized with a sudden
horror when he reflected how little he really knew, and
how possible it was that he had followed the wrong
person when he followed Mr. Vandeleur.

The porter, whom he consulted, could afford him
little information ; but, such as it was, it had a mysterious and questionable sound. The person next door
was an English gentleman of extraordinary wealth, and
proportionately eccentric in his tastes and habits. He
possessed great collections, which he kept in the house
beside him ; and it was to protect these that he had
fitted the place with steel shutters, elaborate fastenings,
and *chevaux-de-frise* along the garden wall. He lived
much alone, in spite of some strange visitors, with whom,
it seemed, he had business to transact ; and there was no
one else in the house, except Mademoiselle and an old
woman servant.

" Is Mademoiselle his daughter ? " inquired Francis.

" Certainly," replied the porter. " Mademoiselle is the
daughter of the house ; and strange it is to see how she
is made to work. For all his riches, it is she who goes to

market; and every day in the week you may see her going by with a basket on her arm."

" And the collections?" asked the other.

" Sir," said the man, " they are immensely valuable. More I cannot tell you. Since M. de Vandeleur's arrival no one in the quarter has so much as passed the door."

"Suppose not," returned Francis, "you must surely have some notion what these famous galleries contain. Is it pictures, silks, statues, jewels, or what?"

"My faith, sir," said the fellow, with a shrug, "it might be carrots, and still I could not tell you. How should I know? The house is kept like a garrison, as you perceive."

And then as Francis was returning disappointed to his room, the porter called him back.

"I have just remembered, sir," said he. "M. de Vandeleur has been in all parts of the world, and I once heard the old woman declare that he had brought many diamonds back with him. If that be the truth, there must be a fine show behind those shutters."

By an early hour on Sunday Francis was in his place at the theatre. The seat which had been taken for him was only two or three numbers from the left-hand side, and directly opposite one of the lower boxes. As the seat had been specially chosen there was doubtless something to be learned from its position; and he judged by an instinct that the box upon his right was, in some way or other, to be connected with the drama in which he ignorantly played a part. Indeed, it was so situated that its occupants could safely observe him from beginning to end of the piece, if they were so minded; while, profiting by the depth, they could screen themselves sufficiently well from any counter-examination on his side. He promised himself not to leave it for a moment out of sight; and whilst he scanned the rest of the theatre, or made a show of attending to the business of the stage, he always kept a corner of an eye upon the empty box.

The second act had been some time in progress, and was even drawing towards a close, when the door opened and two persons entered and ensconced themselves in the darkest of the shade. Francis could hardly control his emotion. It was Mr. Vandeleur and his daughter. The blood came and went in his arteries and veins with stunning activity; his ears sang; his head turned. He dared not look lest he should awake suspicion; his play-bill, which he kept reading from end to end and over and over again, turned from white to red before his eyes; and when he cast a glance upon the stage, it seemed incalculably far away, and he found the voices and gestures of the actors to the last degree impertinent and absurd.

From time to time he risked a momentary look in the direction which principally interested him; and once at least he felt certain that his eyes encountered those of the young girl. A shock passed over his body, and he saw all the colours of the rainbow. What would he not have given to overhear what passed between the Vandeleurs? What would he not have given for the courage to take up his opera-glass and steadily inspect their attitude and expression? There, for aught he knew, his whole life was being decided—and he not able to interfere, not able even to follow the debate, but condemned to sit and suffer where he was, in impotent anxiety.

At last the act came to an end. The curtain fell, and the people around him began to leave their places for the interval. It was only natural that he should follow their example; and if he did so, it was not only· natural but necessary that he should pass immediately in front of the box in question. Summoning all his courage, but keeping his eyes lowered, Francis drew near the spot. His progress was slow, for the old gentleman before him moved with incredible deliberation,

wheezing as he went. What was he to do? Should
he address the Vandeleurs by name as he went by?
Should he take the flower from his button-hole and
throw it into the box? Should he raise his face
and direct one long and affectionate look upon the
lady who was either his sister or his betrothed? As
he found himself thus struggling among so many alter-
natives, he had a vision of his old equable existence
in the bank, and was assailed by a thought of regret
for the past.

By this time he had arrived directly opposite the
box; and although he was still undetermined what to
do or whether to do anything, he turned his head and
lifted his eyes. No sooner had he done so than he
uttered a cry of disappointment and remained rooted
to the spot. The box was empty. During his slow
advance Mr. Vandeleur and his daughter had quietly
slipped away.

A polite person in his rear reminded him that he
was stopping the path; and he moved on again with
mechanical footsteps, and suffered the crowd to carry
him unresisting out of the theatre. Once in the street,
the pressure ceasing, he came to a halt, and the cool
night air speedily restored him to the possession of his
faculties. He was surprised to find that his head ached
violently, and that he remembered not one word of the
two acts which he had witnessed. As the excitement
wore away, it was succeeded by an overmastering appetite for sleep, and he hailed a cab and drove to his
lodging in a state of extreme exhaustion and some
disgust of life.

Next morning he lay in wait for Miss Vandeleur on
her road to market, and by eight o'clock beheld her
stepping down a lane. She was simply, and even
poorly, attired; but in the carriage of her head and
body there was something flexible and noble that would

have lent distinction to the meanest toilette. Even her basket, so aptly did she carry it, became her like an ornament. It seemed to Francis, as he slipped into a doorway, that the sunshine followed and the shadows fled before her as she walked; and he was conscious, for the first time, of a bird singing in a cage above the lane.

He suffered her to pass the doorway, and then, coming forth once more, addressed her by name from behind.

"Miss Vandeleur," said he.

She turned and, when she saw who he was, became deadly pale.

"Pardon me," he continued; "Heaven knows I had no will to startle you; and, indeed, there should be nothing startling in the presence of one who wishes you so well as I do. And, believe me, I am acting rather from necessity than choice. We have many things in common, and I am sadly in the dark. There is much that I should be doing, and my hands are tied. I do not know even what to feel, nor who are my friends and enemies."

She found her voice with an effort.

"I do not know who you are," she said.

"Ah, yes! Miss Vandeleur, you do," returned Francis; "better than I do myself. Indeed, it is on that, above all, that I seek light. Tell me what you know," he pleaded. "Tell me who I am, who you are, and how our destinies are intermixed. Give me a little help with my life, Miss Vandeleur—only a word or two to guide me, only the name of my father, if you will— and I shall be grateful and content."

"I will not attempt to deceive you," she replied. "I know who you are, but I am not at liberty to say."

"Tell me, at least, that you have forgiven my presumption, and I shall wait with all the patience I have," he said. "If I am not to know, I must do without. It is cruel, but I can bear more upon a push. Only do not add to my troubles the thought that I have made an enemy of you."

"You did only what was natural," she said, "and I have nothing to forgive you. Farewell."

"Is it to be *farewell?*" he asked.

"Nay, that I do not know myself," she answered. "Farewell for the present, if you like."

And with these words she was gone.

Francis returned to his lodging in a state of considerable commotion of mind. He made the most trifling progress with his Euclid for that forenoon, and was more often at the window than at his improvised writing-table. But beyond seeing the return of Miss Vandeleur, and the meeting between her and her father, who was smoking a Trichinopoli cigar in the verandah, there was nothing notable in the neighbourhood of the house with the green blinds before the time of the mid-day meal. The young man hastily allayed his appetite in a neighbouring restaurant, and returned with the speed of unallayed curiosity to the house in the Rue Lepic. A mounted servant was leading a saddle-horse to and fro before the garden wall ; and the porter of Francis's lodging was smoking a pipe against the door-post, absorbed in contemplation of the livery and the steeds.

"Look!" he cried to the young man, "what fine cattle! what an elegant costume! They belong to the brother of M. de Vandeleur, who is now within upon a visit. He is a great man, a general, in your country ; and you doubtless know him well by reputation."

"I confess," returned Francis, "that I have never heard of General Vandeleur before. We have many officers of that grade, and my pursuits have been exclusively civil."

"It is he," replied the porter, "who lost the great

diamond of the Indies. Of that at least you must have
read often in the papers."

As soon as Francis could disengage himself from the
porter he ran upstairs and hurried to the window. Immediately below the clear space in the chestnut leaves,
the two gentlemen were seated in conversation over a
cigar. The General, a red, military-looking man, offered
some traces of a family resemblance to his brother; he
had something of the same features, something, although
very little, of the same free and powerful carriage; but
he was older, smaller, and more common in air; his
likeness was that of a caricature, and he seemed altogether a poor and debile being by the side of the Dictator.

They spoke in tones so low, leaning over the table
with every appearance of interest, that Francis could
catch no more than a word or two on an occasion.
For as little as he heard, he was convinced that the
conversation turned upon himself and his own career;
several times the name of Scrymgeour reached his ear,
for it was easy to distinguish, and still more frequently
he fancied he could distinguish the name Francis.

At length the General, as if in a hot anger, broke forth
into several violent exclamations.

" Francis Vandeleur ! " he cried, accentuating the last
word. " Francis Vandeleur, I tell you."

The Dictator made a movement of his whole body,
half affirmative, half contemptuous, but his answer was
inaudible to the young man.

Was he the Francis Vandeleur in question ? he wondered. Were they discussing the name under which he
was to be married ? Or was the whole affair a dream and
a delusion of his own conceit and self-absorption ?

After another interval of inaudible talk, dissension
seemed again to rise between the couple underneath
the chestnut, and again the General raised his voice
angrily so as to be audible to Francis.

"My wife?" he cried. "I have done with my wife for good. I will not hear her name. I am sick of her very name."

And he swore aloud and beat the table with his fist.

The Dictator appeared, by his gestures, to pacify him after a paternal fashion; and a little after he conducted him to the garden gate. The pair shook hands affectionately enough; but as soon as the door had closed behind his visitor, John Vandeleur fell into a fit of laughter which sounded unkindly and even devilish in the ears of Francis Scrymgeour.

So another day had passed, and little more learnt. But the young man remembered that the morrow was Tuesday, and promised himself some curious discoveries; all might be well, or all might be ill; he was sure, at least, to glean some curious information, and perhaps, by good luck, get at the heart of the mystery which surrounded his father and his family.

As the hour of the dinner drew near many preparations were made in the garden of the house with the green blinds. That table, which was partly visible to Francis through the chestnut leaves, was destined to serve as a sideboard, and carried relays of plates and the materials for salad: the other, which was almost entirely concealed, had been set apart for the diners, and Francis could catch glimpses of white cloth and silver plate.

Mr. Rolles arrived, punctual to the minute; he looked like a man upon his guard, and spoke low and sparingly. The Dictator, on the other hand, appeared to enjoy an unusual flow of spirits; his laugh, which was youthful and pleasant to hear, sounded frequently from the garden; by the modulation and the changes of his voice it was obvious that he told many droll stories and imitated the accents of a variety of different nations; and before he and the young clergyman had finished their vermouth all feeling of distrust was at an end, and they were talking together like a pair of school companions.

At length Miss Vandeleur made her appearance, carrying the soup-tureen. Mr. Rolles ran to offer her assistance, which she laughingly refused; and there was an interchange of pleasantries among the trio which seemed to have reference to this primitive manner of waiting by one of the company.

"One is more at one's ease," Mr. Vandeleur was heard to declare.

Next moment they were all three in their places, and Francis could see as little as he could hear of what passed. But the dinner seemed to go merrily; there was a perpetual babble of voices and sound of knives and forks below the chestnut; and Francis, who had no more than a roll to gnaw, was affected with envy by the comfort and deliberation of the meal. The party lingered over one dish after another, and then over a delicate dessert, with a bottle of old wine, carefully uncorked by the hand of the Dictator himself. As it began to grow dark a lamp was set upon the table and a couple of candles on the sideboard; for the night was perfectly pure, starry, and windless. Light overflowed besides from the door and window in the verandah, so that the garden was fairly illuminated and the leaves twinkled in the darkness.

For perhaps the tenth time Miss Vandeleur entered the house; and on this occasion she returned with the coffee-tray, which she placed upon the sideboard. At the same moment her father rose from his seat.

"The coffee is my province," Francis heard him say.

And next moment he saw his supposed father standing by the sideboard in the light of the candles.

Talking over his shoulder all the while, Mr. Vandeleur poured out two cups of the brown stimulant, and then, by a rapid act of prestidigitation, emptied the contents of a tiny phial into the smaller of the two. The thing was so swiftly done that even Francis, who looked straight into his face, had hardly time to perceive the movement before it was completed. And next instant, and still laughing, Mr. Vandeleur had turned again towards the table with a cup in either hand.

"Ere we have done with this," said he, "we may expect our famous Hebrew."

It would be impossible to depict the confusion and distress of Francis Scrymgeour. He saw foul play going forward before his eyes, and he felt bound to interfere, but knew not how. It might be a mere pleasantry, and then how should he look if he were to offer an unnecessary warning? Or again, if it were serious, the criminal might be his own father, and then how should he not lament if he were to bring ruin on the author of his days? For the first time he became conscious of his own position as a spy. To wait inactive at such a juncture and with such a conflict of sentiments in his bosom was to suffer the most acute torture; he clung to the bars of the shutters, his heart beat fast and with irregularity, and he felt a strong sweat break forth upon his body.

Several minutes passed.

He seemed to perceive the conversation die away and grow less and less in vivacity and volume; but still no sign of any alarming or even notable event.

Suddenly the ring of a glass breaking was followed by a faint and dull sound, as of a person who should have fallen forward with his head upon the table. At the same moment a piercing scream rose from the garden.

"What have you done?" cried Miss Vandeleur. "He is dead!"

The Dictator replied in a violent whisper, so strong and sibilant that every word was audible to the watcher at the window.

4—L

"Silence!" said Mr. Vandeleur; "the man is as well as I am. Take him by the heels whilst I carry him by the shoulders."

Francis heard Miss Vandeleur break forth into a passion of tears.

"Do you hear what I say?" resumed the Dictator, in the same tones. "Or do you wish to quarrel with me? I give you your choice, Miss Vandeleur."

There was another pause, and the Dictator spoke again.

"Take that man by the heels," he said. "I must have him brought into the house. If I were a little younger, I could help myself against the world. But now that years and dangers are upon me, and my hands are weakened, I must turn to you for aid."

"It is a crime," replied the girl.

"I am your father," said Mr. Vandeleur.

This appeal seemed to produce its effect. A scuffling noise followed upon the gravel, a chair was overset, and then Francis saw the father and daughter stagger across the walk and disappear under the verandah, bearing the inanimate body of Mr. Rolles embraced about the knees and shoulders. The young clergyman was limp and pallid, and his head rolled upon his shoulders at every step.

Was he alive or dead? Francis, in spite of the Dictator's declaration, inclined to the latter view. A great crime had been committed; a great calamity had fallen upon the inhabitants of the house with the green blinds. To his surprise, Francis found all horror for the deed swallowed up in sorrow for a girl and an old man whom he judged to be in the height of peril. A tide of generous feeling swept into his heart; he, too, would help his father against man and mankind, against fate and justice; and casting open the shutters he closed his eyes and threw himself with outstretched arms into the foliage of the chestnut.

Branch after branch slipped from his grasp or broke under his weight; then he caught a stalwart bough under his armpit, and hung suspended for a second; and then he let himself drop and fell heavily against the table. A cry of alarm from the house warned him that his entrance had not been effected unobserved. He recovered himself with a stagger, and in three bounds crossed the intervening space and stood before the door in the verandah.

In a small apartment, carpeted with matting and surrounded by glazed cabinets full of rare and costly curios, Mr. Vandeleur was stooping over the body of Mr. Rolles. He raised himself as Francis entered, and there was an instantaneous passage of hands. It was the business of a second; as fast as an eye can wink the thing was done; the young man had not the time to be sure, but it seemed to him as if the Dictator had taken something from the curate's breast, looked at it for the least fraction of time as it lay in his hand, and then suddenly and swiftly passed it to his daughter.

All this was over while Francis had still one foot upon the threshold, and the other raised in air. The next instant he was on his knees to Mr. Vandeleur.

"Father!" he cried. "Let me too help you. I will do what you wish and ask no questions; I will obey you with my life; treat me as a son, and you will find I have a son's devotion."

A deplorable explosion of oaths was the Dictator's first reply.

"Son and father?" he cried. "Father and son? What d——d unnatural comedy is all this? How do you come in my garden? What do you want? And who, in God's name, are you?"

Francis, with a stunned and shamefaced aspect, got upon his feet again, and stood in silence.

Then a light seemed to break upon Mr. Vandeleur, and he laughed aloud.

"I see," cried he. "It is the Scrymgeour. Very well,
Mr. Scrymgeour. Let me tell you in a few words how
you stand. You have entered my private residence by
force, or perhaps by fraud, but certainly with no encouragement from me ; and you come at a moment of
some annoyance, a guest having fainted at my table, to
besiege me with your protestations. You are no son of
mine. You are my brother's bastard by a fishwife, if you
want to know. I regard you with an indifference closely
bordering on aversion ; and from what I now see of your
conduct, I judge your mind to be exactly suitable to your
exterior. I recommend you these mortifying reflections
for your leisure ; and, in the meantime, let me beseech
you to rid us of your presence. If I were not occupied,"
added the Dictator, with a terrifying oath, " I should give
you the unholiest drubbing ere you went ! "

Francis listened in profound humiliation. He would
have fled had it been possible ; but as he had no
means of leaving the residence into which he had
so unfortunately penetrated, he could do no more than
stand foolishly where he was.

It was Miss Vandeleur who broke the silence.

"Father," she said, "you speak in anger. Mr.
Scrymgeour may have been mistaken, but he meant
well and kindly."

"Thank you for speaking," returned the Dictator.
"You remind me of some other observations which I
hold it a point of honour to make to Mr. Scrymgeour.
My brother," he continued, addressing the young man,
"has been foolish enough to give you an allowance ; he was foolish enough and presumptuous enough
to propose a match between you and this young lady.
You were exhibited to her two nights ago ; and I
rejoice to tell you that she rejected the idea with disgust. Let me add that I have considerable influence
with your father ; and it shall not be my fault if you

are not beggared of your allowance and sent back to your scrivening ere the week be out."

The tones of the old man's voice were, if possible, more wounding than his language; Francis felt himself exposed to the most cruel, blighting, and unbearable contempt; his head turned, and he covered his face with his hands, uttering at the same time a tearless sob of agony. But Miss Vandeleur once again interfered in his behalf.

"Mr. Scrymgeour," she said, speaking in clear and even tones, "you must not be concerned at my father's harsh expressions. I felt no disgust for you; on the contrary, I asked an opportunity to make your better acquaintance. As for what has passed to-night, believe me it has filled my mind with both pity and esteem."

Just then Mr. Rolles made a convulsive movement with his arm, which convinced Francis that he was only drugged, and was beginning to throw off the influence of the opiate. Mr. Vandeleur stooped over him and examined his face for an instant.

"Come, come!" cried he, raising his head. "Let there be an end of this. And since you are so pleased with his conduct, Miss Vandeleur, take a candle and show the bastard out."

The young lady hastened to obey.

"Thank you," said Francis, as soon as he was alone with her in the garden. "I thank you from my soul. This has been the bitterest evening of my life, but it will have always one pleasant recollection."

"I spoke as I felt," she replied, "and in justice to you. It made my heart sorry that you should be so unkindly used."

By this time they had reached the garden gate; and Miss Vandeleur, having set the candle on the ground, was already unfastening the bolts.

"One word more," said Francis. "This is not for the last time—I shall see you again, shall I not?"

"Alas!" she answered. "You have heard my father. What can I do but obey?"

"Tell me at least that it is not with your consent," returned Francis; "tell me that you have no wish to see the last of me."

"Indeed," replied she, "I have none. You seem to me both brave and honest."

"Then," said Francis, "give me a keepsake."

She paused for a moment, with her hand upon the key; for the various bars and bolts were all undone, and there was nothing left but to open the lock.

"If I agree," she said, "will you promise to do as I tell you from point to point?"

"Can you ask?" replied Francis. "I would do so willingly on your bare word."

She turned the key and threw open the door.

"Be it so," said she. "You do not know what you ask, but be it so. Whatever you hear," she continued, "whatever happens, do not return to this house; hurry fast until you reach the lighted and populous quarters of the city; even there be upon your guard. You are in a greater danger than you fancy. Promise me you will not so much as look at my keepsake until you are in a place of safety."

"I promise," replied Francis.

She put something loosely wrapped in a handkerchief into the young man's hand; and at the same time, with more strength than he could have anticipated, she pushed him into the street.

"Now, run!" she cried.

He heard the door close behind him, and the noise of the bolts being replaced.

"My faith," said he, "since I have promised!"

And he took to his heels down the lane that leads into the Rue Ravignan.

He was not fifty paces from the house with the green blinds when the most diabolical outcry suddenly arose out of the stillness of the night. Mechanically he stood still; another passenger followed his example; in the neighbouring floors he saw people crowding to the windows; a conflagration could not have produced more disturbance in this empty quarter. And yet it seemed to be all the work of a single man, roaring between grief and rage, like a lioness robbed of her whelps; and Francis was surprised and alarmed to hear his own name shouted with English imprecations to the wind.

His first movement was to return to the house; his second, as he remembered Miss Vandeleur's advice, to continue his flight with greater expedition than before; and he was in the act of turning to put his thought in action, when the Dictator, bare-headed, bawling aloud, his white hair blowing about his head, shot past him like a ball out of the cannon's mouth, and went careering down the street.

" That was a close shave," thought Francis to himself. " What he wants with me, and why he should be so disturbed, I cannot think ; but he is plainly not good company for the moment, and I cannot do better than follow Miss Vandeleur's advice."

So saying, he turned to retrace his steps, thinking to double and descend by the Rue Lepic itself while his pursuer should continue to follow after him on the other line of street. The plan was ill-devised : as a matter of fact, he should have taken his seat in the nearest café, and waited there until the first heat of the pursuit was over. But besides that Francis had no experience and little natural aptitude for the small war of private life, he was so unconscious of any evil on his part, that he saw nothing to fear beyond a disagreeable interview.

And to disagreeable interviews he felt he had already served his apprenticeship that evening; nor could he suppose that Miss Vandeleur had left anything unsaid. Indeed, the young man was sore both in body and mind —the one was all bruised, the other was full of smarting arrows; and he owned to himself that Mr. Vandeleur was master of a very deadly tongue.

The thought of his bruises reminded him that he had not only come without a hat, but that his clothes had considerably suffered in his descent through the chestnut. At the first magazine he purchased a cheap wideawake, and had the disorder of his toilet summarily repaired. The keepsake, still rolled in the handkerchief, he thrust in the meantime into his trousers pocket.

Not many steps beyond the shop he was conscious of a sudden shock, a hand upon his throat, an infuriated face close to his own, and an open mouth bawling curses in his ear. The Dictator, having found no trace of his quarry, was returning by the other way. Francis was a stalwart young fellow; but he was no match for his adversary, whether in strength or skill; and after a few ineffectual struggles he resigned himself entirely to his captor.

" What do you want with me ? " said he.

" We will talk of that at home," returned the Dictator grimly.

And he continued to march the young man up hill in the direction of the house with the green blinds.

But Francis, although he no longer struggled, was only waiting an opportunity to make a bold push for freedom. With a sudden jerk he left the collar of his coat in the hands of Mr. Vandeleur, and once more made off at his best speed in the direction of the Boulevards.

The tables were now turned. If the Dictator was the stronger, Francis, in the top of his youth, was the more fleet of foot, and he had soon effected his escape among the crowds. Relieved for a moment, but with a growing sentiment of alarm and wonder in his mind, he walked briskly until he debouched upon the Place de l'Opéra lit up like day with electric lamps.

"This, at least," thought he, "should satisfy Miss Vandeleur."

And turning to his right along the Boulevards, he entered the Café Américain and ordered some beer. It was both late and early for the majority of the frequenters of the establishment. Only two or three persons, all men, were dotted here and there at separate tables in the hall; and Francis was too much occupied by his own thoughts to observe their presence.

He drew the handkerchief from his pocket. The object wrapped in it proved to be a morocco case, clasped and ornamented in gilt, which opened by means of a spring, and disclosed to the horrified young man a diamond of monstrous bigness and extraordinary brilliancy. The circumstance was so inexplicable, the value of the stone was plainly so enormous, that Francis sat staring into the open casket without movement, without conscious thought, like a man stricken suddenly with idiocy.

A hand was laid upon his shoulder, lightly but firmly, and a quiet voice, which yet had in it the ring of command, uttered these words in his ear—

"Close the casket, and compose your face."

Looking up, he beheld a man, still young, of an urbane and tranquil presence, and dressed with rich simplicity. This personage had risen from a neighbouring table, and, bringing his glass with him, had taken a seat beside Francis.

"Close the casket," repeated the stranger, "and put it quietly back into your pocket, where I feel persuaded it should never have been. Try, if you please, to throw off your bewildered air, and act as though I were one of your acquaintances whom you had met by chance. So!

Touch glasses with me. That is better. I fear, sir, you must be an amateur."

And the stranger pronounced these last words with a smile of peculiar meaning, leaned back in his seat and enjoyed a deep inhalation of tobacco.

"For God's sake," said Francis, "tell me who you are and what this means! Why I should obey your most unusual suggestions I am sure I know not; but the truth is, I have fallen this evening into so many perplexing adventures, and all I meet conduct themselves so strangely, that I think I must either have gone mad or wandered into another planet. Your face inspires me with confidence; you seem wise, good, and experienced; tell me, for heaven's sake, why you accost me in so odd a fashion."

"All in due time," replied the stranger. "But I have the first hand, and you must begin by telling me how the Rajah's Diamond is in your possession."

"The Rajah's Diamond!" echoed Francis.

"I would not speak so loud, if I were you," returned the other. "But most certainly you have the Rajah's Diamond in your pocket. I have seen and handled it a score of times in Sir Thomas Vandeleur's collection."

"Sir Thomas Vandeleur! The General! My father!" cried Francis.

"Your father?" repeated the stranger. "I was not aware the General had any family."

"I am illegitimate, sir," replied Francis, with a flush.

The other bowed with gravity. It was a respectful bow, as of a man silently apologising to his equal; and Francis felt relieved and comforted, he scarce knew why. The society of this person did him good; he seemed to touch firm ground; a strong feeling of respect grew up in his bosom, and mechanically he removed his wideawake as though in the presence of a superior.

"I perceive," said the stranger, "that your adventures have not all been peaceful. Your collar is torn, your face is scratched, you have a cut upon your temple ; you will, perhaps, pardon my curiosity when I ask you to explain how you came by these injuries, and how you happen to have stolen property to an enormous value in your pocket."

"I must differ from you !" returned Francis hotly. "I possess no stolen property. And if you refer to the diamond, it was given to me not an hour ago by Miss Vandeleur in the Rue Lepic."

"By Miss Vandeleur in the Rue Lepic !" repeated the other. "You interest me more than you suppose. Pray continue."

"Heavens !" cried Francis.

His memory had made a sudden bound. He had seen Mr. Vandeleur take an article from the breast of his drugged visitor, and that article, he was now persuaded, was a morocco case.

"You have a light ? " inquired the stranger.

"Listen," replied Francis. "I know not who you are, but I believe you to be worthy of confidence and helpful ; I find myself in strange waters ; I must have counsel and support, and since you invite me I shall tell you all."

And he briefly recounted his experience since the day when he was summoned from the bank by his lawyer.

"Yours is indeed a remarkable history," said the stranger, after the young man had made an end of his narrative ; "and your position is full of difficulty and peril. Many would counsel you to seek out your father, and give the diamond to him ; but I have other views. —Waiter ! " he cried.

The waiter drew near.

"Will you ask the manager to speak with me a moment ? " said he ; and Francis observed once more, both in his tone and manner, the evidence of a habit of command.

The waiter withdrew, and returned in a moment with the manager, who bowed with obsequious respect.

"What," said he, "can I do to serve you?"

"Have the goodness," replied the stranger, indicating Francis, "to tell this gentleman my name."

"You have the honour, sir," said the functionary, addressing young Scrymgeour, "to occupy the same table with His Highness Prince Florizel of Bohemia."

Francis rose with precipitation, and made a grateful reverence to the Prince, who bade him resume his seat.

"I thank you," said Florizel, once more addressing the functionary; "I am sorry to have deranged you for so small a matter."

And he dismissed him with a movement of his hand.

"And now," added the Prince, turning to Francis, "give me the diamond."

Without a word the casket was handed over.

"You have done right," said Florizel; "your sentiments have properly inspired you, and you will live to be grateful for the misfortunes of to-night. A man, Mr. Scrymgeour, may fall into a thousand perplexities, but if his heart be upright and his intelligence unclouded, he will issue from them all without dishonour. Let your mind be at rest; your affairs are in my hand; and with the aid of Heaven I am strong enough to bring them to a good end. Follow me, if you please, to my carriage."

So saying the Prince arose, and, having left a piece of gold for the waiter, conducted the young man from the café and along the Boulevard to where an unpretentious brougham and a couple of servants out of livery awaited his arrival.

"This carriage," said he, "is at your disposal; collect your baggage as rapidly as you can make it convenient, and my servants will conduct you to a villa in the neighbourhood of Paris where you can wait in some degree of comfort until I have had time to arrange your situation.

You will find there a pleasant garden, a library of good authors, a cook, a cellar, and some good cigars, which I recommend to your attention. Jérome," he added, turning to one of the servants, "you have heard what I say; I leave Mr. Scrymgeour in your charge; you will, I know, be careful of my friend."

Francis uttered some broken phrases of gratitude.

"It will be time enough to thank me," said the Prince, "when you are acknowledged by your father and married to Miss Vandeleur."

And with that the Prince turned away and strolled leisurely in the direction of Montmartre. He hailed the first passing cab, gave an address, and a quarter of an hour afterwards, having discharged the driver some distance lower, he was knocking at Mr. Vandeleur's garden gate.

It was opened with singular precautions by the Dictator in person.

"Who are you?" he demanded.

"You must pardon me this late visit, Mr. Vandeleur," replied the Prince.

"Your Highness is always welcome," returned Mr. Vandeleur, stepping back.

The Prince profited by the open space, and without waiting for his host walked right into the house and opened the door of the *salon*. Two people were seated there; one was Miss Vandeleur, who bore the marks of weeping about her eyes, and was still shaken from time to time by a sob; in the other the Prince recognised the young man who had consulted him on literary matters about a month before, in a club smoking-room.

"Good evening, Miss Vandeleur," said Florizel; "you look fatigued. Mr. Rolles, I believe? I hope you have profited by the study of Gaboriau, Mr. Rolles."

But the young clergyman's temper was too much

embittered for speech ; and he contented himself with bowing stiffly, and continued to gnaw his lip.

"To what good wind," said Mr. Vandeleur, following his guest, "am I to attribute the honour of your Highness's presence ? "

"I am come on business," returned the Prince ; "on business with you ; as soon as that is settled I shall request Mr. Rolles to accompany me for a walk.—Mr. Rolles," he added, with severity, "let me remind you that I have not yet sat down."

The clergyman sprang to his feet with an apology ; whereupon the Prince took an arm-chair beside the table, handed his hat to Mr. Vandeleur, his cane to Mr. Rolles, and, leaving them standing and thus menially employed upon his service, spoke as follows :—

"I have come here, as I said, upon business ; but, had I come looking for pleasure, I could not have been more displeased with my reception nor more dissatisfied with my company. You, sir," addressing Mr. Rolles, "you have treated your superior in station with discourtesy ; you, Vandeleur, receive me with a smile, but you know right well that your hands are not yet cleansed from misconduct.—I do not desire to be interrupted, sir," he added imperiously ; " I am here to speak, and not to listen ; and I have to ask you to hear me with respect, and to obey punctiliously. At the earliest possible date your daughter shall be married at the Embassy to my friend, Francis Scrymgeour, your brother's acknowledged son. You will oblige me by offering not less than ten thousand pounds dowry. For yourself, I will indicate to you in writing a mission of some importance in Siam which I destine to your care. And now, sir, you will answer me in two words whether or not you agree to these conditions."

"Your Highness will pardon me," said Mr. Vandeleur, "and permit me, with all respect, to submit to him two queries ? "

"The permission is granted," replied the Prince.

"Your Highness," resumed the Dictator, "has called Mr. Scrymgeour his friend. Believe me, had I known he was thus honoured, I should have treated him with proportional respect."

"You interrogate adroitly," said the Prince; "but it will not serve your turn. You have my commands; if I had never seen that gentleman before to-night, it would not render them less absolute."

"Your Highness interprets my meaning with his usual subtlety," returned Vandeleur. "Once more: I have, unfortunately, put the police upon the track of Mr. Scrymgeour on a charge of theft; am I to withdraw or to uphold the accusation?"

"You will please yourself," replied Florizel. "The question is one between your conscience and the laws of this land. Give me my hat; and you, Mr. Rolles, give me my cane and follow me. Miss Vandeleur, I wish you good-evening. I judge," he added to Vandeleur, "that your silence means unqualified assent."

"If I can do no better," replied the old man, "I shall submit; but I warn you openly it shall not be without a struggle."

"You are old," said the Prince; "but years are disgraceful to the wicked. Your age is more unwise than the youth of others. Do not provoke me, or you may find me harder than you dream. This is the first time that I have fallen across your path in anger; take care that it be the last."

With these words, motioning the clergyman to follow, Florizel left the apartment and directed his steps towards the garden gate; and the Dictator, following with a candle, gave them light, and once more undid the elaborate fastenings with which he sought to protect himself from intrusion.

"Your daughter is no longer present," said the Prince,

turning on the threshold. "Let me tell you that I understand your threats; and you have only to lift your hand to bring upon yourself sudden and irremediable ruin."

The Dictator made no reply; but as the Prince turned his back upon him in the lamplight he made a gesture full of menace and insane fury; and the next moment, slipping round a corner, he was running at full speed for the nearest cab-stand.

Here (says my Arabian) *the thread of events is finally diverted from* THE HOUSE WITH THE GREEN BLINDS. *One more adventure,* he adds, *and we have done with* THE RAJAH'S DIAMOND. *That last link in the chain is known among the inhabitants of Bagdad by the name of*

THE ADVENTURE OF PRINCE FLORIZEL AND A DETECTIVE

PRINCE FLORIZEL walked with Mr. Rolles to the door of a small hotel where the latter resided. They spoke much together, and the clergyman was more than once affected to tears by the mingled severity and tenderness of Florizel's reproaches.

"I have made ruin of my life," he said at last. "Help me; tell me what I am to do; I have, alas! neither the virtues of a priest nor the dexterity of a rogue."

"Now that you are humbled," said the Prince, "I command no longer; the repentant have to do with God, and not with Princes. But if you will let me advise you, go to Australia as a colonist, seek menial labour in the open air, and try to forget that you have ever been a clergyman, or that you ever set eyes on that accursed stone."

"Accurst indeed!" replied Mr. Rolles. "Where is it

now ? What further hurt is it not working for mankind ? "

"It will do no more evil," returned the Prince. "It is
here in my pocket. And this," he added kindly, "will
show that I place some faith in your penitence, young
as it is."

"Suffer me to touch your hand," pleaded Mr. Rolles.

"No," replied Prince Florizel, "not yet."

The tone in which he uttered these last words was
eloquent in the ears of the young clergyman ; and for
some minutes after the Prince had turned away he
stood on the threshold following with his eyes the retreating figure and invoking the blessing of Heaven upon
a man so excellent in counsel.

For several hours the Prince walked alone in unfrequented streets. His mind was full of concern ; what
to do with the diamond, whether to return it to its owner,
whom he judged unworthy of this rare possession, or to
take some sweeping and courageous measure and put it
out of the reach of all mankind at once and for ever, was
a problem too grave to be decided in a moment. The
manner in which it had come into his hands appeared
manifestly providential ; and as he took out the jewel and
looked at it under the street lamps, its size and surprising
brilliancy inclined him more and more to think of it as of
an unmixed and dangerous evil for the world.

"God help me ! " he thought ; "if I look at it much
oftener I shall begin to grow covetous myself."

At last, though still uncertain in his mind, he turned
his steps towards the small but elegant mansion on the
river-side which had belonged for centuries to his royal
family. The arms of Bohemia are deeply graved over
the door and upon the tall chimneys ; passengers have
a look into a green court set with the most costly flowers ;
and a stork, the only one in Paris, perches on the gable
all day long and keeps a crowd before the house. Grave

servants are seen passing to and fro within; and from time to time the great gate is thrown open and a carriage rolls below the arch. For many reasons this residence was especially dear to the heart of Prince Florizel; he never drew near to it without enjoying that sentiment of home-coming so rare in the lives of the great; and on the present evening he beheld its tall roof and mildly illuminated windows with unfeigned relief and satisfaction.

As he was approaching the postern door by which he always entered when alone, a man stepped forth from the shadow and presented himself with an obeisance in the Prince's path.

"I have the honour of addressing Prince Florizel of Bohemia?" said he.

"Such is my title," replied the Prince. "What do you want with me?"

"I am," said the man, "a detective, and I have to present your Highness with this billet from the Prefect of Police."

The Prince took the letter and glanced it through by the light of the street lamp. It was highly apologetic, but requested him to follow the bearer to the Prefecture without delay.

"In short," said Florizel, "I am arrested."

"Your Highness," replied the officer, "nothing, I am certain, could be further from the intention of the Prefect. You will observe that he has not granted a warrant. It is mere formality, or call it, if you prefer, an obligation that your Highness lays on the authorities."

"At the same time," asked the Prince, "if I were to refuse to follow you?"

"I will not conceal from your Highness that a considerable discretion has been granted me," replied the detective, with a bow.

"Upon my word," cried Florizel, "your effrontery astounds me! Yourself, as an agent, I must pardon; but your superiors shall dearly smart for their misconduct. What, have you any idea, is the cause of this impolitic and unconstitutional act? You will observe that I have as yet neither refused nor consented, and much may depend on your prompt and ingenuous answer. Let me remind you, officer, that this is an affair of some gravity."

"Your Highness," said the detective humbly, "General Vandeleur and his brother have had the incredible presumption to accuse you of theft. The famous diamond, they declare, is in your hands. A word from you in denial will most amply satisfy the Prefect; nay, I go further: if your Highness would so far honour a subaltern as to declare his ignorance of the matter even to myself, I should ask permission to retire upon the spot."

Florizel, up to the last moment, had regarded his adventure in the light of a trifle, only serious upon international considerations. At the name of Vandeleur the horrible truth broke upon him in a moment; he was not only arrested, but he was guilty. This was not only an annoying incident—it was a peril to his honour. What was he to say? What was he to do? The Rajah's Diamond was indeed an accursed stone; and it seemed as if he were to be the last victim to its influence.

One thing was certain. He could not give the required assurance to the detective. He must gain time.

His hesitation had not lasted a second.

"Be it so," said he, "let us walk together to the Prefecture."

The man once more bowed, and proceeded to follow Florizel at a respectful distance in the rear.

"Approach," said the Prince. "I am in a humour to

talk, and, if I mistake not, now I look at you again, this is not the first time that we have met."

" I count it an honour," replied the officer, " that your Highness should recollect my face. It is eight years since I had the pleasure of an interview."

" To remember faces," returned Florizel, " is as much a part of my profession as it is of yours. Indeed, rightly looked upon, a Prince and a detective serve in the same corps. We are both combatants against crime ; only mine is the more lucrative and yours the more dangerous rank, and there is a sense in which both may be made equally honourable to a good man. I had rather, strange as you may think it, be a detective of character and parts than a weak and ignoble sovereign."

The officer was overwhelmed.

" Your Highness returns good for evil," said he. " To an act of presumption he replies by the most amiable condescension."

" How do you know," replied Florizel, " that I am not seeking to corrupt you ? "

" Heaven preserve me from the temptation ! " cried the detective.

" I applaud your answer," returned the Prince. " It is that of a wise and honest man. The world is a great place, and stocked with wealth and beauty, and there is no limit to the rewards that may be offered. Such an one who would refuse a million of money may sell his honour for an empire or the love of a woman ; and I myself, who speak to you, have seen occasions so tempting, provocations so irresistible to the strength of human virtue, that I have been glad to tread in your steps and recommend myself to the grace of God. It is thus, thanks to that modest and becoming habit alone," he added, " that you and I can walk this town together with untarnished hearts."

" I had always heard that you were brave," replied

the officer, "but I was not aware that you were wise and pious. You speak the truth, and you speak it with an accent that moves me to the heart. This world is indeed a place of trial."

"We are now," said Florizel, "in the middle of the bridge. Lean your elbows on the parapet and look over. As the water rushing below, so the passions and complications of life carry away the honesty of weak men. Let me tell you a story."

"I receive your Highness's commands," replied the man.

And, imitating the Prince, he leaned against the parapet, and disposed himself to listen. The city was already sunk in slumber; had it not been for the infinity of lights and the outline of buildings on the starry sky, they might have been alone beside some country river.

"An officer," began Prince Florizel, "a man of courage and conduct, who had already risen by merit to an eminent rank, and won not only admiration but respect, visited, in an unfortunate hour for his peace of mind, the collections of an Indian Prince. Here he beheld a diamond so extraordinary for size and beauty that from that instant he had only one desire in life: honour, reputation, friendship, the love of country—he was ready to sacrifice all for this lump of sparkling crystal. For three years he served this semi-barbarian potentate as Jacob served Laban; he falsified frontiers, he connived at murders, he unjustly condemned and executed a brother-officer who had the misfortune to displease the Rajah by some honest freedoms; lastly, at a time of great danger to his native land, he betrayed a body of his fellow-soldiers, and suffered them to be defeated and massacred by thousands. In the end he had amassed a magnificent fortune, and brought home with him the coveted diamond.

"Years passed," continued the Prince, "and at length the diamond is accidentally lost. It falls into the hands

of a simple and laborious youth, a student, a minister of
God, just entering on a career of usefulness and even
distinction.   Upon him also the spell is cast; he deserts
everything, his holy calling, his studies, and flees with
the gem into a foreign country.   The officer has a
brother, an astute, daring, unscrupulous man, who learns
the clergyman's secret.   What does he do ?   Tell his
brother, inform the police ?   No ; upon this man also
the Satanic charm has fallen ; he must have the stone
for himself.   At the risk of murder, he drugs the young
priest and seizes the prey.   And now, by an accident
which is not important to my moral, the jewel passes
out of his custody into that of another, who, terrified
at what he sees, gives it into the keeping of a man in
high station and above reproach.

"The officer's name is Thomas Vandeleur," continued
Florizel.   "The stone is called the Rajah's Diamond.
And"—suddenly opening his hand—"you behold it here
before your eyes."

The officer started back with a cry.

"We have spoken of corruption," said the Prince.
"To me this nugget of bright crystal is as loathsome as
though it were crawling with the worms of death ; it
is as shocking as though it were compacted out of innocent blood.   I see it here in my hand, and I know it
is shining with hell-fire.   I have told you but a hundredth
part of its story ; what passed in former ages, to what
crimes and treacheries it incited men of yore, the imagination trembles to conceive ; for years and years it has
faithfully served the powers of hell ; enough, I say, of
blood, enough of disgrace, enough of broken lives and
friendships ; all things come to an end, the evil like the
good ; pestilence as well as beautiful music ; and as for
this diamond, God forgive me if I do wrong, but its
empire ends to-night."

The Prince made a sudden movement with his hand,

and the jewel, describing an arc of light, dived with a splash into the flowing river.

"Amen," said Florizel, with gravity. "I have slain a cockatrice!"

"God pardon me!" cried the detective. "What have you done? I am a ruined man."

"I think," returned the Prince, with a smile, "that many well-to-do people in this city might envy you your ruin."

"Alas! your Highness!" said the officer, "and you corrupt me after all?"

"It seems there was no help for it," replied Florizel. —"And now let us go forward to the Prefecture."

Not long after, the marriage of Francis Scrymgeour and Miss Vandeleur was celebrated in great privacy; and the Prince acted on that occasion as groom's man. The two Vandeleurs surprised some rumour of what had happened to the diamond; and their vast diving operations on the River Seine are the wonder and amusement of the idle. It is true that through some miscalculation they have chosen the wrong branch of the river. As for the Prince, that sublime person, having now served his turn, may go, along with the *Arabian Author*, topsy-turvy into space. But if the reader insists on more specific information, I am happy to say that a recent revolution hurled him from the throne of Bohemia, in consequence of his continued absence and edifying neglect of public business; and that his Highness now keeps a cigar store in Rupert Street, much frequented by other foreign refugees. I go there from time to time to smoke and have a chat, and find him as great a creature as in the days of his prosperity; he has an Olympian air behind the counter; and although a sedentary life is beginning to tell upon his waistcoat, he is probably, take him for all in all, the handsomest tobacconist in London.

THE PAVILION ON THE LINKS

CHAPTER I

TELLS HOW I CAMPED IN GRADEN SEA-WOOD, AND BEHELD A LIGHT IN THE PAVILION

I WAS a great solitary when I was young. I made it my pride to keep aloof and suffice for my own entertainment; and I may say that I had neither friends nor acquaintances until I met that friend who became my wife and the mother of my children. With one man only was I on private terms : this was R. Northmour, Esquire, of Graden-Easter, in Scotland. We had met at college ; and though there was not much liking between us, nor even much intimacy, we were so nearly of a humour that we could associate with ease to both. Misanthropes we believed ourselves to be ; but I have thought since that we were only sulky fellows. It was scarcely a companionship, but a co-existence in unsociability. Northmour's exceptional violence of temper made it no easy affair for him to keep the peace with any one but me ; and as he respected my silent ways, and let me come and go as I pleased, I could tolerate his presence without concern. I think we called each other friends.

When Northmour took his degree and I decided to leave the University without one, he invited me on a long visit to Graden-Easter ; and it was thus that I first became acquainted with the scene of my adventures. The mansion-house of Graden stood in a bleak stretch of country some three miles from the shore of the German Ocean. It was as large as a barrack; and as it had been built of a soft stone, liable to consume in the eager air of the seaside, it was damp and draughty within and half-ruinous without. It was impossible for two young men to lodge with comfort in such a dwelling. But there stood in the northern part of the estate, in a wilderness of links and blowing sand-hills, and between a plantation and the sea, a small Pavilion or Belvidere, of modern design, which was exactly suited to our wants; and in this hermitage, speaking little, reading much, and rarely associating except at meals, Northmour and I spent four tempestuous winter months. I might have stayed longer; but one March night there sprang up between us a dispute, which rendered my departure necessary. Northmour spoke hotly, I remember, and I suppose I must have made some tart rejoinder. He leaped from his chair and grappled me; I had to fight, without exaggeration, for my life; and it was only with a great effort that I mastered him, for he was near as strong in body as myself, and seemed filled with the devil. The next morning we met on our usual terms; but I judged it more delicate to withdraw; nor did he attempt to dissuade me.

It was nine years before I revisited the neighbourhood. I travelled at that time with a tilt-cart, a tent, and a cooking-stove, tramping all day beside the waggon, and at night, whenever it was possible, gipsying in a cove of the hills, or by the side of a wood. I believe I visited in this manner most of the wild and desolate regions both in England and Scotland; and, as I had neither friends nor relations, I was troubled with no correspondence, and had nothing in the nature of headquarters, unless it was the office of my solicitors, from whom I drew my income twice a year. It was a life in which I delighted; and I fully thought to have grown old upon the march, and at last died in a ditch.

It was my whole business to find desolate corners, where I could camp without the fear of interruption ; and hence, being in another part of the same shire, I bethought me suddenly of the Pavilion on the Links. No thoroughfare passed within three miles of it. The nearest town, and that was but a fisher village, was at a distance of six or seven. For ten miles of length, and from a depth varying from three miles to half a mile, this belt of barren country lay along the sea. The beach, which was the natural approach, was full of quicksands. Indeed, I may say there is hardly a better place of concealment in the United Kingdom. I determined to pass a week in the Sea-Wood of Graden-Easter, and making a long stage, reached it about sundown on a wild September day.

The country, I have said, was mixed sand-hill and links ; *links* being a Scottish name for sand which has ceased drifting and become more or less solidly covered with turf. The pavilion stood on an even space ; a little behind it, the wood began in a hedge of elders huddled together by the wind ; in front, a few tumbled sand-hills stood between it and the sea. An outcropping of rock had formed a bastion for the sand, so that there was here a promontory in the coast-line between two shallow bays ; and just beyond the tides, the rock again cropped out and formed an islet of small dimensions but strikingly designed. The quicksands were of great extent at low water, and had an infamous reputation in the country. Close inshore, between the islet and the promontory, it was said they would swallow a man in four minutes and a half ; but there may have been little ground for this precision. The district was alive with rabbits, and haunted by gulls which made a continual piping about the pavilion. On summer days the outlook was bright, and even gladsome ; but at sundown in September, with a high wind, and a heavy surf rolling in close along the links, the place told of nothing but dead mariners and sea disaster. A ship beating to windward on the horizon, and a huge truncheon of wreck half-buried in the sands at my feet, completed the innuendo of the scene.

The pavilion—it had been built by the last proprietor, Northmour's uncle, a silly and prodigal virtuoso—presented little signs of age. It was two stories in height, Italian in design, surrounded by a patch of garden in which nothing had prospered but a few coarse flowers, and looked, with its shuttered windows, not like a house that had been deserted, but like one that had never been tenanted by man. Northmour was plainly from home ; whether, as usual, sulking in the cabin of his yacht, or in one of his fitful and extravagant appearances in the world of society, I had, of course, no means of guessing. The place had an air of solitude that daunted even a solitary like myself ; the wind cried in the chimneys with a strange and wailing note ; and it was with a sense of escape, as if I were going indoors, that I turned away and, driving my cart before me, entered the skirts of the wood.

The Sea-Wood of Graden had been planted to shelter the cultivated fields behind, and check the encroachments of the blowing sand. As you advanced into it from coastward, elders were succeeded by other hardy shrubs ; but the timber was all stunted and bushy ; it led a life of conflict ; the trees were accustomed to swing there all night long in fierce winter tempests ; and even in early spring the leaves were already flying, and autumn was beginning, in this exposed plantation. Inland the ground rose into a little hill, which, along with the islet, served as a sailing mark for seamen. When the hill was open of the islet to the north, vessels must bear well to

the eastward to clear Graden Ness and the Graden Bullers.
In the lower ground, a streamlet ran among the trees, and,
being dammed with dead leaves and clay of its own carrying, spread out every here and there, and lay in stagnant
pools.   One or two ruined cottages were dotted about
the wood ; and, according to Northmour, these were
ecclesiastical foundations, and in their time had sheltered
pious hermits.

I found a den, or small hollow, where there was
a spring of pure water ; and there, clearing away the
brambles, I pitched the tent, and made a fire to cook
my supper. My horse I picketed farther in the wood
where there was a patch of sward. The banks of the
den not only concealed the light of my fire, but
sheltered me from the wind, which was cold as well
as high.

The life I was leading made me both hardy and
frugal.   I never drank but water, and rarely ate anything more costly than oatmeal ; and I required so
little sleep that, although I rose with the peep of day,
I would often lie long awake in the dark or starry
watches of the night. Thus in Graden Sea-Wood,
although I fell thankfully asleep by eight in the evening,
I was awake again before eleven with a full possession
of my faculties, and no sense of drowsiness or fatigue.
I rose and sat by the fire, watching the trees and
clouds tumultuously tossing and fleeing overhead, and
hearkening to the wind and the rollers along the shore ;
till at length, growing weary of inaction, I quitted the
den, and strolled towards the borders of the wood. A
young moon, buried in mist, gave a faint illumination
to my steps ; and the light grew brighter as I walked
forth into the links. At the same moment, the wind,
smelling salt of the open ocean, and carrying particles
of sand, struck me with its full force, so that I had to
bow my head.

When I raised it again to look about me, I was aware of a light in the pavilion. It was not stationary; but passed from one window to another as though some one were reviewing the different apartments with a lamp or candle. I watched it for some seconds in great surprise. When I had arrived in the afternoon the house had been plainly deserted; now it was as plainly occupied. It was my first idea that a gang of thieves might have broken in and be now ransacking Northmour's cupboards, which were many and not ill supplied. But what should bring thieves to Graden-Easter? And, again, all the shutters had been thrown open, and it would have been more in the character of such gentry to close them. I dismissed the notion, and fell back upon another: Northmour himself must have arrived, and was now airing and inspecting the pavilion.

I have said that there was no real affection between this man and me; but, had I loved him like a brother, I was then so much more in love with solitude that I should none the less have shunned his company. As it was, I turned and ran for it; and it was with genuine satisfaction that I found myself safely back beside the fire. I had escaped an acquaintance: I should have one more night in comfort. In the morning I might either slip away before Northmour was abroad, or pay him as short a visit as I chose.

But when morning came I thought the situation so diverting that I forgot my shyness. Northmour was at my mercy; I arranged a good practical jest, though I knew well that my neighbour was not the man to jest with in security; and, chuckling beforehand over its success, took my place among the elders at the edge of the wood, whence I could command the door of the pavilion. The shutters were all once more closed, which I remember thinking odd; and the house, with its white walls and green venetians, looked spruce and habitable in the morning light. Hour after hour passed, and still no sign of Northmour. I knew him for a sluggard in the morning; but, as it drew on towards noon, I lost my patience. To say the truth, I had promised myself to break my fast in the pavilion, and hunger began to prick me sharply. It was a pity to let the opportunity go by without some cause for mirth; but the grosser appetite prevailed, and I relinquished my jest with regret, and sallied from the wood.

The appearance of the house affected me, as I drew near, with disquietude. It seemed unchanged since last evening; and I had expected it, I scarce knew why, to wear some external signs of habitation. But no: the windows were all closely shuttered, the chimneys breathed no smoke, and the front door itself was closely padlocked. Northmour therefore had entered by the back; this was the natural, and indeed the necessary, conclusion; and you may judge of my surprise when, on turning the house, I found the back-door similarly secured.

My mind at once reverted to the original theory of thieves; and I blamed myself sharply for my last night's inaction. I examined all the windows on the lower story, but none of them had been tampered with; I tried the padlocks, but they were both secure. It thus became a problem how the thieves, if thieves they were, had managed to enter the house. They must have got, I reasoned, upon the roof of the outhouse where Northmour used to keep his photographic battery; and from thence, either by the window of the study or that of my old bedroom, completed their burglarious entry.

I followed what I supposed was their example; and, getting on the roof, tried the shutters of each room. Both were secure; but I was not to be beaten; and, with a little force, one of them flew open, grazing, as it did so, the back of my hand. I remember I put the wound to my mouth and stood for perhaps half a minute licking it like a dog, and mechanically gazing behind me over the waste links and the sea ; and in that space of time my eye made note of a large schooner yacht some miles to the north-east. Then I threw up the window and climbed in.

I went over the house, and nothing can express my mystification. There was no sign of disorder, but, on the contrary, the rooms were unusually clean and pleasant. I found fires laid ready for lighting ; three bedrooms prepared with a luxury quite foreign to Northmour's habits, and with water in the ewers and the beds turned down ; a table set for three in the dining-room ; and an ample supply of cold meats, game, and vegetables on the pantry shelves. There were guests expected, that was plain ; but why guests when Northmour hated society ? And, above all, why was the house thus stealthily prepared at dead of night ? and why were the shutters closed and the doors padlocked ?

I effaced all traces of my visit, and came forth from the window feeling sobered and concerned.

The schooner yacht was still in the same place ; and it flashed for a moment through my mind that this might be the *Red Earl* bringing the owner of the pavilion and his guests. But the vessel's head was set the other way.

CHAPTER II

TELLS OF THE NOCTURNAL LANDING FROM THE YACHT

I RETURNED to the den to cook myself a meal, of which I stood in great need, as well as to care for my horse, which I had somewhat neglected in the morning. From time to time I went down to the edge of the wood ; but

there was no change in the pavilion, and not a human
creature was seen all day upon the links. The schooner
in the offing was the one touch of life within my range of
vision. She, apparently with no set object, stood off and on
or lay to, hour after hour ; but as the evening deepened
she drew steadily nearer. I became more convinced that
she carried Northmour and his friends, and that they
would probably come ashore after dark ; not only because
that was of a piece with the secrecy of the preparations,
but because the tide would not have flowed sufficiently
before eleven to cover Graden Floe and the other sea
quags that fortified the shore against invaders.

All day the wind had been going down, and the sea
along with it ; but there was a return towards sunset of
the heavy weather of the day before. The night set in
pitch dark. The wind came off the sea in squalls, like the
firing of a battery of cannon ; now and then there was a
flaw of rain, and the surf rolled heavier with the rising tide,
I was down at my observatory among the elders, when a
light was run up to the mast-head of the schooner, and
showed she was closer in than when I had last seen her
by the dying daylight. I concluded that this must be a
signal to Northmour's associates on shore ; and, stepping
forth into the links, looked around me for something in
response.

A small footpath ran along the margin of the wood,
and formed the most direct communication between the
pavilion and the mansion-house ; and as I cast my eyes
to that side I saw a spark of light, not a quarter of a mile
away, and rapidly approaching. From its uneven course it
appeared to be the light of a lantern carried by a person who
followed the windings of the path, and was often staggered
and taken aback by the more violent squalls. I concealed
myself once more among the elders, and waited eagerly
for the new-comer's advance. It proved to be a woman ;
and as she passed within half a rod of my ambush I was

able to recognise the features. The deaf and silent old dame who had nursed Northmour in his childhood was his associate in this underhand affair.

I followed her at a little distance, taking advantage of the innumerable heights and hollows, concealed by the darkness, and favoured not only by the nurse's deafness, but by the uproar of the wind and surf. She entered the pavilion, and, going at once to the upper story, opened and set a light in one of the windows that looked towards the sea. Immediately afterwards the light at the schooner's mast-head was run down and extinguished. Its purpose had been attained, and those on board were sure that they were expected. The old woman resumed her preparations ; although the other shutters remained closed, I could see a glimmer going to and fro about the house; and a gush of sparks from one chimney after another soon told me that the fires were being kindled.

Northmour and his guests, I was now persuaded, would come ashore as soon as there was water on the floe. It was a wild night for boat service ; and I felt some alarm mingle with my curiosity as I reflected on the danger of the landing. My old acquaintance, it was true, was the most eccentric of men; but the present eccentricity was both disquieting and lugubrious to consider. A variety of feelings thus led me towards the beach, where I lay flat on my face in a hollow within six feet of the track that led to the pavilion. Thence, I should have the satisfaction of recognising the arrivals, and, if they should prove to be acquaintances, greeting them as soon as they had landed.

Some time before eleven, while the tide was still dangerously low, a boat's lantern appeared close inshore ; and, my attention being thus awakened, I could perceive another still far to seaward, violently tossed, and sometimes hidden by the billows. The weather, which was getting dirtier as the night went on, and the perilous situation of the yacht upon a lee-shore, had

4—N

probably driven them to attempt a landing at the earliest possible moment.

A little afterwards, four yachtsmen carrying a very heavy chest, and guided by a fifth with a lantern, passed close in front of me as I lay, and were admitted to the pavilion by the nurse. They returned to the beach, and passed me a second time with another chest, larger but apparently not so heavy as the first. A third time they made the transit; and on this occasion one of the yachtsmen carried a leather portmanteau, and the others a lady's trunk and carriage bag. My curiosity was sharply excited. If a woman were among the guests of Northmour, it would show a change in his habits and an apostasy from his pet theories of life, well calculated to fill me with surprise. When he and I dwelt there together, the pavilion had been a temple of misogyny. And now, one of the detested sex was to be installed under its roof. I remembered one or two particulars, a few notes of daintiness and almost of coquetry which had struck me the day before as I surveyed the preparations in the house; their purpose was now clear, and I thought myself dull not to have perceived it from the first.

While I was thus reflecting, a second lantern drew near me from the beach. It was carried by a yachtsman whom I had not yet seen, and who was conducting two other persons to the pavilion. These two persons were unquestionably the guests for whom the house was made ready; and, straining eye and ear, I set myself to watch them as they passed. One was an unusually tall man, in a travelling hat slouched over his eyes, and a highland cape closely buttoned and turned up so as to conceal his face. You could make out no more of him than that he was, as I have said, unusually tall, and walked feebly with a heavy stoop. By his side, and either clinging to him or giving him support—I could not make out which—was a young, tall, and slender figure of a woman. She was extremely pale; but in the light of the lantern her face was so marred by strong and changing shadows that she might equally well have been as ugly as sin or as beautiful as I afterwards found her to be. When they were just abreast of me, the girl made some remark which was drowned by the noise of the wind.

"Hush!" said her companion; and there was something in the tone with which the word was uttered that thrilled and rather shook my spirits. It seemed to breathe from a bosom labouring under the deadliest terror; I have never heard another syllable so expressive; and I still hear it again when I am feverish at night, and my mind runs upon old times. The man turned towards the girl as he spoke; I had a glimpse of much red beard and a nose which seemed to have been broken in youth; and his light eyes seemed shining in his face with some strong and unpleasant emotion.

But these two passed on and were admitted in their turn to the pavilion.

One by one, or in groups, the seamen returned to the beach. The wind brought me the sound of a rough voice crying, "Shove off!" Then, after a pause, another lantern drew near. It was Northmour alone.

My wife and I, a man and a woman, have often agreed to wonder how a person could be, at the same time, so handsome and so repulsive as Northmour. He had the appearance of a finished gentleman; his face bore every mark of intelligence and courage; but you had only to look at him, even in his most amiable moment, to see that he had the temper of a slaver captain. I never knew a character that was both explosive and revengeful to the same degree; he combined the vivacity of the South with the sustained and deadly hatreds of the North; and both traits were plainly written on his face, which was a sort of danger-signal.

In person he was tall, strong, and active ; his hair and complexion very dark ; his features handsomely designed, but spoiled by a menacing expression.

At that moment he was somewhat paler than by nature ; he wore a heavy frown ; and his lips worked, and he looked sharply round him as he walked, like a man besieged with apprehensions. And yet I thought he had a look of triumph underlying all, as though he had already done much, and was near the end of an achievement.

Partly from a scruple of delicacy—which I daresay came too late—partly from the pleasure of startling an acquaintance, I desired to make my presence known to him without delay.

I got suddenly to my feet, and stepped forward.

"Northmour !" said I.

I have never had so shocking a surprise in all my days. He leaped on me without a word ; something shone in his hand ; and he struck for my heart with a dagger. At the same moment I knocked him head over heels. Whether it was my quickness, or his own uncertainty, I know not ; but the blade only grazed my shoulder, while the hilt and his fist struck me violently on the mouth.

I fled, but not far. I had often and often observed the capabilities of the sand-hills for protracted ambush or stealthy advances and retreats ; and, not ten yards from the scene of the scuffle, plumped down again upon the grass. The lantern had fallen and gone out. But what was my astonishment to see Northmour slip at a bound into the pavilion, and hear him bar the door behind him with a clang of iron !

He had not pursued me. He had run away. Northmour, whom I knew for the most implacable and daring of men, had run away ! I could scarce believe my reason ; and yet in this strange business, where all was incredible, there was nothing to make a work about in an incredibility more or less. For why was the pavilion secretly prepared? Why had Northmour landed with his guests at dead of night, in half a gale of wind, and with the floe scarce covered? Why had he sought to kill me? Had he not recognised my voice? I wondered. And, above all, how had he come to have a dagger ready in his hand? A dagger, or even a sharp knife, seemed out of keeping with the age in which we lived; and a gentleman landing from his yacht on the shore of his own estate, even although it was at night and with some mysterious circumstances, does not usually, as a matter of fact, walk thus prepared for deadly onslaught. The more I reflected, the further I felt at sea. I recapitulated the elements of mystery, counting them on my fingers: the pavilion secretly prepared for guests; the guests landed at the risk of their lives and to the imminent peril of the yacht; the guests, or at least one of them, in undisguised and seemingly causeless terror; Northmour with a naked weapon; Northmour stabbing his most intimate acquaintance at a word; last, and not least strange, Northmour fleeing from the man whom he had sought to murder, and barricading himself, like a hunted creature, behind the door of the pavilion. Here were at least six separate causes for extreme surprise; each part and parcel with the others, and forming all together one consistent story. I felt almost ashamed to believe my own senses.

As I thus stood, transfixed with wonder, I began to grow painfully conscious of the injuries I had received in the scuffle; skulked round among the sand-hills; and, by a devious path, regained the shelter of the wood. On the way, the old nurse passed again within several yards of me, still carrying her lantern, on the return journey to the mansion-house of Graden. This made a seventh suspicious feature in the case. Northmour and his guests, it appeared, were to cook and do the cleaning for themselves, while the old woman continued to inhabit the big empty barrack among the policies. There must surely be great cause for secrecy when so many inconveniences were confronted to preserve it.

So thinking, I made my way to the den. For greater security I trod out the embers of the fire, and lit my lantern to examine the wound upon my shoulder. It was a trifling hurt, although it bled somewhat freely, and I dressed it as well as I could (for its position made it difficult to reach) with some rag and cold water from the spring. While I was thus busied I mentally declared war against Northmour and his mystery. I am not an angry man by nature, and I believe there was more curiosity than resentment in my heart. But war I certainly declared ; and, by way of preparation, I got out my revolver, and, having drawn the charges, cleaned and reloaded it with scrupulous care. Next I became preoccupied about my horse. It might break loose, or fall to neighing, and so betray my camp in the Sea-Wood. I determined to rid myself of its neighbourhood ; and long before dawn I was leading it over the links in the direction of the fisher village.

CHAPTER III

TELLS HOW I BECAME ACQUAINTED WITH MY WIFE

FOR two days I skulked round the pavilion, profiting by the uneven surface of the links. I became an adept in the necessary tactics. These low hillocks and shallow dells, running one into another, became a kind of cloak of darkness for my enthralling, but perhaps dishonourable, pursuit. Yet, in spite of this advantage, I could learn but little of Northmour or his guests.

Fresh provisions were brought under cover of darkness by the old woman from the mansion-house. Northmour and the young lady, sometimes together, but more often singly, would walk for an hour or two at a time on the beach beside the quicksand. I could not but conclude that this promenade was chosen with an eye to secrecy; for the spot was open only to the seaward. But it suited me not less excellently; the highest and most accidented of the sand-hills immediately adjoined; and from these, lying flat in a hollow, I could overlook Northmour or the young lady as they walked.

The tall man seemed to have disappeared. Not only did he never cross the threshold, but he never so much as showed face at a window; or, at least, not so far as I could see; for I dared not creep forward beyond a certain distance in the day, since the upper floor commanded the bottoms of the links; and at night, when I could venture farther, the lower windows were barricaded as if to stand a siege. Sometimes I thought the tall man must be confined to bed, for I remembered the feebleness of his gait; and sometimes I thought he must have gone clear away, and that Northmour and the young lady remained alone together in the pavilion. The idea, even then, displeased me.

Whether or not this pair were man and wife, I had seen abundant reason to doubt the friendliness of their relation. Although I could hear nothing of what they said, and rarely so much as glean a decided expression on the face of either, there was a distance, almost a stiffness, in their bearing which showed them to be either unfamiliar or at enmity. The girl walked faster when she was with Northmour than when she was alone; and I conceived that any inclination between a man and a woman would rather delay than accelerate the step. Moreover, she kept a good yard free of him, and trailed her umbrella, as if it were a barrier, on the side between them. Northmour kept sidling closer; and, as the girl retired from his advance, their course lay at a sort of diagonal across the beach, and would have landed them in the surf had it been long enough continued. But when this was imminent, the girl would unostentatiously change sides and put Northmour between her and the sea. I watched these manœuvres, for my part, with high enjoyment and approval, and chuckled to myself at every move.

On the morning of the third day she walked alone for some time, and I perceived, to my great concern, that she was more than once in tears. You will see that my heart was already interested more than I supposed. She had a firm yet airy motion of the body, and carried her head with unimaginable grace; every step was a thing to look at, and she seemed in my eyes to breathe sweetness and distinction.

The day was so agreeable, being calm and sunshiny, with a tranquil sea, and yet with a healthful piquancy and vigour in the air, that, contrary to custom, she was tempted forth a second time to walk. On this occasion she was accompanied by Northmour, and they had been but a short while on the beach, when I saw him take forcible possession of her hand. She struggled, and uttered a cry that was almost a scream. I sprang to my feet, unmindful of my strange position; but, ere I had taken a step, I saw Northmour bareheaded and bowing very low, as if to apologise; and dropped again at once into my ambush. A few words were interchanged; and then, with another bow, he left the beach to return to the pavilion. He passed not far from me, and I could see him, flushed and lowering, and cutting savagely with his cane among the grass. It was not without satisfaction that I recognised my own handiwork in a great cut under his right eye, and a considerable discoloration round the socket.

For some time the girl remained where he had left her, looking out past the islet and over the bright sea. Then with a start, as one who throws off preoccupation and puts energy again upon its mettle, she broke into a rapid and decisive walk. She also was much incensed by what had passed. She had forgotten where she was. And I beheld her walk straight into the borders of the quicksand where it is most abrupt and dangerous. Two or three steps farther and her life would have been in serious jeopardy, when I slid down the face of the sand - hill, which is there precipitous, and, running half-way forward, called to her to stop.

She did so, and turned round. There was not a tremor of fear in her behaviour, and she marched directly up to me like a queen. I was barefoot, and clad like a common sailor, save for an Egyptian scarf round my waist; and she probably took me at first for some one from the fisher village, straying after bait. As for her, when I thus saw her face to face, her eyes set steadily and imperiously upon mine, I was filled with admiration and astonishment, and thought her even more beautiful than I had looked to find her. Nor could I think enough of one who, acting with so much boldness, yet preserved a maidenly air that was both quaint and engaging; for my wife kept an old-fashioned precision of manner through all her admirable life—an excellent thing in woman, since it sets another value on her sweet familiarities.

"What does this mean?" she asked.

"You were walking," I told her, "directly into Graden Floe."

"You do not belong to these parts," she said again. "You speak like an educated man."

"I believe I have right to that name," said I, "although in this disguise."

But her woman's eye had already detected the sash.

"Oh!" she said; "your sash betrays you."

"You have said the word *betray*," I resumed. "May I ask you not to betray me? I was obliged to disclose myself in your interest; but if Northmour learned my presence it might be worse than disagreeable for me."

"Do you know," she asked, "to whom you are speaking?"

"Not to Mr. Northmour's wife?" I asked, by way of answer.

She shook her head. All this while she was studying my face with an embarrassing intentness. Then she broke out—

"You have an honest face. Be honest like your face, sir, and tell me what you want and what you are afraid of. Do you think I could hurt you? I believe you have far more power to injure me! And yet you do not look unkind. What do you mean—you, a gentleman—by skulking like a spy about this desolate place? Tell me," she said, "who is it you hate?"

"I hate no one," I answered; "and I fear no one face to face. My name is Cassilis—Frank Cassilis. I lead the life of a vagabond for my own good pleasure. I am one of Northmour's oldest friends; and three nights ago, when I addressed him on these links, he stabbed me in the shoulder with a knife."

"It was you!" she said.

"Why he did so," I continued, disregarding the interruption, "is more than I can guess, and more than I care to know. I have not many friends, nor am I very susceptible to friendship; but no man shall drive me from a place by terror. I had camped in Graden Sea-Wood ere he came; I camp in it still. If you think I mean harm to you or yours, madam, the remedy is in your hand. Tell him that my camp is in the Hemlock Den, and to-night he can stab me in safety while I sleep."

With this I doffed my cap to her, and scrambled up once more among the sand-hills. I do not know why, but I felt a prodigious sense of injustice, and felt like a hero and a martyr ; while, as a matter of fact, I had not a word to say in my defence, nor so much as one plausible reason to offer for my conduct. I had stayed at Graden out of a curiosity natural enough, but undignified ; and though there was another motive growing in along with the first, it was not one which, at that period, I could have properly explained to the lady of my heart.

Certainly, that night, I thought of no one else ; and, though her whole conduct and position seemed suspicious, I could not find it in my heart to entertain a doubt of her integrity. I could have staked my life that she was clear of blame, and, though all was dark at the present, that the explanation of the mystery would show her part in these events to be both right and needful. It was true, let me cudgel my imagination as I pleased, that I could invent no theory of her relations to Northmour ; but I felt none the less sure of my conclusion because it was founded on instinct in place of reason, and, as I may say, went to sleep that night with the thought of her under my pillow.

Next day she came out about the same hour alone, and, as soon as the sand-hills concealed her from the pavilion, drew nearer to the edge, and called me by name in guarded tones. I was astonished to observe that she was deadly pale, and seemingly under the influence of strong emotion.

"Mr. Cassilis !" she cried ; "Mr. Cassilis !"

I appeared at once, and leaped down upon the beach. A remarkable air of relief overspread her countenance as soon as she saw me.

"Oh !" she cried, with a hoarse sound, like one whose bosom has been lightened of a weight. And then, "Thank God you are still safe!" she added; "I knew, if you were, you would be here." (Was not this strange? So swiftly and wisely does Nature prepare our hearts for these great life-long intimacies, that both my wife and I had been given a presentiment on this the second day of our acquaintance. I had even then hoped that she would seek me; she had felt sure that she would find me.) "Do not," she went on swiftly, "do not stay in this place. Promise me that you will sleep no longer in that wood. You do not know how I suffer; all last night I could not sleep for thinking of your peril."

"Peril?" I repeated. "Peril from whom? From Northmour?"

"Not so," she said. "Did you think I would tell him after what you said?"

"Not from Northmour?" I repeated. "Then how? From whom? I see none to be afraid of."

"You must not ask me," was her reply, "for I am not free to tell you. Only believe me, and go hence— believe me, and go away quickly, quickly, for your life!"

An appeal to his alarm is never a good plan to rid oneself of a spirited young man. My obstinacy was but increased by what she said, and I made it a point of honour to remain. And her solicitude for my safety still more confirmed me in the resolve.

"You must not think me inquisitive, madam," I replied; "but, if Graden is so dangerous a place, you yourself perhaps remain here at some risk."

She only looked at me reproachfully.

"You and your father—" I resumed; but she interrupted me almost with a gasp.

"My father! How do you know that?" she cried.

"I saw you together when you landed," was my

answer; and I do not know why, but it seemed satisfactory to both of us, as indeed it was the truth. "But," I continued, "you need have no fear from me. I see you have some reason to be secret, and, you may believe me, your secret is as safe with me as if I were in Graden Floe. I have scarce spoken to any one for years; my horse is my only companion, and even he, poor beast, is not beside me. You see, then, you may count on me for silence. So tell me the truth, my dear young lady, are you not in danger?"

"Mr. Northmour says you are an honourable man," she returned, "and I believe it when I see you. I will tell you so much; you are right; we are in dreadful, dreadful danger, and you share it by remaining where you are."

"Ah!" said I; "you have heard of me from Northmour? And he gives me a good character?"

"I asked him about you last night," was her reply. "I pretended," she hesitated, "I pretended to have met you long ago, and spoken to you of him. It was not true; but I could not help myself without betraying you, and you had put me in a difficulty. He praised you highly."

"And—you may permit me one question—does this danger come from Northmour?" I asked.

"From Mr. Northmour?" she cried. "Oh, no; he stays with us to share it."

"While you propose that I should run away?" I said. "You do not rate me very high."

"Why should you stay?" she asked. "You are no friend of ours."

I know not what came over me, for I had not been conscious of a similar weakness since I was a child, but I was so mortified by this retort that my eyes pricked and filled with tears, as I continued to gaze upon her face.

"No, no," she said, in a changed voice; "I did not
mean the words unkindly."

"It was I who offended," I said; and I held out
my hand with a look of appeal that somehow touched
her, for she gave me hers at once, and even eagerly. I
held it for a while in mine, and gazed into her eyes. It
was she who first tore her hand away, and, forgetting all
about her request and the promise she had sought to
extort, ran at the top of her speed, and without turning,
till she was out of sight. And then I knew that I loved
her, and thought in my glad heart that she—she herself
—was not indifferent to my suit. Many a time she has
denied it in after days, but it was with a smiling and
not a serious denial. For my part, I am sure our hands
would not have lain so closely in each other if she had
not begun to melt to me already. And, when all is
said, it is no great contention, since, by her own avowal,
she began to love me on the morrow.

And yet on the morrow very little took place. She
came and called me down as on the day before, up-
braided me for lingering at Graden, and, when she found
I was still obdurate, began to ask me more particularly
as to my arrival. I told her by what series of accidents I had come to witness their disembarkation, and
how I had determined to remain, partly from the interest which had been wakened in me by Northmour's
guests, and partly because of his own murderous attack.
As to the former, I fear I was disingenuous, and led
her to regard herself as having been an attraction to
me from the first moment that I saw her on the links.
It relieves my heart to make this confession even
now, when my wife is with God, and already knows
all things, and the honesty of my purpose even in
this; for while she lived, although it often pricked
my conscience, I had never the hardihood to undeceive
her. Even a little secret, in such a married life as

ours, is like the rose-leaf which kept the Princess from her sleep.

From this the talk branched into other subjects, and I told her much about my lonely and wandering existence; she, for her part, giving ear and saying little. Although we spoke very naturally, and latterly on topics that might seem indifferent, we were both sweetly agitated. Too soon it was time for her to go; and we separated, as if by mutual consent, without shaking hands, for both knew that, between us, it was no idle ceremony.

The next, and that was the fourth day of our acquaintance, we met in the same spot, but early in the morning, with much familiarity and yet much timidity on either side. When she had once more spoken about my danger—and that, I understood, was her excuse for coming—I, who had prepared a great deal of talk during the night, began to tell her how highly I valued her kind interest, and how no one had ever cared to hear about my life, nor had I ever cared to relate it, before yesterday. Suddenly she interrupted me, saying with vehemence—

"And yet, if you knew who I was, you would not so much as speak to me!"

I told her such a thought was madness, and, little as we had met, I counted her already a dear friend; but my protestations seemed only to make her more desperate.

"My father is in hiding!" she cried.

"My dear," I said, forgetting for the first time to add "young lady," "what do I care? If he were in hiding twenty times over, would it make one thought of change in you?"

"Ah, but the cause!" she cried, "the cause! It is——" she faltered for a second—"it is disgraceful to us."

CHAPTER IV

TELLS IN WHAT A STARTLING MANNER I LEARNED THAT I WAS NOT ALONE IN GRADEN SEA-WOOD

This was my wife's story, as I drew it from her among tears and sobs. Her name was Clara Huddlestone : it sounded very beautiful in my ears ; but not so beautiful as that other name of Clara Cassilis, which she wore during the longer, and I thank God the happier, portion of her life. Her father, Bernard Huddlestone, had been a private banker in a very large way of business. Many years before, his affairs becoming disordered, he had been led to try dangerous, and at last criminal, expedients to retrieve himself from ruin. All was in vain ; he became more and more cruelly involved, and found his honour lost at the same moment with his fortune. About this period Northmour had been courting his daughter with great assiduity, though with small encouragement ; and to him, knowing him thus disposed in his favour, Bernard Huddlestone turned for help in his extremity. It was not merely ruin and dishonour, nor merely a legal condemnation, that the unhappy man had brought upon his head. It seems he could have gone to prison with a light heart. What he feared, what kept him awake at night or recalled him from slumber into frenzy, was some secret, sudden, and unlawful attempt upon his life. Hence he desired to bury his existence and escape to one of the islands in the South Pacific, and it was in Northmour's yacht, the *Red Earl*, that he designed to go. The yacht picked them up clandestinely upon the coast of Wales, and had once more deposited them at Graden, till she could be refitted and provisioned for the longer voyage. Nor could Clara doubt that her hand had been stipulated as the price of passage. For, although Northmour was neither unkind nor even discourteous, he had shown himself in several instances somewhat over-bold in speech and manner.

I listened, I need not say, with fixed attention, and put many questions as to the more mysterious part. It was in vain. She had no clear idea of what the blow was, nor of how it was expected to fall. Her father's alarm was unfeigned and physically prostrating, and he had thought more than once of making an unconditional surrender to the police. But the scheme was finally abandoned, for he was convinced that not even the strength of our English prisons could shelter him from his pursuers. He had had many affairs with Italy, and with Italians resident in London, in the later years of his business, and these last, as Clara fancied, were somehow connected with the doom that threatened him. He had shown great terror at the presence of an Italian seaman on board the *Red Earl*, and had bitterly and repeatedly accused Northmour in consequence. The latter had protested that Beppo (that was the seaman's name) was a capital fellow, and could be trusted to the death ; but Mr. Huddlestone had continued ever since to declare that all was lost, that it was only a question of days, and that Beppo would be the ruin of him yet.

I regarded the whole story as the hallucination of a mind shaken by calamity. He had suffered heavy loss by his Italian transactions; and hence the sight of an Italian was hateful to him, and the principal part in his nightmare would naturally enough be played by one of that nation.

"What your father wants," I said, "is a good doctor and some calming medicine."

"But Mr. Northmour ? " objected your mother. "He is untroubled by losses, and yet he shares in this terror."

I could not help laughing at what I considered her simplicity.

"My dear," said I, "you have told me yourself what

4—o

reward he has to look for. All is fair in love, you must remember; and if Northmour foments your father's terrors, it is not at all because he is afraid of any Italian man, but simply because he is infatuated with a charming English woman."

She reminded me of his attack upon myself on the night of the disembarkation, and this I was unable to explain. In short, and from one thing to another, it was agreed between us that I should set out at once for the fisher village, Graden-Wester, as it is called, look up all the newspapers I could find, and see for myself if there seemed any basis of fact for these continued alarms. The next morning, at the same hour and place, I was to make my report to Clara. She said no more on that occasion about my departure ; nor, indeed, did she make it a secret that she clung to the thought of my proximity as something helpful and pleasant; and, for my part, I could not have left her, if she had gone upon her knees to ask it.

I reached Graden-Wester before ten in the forenoon; for in those days I was an excellent pedestrian, and the distance, as I think I have said, was little over seven miles; fine walking all the way upon the springy turf. The village is one of the bleakest on that coast, which is saying much : there is a church in a hollow ; a miserable haven in the rocks, where many boats have been lost as they returned from fishing ; two or three score of stone houses arranged along the beach and in two streets, one leading from the harbour, and another striking out from it at right angles ; and, at the corner of these two, a very dark and cheerless tavern, by way of principal hotel.

I had dressed myself somewhat more suitably to my station in life, and at once called upon the minister in his little manse beside the graveyard. He knew me, although it was more than nine years since we had met;

and when I told him that I had been long upon a walking tour, and was behind with the news, readily lent me an armful of newspapers, dating from a month back to the day before. With these I sought the tavern, and, ordering some breakfast, sat down to study the "Huddlestone Failure."

It had been, it appeared, a very flagrant case. Thousands of persons were reduced to poverty; and one in particular had blown out his brains as soon as payment was suspended. It was strange to myself that, while I read these details, I continued rather to sympathise with Mr. Huddlestone than with his victims; so complete already was the empire of my love for my wife. A price was naturally set upon the banker's head; and, as the case was inexcusable and the public indignation thoroughly aroused, the unusual figure of £750 was offered for his capture. He was reported to have large sums of money in his possession. One day he had been heard of in Spain; the next, there was sure intelligence that he was still lurking between Manchester and Liverpool, or along the border of Wales; and the day after, a telegram would announce his arrival in Cuba or Yucatan. But in all this there was no word of an Italian, nor any sign of mystery.

In the very last paper, however, there was one item not so clear. The accountants who were charged to verify the failure had, it seemed, come upon the traces of a very large number of thousands, which figured for some time in the transactions of the house of Huddlestone; but which came from nowhere, and disappeared in the same mysterious fashion. It was only once referred to by name, and then under the initials "X. X."; but it had plainly been floated for the first time into the business at a period of great depression some six years ago. The name of a distinguished Royal personage had been mentioned by rumour in connection with this sum. "The cowardly desperado"—such, I remember, was the editorial expression—was supposed to have escaped with a large part of this mysterious fund still in his possession.

I was still brooding over the fact, and trying to torture it into some connection with Mr. Huddlestone's danger, when a man entered the tavern and asked for some bread and cheese with a decided foreign accent.

"*Siete Italiano ?*" said I.

"*Sì, signor,*" was his reply.

I said it was unusually far north to find one of his compatriots ; at which he shrugged his shoulders, and replied that a man would go anywhere to find work. What work he could hope to find at Graden-Wester, I was totally unable to conceive ; and the incident struck so unpleasantly upon my mind that I asked the landlord, while he was counting me some change, whether he had ever before seen an Italian in the village. He said he had once seen some Norwegians, who had been shipwrecked on the other side of Graden Ness and rescued by the lifeboat from Cauldhaven.

"No!" said I ; "but an Italian, like the man who had just had bread and cheese."

"What ?" cried he, "yon black-avised fellow wi' the teeth ? Was he an I-talian ? Weel, yon's the first that ever I saw, an' I daresay he's like to be the last."

Even as he was speaking, I raised my eyes, and, casting a glance into the street, beheld three men in earnest conversation together, and not thirty yards away. One of them was my recent companion in the tavern parlour ; the other two, by their handsome, sallow features and soft hats, should evidently belong to the same race. A crowd of village children stood around them, gesticulating and talking gibberish in imitation. The trio looked singularly foreign to the bleak dirty street in which they were standing, and the dark grey heaven that overspread them; and I confess my incredulity received at that moment a shock from which it never recovered. I might reason with myself as I pleased, but I could not argue down the effect of what I had seen, and I began to share in the Italian terror. It was already drawing towards the close of the day before I had returned the newspapers at the manse, and got well forward on to the links on my way home. I shall never forget that walk. It grew very cold and boisterous; the wind sang in the short grass about my feet; thin rain showers came running on the gusts; and an immense mountain range of clouds began to arise out of the bosom of the sea. It would be hard to imagine a more dismal evening; and whether it was from these external influences, or because my nerves were already affected by what I had heard and seen, my thoughts were as gloomy as the weather.

The upper windows of the pavilion commanded a considerable spread of links in the direction of Graden-Wester. To avoid observation, it was necessary to hug the beach until I had gained cover from the higher sand-hills on the little headland, when I might strike across, through the hollows, for the margin of the wood. The sun was about setting; the tide was low, and all the quicksands uncovered; and I was moving along, lost in unpleasant thought, when I was suddenly thunderstruck to perceive the prints of human feet. They ran parallel to my own course, but low down upon the beach instead of along the border of the turf; and, when I examined them, I saw at once, by the size and coarseness of the impression, that it was a stranger to me and to those in the pavilion who had recently passed that way. Not only so; but from the recklessness of the course which he had followed, steering near to the most formidable portions of the sand, he was as evidently a stranger to the country and to the ill-repute of Graden beach.

Step by step I followed the prints; until, a quarter of a mile farther, I beheld them die away into the south-eastern boundary of Graden Floe. There, whoever he was, the miserable man had perished. One or two gulls, who had, perhaps, seen him disappear, wheeled over his sepulchre with their usual melancholy piping. The sun had broken through the clouds by a last effort, and coloured the wide level of quicksands with a dusky purple. I stood for some time gazing at the spot, chilled and disheartened by my own reflections, and with a strong and commanding consciousness of death. I remember wondering how long the tragedy had taken, and whether his screams had been audible at the pavilion. And then, making a strong resolution, I was about to tear myself away, when a gust fiercer than usual fell upon this quarter of the beach, and I saw, now whirling high in air, now skimming lightly across the surface of the sands, a soft, black, felt hat, somewhat conical in shape, such as I had remarked already on the heads of the Italians.

I believe, but I am not sure, that I uttered a cry. The wind was driving the hat shoreward, and I ran round the border of the floe to be ready against its arrival. The gust fell, dropping the hat for a while upon the quicksand, and then, once more freshening, landed it a few yards from where I stood. I seized it with the interest you may imagine. It had seen some service; indeed, it was rustier than either of those I had seen that day upon the street. The lining was red, stamped with the name of the maker, which I have forgotten, and that of the place of manufacture, *Venedig*. This (it is not yet forgotten) was the name given by the Austrians to the beautiful city of Venice, then, and for long after, a part of their dominions.

The shock was complete. I saw imaginary Italians upon every side; and, for the first, and, I may say, for the last time in my experience, became overpowered by what is called a panic terror. I knew nothing, that is, to be afraid of, and yet I admit that I was heartily afraid ; and it was with a sensible reluctance that I returned to my exposed and solitary camp in the Sea-Wood.

There I ate some cold porridge which had been left over from the night before, for I was disinclined to make a fire ; and, feeling strengthened and reassured, dismissed all these fanciful terrors from my mind, and lay down to sleep with composure.

How long I may have slept it is impossible for me to guess ; but I was awakened at last by a sudden, blinding flash of light into my face. It woke me like a blow. In an instant I was upon my knees. But the light had gone as suddenly as it came. The darkness was intense. And, as it was blowing great guns from the sea and pouring with rain, the noises of the storm effectually concealed all others.

It was, I daresay, half a minute before I regained my self-possession. But for two circumstances, I should have thought I had been awakened by some new and vivid form of nightmare. First, the flap of my tent, which I had shut carefully when I retired, was now unfastened ; and, second, I could still perceive, with a sharpness that excluded any theory of hallucination, the smell of hot metal and of burning oil. The conclusion was obvious. I had been wakened by some one flashing a bull's-eye lantern in my face. It had been but a flash, and away. He had seen my face, and then gone. I asked myself the object of so strange a proceeding, and the answer came pat. The man, whoever he was, had thought to recognise me, and he had not. There was yet another question unresolved : and to this, I may say, I feared to give an answer ; if he had recognised me, what would he have done ?

My fears were immediately diverted from myself, for

I saw that I had been visited in a mistake ; and I became persuaded that some dreadful danger threatened the pavilion. It required some nerve to issue forth into the black and intricate thicket which surrounded and overhung the den ; but I groped my way to the links, drenched with rain, beaten upon and deafened by the gusts, and fearing at every step to lay my hand upon some lurking adversary. The darkness was so complete that I might have been surrounded by an army and yet none the wiser, and the uproar of the gale so loud that my hearing was as useless as my sight.

For the rest of that night, which seemed interminably long, I patrolled the vicinity of the pavilion, without seeing a living creature or hearing any noise but the concert of the wind, the sea, and the rain. A light in the upper story filtered through a cranny of the shutter, and kept me company till the approach of dawn.

CHAPTER V

TELLS OF AN INTERVIEW BETWEEN NORTHMOUR, CLARA, AND MYSELF

WITH the first peep of day, I retired from the open to my old lair among the sand-hills, there to await the coming of my wife. The morning was grey, wild, and melancholy ; the wind moderated before sunrise, and then went about, and blew in puffs from the shore ; the sea began to go down, but the rain still fell without mercy. Over all the wilderness of links there was not a creature to be seen. Yet I felt sure the neighbourhood was alive with skulking foes. The light had been so suddenly and surprisingly flashed upon my face as I lay sleeping, and the hat that had been blown ashore by the wind from over Graden Floe, were two speaking signals of the peril that environed Clara and the party in the pavilion.

It was perhaps half-past seven, or nearer eight, before I saw the door open, and that dear figure come towards me in the rain. I was waiting for her on the beach before she had crossed the sand-hills.

"I have had such trouble to come!" she cried. "They did not wish me to go walking in the rain."

"Clara," I said, "you are not frightened!"

"No," said she, with a simplicity that filled my heart with confidence. For my wife was the bravest as well as the best of women; in my experience I have not found the two go always together, but with her they did; and she combined the extreme of fortitude with the most endearing and beautiful virtues.

I told her what had happened; and, though her cheek grew visibly paler, she retained perfect control over her senses.

"You see now that I am safe," said I, in conclusion. "They do not mean to harm me; for, had they chosen, I was a dead man last night."

She laid her hand upon my arm.

"And I had no presentiment!" she cried.

Her accent thrilled me with delight. I put my arm about her, and strained her to my side; and before either of us was aware, her hands were on my shoulders, and my lips upon her mouth. Yet up to that moment no word of love had passed between us. To this day I remember the touch of her cheek, which was wet and cold with the rain; and many a time since, when she has been washing her face, I have kissed it again for the sake of that morning on the beach. Now that she is taken from me, and I finish my pilgrimage alone, I recall our old loving-kindnesses and the deep honesty and affection which united us, and my present loss seems but a trifle in comparison.

We may have thus stood for some seconds—for time passes quickly with lovers—before we were startled by a peal of laughter close at hand. It was not natural mirth, but seemed to be affected in order to conceal an angrier feeling. We both turned, though I still kept my left arm about Clara's waist; nor did she seek to withdraw herself; and there, a few paces off upon the beach, stood Northmour, his head lowered, his hands behind his back, his nostrils white with passion.

"Ah! Cassilis!" he said, as I disclosed my face.

"That same," said I; for I was not at all put about.

"And so, Miss Huddlestone," he continued slowly but savagely, "this is how you keep your faith to your father and to me? This is the value you set upon your father's life? And you are so infatuated with this young gentleman that you must brave ruin, and decency, and common human caution——"

"Miss Huddlestone——" I was beginning to interrupt him, when he, in his turn, cut in brutally—

"You hold your tongue," said he; "I am speaking to that girl."

"That girl, as you call her, is my wife," said I; and my wife only leaned a little nearer, so that I knew she had affirmed my words.

"Your what?" he cried. "You lie!"

"Northmour," I said, "we all know you have a bad temper, and I am the last man to be irritated by words. For all that, I propose that you speak lower, for I am convinced that we are not alone."

He looked round him, and it was plain my remark had in some degree sobered his passion. "What do you mean?" he asked.

I only said one word: "Italians."

He swore a round oath, and looked at us, from one to the other.

" Mr. Cassilis knows all that I know," said my wife.

" What I want to know," he broke out, " is where the devil Mr. Cassilis comes from, and what the devil Mr. Cassilis is doing here. You say you are married ; that I do not believe. If you were, Graden Floe would soon divorce you ; four minutes and a half, Cassilis. I keep my private cemetery for my friends."

" It took somewhat longer," said I, " for that Italian."

He looked at me for a moment half-daunted, and then, almost civilly, asked me to tell my story. " You have too much the advantage of me, Cassilis," he added. I complied, of course ; and he listened, with several ejaculations, while I told him how I had come to Graden : that it was I whom he had tried to murder on the night of landing ; and what I had subsequently seen and heard of the Italians.

" Well," said he, when I had done, " it is here at last ; there is no mistake about that. And what, may I ask, do you propose to do ? "

" I propose to stay with you and lend a hand," said I.

" You are a brave man," he returned, with a peculiar intonation.

" I am not afraid," said I.

" And so," he continued, " I am to understand that you two are married ? And you stand up to it before my face, Miss Huddlestone ? "

" We are not yet married," said Clara ; " but we shall be as soon as we can."

" Bravo ! " cried Northmour. " And the bargain ? D—n it, you're not a fool, young woman ; I may call a spade a spade with you. How about the bargain ? You know as well as I do what your father's life depends upon. I have only to put my hands under my coat-tails and walk away, and his throat would be cut before the evening."

"Yes, Mr. Northmour," returned Clara, with great spirit; "but that is what you will never do. You made a bargain that was unworthy of a gentleman; but you are gentleman for all that, and you will never desert a man whom you have begun to help."

"Aha!" said he. "You think I will give my yacht for nothing? You think I will risk my life and liberty for love of the old gentleman; and then, I suppose, be best-man at the wedding, to wind up? Well," he added, with an odd smile, "perhaps you are not altogether wrong. But ask Cassilis here. *He* knows me. Am I a man to trust? Am I safe and scrupulous? Am I kind?"

"I know you talk a great deal, and sometimes, I think, very foolishly," replied Clara, "but I know you are a gentleman, and I am not the least afraid."

He looked at her with a peculiar approval and admiration; then, turning to me, "Do you think I would give her up without a struggle, Frank?" said he. "I tell you plainly, you look out. The next time we come to blows——"

"Will make the third," I interrupted, smiling.

"Ay, true; so it will," he said. "I had forgotten. Well, the third time's lucky."

"The third time, you mean, you will have the crew of the *Red Earl* to help," I said.

"Do you hear him?" he asked, turning to my wife.

"I hear two men speaking like cowards," said she. "I should despise myself either to think or speak like that. And neither of you believe one word that you are saying, which makes it the more wicked and silly."

"She's a trump!" cried Northmour. "But she's not yet Mrs. Cassilis. I say no more. The present is not for me."

Then my wife surprised me.

"I leave you here," she said suddenly. "My father

has been too long alone. But remember this : you are to be friends, for you are both good friends to me."

She has since told me her reason for this step. As long as she remained, she declares that we two would have continued to quarrel ; and I suppose that she was right, for when she was gone we fell at once into a sort of confidentiality.

Northmour stared after her as she went away over the sand-hill.

"She is the only woman in the world ! " he exclaimed, with an oath. "Look at her action."

I, for my part, leaped at this opportunity for a little further light.

"See here, Northmour," said I ; "we are all in a tight place, are we not ? "

"I believe you, my boy," he answered, looking me in the eyes, and with great emphasis. "We have all hell upon us, that's the truth. You may believe me or not, but I'm afraid of my life."

"Tell me one thing," said I. "What are they after, these Italians ? What do they want with Mr. Huddlestone ? "

"Don't you know ?" he cried. " The black old scamp had *carbonaro* funds on a deposit—two hundred and eighty thousand ; and of course he gambled it away on stocks. There was to have been a revolution in the Tridentino, or Parma ; but the revolution is off, and the whole wasps' nest is after Huddlestone. We shall all be lucky if we can save our skins."

"The *carbonari !*" I exclaimed ; " God help him indeed ! "

"Amen !" said Northmour. "And now, look here : I have said that we are in a fix ; and, frankly, I shall be glad of your help. If I can't save Huddlestone, I want at least to save the girl. Come and stay in the pavilion ; and, there's my hand on it, I shall act as your friend until the old man is either clear or dead. But," he added, "once that is settled, you become my rival once again, and I warn you—mind yourself."

"Done!" said I; and we shook hands.

"And now let us go directly to the fort," said Northmour; and he began to lead the way through the rain.

CHAPTER VI

TELLS OF MY INTRODUCTION TO THE TALL MAN

WE were admitted to the pavilion by Clara, and I was surprised by the completeness and security of the defences. A barricade of great strength, and yet easy to displace, supported the door against any violence from without; and the shutters of the dining-room, into which I was led directly, and which was feebly illuminated by a lamp, were even more elaborately fortified. The panels were strengthened by bars and cross-bars; and these, in their turn, were kept in position by a system of braces and struts, some abutting on the floor, some on the roof, and others, in fine, against the opposite wall of the apartment. It was at once a solid and well-designed piece of carpentry; and I did not seek to conceal my admiration.

"I am the engineer," said Northmour. "You remember the planks in the garden? Behold them!"

"I did not know you had so many talents," said I.

"Are you armed?" he continued, pointing to an array of guns and pistols, all in admirable order, which stood in line against the wall or were displayed upon the sideboard.

"Thank you," I returned; "I have gone armed since our last encounter. But, to tell you the truth, I have had nothing to eat since early yesterday evening."

Northmour produced some cold meat, to which I

eagerly set myself, and a bottle of good Burgundy, by which, wet as I was, I did not scruple to profit. I have always been an extreme temperance man on principle; but it is useless to push principle to excess, and on this occasion I believe that I finished three-quarters of the bottle. As I ate, I still continued to admire the preparations for defence.

"We could stand a siege," I said at length.

"Ye—es," drawled Northmour; "a very little one, per—haps. It is not so much the strength of the pavilion I misdoubt; it is the double danger that kills me. If we get to shooting, wild as the country is, some one is sure to hear it, and then—why, then it's the same thing, only different, as they say: caged by law, or killed by *carbonari*. There's the choice. It is a devilish bad thing to have the law against you in this world, and so I tell the old gentleman upstairs. He is quite of my way of thinking."

"Speaking of that," said I, "what kind of person is he?"

"Oh, he!" cried the other; "he's a rancid fellow, as far as he goes. I should like to have his neck wrung to-morrow by all the devils in Italy. I am not in this affair for him. You take me? I made a bargain for Missy's hand, and I mean to have it too."

"That by the way," said I. "I understand. But how will Mr. Huddlestone take my intrusion?"

"Leave that to Clara," returned Northmour.

I could have struck him in the face for this coarse familiarity; but I respected the truce, as, I am bound to say, did Northmour, and so long as the danger continued not a cloud arose in our relation. I bear him this testimony with the most unfeigned satisfaction; nor am I without pride when I look back upon my own behaviour. For surely no two men were ever left in a position so invidious and irritating.

As soon as I had done eating, we proceeded to inspect the lower floor. Window by window we tried the different supports, now and then making an inconsiderable change ; and the strokes of the hammer sounded with startling loudness through the house. I proposed, I remember, to make loopholes ; but he told me they were already made in the windows of the upper story. It was an anxious business, this inspection, and left me down-hearted. There were two doors and five windows to protect, and, counting Clara, only four of us to defend them against an unknown number of foes. I communicated my doubts to Northmour, who assured me, with unmoved composure, that he entirely shared them.

" Before morning," said he, " we shall all be butchered and buried in Graden Floe. For me, that is written."

I could not help shuddering at the mention of the quicksand, but reminded Northmour that our enemies had spared me in the wood.

" Do not flatter yourself," said he. " Then you were not in the same boat with the old gentleman ; now you are. It's the floe for all of us, mark my words."

I trembled for Clara ; and just then her dear voice was heard calling us to come upstairs. Northmour showed me the way, and, when he had reached the landing, knocked at the door of what used to be called *My Uncle's Bedroom*, as the founder of the pavilion had designed it especially for himself.

" Come in, Northmour ; come in, dear Mr. Cassilis," said a voice from within.

Pushing open the door, Northmour admitted me before him into the apartment. As I came in I could see the daughter slipping out by the side-door into the study, which had been prepared as her bedroom. In the bed, which was drawn back against the wall, instead of standing, as I had last seen it, boldly across the window, sat Bernard Huddlestone, the defaulting banker. Little as I had seen of him by the shifting light of the lantern on the links, I had no difficulty in recognising him for the same. He had a long and sallow countenance, surrounded by a long red beard and side-whiskers. His broken nose and high cheek-bones gave him somewhat the air of a Kalmuck, and his light eyes shone with the excitement of a high fever. He wore a skull-cap of black silk; a huge Bible lay open before him on the bed, with a pair of gold spectacles in the place, and a pile of other books lay on the stand by his side. The green curtains lent a cadaverous shade to his cheek; and, as he sat propped on pillows, his great stature was painfully hunched, and his head protruded till it overhung his knees. I believe if he had not died otherwise, he must have fallen a victim to consumption in the course of but a very few weeks.

He held out to me a hand, long, thin, and disagreeably hairy.

" Come in, come in, Mr. Cassilis," said he. " Another protector—ahem !—another protector. Always welcome as a friend of my daughter's, Mr. Cassilis. How they have rallied about me, my daughter's friends ! May God in Heaven bless and reward them for it ! "

I gave him my hand, of course, because I could not help it ; but the sympathy I had been prepared to feel for Clara's father was immediately soured by his appearance, and the wheedling, unreal tones in which he spoke.

" Cassilis is a good man," said Northmour ; " worth ten."

" So I hear," cried Mr. Huddlestone eagerly ; " so my girl tells me. Ah, Mr. Cassilis, my sin has found me out, you see ! I am very low, very low ; but I hope equally penitent. We must all come to the throne of grace at last, Mr. Cassilis. For my part, I come late indeed ; but with unfeigned humility, I trust."

4—P

"Fiddle-de-dee!" said Northmour roughly.

"No, no, dear Northmour!" cried the banker. "You must not say that; you must not try to shake me. You forget, my dear, good boy, you forget I may be called this very night before my Maker."

His excitement was pitiful to behold; and I felt myself grow indignant with Northmour, whose infidel opinions I well knew, and heartily derided, as he continued to taunt the poor sinner out of his humour of repentance.

"Pooh, my dear Huddlestone!" said he. "You do yourself injustice. You are a man of the world, inside and out, and were up to all kinds of mischief before I was born. Your conscience is tanned like South American leather—only you forgot to tan your liver, and that, if you will believe me, is the seat of the annoyance."

"Rogue, rogue! bad boy!" said Mr. Huddlestone, shaking his finger, "I am no precisian, if you come to that; I always hated a precisian; but I never lost hold of something better through it all. I have been a bad boy, Mr. Cassilis; I do not seek to deny that; but it was after my wife's death, and you know, with a widower, it's a different thing: sinful—I won't say no; but there is a gradation, we shall hope. And talking of that—— Hark!" he broke out suddenly, his hand raised, his fingers spread, his face racked with interest and terror. "Only the rain, bless God!" he added, after a pause, and with indescribable relief.

For some seconds he lay back among the pillows like a man near to fainting; then he gathered himself together, and, in somewhat tremulous tones, began once more to thank me for the share I was prepared to take in his defence.

"One question, sir," said I, when he had paused. "Is it true that you have money with you?"

He seemed annoyed by the question, but admitted with reluctance that he had a little.

"Well," I continued, "it is their money they are after, is it not? Why not give it up to them?"

"Ah!" replied he, shaking his head, "I have tried that already, Mr. Cassilis; and alas that it should be so! but it is blood they want."

"Huddlestone, that's a little less than fair," said Northmour. "You should mention that what you offered them was upwards of two hundred thousand short. The deficit is worth a reference; it is for what they call a cool sum, Frank. Then, you see, the fellows reason in their clear Italian way; and it seems to them, as indeed it seems to me, that they may just as well have both while they're about it—money and blood together, by George, and no more trouble for the extra pleasure."

"Is it in the pavilion?" I asked.

"It is; and I wish it were in the bottom of the sea instead," said Northmour; and then suddenly—"What are you making faces at me for?" he cried to Mr. Huddlestone, on whom I had unconsciously turned my back. "Do you think Cassilis would sell you?"

Mr. Huddlestone protested that nothing had been further from his mind.

"It is a good thing," retorted Northmour in his ugliest manner. "You might end by wearying us.—What were you going to say?" he added, turning to me.

"I was going to propose an occupation for the afternoon," said I. "Let us carry that money out, piece by piece, and lay it down before the pavilion door. If the *carbonari* come, why, it's theirs at any rate."

"No, no," cried Mr. Huddlestone; "it does not, it cannot belong to them! It should be distributed *pro rata* among all my creditors."

"Come now, Huddlestone," said Northmour, "none of that."

"Well, but my daughter," moaned the wretched man.
"Your daughter will do well enough. Here are two
suitors, Cassilis and I, neither of us beggars, between
whom she has to choose. And as for yourself, to make
an end of arguments, you have no right to a farthing,
and, unless I'm much mistaken, you are going to die."

It was certainly very cruelly said; but Mr. Huddlestone was a man who attracted little sympathy; and,
although I saw him wince and shudder, I mentally
endorsed the rebuke; nay, I added a contribution of
my own.

"Northmour and I," I said, "are willing enough to
help you to save your life, but not to escape with stolen
property."

He struggled for a while with himself, as though he
were on the point of giving way to anger, but prudence
had the best of the controversy.

"My dear boys," he said, "do with me or my money
what you will. I leave all in your hands. Let me
compose myself."

And so we left him, gladly enough I am sure. The
last that I saw, he had once more taken up his great
Bible, and with tremulous hands was adjusting his spectacles to read.

CHAPTER VII

TELLS HOW A WORD WAS CRIED THROUGH THE
PAVILION WINDOW

THE recollection of that afternoon will always be graven
on my mind. Northmour and I were persuaded that an
attack was imminent; and if it had been in our power
to alter in any way the order of events, that power
would have been used to precipitate rather than delay
the critical moment. The worst was to be anticipated;

yet we could conceive no extremity so miserable as the suspense we were now suffering. I have never been an eager, though always a great, reader ; but I never knew books so insipid as those which I took up and cast aside that afternoon in the pavilion. Even talk became impossible as the hours went on. One or other was always listening for some sound, or peering from an upstairs window over the links. And yet not a sign indicated the presence of our foes.

We debated over and over again my proposal with regard to the money ; and had we been in complete possession of our faculties, I am sure we should have condemned it as unwise ; but we were flustered with alarm, grasped at a straw, and determined, although it was as much as advertising Mr. Huddlestone's presence in the pavilion, to carry my proposal into effect.

The sum was part in specie, part in bank paper, and part in circular notes payable to the name of James Gregory. We took it out, counted it, enclosed it once more in a despatch-box belonging to Northmour, and prepared a letter in Italian which he tied to the handle. It was signed by both of us under oath, and declared that this was all the money which had escaped the failure of the house of Huddlestone. This was, perhaps, the maddest action ever perpetrated by two persons professing to be sane. Had the despatch-box fallen into other hands than those for which it was intended, we stood criminally convicted on our own written testimony; but as I have said, we were neither of us in a condition to judge soberly, and had a thirst for action that drove us to do something, right or wrong, rather than endure the agony of waiting. Moreover, as we were both convinced that the hollows of the links were alive with hidden spies upon our movements, we hoped that our appearance with the box might lead to a parley, and perhaps a compromise.

It was nearly three when we issued from the pavilion. The rain had taken off; the sun shone quite cheerfully. I have never seen the gulls fly so close about the house or approach so fearlessly to human beings. On the very doorstep one flapped heavily past our heads, and uttered its wild cry in my very ear.

"There is an omen for you," said Northmour, who, like all freethinkers, was much under the influence of superstition. "They think we are already dead."

I made some light rejoinder, but it was with half my heart; for the circumstance had impressed me.

A yard or two before the gate, on a patch of smooth turf, we set down the despatch-box; and Northmour waved a white handkerchief over his head. Nothing replied. We raised our voices, and cried aloud in Italian that we were there as ambassadors to arrange the quarrel; but the stillness remained unbroken save by the sea-gulls and the surf. I had a weight at my heart when we desisted; and I saw that even Northmour was unusually pale. He looked over his shoulder nervously, as though he feared that some one had crept between him and the pavilion door.

"By God," he said in a whisper, "this is too much for me!"

I replied in the same key: "Suppose there should be none, after all?"

"Look there," he returned, nodding with his head, as though he had been afraid to point.

I glanced in the direction indicated; and there, from the northern quarter of the Sea-Wood, beheld a thin column of smoke rising steadily against the now cloudless sky.

"Northmour," I said (we still continued to talk in whispers), "it is not possible to endure this suspense. I prefer death fifty times over. Stay you here to watch the pavilion; I will go forward and make sure, if I have to walk right into their camp."

He looked once again all round him with puckered eyes, and then nodded assentingly to my proposal. My heart beat like a sledge-hammer as I set out walking rapidly in the direction of the smoke ; and, though up to that moment I had felt chill and shivering, I was suddenly conscious of a glow of heat over all my body. The ground in this direction was very uneven ; a hundred men might have lain hidden in as many square yards about my path. But I had not practised the business in vain, chose such routes as cut at the very root of concealment, and, by keeping along the most convenient ridges, commanded several hollows at a time. It was not long before I was rewarded for my caution. Coming suddenly on to a mound somewhat more elevated than the surrounding hummocks, I saw, not thirty yards away, a man bent almost double, and running as fast as his attitude permitted along the bottom of a gully. I had dislodged one of the spies from his ambush. As soon as I sighted him, I called loudly both in English and Italian ; and he, seeing concealment was no longer possible, straightened himself out, leaped from the gully, and made off as straight as an arrow for the borders of the wood.

It was none of my business to pursue ; I had learned what I wanted—that we were beleaguered and watched in the pavilion ; and I returned at once, and walking as nearly as possible in my old footsteps, to where Northmour awaited me beside the despatch-box. He was even paler than when I had left him, and his voice shook a little.

"Could you see what he was like ?" he asked.

"He kept his back turned," I replied.

"Let us get into the house, Frank. I don't think I'm a coward, but I can stand no more of this," he whispered.

All was still and sunshiny about the pavilion as we

turned to re-enter it; even the gulls had flown in a
wider circuit, and were seen flickering along the beach
and sand-hills; and this loneliness terrified me more than
a regiment under arms. It was not until the door was
barricaded that I could draw a full inspiration and re-
lieve the weight that lay upon my bosom. Northmour
and I exchanged a steady glance; and I suppose each
made his own reflections on the white and startled aspect
of the other.

"You were right," I said. "All is over. Shake
hands, old man, for the last time."

"Yes," replied he, "I will shake hands; for, as sure
as I am here, I bear no malice. But remember, if, by
some impossible accident, we should give the slip to
these blackguards, I'll take the upper hand of you by
fair or foul."

"Oh," said I, "you weary me."

He seemed hurt, and walked away in silence to the
foot of the stairs, where he paused.

"You do not understand," said he. "I am not a
swindler, and I guard myself; that is all. It may weary
you or not, Mr. Cassilis, I do not care a rush; I speak
for my own satisfaction, and not for your amusement.
You had better go upstairs and court the girl; for my
part, I stay here."

"And I stay with you," I returned. "Do you think
I would steal a march, even with your permission?"

"Frank," he said, smiling, "it's a pity you are an
ass, for you have the makings of a man. I think I
must be *fey* to-day; you cannot irritate me even when
you try. Do you know," he continued softly, "I think
we are the two most miserable men in England, you
and I? we have got on to thirty without wife or child,
or so much as a shop to look after—poor, pitiful, lost
devils, both! And now we clash about a girl! As if
there were not several millions in the United Kingdom!

Ah, Frank, Frank, the one who loses this throw, be it you or me, he has my pity! It were better for him — how does the Bible say? — that a millstone were hanged about his neck and he were cast into the depth of the sea. Let us take a drink," he concluded suddenly, but without any levity of tone.

I was touched by his words, and consented. He sat down on the table in the dining-room, and held up the glass of sherry to his eye.

"If you beat me, Frank," he said, "I shall take to drink. What will you do, if it goes the other way?"

"God knows," I returned.

"Well," said he, "here is a toast in the meantime: '*Italia irredenta!*'"

The remainder of the day was passed in the same dreadful tedium and suspense. I laid the table for dinner, while Northmour and Clara prepared the meal together in the kitchen. I could hear their talk as I went to and fro, and was surprised to find it ran all the time upon myself. Northmour again bracketed us together, and rallied Clara on a choice of husbands; but he continued to speak of me with some feeling, and uttered nothing to my prejudice unless he included himself in the condemnation. This awakened a sense of gratitude in my heart, which combined with the immediateness of our peril to fill my eye with tears. After all, I thought—and perhaps the thought was laughably vain—we were here three very noble human beings to perish in defence of a thieving banker.

Before we sat down to table I looked forth from an upstairs window. The day was beginning to decline; the links were utterly deserted; the despatch-box still lay untouched where we had left it hours before.

Mr. Huddlestone, in a long yellow dressing-gown, took one end of the table, Clara the other; while Northmour and I faced each other from the sides. The lamp was brightly trimmed; the wine was good; the viands, although mostly cold, excellent of their sort. We seemed to have agreed tacitly; all reference to the impending catastrophe was carefully avoided; and, considering our tragic circumstances, we made a merrier party than could have been expected. From time to time, it is true, Northmour or I would rise from table and make a round of the defences; and, on each of these occasions, Mr. Huddlestone was recalled to a sense of his tragic predicament, glanced up with ghastly eyes, and bore for an instant on his countenance the stamp of terror. But he hastened to empty his glass, wiped his forehead with his handkerchief, and joined again in the conversation.

I was astonished at the wit and information he displayed. Mr. Huddlestone's was certainly no ordinary character; he had read and observed for himself; his gifts were sound; and, though I could never have learned to love the man, I began to understand his success in business, and the great respect in which he had been held before his failure. He had, above all, the talent of society; and though I never heard him speak but on this one and most unfavourable occasion, I set him down among the most brilliant conversationalists I ever met.

He was relating with great gusto, and seemingly no feeling of shame, the manœuvres of a scoundrelly commission merchant whom he had known and studied in his youth, and we were all listening with an odd mixture of mirth and embarrassment, when our little party was brought abruptly to an end in the most startling manner.

A noise like that of a wet finger on the window-pane interrupted Mr. Huddlestone's tale; and in an instant we were all four as white as paper, and sat tongue-tied and motionless round the table.

"A snail," I said at last; for I had heard that these animals make a noise somewhat similar in character.

"Snail be d—d!" said Northmour. "Hush!"

The same sound was repeated twice at regular intervals; and then a formidable voice shouted through the shutters the Italian word *"Traditore!"*

Mr. Huddlestone threw his head in the air; his eyelids quivered; next moment he fell insensible below the table. Northmour and I had each run to the armoury and seized a gun. Clara was on her feet with her hand at her throat.

So we stood waiting, for we thought the hour of attack was certainly come; but second passed after second, and all but the surf remained silent in the neighbourhood of the pavilion.

"Quick," said Northmour; "upstairs with him before they come."

CHAPTER VIII

TELLS THE LAST OF THE TALL MAN

SOMEHOW or other, by hook and crook, and between the three of us, we got Bernard Huddlestone bundled upstairs and laid upon the bed in *My Uncle's Room.* During the whole process, which was rough enough, he gave no sign of consciousness, and he remained, as we had thrown him, without changing the position of a finger. His daughter opened his shirt and began to wet his head and bosom; while Northmour and I ran to the window. The weather continued clear; the moon, which was now about full, had risen and shed a very clear light upon the links; yet, strain our eyes as we might, we could distinguish nothing moving. A few dark spots, more or less, on the uneven expanse, were not to be identified; they might be crouching men, they might be shadows; it was impossible to be sure.

"Thank God," said Northmour, "Aggie is not coming to-night."

Aggie was the name of the old nurse; he had not thought of her till now; but that he should think of her at all was a trait that surprised me in the man.

We were again reduced to waiting. Northmour went to the fireplace and spread his hands before the red embers, as if he were cold. I followed him mechanically with my eyes, and in so doing turned my back upon the window. At that moment a very faint report was audible from without, and a ball shivered a pane of glass, and buried itself in the shutter two inches from my head. I heard Clara scream; and though I whipped instantly out of range and into a corner, she was there, so to speak, before me, beseeching to know if I were hurt. I felt that I could stand to be shot at every day and all day long, with such marks of solicitude for a reward; and I continued to reassure her, with the tenderest caresses and in complete forgetfulness of our situation, till the voice of Northmour recalled me to myself.

"An air-gun," he said. "They wish to make no noise."

I put Clara aside, and looked at him. He was standing with his back to the fire and his hands clasped behind him; and I knew by the black look on his face that passion was boiling within. I had seen just such a look before he attacked me, that March night, in the adjoining chamber; and, though I could make every allowance for his anger, I confess I trembled for the consequences. He gazed straight before him; but he could see us with the tail of his eye, and his temper kept rising like a gale of wind. With regular battle awaiting us outside, this prospect of an internecine strife within the walls began to daunt me.

Suddenly, as I was thus closely watching his expression

and prepared against the worst, I saw a change, a flash, a look of relief, upon his face. He took up the lamp which stood beside him on the table, and turned to us with an air of some excitement.

"There is one point that we must know," said he. "Are they going to butcher the lot of us, or only Huddlestone ? Did they take you for him, or fire at you for your own *beaux yeux* ? "

"They took me for him, for certain," I replied. " I am near as tall, and my head is fair."

" I am going to make sure," returned Northmour; and he stepped up to the window, holding the lamp above his head, and stood there, quietly affronting death, for half a minute.

Clara sought to rush forward and pull him from the place of danger ; but I had the pardonable selfishness to hold her back by force.

"Yes," said Northmour, turning coolly from the window ; "it's only Huddlestone they want."

"Oh, Mr. Northmour ! " cried Clara ; but found no more to add ; the temerity she had just witnessed seeming beyond the reach of words.

He, on his part, looked at me, cocking his head, with a fire of triumph in his eyes ; and I understood at once that he had thus hazarded his life, merely to attract Clara's notice, and depose me from my position as the hero of the hour. He snapped his fingers.

" The fire is only beginning," said he. " When they warm up to their work they won't be so particular."

A voice was now heard hailing us from the entrance. From the window we could see the figure of a man in the moonlight ; he stood motionless, his face uplifted to ours, and a rag of something white on his extended arm ; and as we looked right down upon him, though he was a good many yards distant on the links, we could see the moonlight glitter on his eyes.

He opened his lips again, and spoke for some minutes on end, in a key so loud that he might have been heard in every corner of the pavilion, and as far away as the borders of the wood. It was the same voice that had already shouted "*Traditore!*" through the shutters of the dining-room; this time it made a complete and clear statement. If the traitor "Oddlestone" were given up, all others should be spared; if not, no one should escape to tell the tale.

"Well, Huddlestone, what do you say to that?" asked Northmour, turning to the bed.

Up to that moment the banker had given no sign of life, and I, at least, had supposed him to be still lying in a faint; but he replied at once, and in such tones as I have never heard elsewhere, save from a delirious patient, adjured and besought us not to desert him. It was the most hideous and abject performance that my imagination can conceive.

"Enough," cried Northmour; and then he threw open the window, leaned out into the night, and in a tone of exultation, and with a total forgetfulness of what was due to the presence of a lady, poured out upon the ambassador a string of the most abominable raillery both in English and Italian, and bade him be gone where he had come from. I believe that nothing so delighted Northmour at that moment as the thought that we must all infallibly perish before the night was out.

Meantime the Italian put his flag of truce into his pocket, and disappeared, at a leisurely pace, among the sand-hills.

"They make honourable war," said Northmour. "They are all gentlemen and soldiers. For the credit of the thing, I wish we could change sides—you and I, Frank, and you too, Missy my darling—and leave that being on the bed to some one else. Tut! Don't look shocked! We are all going post to what they call eternity, and may as well be above-board while there's time. As far as I'm concerned, if I could first strangle Huddlestone and then get Clara in my arms, I could die with some pride and satisfaction. And as it is, by God, I'll have a kiss!"

Before I could do anything to interfere, he had rudely embraced and repeatedly kissed the resisting girl. Next moment I had pulled him away with fury, and flung him heavily against the wall. He laughed loud and long, and I feared his wits had given way under the strain; for even in the best of days he had been a sparing and a quiet laugher.

"Now, Frank," said he, when his mirth was somewhat appeased, "it's your turn. Here's my hand. Good-bye; farewell!" Then, seeing me stand rigid and indignant, and holding Clara to my side—"Man!" he broke out, "are you angry? Did you think we were going to die with all the airs and graces of society? I took a kiss; I'm glad I had it; and now you can take another if you like, and square accounts."

I turned from him with a feeling of contempt which I did not seek to dissemble.

"As you please," said he. "You've been a prig in life; a prig you'll die."

And with that he sat down in a chair, a rifle over his knee, and amused himself with snapping the lock; but I could see that his ebullition of light spirits (the only one I ever knew him to display) had already come to an end, and was succeeded by a sullen, scowling humour.

All this time our assailants might have been entering the house, and we been none the wiser; we had in truth almost forgotten the danger that so imminently overhung our days. But just then Mr. Huddlestone uttered a cry, and leaped from the bed.

I asked him what was wrong.

"Fire!" he cried. "They have set the house on fire!"

Northmour was on his feet in an instant, and he and I ran through the door of communication with the study. The room was illuminated by a red and angry light. Almost at the moment of our entrance, a tower of flame arose in front of the window, and, with a tingling report, a pane fell inwards on the carpet. They had set fire to the lean-to outhouse, where Northmour used to nurse his negatives.

"Hot work," said Northmour. "Let us try in your old room."

We ran thither in a breath, threw up the casement, and looked forth. Along the whole back wall of the pavilion piles of fuel had been arranged and kindled; and it is probable they had been drenched with mineral oil, for, in spite of the morning's rain, they all burned bravely. The fire had taken a firm hold already on the outhouse, which blazed higher and higher every moment; the back-door was in the centre of a red-hot bonfire; the eaves, we could see, as we looked upward, were already smouldering, for the roof overhung, and was supported by considerable beams of wood. At the same time, hot, pungent, and choking volumes of smoke began to fill the house. There was not a human being to be seen to right or left.

"Ah, well!" said Northmour, "here's the end, thank God."

And we returned to *My Uncle's Room*. Mr. Huddlestone was putting on his boots, still violently trembling, but with an air of determination such as I had not hitherto observed. Clara stood close by him, with her cloak in both hands ready to throw about her shoulders, and a strange look in her eyes, as if she were half-hopeful, half-doubtful of her father.

"Well, boys and girls," said Northmour, "how about

a sally? The oven is heating; it is not good to stay here and be baked; and, for my part, I want to come to my hands with them, and be done."

"There is nothing else left," I replied.

And both Clara and Mr. Huddlestone, though with a very different intonation, added, "Nothing."

As we went downstairs the heat was excessive, and the roaring of the fire filled our ears; and we had scarce reached the passage before the stairs window fell in, a branch of flame shot brandishing through the aperture, and the interior of the pavilion became lit up with that dreadful and fluctuating glare. At the same moment we heard the fall of something heavy and inelastic in the upper story. The whole pavilion, it was plain, had gone alight like a box of matches, and now not only flamed sky-high to land and sea, but threatened with every moment to crumble and fall in about our ears.

Northmour and I cocked our revolvers. Mr. Huddlestone, who had already refused a firearm, put us behind him with a manner of command.

"Let Clara open the door," said he. "So, if they fire a volley, she will be protected. And in the meantime stand behind me. I am the scapegoat; my sins have found me out."

I heard him, as I stood breathless by his shoulder, with my pistol ready, pattering off prayers in a tremulous, rapid whisper; and I confess, horrid as the thought may seem, I despised him for thinking of supplications in a moment so critical and thrilling. In the meantime, Clara, who was dead white, but still possessed her faculties, had displaced the barricade from the front door. Another moment, and she had pulled it open. Firelight and moonlight illuminated the links with confused and changeful lustre, and far away against the sky we could see a long trail of glowing smoke.

Mr. Huddlestone, filled for the moment with a strength

4—Q

greater than his own, struck Northmour and myself a back-hander in the chest; and while we were thus for the moment incapacitated from action, lifting his arms above his head like one about to dive, he ran straight forward out of the pavilion.

"Here am I!" he cried—"Huddlestone! Kill me, and spare the others!"

His sudden appearance daunted, I suppose, our hidden enemies; for Northmour and I had time to recover, to seize Clara between us, one by each arm, and to rush forth to his assistance, ere anything further had taken place. But scarce had we passed the threshold when there came near a dozen reports and flashes from every direction among the hollows of the links. Mr. Huddlestone staggered, uttered a weird and freezing cry, threw up his arms over his head, and fell backward on the turf.

"*Traditore! Traditore!*" cried the invisible avengers.

And just then a part of the roof of the pavilion fell in, so rapid was the progress of the fire. A loud, vague, and horrible noise accompanied the collapse, and a vast volume of flame went soaring up to heaven. It must have been visible at that moment from twenty miles out at sea, from the shore at Graden-Wester, and far inland from the peak of Graystiel, the most eastern summit of the Caulder Hills. Bernard Huddlestone, although God knows what were his obsequies, had a fine pyre at the moment of his death.

CHAPTER IX

TELLS HOW NORTHMOUR CARRIED OUT HIS THREAT

I SHOULD have the greatest difficulty to tell you what followed next after this tragic circumstance. It is all to me, as I look back upon it, mixed, strenuous, and ineffectual, like the struggles of a sleeper in a nightmare. Clara, I remember, uttered a broken sigh and would have fallen forward to earth, had not Northmour and I supported her insensible body. I do not think we were attacked; I do not remember even to have seen an assailant; and I believe we deserted Mr. Huddlestone without a glance. I only remember running like a man in a panic, now carrying Clara altogether in my own arms, now sharing her weight with Northmour, now scuffling confusedly for the possession of that dear burden. Why we should have made for my camp in the Hemlock Den, or how we reached it, are points lost for ever to my recollection. The first moment at which I became definitely sure, Clara had been suffered to fall against the outside of my little tent, Northmour and I were tumbling together on the ground, and he, with contained ferocity, was striking for my head with the butt of his revolver. He had already twice wounded me on the scalp; and it is to the consequent loss of blood that I am tempted to attribute the sudden clearness of my mind.

I caught him by the wrist.

"Northmour," I remember saying, "you can kill me afterwards. Let us first attend to Clara."

He was at that moment uppermost. Scarcely had the words passed my lips, when he had leaped to his feet and ran towards the tent; and the next moment he was straining Clara to his heart and covering her unconscious hands and face with his caresses.

"Shame!" I cried. "Shame to you, Northmour!"

And, giddy though I still was, I struck him repeatedly upon the head and shoulders.

He relinquished his grasp, and faced me in the broken moonlight.

"I had you under, and I let you go," said he; "and now you strike me! Coward!"

"You are the coward," I retorted. "Did she wish your kisses while she was still sensible of what she wanted? Not she! And now she may be dying; and you waste this precious time, and abuse her helplessness. Stand aside, and let me help her."

He confronted me for a moment, white and menacing; then suddenly he stepped aside.

"Help her, then," said he.

I threw myself on my knees beside her, and loosened, as well as I was able, her dress and corset; but while I was thus engaged, a grasp descended on my shoulder.

"Keep your hands off her," said Northmour fiercely. "Do you think I have no blood in my veins?"

"Northmour," I cried, "if you will neither help her yourself, nor let me do so, do you know that I shall have to kill you?"

"That is better!" he cried. "Let her die also—where's the harm? Step aside from that girl, and stand up to fight!"

"You will observe," said I, half-rising, "that I have not kissed her yet."

"I dare you to," he cried.

I do not know what possessed me; it was one of the things I am most ashamed of in my life, though, as my wife used to say, I knew that my kisses would be always welcome were she dead or living; down I fell again upon my knees, parted the hair from her forehead, and, with the dearest respect, laid my lips for a moment on that cold brow. It was such a caress as a father might have given; it was such a one as was not unbecoming from a man soon to die to a woman already dead.

"And now," said I, "I am at your service, Mr. Northmour."

But I saw, to my surprise, that he had turned his back upon me.

"Do you hear?" I asked.

"Yes," said he, "I do. If you wish to fight, I am ready. If not, go on and save Clara. All is one to me."

I did not wait to be twice bidden; but, stooping again over Clara, continued my efforts to revive her. She still lay white and lifeless; I began to fear that her sweet spirit had indeed fled beyond recall, and horror and a sense of utter desolation seized upon my heart. I called her by name with the most endearing inflections; I chafed and beat her hands; now I laid her head low, now supported it against my knee; but all seemed to be in vain, and the lids still lay heavy on her eyes.

"Northmour," I said, "there is my hat. For God's sake bring some water from the spring."

Almost in a moment he was by my side with the water.

"I have brought it in my own," he said. "You do not grudge me the privilege?"

"Northmour," I was beginning to say, as I laved her head and breast; but he interrupted me savagely.

"Oh, you hush up!" he said. "The best thing you can do is to say nothing."

I had certainly no desire to talk, my mind being swallowed up in concern for my dear love and her condition; so I continued in silence to do my best towards her recovery, and, when the hat was empty, returned it to him with one word—"More." He had, perhaps, gone several times upon this errand, when Clara reopened her eyes.

"Now," said he, "since she is better, you can spare me, can you not? I wish you a good-night, Mr. Cassilis."

And with that he was gone among the thicket. I made a fire, for I had now no fear of the Italians, who had even spared all the little possessions left in my encampment; and, broken as she was by the excitement and the hideous catastrophe of the evening, I managed, in one way or another—by persuasion, encouragement, warmth, and such simple remedies as I could lay my hand on—to bring her back to some composure of mind and strength of body.

Day had already come, when a sharp "Hist!" sounded from the thicket. I started from the ground; but the voice of Northmour was heard adding, in the most tranquil tones: "Come here, Cassilis, and alone; I want to show you something."

I consulted Clara with my eyes, and, receiving her tacit permission, left her alone, and clambered out of the den. At some distance off I saw Northmour leaning against an elder; and, as soon as he perceived me, he began walking seaward. I had almost overtaken him as he reached the outskirts of the wood.

"Look," said he, pausing.

A couple of steps more brought me out of the foliage. The light of the morning lay cold and clear over that well-known scene. The pavilion was but a blackened wreck; the roof had fallen in, one of the gables had fallen out; and, far and near, the face of the links was cicatrised with little patches of burnt furze. Thick smoke still went straight upwards in the windless air of the morning, and a great pile of ardent cinders filled the bare walls of the house, like coals in an open grate. Close by the islet a schooner yacht lay-to, and a well-manned boat was pulling vigorously for the shore.

"The *Red Earl!*" I cried. "The *Red Earl* twelve hours too late!"

"Feel in your pocket, Frank. Are you armed?" asked Northmour.

I obeyed him, and I think I must have become deadly pale. My revolver had been taken from me.

"You see I have you in my power," he continued. "I disarmed you last night while you were nursing Clara ; but this morning—here—take your pistol. No thanks !" he cried, holding up his hand. "I do not like them ; that is the only way you can annoy me now."

He began to walk forward across the links to meet the boat, and I followed a step or two behind. In front of the pavilion I paused to see where Mr. Huddlestone had fallen ; but there was no sign of him, nor so much as a trace of blood.

"Graden Floe," said Northmour.

He continued to advance till we had come to the head of the beach.

"No farther, please," said he. "Would you like to take her to Graden House ? "

"Thank you," replied I ; "I shall try to get her to the minister's at Graden-Wester."

The prow of the boat here grated on the beach, and a sailor jumped ashore with a line in his hand.

"Wait a minute, lads !" cried Northmour ; and then lower and to my private ear : "You had better say nothing of all this to her," he added.

"On the contrary !" I broke out, "she shall know everything that I can tell."

"You do not understand," he returned, with an air of great dignity. "It will be nothing to her ; she expects it of me. Good-bye !" he added, with a nod.

I offered him my hand.

"Excuse me," said he. "It's small, I know ; but I can't push things quite so far as that. I don't wish any sentimental business, to sit by your hearth a white-haired wanderer, and all that. Quite the contrary : I hope to God I shall never again clap eyes on either one of you."

"Well, God bless you, Northmour!" I said heartily.

"Oh, yes," he returned.

He walked down the beach; and the man who was ashore gave him an arm on board, and then shoved off and leaped into the bows himself. Northmour took the tiller; the boat rose to the waves, and the oars between the thole-pins sounded crisp and measured in the morning air.

They were not yet half-way to the *Red Earl*, and I was still watching their progress, when the sun rose out of the sea.

One word more, and my story is done. Years after, Northmour was killed fighting under the colours of Garibaldi for the liberation of the Tyrol.

A LODGING FOR THE NIGHT

A STORY OF FRANCIS VILLON

IT was late in November 1456. The snow fell over
Paris with rigorous, relentless persistence; sometimes
the wind made a sally and scattered it in flying vor-
tices; sometimes there was a lull, and flake after flake
descended out of the black night air, silent, circuitous,
interminable. To poor people, looking up under moist
eyebrows, it seemed a wonder where it all came from.
Master Francis Villon had propounded an alternative
that afternoon at a tavern window : was it only Pagan
Jupiter plucking geese upon Olympus ? or were the holy
angels moulting ? He was only a poor Master of Arts,
he went on; and as the question somewhat touched
upon divinity, he durst not venture to conclude. A
silly old priest from Montargis, who was among the
company, treated the young rascal to a bottle of wine
in honour of the jest and the grimaces with which it
was accompanied, and swore on his own white beard
that he had been just such another irreverent dog when
he was Villon's age.

The air was raw and pointed, but not far below
freezing; and the flakes were large, damp, and adhesive. The whole city was sheeted up. An army might
have marched from end to end and not a footfall given
the alarm. If there were any belated birds in heaven,
they saw the island like a large white patch, and the
bridges like slim white spars, on the black ground of
the river. High up overhead the snow settled among
the tracery of the cathedral towers. Many a niche was

drifted full; many a statue wore a long white bonnet
on its grotesque or sainted head. The gargoyles had
been transformed into great false noses, drooping towards the point. The crockets were like upright pillows
swollen on one side. In the intervals of the wind
there was a dull sound of dripping about the precincts
of the church.

The cemetery of St. John had taken its own share
of the snow. All the graves were decently covered;
tall white housetops stood around in grave array; worthy
burghers were long ago in bed, be-nightcapped like their
domiciles; there was no light in all the neighbourhood
but a little peep from a lamp that hung swinging in the
church choir, and tossed the shadows to and fro in time
to its oscillations. The clock was hard on ten when
the patrol went by with halberds and a lantern, beating their hands; and they saw nothing suspicious about
the cemetery of St. John.

Yet there was a small house, backed up against the
cemetery wall, which was still awake, and awake to
evil purpose, in that snoring district. There was not
much to betray it from without; only a stream of warm
vapour from the chimney-top, a patch where the snow
melted on the roof, and a few half-obliterated footprints
at the door. But within, behind the shuttered windows,
Master Francis Villon the poet, and some of the thievish
crew with whom he consorted, were keeping the night
alive and passing round the bottle.

A great pile of living embers diffused a strong and
ruddy glow from the arched chimney. Before this
straddled Dom Nicolas, the Picardy monk, with his
skirts picked up and his fat legs bared to the comfortable warmth. His dilated shadow cut the room in
half; and the firelight only escaped on either side of
his broad person, and in a little pool between his outspread feet. His face had the beery, bruised appearance

of the continual drinker's; it was covered with a network of congested veins, purple in ordinary circumstances, but now pale violet, for even with his back to the fire the cold pinched him on the other side. His cowl had half-fallen back, and made a strange excrescence on either side of his bull-neck. So he straddled, grumbling, and cut the room in half with the shadow of his portly frame.

On the right, Villon and Guy Tabary were huddled together over a scrap of parchment; Villon making a ballade which he was to call the " Ballade of Roast Fish," and Tabary spluttering admiration at his shoulder. The poet was a rag of a man, dark, little, and lean, with hollow cheeks and thin black locks. He carried his four-and-twenty years with feverish animation. Greed had made folds about his eyes, evil smiles had puckered his mouth. The wolf and pig struggled together in his face. It was an eloquent, sharp, ugly, earthly countenance. His hands were small and prehensile, with fingers knotted like a cord; and they were continually flickering in front of him in violent and expressive pantomime. As for Tabary, a broad, complacent, admiring imbecility breathed from his squash nose and slobbering lips: he had become a thief, just as he might have become the most decent of burgesses, by the imperious chance that rules the lives of human geese and human donkeys.

At the monk's other hand, Montigny and Thevenin Pensete played a game of chance. About the first there clung some flavour of good birth and training, as about a fallen angel; something long, lithe, and courtly in the person; something aquiline and darkling in the face. Thevenin, poor soul, was in great feather: he had done a good stroke of knavery that afternoon in the Faubourg St. Jacques, and all night he had been gaining from Montigny. A flat smile illuminated his face; his bald head shone rosily in a garland of red curls; his little protuberant stomach shook with silent chucklings as he swept in his gains.

"Doubles or quits?" said Thevenin.

Montigny nodded grimly.

"*Some may prefer to dine in state*," wrote Villon, "*On bread and cheese on silver plate.* Or—or—help me out, Guido!"

Tabary giggled.

"*Or parsley on a golden dish,*" scribbled the poet.

The wind was freshening without; it drove the snow before it, and sometimes raised its voice in a victorious whoop, and made sepulchral grumblings in the chimney. The cold was growing sharper as the night went on. Villon, protruding his lips, imitated the gust with something between a whistle and a groan. It was an eerie, uncomfortable talent of the poet's, much detested by the Picardy monk.

"Can't you hear it rattle in the gibbet?" said Villon. "They are all dancing the devil's jig on nothing, up there. You may dance, my gallants, you'll be none the warmer! Whew! what a gust! Down went somebody just now! A medlar the fewer on the three-legged medlar-tree!— I say, Dom Nicolas, it'll be cold to-night on the St. Denis Road?" he asked.

Dom Nicolas winked both his big eyes, and seemed to choke upon his Adam's apple. Montfaucon, the great grisly Paris gibbet, stood hard by the St. Denis Road, and the pleasantry touched him on the raw. As for Tabary, he laughed immoderately over the medlars; he had never heard anything more light-hearted; and he held his sides and crowed. Villon fetched him a fillip on the nose, which turned his mirth into an attack of coughing.

"Oh, stop that row," said Villon, "and think of rhymes to 'fish.'"

"Doubles or quits?" said Montigny doggedly.

"With all my heart," quoth Thevenin.

"Is there any more in that bottle?" asked the monk.

"Open another," said Villon. "How do you ever hope to fill that big hogshead, your body, with little things like bottles? And how do you expect to get to heaven? How many angels, do you fancy, can be spared to carry up a single monk from Picardy? Or do you think yourself another Elias—and they'll send the coach for you?"

"*Hominibus impossibile,*" replied the monk, as he filled his glass.

Tabary was in ecstasies.

Villon filliped his nose again.

"Laugh at my jokes, if you like," he said.

"It was very good," objected Tabary.

Villon made a face at him. "Think of rhymes to 'fish,'" he said. "What have you to do with Latin? You'll wish you knew none of it at the great assizes, when the devil calls for Guido Tabary, clericus—the devil with the hump-back and red-hot finger-nails. Talking of the devil," he added in a whisper, "look at Montigny!"

All three peered covertly at the gamester. He did not seem to be enjoying his luck. His mouth was a little to a side; one nostril nearly shut, and the other much inflated. The black dog was on his back, as people say, in terrifying nursery metaphor; and he breathed hard under the gruesome burden.

"He looks as if he could knife him," whispered Tabary, with round eyes.

The monk shuddered, and turned his face and spread his open hands to the red embers. It was the cold that thus affected Dom Nicolas, and not any excess of moral sensibility.

"Come now," said Villon—"about this ballade. How does it run so far?" And beating time with his hand, he read it aloud to Tabary.

They were interrupted at the fourth rhyme by a brief and fatal movement among the gamesters. The round was completed, and Thevenin was just opening his mouth to claim another victory, when Montigny leaped up, swift as an adder, and stabbed him to the heart. The blow took effect before he had time to utter a cry, before he had time to move. A tremor or two convulsed his frame; his hands opened and shut, his heels rattled on the floor; then his head rolled backward over one shoulder with the eyes wide open; and Thevenin Pensete's spirit had returned to Him who made it.

Every one sprang to his feet; but the business was over in two twos. The four living fellows looked at each other in rather a ghastly fashion; the dead man contemplating a corner of the roof with a singular and ugly leer.

"My God!" said Tabary; and he began to pray in Latin.

Villon broke out into hysterical laughter. He came a step forward and ducked a ridiculous bow at Thevenin, and laughed still louder. Then he sat down suddenly, all of a heap, upon a stool, and continued laughing bitterly as though he would shake himself to pieces.

Montigny recovered his composure first.

"Let's see what he has about him," he remarked; and he picked the dead man's pockets with a practised hand, and divided the money into four equal portions on the table. "There's for you," he said.

The monk received his share with a deep sigh, and a single stealthy glance at the dead Thevenin, who was beginning to sink into himself and topple sideways off the chair.

"We're all in for it," cried Villon, swallowing his mirth. "It's a hanging job for every man jack of us that's here—not to speak of those who aren't." He made a shocking gesture in the air with his raised right hand, and put out his tongue and threw his head on one side, so as to counterfeit the appearance of one who has been hanged. Then he pocketed his share of the spoil, and executed a shuffle with his feet as if to restore the circulation.

Tabary was the last to help himself; he made a dash at the money, and retired to the other end of the apartment.

Montigny stuck Thevenin upright in the chair, and drew out the dagger, which was followed by a jet of blood.

"You fellows had better be moving," he said, as he wiped the blade on his victim's doublet.

"I think we had," returned Villon, with a gulp. "Damn his fat head!" he broke out. "It sticks in my throat like phlegm. What right has a man to have red hair when he is dead?" And he fell all of a heap again upon the stool, and fairly covered his face with his hands.

Montigny and Dom Nicolas laughed aloud, even Tabary feebly chiming in.

"Cry baby," said the monk.

"I always said he was a woman," added Montigny with a sneer. "Sit up, can't you?" he went on, giving another shake to the murdered body. "Tread out that fire, Nick!"

But Nick was better employed; he was quietly taking Villon's purse, as the poet sat, limp and trembling, on the stool where he had been making a ballade not three minutes before. Montigny and Tabary dumbly demanded a share of the booty, which the monk silently promised as he passed the little bag into the bosom of his gown.

In many ways an artistic nature unfits a man for practical existence.

No sooner had the theft been accomplished than Villon shook himself, jumped to his feet, and began helping to scatter and extinguish the embers. Meanwhile Montigny opened the door and cautiously peered into the street. The coast was clear; there was no meddlesome patrol in sight. Still it was judged wiser to slip out severally; and as Villon was himself in a hurry to escape from the neighbourhood of the dead Thevenin, and the rest were in a still greater hurry to get rid of him before he should discover the loss of his money, he was the first by general consent to issue forth into the street.

The wind had triumphed and swept all the clouds from heaven. Only a few vapours, as thin as moonlight, fleeted rapidly across the stars. It was bitter cold; and by a common optical effect, things seemed almost more definite than in the broadest daylight. The sleeping city was absolutely still: a company of white hoods, a field full of little Alps, below the twinkling stars. Villon cursed his fortune. Would it were still snowing! Now, wherever he went, he left an indelible trail behind him on the glittering streets; wherever he went he was still tethered to the house by the cemetery of St. John; wherever he went he must weave, with his own plodding feet, the rope that bound him to the crime and would bind him to the gallows. The leer of the dead man came back to him with a new significance. He snapped his fingers as if to pluck up his own spirits, and choosing a street at random, stepped boldly forward in the snow.

Two things preoccupied him as he went: the aspect of the gallows at Montfaucon in this bright windy phase of the night's existence, for one; and for another, the look of the dead man with his bald head and garland of red curls. Both struck cold upon his heart, and he kept quickening his pace as if he could escape from unpleasant thoughts by mere fleetness of foot. Sometimes he looked back over his shoulder with a sudden nervous jerk ; but he was the only moving thing in the white streets, except when the wind swooped round a corner and threw up the snow, which was beginning to freeze, in spouts of glittering dust.

Suddenly he saw, a long way before him, a black clump and a couple of lanterns. The clump was in motion, and the lanterns swung as though carried by men walking. It was a patrol. And though it was merely crossing his line of march, he judged it wiser to get out of eyeshot as speedily as he could. He was not in the humour to be challenged, and he was conscious of making a very conspicuous mark upon the snow. Just on his left hand there stood a great hotel, with some turrets and a large porch before the door ; it was half-ruinous, he remembered, and had long stood empty ; and so he made three steps of it and jumped into the shelter of the porch. It was pretty dark inside, after the glimmer of the snowy streets, and he was groping forward with outspread hands, when he stumbled over some substance which offered an indescribable mixture of resistances, hard and soft, firm and loose. His heart gave a leap, and he sprang two steps back and stared dreadfully at the obstacle. Then he gave a little laugh of relief. It was only a woman, and she dead. He knelt beside her to make sure upon this latter point. She was freezing cold, and rigid like a stick. A little ragged finery fluttered in the wind about her hair, and her cheeks had been heavily rouged that same afternoon. Her pockets were quite empty ; but in her stocking, underneath the garter, Villon found two of the small coins that went by the name of whites. It was little enough ; but it was always something ; and the

4—R

poet was moved with a deep sense of pathos that she should have died before she had spent her money. That seemed to him a dark and pitiable mystery; and he looked from the coins in his hand to the dead woman, and back again to the coins, shaking his head over the riddle of man's life. Henry V. of England, dying at Vincennes just after he had conquered France, and this poor jade cut off by a cold draught in a great man's doorway, before she had time to spend her couple of whites—it seemed a cruel way to carry on the world. Two whites would have taken such a little while to squander; and yet it would have been one more good taste in the mouth, one more smack of the lips, before the devil got the soul, and the body was left to birds and vermin. He would like to use all his tallow before the light was blown out and the lantern broken.

While these thoughts were passing through his mind, he was feeling, half mechanically, for his purse. Suddenly his heart stopped beating; a feeling of cold scales passed up the back of his legs, and a cold blow seemed to fall upon his scalp. He stood petrified for a moment; then he felt again with one feverish movement; and then his loss burst upon him, and he was covered at once with perspiration. To spendthrifts money is so living and actual—it is such a thin veil between them and their pleasures! There is only one limit to their fortune —that of time; and a spendthrift with only a few crowns is the Emperor of Rome until they are spent. For such a person to lose his money is to suffer the most shocking reverse, and fall from heaven to hell, from all to nothing, in a breath. And all the more if he has put his head in the halter for it; if he may be hanged to-morrow for that same purse so dearly earned, so foolishly departed! Villon stood and cursed; he threw the two whites into the street; he shook his fist at heaven; he stamped, and was not horrified to find himself trampling the poor corpse. Then he began rapidly to retrace his steps towards the house beside the cemetery. He had forgotten all fear of the patrol, which was long gone by at any rate, and had no idea but that of his lost purse. It was in vain that he looked right and left upon the snow: nothing was to be seen. He had not dropped it in the streets. Had it fallen in the house? He would have liked dearly to go in and see; but the idea of the grisly occupant unmanned him. And he saw besides, as he drew near, that their efforts to put out the fire had been unsuccessful; on the contrary, it had broken into a blaze, and a changeful light played in the chinks of door and window, and revived his terror for the authorities and Paris gibbet.

He returned to the hotel with the porch, and groped about upon the snow for the money he had thrown away in his childish passion. But he could only find one white; the other had probably struck sideways and sunk deeply in. With a single white in his pocket, all his projects for a rousing night in some wild tavern vanished utterly away. And it was not only pleasure that fled laughing from his grasp; positive discomfort, positive pain, attacked him as he stood ruefully before the porch. His perspiration had dried upon him; and though the wind had now fallen, a binding frost was setting in stronger with every hour, and he felt benumbed and sick at heart. What was to be done? Late as was the hour, improbable as was success, he would try the house of his adopted father, the chaplain of St. Benoît.

He ran there all the way, and knocked timidly. There was no answer. He knocked again and again, taking heart with every stroke; and at last steps were heard approaching from within. A barred wicket fell open in the iron-studded door, and emitted a gush of yellow light.

" Hold up your face to the wicket," said the chaplain
from within.

" It's only me," whimpered Villon.

" Oh, it's only you, is it ?" returned the chaplain ;
and he cursed him with foul unpriestly oaths for disturbing him at such an hour, and bade him be off to
hell, where he came from.

" My hands are blue to the wrist," pleaded Villon ;
" my feet are dead and full of twinges : my nose
aches with the sharp air ; the cold lies at my heart.   I
may be dead before morning. Only this once, father,
and before God I will never ask again ! "

" You should have come earlier," said the ecclesiastic
coolly.   " Young men require a lesson now and then."
He shut the wicket and retired deliberately into the
interior of the house.

Villon was beside himself ; he beat upon the door
with his hands and feet, and shouted hoarsely after the
chaplain.

" Wormy old fox ! " he cried.   " If I had my hand
under your twist, I would send you flying headlong into
the bottomless pit."

A door shut in the interior, faintly audible to the
poet down long passages.   He passed his hand over
his mouth with an oath. And then the humour of the
situation struck him, and he laughed and looked lightly
up to heaven, where the stars seemed to be winking
over his discomfiture.

What was to be done ? It looked very like a night
in the frosty streets. The idea of the dead woman
popped into his imagination, and gave him a hearty
fright ; what had happened to her in the early night
might very well happen to him before morning. And
he so young ! and with such immense possibilities of
disorderly amusement before him !   He felt quite
pathetic over the notion of his own fate, as if it had

been some one else's, and made a little imaginative vignette of the scene in the morning, when they should find his body.

He passed all his chances under review, turning the white between his thumb and forefinger. Unfortunately he was on bad terms with some old friends who would once have taken pity on him in such a plight. He had lampooned them in verses, he had beaten and cheated them ; and yet now, when he was in so close a pinch, he thought there was at least one who might perhaps relent. It was a chance. It was worth trying at least, and he would go and see.

On the way, two little accidents happened to him which coloured his musings in a very different manner. For, first, he fell in with the track of a patrol, and walked in it for some hundred yards, although it lay out of his direction. And this spirited him up ; at least he had confused his trail ; for he was still possessed with the idea of people tracking him all about Paris over the snow, and collaring him next morning before he was awake. The other matter affected him very differently. He passed a street corner, where, not so long before, a woman and her child had been devoured by wolves. This was just the kind of weather, he reflected, when wolves might take it into their heads to enter Paris again ; and a lone man in these deserted streets would run the chance of something worse than a mere scare. He stopped and looked upon the place with an unpleasant interest—it was a centre where several lanes intersected each other ; and he looked down them all one after another, and held his breath to listen, lest he should detect some galloping black things on the snow, or hear the sound of howling between him and the river. He remembered his mother telling him the story and pointing out the spot, while he was yet a child. His mother ! If he only knew where she lived, he might make sure at least of shelter. He determined he would inquire upon the morrow; nay, he would go and see her too, poor old girl! So thinking, he arrived at his destination—his last hope for the night.

The house was quite dark, like its neighbours, and yet after a few taps, he heard a movement overhead, a door opening, and a cautious voice asking who was there. The poet named himself in a loud whisper, and waited, not without some trepidation, the result. Nor had he to wait long. A window was suddenly opened, and a pailful of slops splashed down upon the doorstep. Villon had not been unprepared for something of the sort, and had put himself as much in shelter as the nature of the porch admitted ; but for all that, he was deplorably drenched below the waist. His hose began to freeze almost at once. Death from cold and exposure stared him in the face ; he remembered he was of phthisical tendency, and began coughing tentatively. But the gravity of the danger steadied his nerves. He stopped a few hundred yards from the door where he had been so rudely used, and reflected with his finger to his nose. He could only see one way of getting a lodging, and that was to take it. He had noticed a house not far away, which looked as if it might be easily broken into, and thither he betook himself promptly, entertaining himself on the way with the idea of a room still hot, with a table still loaded with the remains of supper, where he might pass the rest of the black hours, and whence he should issue, on the morrow, with an armful of valuable plate. He even considered on what viands and what wines he should prefer ; and as he was calling the roll of his favourite dainties, roast fish presented itself to his mind with an odd mixture of amusement and horror.

"I shall never finish that ballade," he thought to himself; and then, with another shudder at the recollection, " Oh, damn his fat head ! " he repeated fervently, and spat upon the snow.

The house in question looked dark at first sight ; but as Villon made a preliminary inspection in search of the handiest point of attack, a little twinkle of light caught his eye from behind a curtained window. "The devil ! " he thought. " People awake ! Some student or some saint, confound the crew ! Can't they get drunk and lie in bed snoring like their neighbours ! What's the good of curfew, and poor devils of bell-ringers jumping at a rope's-end in bell-towers ? What's the use of day, if people sit up all night ? The gripes to them ! " He grinned as he saw where his logic was leading him. " Every man to his business, after all," added he, " and if they're awake, by the lord, I may come by a supper honestly for this once, and cheat the devil."

He went boldly to the door and knocked with an assured hand. On both previous occasions, he had knocked timidly and with some dread of attracting notice ; but now, when he had just discarded the thought of a burglarious entry, knocking at a door seemed a mighty simple and innocent proceeding. The sound of his blows echoed through the house with thin, phantasmal reverberations, as though it were quite empty ; but these had scarcely died away before a measured tread drew near, a couple of bolts were withdrawn, and one wing was opened broadly, as though no guile or fear of guile were known to those within. A tall figure of a man, muscular and spare, but a little bent, confronted Villon. The head was massive in bulk, but finely sculptured ; the nose blunt at the bottom, but refining upward to where it joined a pair of strong and honest eyebrows ; the mouth and eyes surrounded with delicate markings, and the whole face based upon a thick white beard, boldly and squarely trimmed. Seen as it was by the light of a flickering hand-lamp, it looked perhaps nobler than it had a right to do ; but it was a fine face, honourable rather than intelligent, strong, simple, and righteous.

"You knock late, sir," said the old man in resonant, courteous tones.

Villon cringed, and brought up many servile words of apology ; at a crisis of this sort the beggar was uppermost in him, and the man of genius hid his head with confusion.

"You are cold," repeated the old man, "and hungry ? Well, step in." And he ordered him into the house with a noble enough gesture.

"Some great seigneur," thought Villon, as his host setting down the lamp on the flagged pavement of the entry, shot the bolts once more into their places.

"You will pardon me if I go in front," he said, when this was done ; and he preceded the poet upstairs into a large apartment, warmed with a pan of charcoal and lit by a great lamp hanging from the roof. It was very bare of furniture : only some gold plate on a sideboard ; some folios ; and a stand of armour between the windows. Some smart tapestry hung upon the walls, representing the crucifixion of our Lord in one piece, and in another a scene of shepherds and shepherdesses by a running stream. Over the chimney was a shield of arms.

"Will you seat yourself," said the old man, "and forgive me if I leave you ? I am alone in my house to-night, and if you are to eat I must forage for you myself."

No sooner was his host gone than Villon leaped from the chair on which he had just seated himself, and began examining the room, with the stealth and passion of a cat. He weighed the gold flagons in his hand, opened all the folios, and investigated the arms upon the shield, and the stuff with which the seats were lined. He raised the window curtains, and saw that the windows were set with rich stained glass in figures, so far as he could see, of martial import. Then he stood in the middle of the room, drew a long breath, and retaining it with puffed cheeks, looked round and round him, turning on his heels, as if to impress every feature of the apartment on his memory.

"Seven pieces of plate," he said. "If there had been ten, I would have risked it. A fine house, and a fine old master, so help me all the saints!"

And just then, hearing the old man's tread returning along the corridor, he stole back to his chair, and began humbly toasting his wet legs before the charcoal pan.

His entertainer had a plate of meat in one hand and a jug of wine in the other. He set down the plate upon the table, motioning Villon to draw in his chair, and going to the sideboard, brought back two goblets, which he filled.

"I drink to your better fortune," he said, gravely touching Villon's cup with his own.

"To our better acquaintance," said the poet, growing bold. A mere man of the people would have been awed by the courtesy of the old seigneur, but Villon was hardened in that matter; he had made mirth for great lords before now, and found them as black rascals as himself. And so he devoted himself to the viands with a ravenous gusto, while the old man, leaning backward, watched him with steady, curious eyes.

"You have blood on your shoulder, my man," he said.

Montigny must have laid his wet right hand upon him as he left the house. He cursed Montigny in his heart.

"It was none of my shedding," he stammered.

"I had not supposed so," returned his host quietly.

"A brawl?"

"Well, something of that sort," Villon admitted with a quaver.

"Perhaps a fellow murdered?"

"Oh, no—not murdered," said the poet, more and more confused. "It was all fair play—murdered by accident. I had no hand in it, God strike me dead!" he added fervently.

"One rogue the fewer, I daresay," observed the master of the house.

"You may dare to say that," agreed Villon, infinitely relieved. "As big a rogue as there is between here and Jerusalem. He turned up his toes like a lamb. But it was a nasty thing to look at. I daresay you've seen dead men in your time, my lord?" he added, glancing at the armour.

"Many," said the old man. "I have followed the wars, as you imagine."

Villon laid down his knife and fork, which he had just taken up again.

"Were any of them bald?" he asked.

"Oh yes, and with hair as white as mine."

"I don't think I should mind the white so much," said Villon. "His was red." And he had a return of his shuddering and tendency to laughter, which he drowned with a great draught of wine. "I'm a little put out when I think of it," he went on. "I knew him—damn him! And then the cold gives a man fancies—or the fancies give a man cold, I don't know which."

"Have you any money?" asked the old man.

"I have one white," returned the poet, laughing. "I got it out of a dead jade's stocking in a porch. She was as dead as Cæsar, poor wench, and as cold as a church, with bits of ribbon sticking in her hair. This is a hard world in winter for wolves and wenches and poor rogues like me."

"I," said the old man, "am Enguerrand de la Feuillée, seigneur de Brisetout, bailly du Patatrac. Who and what may you be?"

Villon rose and made a suitable reverence. "I am called Francis Villon," he said, "a poor Master of Arts of this university. I know some Latin, and a deal of vice. I can make chansons, ballades, lais, virelais, and roundels, and I am very fond of wine. I was born in a garret, and I shall not improbably die upon the gallows. I may add, my lord, that from this night forward I am your lordship's very obsequious servant to command."

"No servant of mine," said the knight; "my guest for this evening, and no more."

"A very grateful guest," said Villon politely; and he drank in dumb show to his entertainer.

"You are shrewd," began the old man, tapping his forehead, "very shrewd; you have learning; you are a clerk; and yet you take a small piece of money off a dead woman in the street. Is it not a kind of theft?"

"It is a kind of theft much practised in the wars, my lord."

"The wars are the field of honour," returned the old man proudly. "There a man plays his life upon the cast; he fights in the name of his lord the king, his Lord God, and all their lordships the holy saints and angels."

"Put it," said Villon, "that I were really a thief, should I not play my life also, and against heavier odds?"

"For gain, but not for honour."

"Gain?" repeated Villon, with a shrug. "Gain! The poor fellow wants supper, and takes it. So does the soldier in a campaign. Why, what are all these

requisitions we hear so much about ? If they are not
gain to those who take them, they are loss enough to
the others. The men-at-arms drink by a good fire, while
the burgher bites his nails to buy them wine and wood.
I have seen a good many ploughmen swinging on trees
about the country ; ay, I have seen thirty on one elm,
and a very poor figure they made ; and when I asked
some one how all these came to be hanged, I was told
it was because they could not scrape together enough
crowns to satisfy the men-at-arms."

"These things are a necessity of war, which the
low-born must endure with constancy. It is true that
some captains drive overhard ; there are spirits in every
rank not easily moved by pity; and indeed many follow
arms who are no better than brigands."

"You see," said the poet, "you cannot separate the
soldier from the brigand ; and what is a thief but an
isolated brigand with circumspect manners ? I steal a
couple of mutton chops, without so much as disturbing
people's sleep; the farmer grumbles a bit, but sups none
the less wholesomely on what remains. You come up
blowing gloriously on a trumpet, take away the whole
sheep, and beat the farmer pitifully into the bargain. I
have no trumpet; I am only Tom, Dick, or Harry; I am
a rogue and a dog, and hanging's too good for me—with
all my heart ; but just you ask the farmer which of us
he prefers, just find out which of us he lies awake to
curse on cold nights."

"Look at us two," said his lordship. "I am old,
strong, and honoured. If I were turned from my house
to-morrow, hundreds would be proud to shelter me. Poor
people would go out and pass the night in the streets
with their children if I merely hinted that I wished to
be alone. And I find you up, wandering homeless, and
picking farthings off dead women by the wayside ! I
fear no man and nothing ; I have seen you tremble and

lose countenance at a word. I wait God's summons contentedly in my own house, or, if it please the king to call me out again, upon the field of battle. You look for the gallows ; a rough, swift death, without hope or honour. Is there no difference between these two ? "

"As far as to the moon," Villon acquiesced. "But if I had been born lord of Brisetout, and you had been the poor scholar Francis, would the difference have been any the less ? Should not I have been warming my knees at this charcoal pan, and would not you have been groping for farthings in the snow ? Should not I have been the soldier, and you the thief ? "

"A thief!" cried the old man. "I a thief! If you understood your words, you would repent them."

Villon turned out his hands with a gesture of inimitable impudence. "If your lordship had done me the honour to follow my argument ! " he said.

"I do you too much honour in submitting to your presence," said the knight. "Learn to curb your tongue when you speak with old and honourable men, or some one hastier than I may reprove you in a sharper fashion." And he rose and paced the lower end of the apartment, struggling with anger and antipathy. Villon surreptitiously refilled his cup, and settled himself more comfortably in the chair, crossing his knees and leaning his head upon one hand and the elbow against the back of the chair. He was now replete and warm ; and he was in nowise frightened for his host, having gauged him as justly as was possible between two such different characters. The night was far spent, and in a very comfortable fashion after all ; and he felt morally certain of a safe departure on the morrow.

"Tell me one thing," said the old man, pausing in his walk. "Are you really a thief ? "

"I claim the sacred rights of hospitality," returned the poet. "My lord, I am."

"You are very young," the knight continued.

"I should never have been so old," replied Villon, showing his fingers, "if I had not helped myself with these ten talents. They have been my nursing-mothers and my nursing-fathers."

"You may still repent and change."

"I repent daily," said the poet. "There are few people more given to repentance than poor Francis. As for change, let somebody change my circumstances. A man must continue to eat, if it were only that he may continue to repent."

"The change must begin in the heart," returned the old man solemnly.

"My dear lord," answered Villon, "do you really fancy that I steal for pleasure? I hate stealing, like any other piece of work or of danger. My teeth chatter when I see a gallows. But I must eat, I must drink, I must mix in society of some sort. What the devil! Man is not a solitary animal—*Cui Deus fœminam tradit.* Make me king's pantler—make me abbot of St. Denis; make me bailly of the Patatrac; and then I shall be changed indeed. But as long as you leave me the poor scholar Francis Villon, without a farthing, why, of course, I remain the same."

"The grace of God is all-powerful."

"I should be a heretic to question it," said Francis. "It has made you lord of Brisetout and bailly of the Patatrac; it has given me nothing but the quick wits under my hat and these ten toes upon my hands. May I help myself to wine? I thank you respectfully. By God's grace, you have a very superior vintage."

The lord of Brisetout walked to and fro with his hands behind his back. Perhaps he was not yet quite settled in his mind about the parallel between thieves and soldiers; perhaps Villon had interested him by some cross-thread of sympathy; perhaps his wits were simply muddled by so much unfamiliar reasoning ; but whatever the cause, he somehow yearned to convert the young man to a better way of thinking, and could not make up his mind to drive him forth again into the street.

"There is something more than I can understand in this," he said at length. "Your mouth is full of subtleties, and the devil has led you very far astray; but the devil is only a very weak spirit before God's truth, and all his subtleties vanish at a word of true honour, like darkness at morning. Listen to me once more. I learned long ago that a gentleman should live chivalrously and lovingly to God, and the king, and his lady; and though I have seen many strange things done, I have still striven to command my ways upon that rule. It is not only written in all noble histories, but in every man's heart, if he will take care to read. You speak of food and wine, and I know very well that hunger is a difficult trial to endure ; but you do not speak of other wants ; you say nothing of honour, of faith to God and other men, of courtesy, of love without reproach. It may be that I am not very wise—and yet I think I am —but you seem to me like one who has lost his way and made a great error in life. You are attending to the little wants, and you have totally forgotten the great and only real ones, like a man who should be doctoring a toothache on the Judgment Day. For such things as honour and love and faith are not only nobler than food and drink, but indeed I think that we desire them more, and suffer more sharply for their absence. I speak to you as I think you will most easily understand me. Are you not, while careful to fill your belly, disregarding another appetite in your heart, which spoils the pleasure of your life and keeps you continually wretched ? "

Villon was sensibly nettled under all this sermonising. " You think I have no sense of honour! " he cried. " I'm

poor enough, God knows! It's hard to see rich people
with their gloves, and you blowing in your hands. An
empty belly is a bitter thing, although you speak so
lightly of it. If you had had as many as I, perhaps
you would change your tune. Any way I'm a thief—
make the most of that—but I'm not a devil from hell,
God strike me dead! I would have you to know I've
an honour of my own, as good as yours, though I don't
prate about it all day long, as if it was a God's miracle
to have any. It seems quite natural to me; I keep it
in its box till it's wanted. Why now, look you here,
how long have I been in this room with you? Did
you not tell me you were alone in the house? Look
at your gold plate! You're strong, if you like, but
you're old and unarmed, and I have my knife. What
did I want but a jerk of the elbow and here would
have been you with the cold steel in your bowels, and
there would have been me, linking in the streets, with
an armful of gold cups! Did you suppose I hadn't wit
enough to see that? And I scorned the action. There
are your damned goblets, as safe as in a church; there
are you, with your heart ticking as good as new; and
here am I, ready to go out again as poor as I came in,
with my one white that you threw in my teeth! And
you think I have no sense of honour—God strike me
dead!"

The old man stretched out his right arm. "I will
tell you what you are," he said. "You are a rogue,
my man, an impudent and a black-hearted rogue and
vagabond. I have passed an hour with you. Oh!
believe me, I feel myself disgraced! And you have
eaten and drunk at my table. But now I am sick at
your presence; the day has come, and the night-bird
should be off to his roost. Will you go before, or after?"

"Which you please," returned the poet, rising. "I
believe you to be strictly honourable." He thoughtfully

emptied his cup. " I wish I could add you were intelligent," he went on, knocking on his head with his knuckles. " Age, age ! the brains stiff and rheumatic."

The old man preceded him from a point of self-respect; Villon followed, whistling, with his thumbs in his girdle.

" God pity you," said the lord of Brisetout at the door.

" Good-bye, papa," returned Villon, with a yawn. " Many thanks for the cold mutton."

The door closed behind him. The dawn was breaking over the white roofs. A chill, uncomfortable morning ushered in the day. Villon stood and heartily stretched himself in the middle of the road.

" A very dull old gentleman," he thought. "I wonder what his goblets may be worth."

THE SIRE DE MALÉTROIT'S DOOR

DENIS DE BEAULIEU was not yet two-and-twenty, but
he counted himself a grown man, and a very accomplished cavalier into the bargain. Lads were early
formed in that rough, war-faring epoch; and when one
has been in a pitched battle and a dozen raids, has
killed one's man in an honourable fashion, and knows a
thing or two of strategy and mankind, a certain swagger
in the gait is surely to be pardoned. He had put up
his horse with due care, and supped with due deliberation; and then, in a very agreeable frame of mind, went
out to pay a visit in the grey of the evening. It was
not a very wise proceeding on the young man's part.
He would have done better to remain beside the fire
or go decently to bed. For the town was full of the
troops of Burgundy and England under a mixed command; and though Denis was there on safe-conduct, his
safe-conduct was like to serve him little on a chance
encounter.

It was September 1429; the weather had fallen sharp;
a flighty piping wind, laden with showers, beat about
the township; and the dead leaves ran riot along the
streets. Here and there a window was already lighted
up; and the noise of men-at-arms making merry over
supper within came forth in fits and was swallowed up
and carried away by the wind. The night fell swiftly;
the flag of England, fluttering on the spire-top, grew
ever fainter and fainter against the flying clouds—a black
speck like a swallow in the tumultuous, leaden chaos of
the sky. As the night fell the wind rose, and began to
hoot under archways and roar amid the tree-tops in the
valley below the town.

Denis de Beaulieu walked fast, and was soon knocking at his friend's door; but though he promised himself to stay only a little while and make an early return, his welcome was so pleasant, and he found so much to delay him, that it was already long past midnight before he said good-bye upon the threshold. The wind had fallen again in the meanwhile; the night was as black as the grave; not a star, nor a glimmer of moonshine, slipped through the canopy of cloud. Denis was ill-acquainted with the intricate lanes of Château Landon; even by daylight he had found some trouble in picking his way; and in this absolute darkness he soon lost it altogether. He was certain of one thing only—to keep mounting the hill; for his friend's house lay at the lower end, or tail, of Château Landon, while the inn was up at the head, under the great church spire. With this clue to go upon he stumbled and groped forward, now breathing more freely in open places where there was a good slice of sky overhead, now feeling along the wall in stifling closes. It is an eerie and mysterious position to be thus submerged in opaque blackness in an almost unknown town. The silence is terrifying in its possibilities. The touch of cold window-bars to the exploring hand startles the man like the touch of a toad; the inequalities of the pavement shake his heart into his mouth; a piece of denser darkness threatens an ambuscade or a chasm in the pathway; and where the air is brighter, the houses put on strange and bewildering appearances, as if to lead him farther from his way. For Denis, who had to regain his inn without attracting notice, there was real danger as well as mere discomfort in the walk; and he went warily and boldly at once, and at every corner paused to make an observation.

He had been for some time threading a lane so narrow that he could touch a wall with either hand, when it began to open out and go sharply downward. Plainly this lay no longer in the direction of his inn; but the hope of a little more light tempted him forward to reconnoitre. The lane ended in a terrace with a bartizan wall, which gave an outlook between high houses, as out of an embrasure, into the valley lying dark and formless several hundred feet below. Denis looked down, and could discern a few tree-tops waving and a single speck of brightness where the river ran across a weir. The weather was clearing up, and the sky had lightened, so as to show the outline of the heavier clouds and the dark margin of the hills. By the uncertain glimmer, the house on his left hand should be a place of some pretensions; it was surmounted by several pinnacles and turret-tops; the round stern of a chapel, with a fringe of flying buttresses, projected boldly from the main block ; and the door was sheltered under a deep porch carved with figures and overhung by two long gargoyles. The windows of the chapel gleamed through their intricate tracery with a light as of many tapers, and threw out the buttresses and the peaked roof in a more intense blackness against the sky. It was plainly the hotel of some great family of the neighbourhood; and as it reminded Denis of a town-house of his own at Bourges, he stood for some time gazing up at it and mentally gauging the skill of the architects and the consideration of the two families.

There seemed to be no issue to the terrace but the lane by which he had reached it; he could only retrace his steps, but he had gained some notion of his whereabouts, and hoped by this means to hit the main thoroughfare and speedily regain the inn. He was reckoning without that chapter of accidents which was to make this night memorable above all others in his career ; for he had not gone back above a hundred yards before he saw a light coming to meet him, and heard loud voices speaking together in the echoing narrows of the lane. It was a party of men-at-arms going the night-round with torches. Denis assured himself that they had all been making free with the wine-bowl, and were in no mood to be particular about safe-conducts or the niceties of chivalrous war. It was as like as not that they would kill him like a dog and leave him where he fell. The situation was inspiriting, but nervous. Their own torches would conceal him from sight, he reflected; and he hoped that they would drown the noise of his footsteps with their own empty voices. If he were but fleet and silent, he might evade their notice altogether.

Unfortunately, as he turned to beat a retreat, his foot rolled upon a pebble; he fell against the wall with an ejaculation, and his sword rang loudly on the stones. Two or three voices demanded who went there —some in French, some in English; but Denis made no reply, and ran the faster down the lane. Once upon the terrace, he paused to look back. They still kept calling after him, and just then began to double the pace in pursuit, with a considerable clank of armour, and great tossing of the torchlight to and fro in the narrow jaws of the passage.

Denis cast a look around and darted into the porch. There he might escape observation, or—if that were too much to expect—was in a capital posture whether for parley or defence. So thinking, he drew his sword and tried to set his back against the door. To his surprise, it yielded behind his weight; and though he turned in a moment, continued to swing back on oiled and noise-less hinges, until it stood wide open on a black interior. When things fall out opportunely for the person con-cerned, he is not apt to be critical about the how or why, his own immediate personal convenience seeming a sufficient reason for the strangest oddities and revo-lutions in our sublunary things; and so Denis, without a moment's hesitation, stepped within and partly closed the door behind him to conceal his place of refuge. Nothing was further from his thoughts than to close it altogether ; but for some inexplicable reason—perhaps by a spring or a weight—the ponderous mass of oak whipped itself out of his fingers and clanked to, with a formidable rumble and noise like the falling of an automatic bar.

The round, at that very moment, debouched upon the terrace, and proceeded to summon him with shouts and curses. He heard them ferreting in the dark corners ; the stock of a lance even rattled along the outer surface of the door behind which he stood ; but these gentlemen were in too high a humour to be long delayed, and soon made off down a corkscrew pathway which had escaped Denis's observation, and passed out of sight and hearing along the battlements of the town.

Denis breathed again. He gave them a few minutes' grace for fear of accidents, and then groped about for some means of opening the door and slipping forth again. The inner surface was quite smooth, not a handle, not a moulding, not a projection of any sort. He got his finger-nails round the edges and pulled, but the mass was immovable. He shook it ; it was as firm as a rock. Denis de Beaulieu frowned and gave vent to a little noiseless whistle. What ailed the door ? he wondered. Why was it open ? How came it to shut so easily and so effectually after him ? There was something obscure and underhand about all this that was little to the young man's fancy. It looked like a snare ; and yet who could suppose a snare in such a quiet by-street and in a house of so prosperous and even noble an exterior ? And yet—snare or no snare, intentionally or unintentionally — here he was, prettily trapped ; and for the life of him he could see no way out of it again. The darkness began to weigh upon him. He gave ear; all was silent without, but within and close by he seemed to catch a faint sighing, a faint sobbing rustle, a little stealthy creak—as though many persons were at his side, holding themselves quite still, and governing even their respiration with the extreme of slyness. The idea went to his vitals with a shock, and he faced about suddenly as if to defend his life. Then, for the first time, he became aware of a light about the level of his eyes, and at some distance in the interior of the house—a vertical thread of light, widening towards the bottom, such as might escape between two wings of arras over a doorway. To see anything was a relief to Denis; it was like a piece of solid ground to a man labouring in a morass; his mind seized upon it with avidity; and he stood staring at it and trying to piece together some logical conception of his surroundings. Plainly there was a flight of steps ascending from his own level to that of this illuminated doorway; and indeed he thought he could make out another thread of light, as fine as a needle, and as faint as phosphorescence, which might very well be reflected along the polished wood of a handrail. Since he had begun to suspect that he was not alone, his heart had continued to beat with smothering violence, and an intolerable desire for action of any sort had possessed itself of his spirit. He was in deadly peril, he believed. What could be more natural than to mount the staircase, lift the curtain, and confront his difficulty at once? At least he would be dealing with something tangible; at least he would be no longer in the dark. He stepped slowly forward with outstretched hands, until his foot struck the bottom step; then he rapidly scaled the stairs, stood for a moment to compose his expression, lifted the arras, and went in.

He found himself in a large apartment of polished stone. There were three doors; one on each of three sides ; all similarly curtained with tapestry. The fourth side was occupied by two large windows and a great stone chimney-piece, carved with the arms of the Malé-troits. Denis recognised the bearings, and was gratified to find himself in such good hands. The room was strongly illuminated ; but it contained little furniture except a heavy table and a chair or two, the hearth was innocent of fire, and the pavement was but sparsely strewn with rushes clearly many days old.

On a high chair beside the chimney, and directly facing Denis as he entered, sat a little old gentleman in a fur tippet. He sat with his legs crossed and his hands folded, and a cup of spiced wine stood by his elbow on a bracket on the wall. His countenance had a strongly masculine cast ; not properly human, but such as we see in the bull, the goat, or the domestic boar ; something equivocal and wheedling, something greedy, brutal, and dangerous. The upper lip was inordinately full, as though swollen by a blow or a toothache ; and the smile, the peaked eyebrows, and the small, strong eyes were quaintly and almost comically evil in expression. Beautiful white hair hung straight all round his head, like a saint's, and fell in a single curl upon the tippet. His beard and moustache were the pink of venerable sweetness. Age, probably in con-sequence of inordinate precautions, had left no mark upon his hands ; and the Malétroit hand was famous. It would be difficult to imagine anything at once so fleshy and so delicate in design ; the taper, sensual fingers were like those of one of Leonardo's women ; the fork of the thumb made a dimpled protuberance when closed ; the nails were perfectly shaped, and of a dead, surprising whiteness. It rendered his aspect ten-fold more redoubtable, that a man with hands like these should keep them devoutly folded in his lap like a virgin martyr—that a man with so intense and startling an expression of face should sit patiently on his seat and contemplate people with an unwinking stare, like a god, or a god's statue. His quiescence seemed ironical and treacherous, it fitted so poorly with his looks. Such was Alain, Sire de Malétroit.

Denis and he looked silently at each other for a second or two.

"Pray step in," said the Sire de Malétroit. "I have been expecting you all the evening."

He had not risen, but he accompanied his words with a smile and a slight but courteous inclination of the head. Partly from the smile, partly from the strange musical murmur with which the Sire prefaced his observation, Denis felt a strong shudder of disgust go through his marrow. And what with disgust and honest confusion of mind, he could scarcely get words together in reply.

"I fear," he said, "that this is a double accident. I am not the person you suppose me. It seems you were looking for a visit; but for my part, nothing was further from my thoughts—nothing could be more contrary to my wishes—than this intrusion."

"Well, well," replied the old gentleman indulgently, "here you are, which is the main point. Seat yourself, my friend, and put yourself entirely at your ease. We shall arrange our little affairs presently."

Denis perceived that the matter was still complicated with some misconception, and he hastened to continue his explanations.

"Your door——" he began.

"About my door?" asked the other, raising his peaked eyebrows. "A little piece of ingenuity." And he shrugged his shoulders. "A hospitable fancy! By your own account, you were not desirous of making my acquaintance. We old people look for such reluctance now and then; and when it touches our honour, we cast

about until we find some way of overcoming it.   You
arrive uninvited, but believe me, very welcome."

"You persist in error, sir," said Denis.   "There can
be no question between you and me.   I am a stranger
in this countryside.   My name is Denis, damoiseau de
Beaulieu.   If you see me in your house, it is only——"

"My young friend," interrupted the other, "you
will permit me to have my own ideas on that subject.
They probably differ from yours at the present moment,"
he added, with a leer, "but time will show which of us
is in the right."

Denis was convinced he had to do with a lunatic.
He seated himself with a shrug, content to wait the
upshot; and a pause ensued, during which he thought
he could distinguish a hurried gabbling as of prayer.
from behind the arras immediately opposite him.   Sometimes there seemed to be but one person engaged,
sometimes two ; and the vehemence of the voice, low
as it was, seemed to indicate either great haste or an
agony of spirit.   It occurred to him that this piece of
tapestry covered the entrance to the chapel he had
noticed from without.

The old gentleman meanwhile surveyed Denis from
head to foot with a smile, and from time to time emitted
little noises like a bird or a mouse, which seemed to
indicate a high degree of satisfaction.   This state of
matters became rapidly insupportable ; and Denis, to
put an end to it, remarked politely that the wind had
gone down.

The old gentleman fell into a fit of silent laughter,
so prolonged and violent that he became quite red in
the face.   Denis got upon his feet at once, and put on
his hat with a flourish.

"Sir," he said, "if you are in your wits, you have
affronted me grossly.   If you are out of them, I flatter
myself I can find better employment for my brains

than to talk with lunatics. My conscience is clear; you have made a fool of me from the first moment; you have refused to hear my explanations; and now there is no power under God will make me stay here any longer; and if I cannot make my way out in a more decent fashion, I will hack your door in pieces with my sword."

The Sire de Malétroit raised his right hand and wagged it at Denis with the fore and little fingers extended.

"My dear nephew," he said, "sit down."

"Nephew!" retorted Denis, "you lie in your throat"; and he snapped his fingers in his face.

"Sit down, you rogue!" cried the old gentleman, in a sudden, harsh voice, like the barking of a dog. "Do you fancy," he went on, "that when I had made my little contrivance for the door I had stopped short with that? If you prefer to be bound hand and foot till your bones ache, rise and try to go away. If you choose to remain a free young buck, agreeably conversing with an old gentleman—why, sit where you are in peace, and God be with you."

"Do you mean I am a prisoner?" demanded Denis.

"I state the facts," replied the other. "I would rather leave the conclusion to yourself."

Denis sat down again. Externally he managed to keep pretty calm; but within, he was now boiling with anger, now chilled with apprehension. He no longer felt convinced that he was dealing with a madman. And if the old gentleman was sane, what, in God's name, had he to look for? What absurd or tragical adventure had befallen him? What countenance was he to assume?

While he was thus unpleasantly reflecting, the arras that overhung the chapel door was raised, and a tall priest in his robes came forth, and, giving a long, keen

stare at Denis, said something in an undertone to Sire
de Malétroit.

"She is in a better frame of spirit?" asked the
latter.

"She is more resigned, messire," replied the priest.

"Now the Lord help her, she is hard to please!"
sneered the old gentleman. "A likely stripling—not ill-
born—and of her own choosing too? Why, what more
would the jade have?"

"The situation is not usual for a young damsel,"
said the other, "and somewhat trying to her blushes."

"She should have thought of that before she began
the dance! It was none of my choosing, God knows
that: but since she is in it, by Our Lady, she shall
carry it to the end." And then addressing Denis, "Monsieur de Beaulieu," he asked, "may I present you to
my niece? She has been waiting your arrival, I may
say, with even greater impatience than myself."

Denis had resigned himself with a good grace—all
he desired was to know the worst of it as speedily as
possible; so he rose at once, and bowed in acquies-
cence. The Sire de Malétroit followed his example, and
limped, with the assistance of the chaplain's arm, towards
the chapel door. The priest pulled aside the arras, and
all three entered. The building had considerable archi-
tectural pretensions. A light groining sprang from six
stout columns, and hung down in two rich pendants from
the centre of the vault. The place terminated behind
the altar in a round end, embossed and honeycombed
with a superfluity of ornament in relief, and pierced by
many little windows shaped like stars, trefoils, or wheels.
These windows were imperfectly glazed, so that the
night-air circulated freely in the chapel. The tapers,
of which there must have been half a hundred burning
on the altar, were unmercifully blown about; and the
light went through many different phases of brilliancy

and semi-eclipse. On the steps in front of the altar knelt a young girl richly attired as a bride. A chill settled over Denis as he observed her costume; he fought with desperate energy against the conclusion that was being thrust upon his mind; it could not—it should not—be as he feared.

"Blanche," said the Sire, in his most flute-like tones, "I have brought a friend to see you, my little girl; turn round and give him your pretty hand. It is good to be devout; but it is necessary to be polite, my niece."

The girl rose to her feet and turned towards the newcomers. She moved all of a piece; and shame and exhaustion were expressed in every line of her fresh young body; and she held her head down and kept her eyes upon the pavement, as she came slowly forward. In the course of her advance, her eyes fell upon Denis de Beaulieu's feet—feet of which he was justly vain, be it remarked, and wore in the most elegant accoutrement even while travelling. She paused—started, as if his yellow boots had conveyed some shocking meaning—and glanced suddenly up into the wearer's countenance. Their eyes met; shame gave place to horror and terror in her looks; the blood left her lips; with a piercing scream she covered her face with her hands and sank upon the chapel floor.

"That is not the man!" she cried. "My uncle, that is not the man!"

The Sire de Malétroit chirped agreeably. "Of course not," he said, "I expected as much. It was so unfortunate you could not remember his name."

"Indeed," she cried, "indeed, I have never seen this person till this moment—I have never so much as set eyes upon him—I never wish to see him again. Sir," she said, turning to Denis, "if you are a gentleman, you will bear me out. Have I ever seen you—have you ever seen me—before this accursed hour?"

" To speak for myself, I have never had that pleasure,"
answered the young man. "This is the first time, messire, that I have met with your engaging niece."

The old gentleman shrugged his shoulders.

"I am distressed to hear it," he said. "But it is
never too late to begin. I had little more acquaintance
with my own late lady ere I married her ; which proves,"
he added with a grimace, "that these impromptu marriages may often produce an excellent understanding in
the long-run. As the bridegroom is to have a voice in
the matter, I will give him two hours to make up for
lost time before we proceed with the ceremony." And
he turned towards the door, followed by the clergyman.

The girl was on her feet in a moment. "My uncle,
you cannot be in earnest," she said. "I declare before
God I will stab myself rather than be forced on that
young man. The heart rises at it ; God forbids such
marriages ; you dishonour your white hair. Oh, my
uncle, pity me! There is not a woman in all the world
but would prefer death to such a nuptial. Is it possible,"
she added, faltering—" is it possible that you do not
believe me—that you still think this "—and she pointed
at Denis with a tremor of anger and contempt—"that
you still think *this* to be the man ? "

" Frankly," said the old gentleman, pausing on the
threshold, "I do. But let me explain to you once for
all, Blanche de Malétroit, my way of thinking about this
affair. When you took it into your head to dishonour
my family and the name that I have borne, in peace and
war, for more than threescore years, you forfeited, not
only the right to question my designs, but that of looking me in the face. If your father had been alive, he
would have spat on you and turned you out of doors.
His was the hand of iron. You may bless your God
you have only to deal with the hand of velvet, mademoiselle. It was my duty to get you married without.

delay. Out of pure goodwill, I have tried to find your own gallant for you. And I believe I have succeeded. But before God and all the holy angels, Blanche de Malétroit, if I have not, I care not one jack-straw. So let me recommend you to be polite to our young friend ; for upon my word, your next groom may be less appetising."

And with that he went out, with the chaplain at his heels ; and the arras fell behind the pair.

The girl turned upon Denis with flashing eyes.

"And what, sir," she demanded, "may be the meaning of all this ? "

"God knows," returned Denis gloomily. "I am a prisoner in this house, which seems full of mad people. More I know not, and nothing do I understand."

"And pray how came you here ? " she asked.

He told her as briefly as he could. "For the rest," he added, "perhaps you will follow my example, and tell me the answer to all these riddles, and what, in God's name, is like to be the end of it."

She stood silent for a little, and he could see her lips tremble and her tearless eyes burn with a feverish lustre. Then she pressed her forehead in both hands.

"Alas, how my head aches ! " she said wearily—"to say nothing of my poor heart ! But it is due to you to know my story, unmaidenly as it must seem. I am called Blanche de Malétroit ; I have been without father or mother for—oh ! for as long as I can recollect, and indeed I have been most unhappy all my life. Three months ago a young captain began to stand near me every day in church. I could see that I pleased him ; I am much to blame, but I was so glad that any one should love me ; and when he passed me a letter, I took it home with me and read it with great pleasure. Since that time he has written many. He was so anxious to speak with me, poor fellow! and kept asking me to leave the door open some evening that we might have two words upon the stair. For he knew how much my uncle trusted me." She gave something like a sob at that, and it was a moment before she could go on. "My uncle is a hard man, but he is very shrewd," she said at last. "He has performed many feats in war, and was a great person at court, and much trusted by Queen Isabeau in old days. How he came to suspect me I cannot tell; but it is hard to keep anything from his knowledge; and this morning, as we came from mass, he took my hand in his, forced it open, and read my little billet, walking by my side all the while. When he had finished, he gave it back to me with great politeness. It contained another request to have the door left open; and this has been the ruin of us all. My uncle kept me strictly in my room until evening, and then ordered me to dress myself as you see me—a hard mockery for a young girl, do you not think so? I suppose, when he could not prevail with me to tell him the young captain's name, he must have laid a trap for him: into which, alas! you have fallen in the anger of God. I looked for much confusion; for how could I tell whether he was willing to take me for his wife on these sharp terms? He might have been trifling with me from the first; or I might have made myself too cheap in his eyes. But truly I had not looked for such a shameful punishment as this! I could not think that God would let a girl be so disgraced before a young man. And now I have told you all; and I can scarcely hope that you will not despise me."

Denis made her a respectful inclination.

"Madam," he said, "you have honoured me by your confidence. It remains for me to prove that I am not unworthy of the honour. Is Messire de Malétroit at hand?"

"I believe he is writing in the salle without," she answered.

"May I lead you thither, madam?" asked Denis, offering his hand with his most courtly bearing.

She accepted it ; and the pair passed out of the chapel, Blanche in a very drooping and shamefast condition, but Denis strutting and ruffling in the consciousness of a mission, and a boyish certainty of accomplishing it with honour.

The Sire de Malétroit rose to meet them with an ironical obeisance.

"Sir," said Denis, with the grandest possible air, "I believe I am to have some say in the matter of this marriage ; and let me tell you at once, I will be no party to forcing the inclination of this young lady. Had it been freely offered to me, I should have been proud to accept her hand, for I perceive she is as good as she is beautiful ; but as things are, I have now the honour, messire, of refusing."

Blanche looked at him with gratitude in her eyes ; but the old gentleman only smiled and smiled, until his smile grew positively sickening to Denis.

"I am afraid," he said, "Monsieur de Beaulieu, that you do not perfectly understand the choice I have to offer you. Follow me, I beseech you, to this window." And he led the way to one of the large windows which stood open on the night. "You observe," he went on, "there is an iron ring in the upper masonry, and reeved through that a very efficacious rope. Now, mark my words : if you should find your disinclination to my niece's person insurmountable, I shall have you hanged out of this window before sunrise. I shall only proceed to such an extremity with the greatest regret, you may believe me. For it is not at all your death that I desire, but my niece's establishment in life. At the same time, it must come to that if you prove obstinate. Your family, Monsieur de Beaulieu, is very well in its way; but if you sprang from Charlemagne, you should not refuse the hand of a Malétroit with impunity—not if she had been as common as the Paris road—not if she were as hideous as the gargoyle over my door. Neither my niece nor you, nor my own private feelings, move me at all in this matter. The honour of my house has been compromised; I believe you to be the guilty person; at least you are now in the secret; and you can hardly wonder if I request you to wipe out the stain. If you will not, your blood be on your own head! It will be no great satisfaction to me to have your interesting relics kicking their heels in the breeze below my windows; but half a loaf is better than no bread, and if I cannot cure the dis-honour, I shall at least stop the scandal."

There was a pause.

"I believe there are other ways of settling such im-broglios among gentlemen," said Denis. "You wear a sword, and I hear you have used it with distinction."

The Sire de Malétroit made a signal to the chap-lain, who crossed the room with long, silent strides and raised the arras over the third of the three doors. It was only a moment before he let it fall again; but Denis had time to see a dusky passage full of armed men.

"When I was a little younger, I should have been delighted to honour you, Monsieur de Beaulieu," said Sire Alain; "but I am now too old. Faithful retainers are the sinews of age, and I must employ the strength I have. This is one of the hardest things to swallow as a man grows up in years; but with a little patience, even this becomes habitual. You and the lady seem to prefer the salle for what remains of your two hours; and as I have no desire to cross your preference, I shall resign it to your use with all the pleasure in the world. No haste!" he added, holding up his hand, as he saw a dangerous look come into Denis de Beaulieu's face. " If your mind revolts against hanging, it will be time enough two hours hence to throw yourself out of the window or upon the pikes of my retainers. Two hours of life are always two hours. A great many things may turn up in even as little a while as that. And, besides, if I understand her appearance, my niece has still something to say to you. You will not disfigure your last hours by a want of politeness to a lady ? "

Denis looked at Blanche, and she made him an imploring gesture.

It is likely that the old gentleman was hugely pleased at this symptom of an understanding ; for he smiled on both, and added sweetly : "If you will give me your word of honour, Monsieur de Beaulieu, to await my return at the end of the two hours before attempting anything desperate, I shall withdraw my retainers, and let you speak in greater privacy with mademoiselle."

Denis again glanced at the girl, who seemed to beseech him to agree.

" I give you my word of honour," he said.

Messire de Malétroit bowed, and proceeded to limp about the apartment, clearing his throat the while with that odd musical chirp which had already grown so irritating in the ears of Denis de Beaulieu. He first possessed himself of some papers which lay upon the table ; then he went to the mouth of the passage and appeared to give an order to the men behind the arras ; and lastly he hobbled out through the door by which Denis had come in, turning upon the threshold to address a last smiling bow to the young couple, and followed by the chaplain with a hand-lamp.

No sooner were they alone than Blanche advanced towards Denis with her hands extended. Her face was flushed and excited, and her eyes shone with tears.

"You shall not die!" she cried, "you shall marry me after all."

"You seem to think, madam," replied Denis, "that I stand much in fear of death."

"Oh, no, no," she said; "I see you are no poltroon. It is for my own sake—I could not bear to have you slain for such a scruple."

"I am afraid," returned Denis, "that you underrate the difficulty, madam. What you may be too generous to refuse, I may be too proud to accept. In a moment of noble feeling towards me, you forgot what you perhaps owe to others."

He had the decency to keep his eyes upon the floor as he said this, and after he had finished, so as not to spy upon her confusion. She stood silent for a moment, then walked suddenly away, and falling on her uncle's chair, fairly burst out sobbing. Denis was in the acme of embarrassment. He looked round, as if to seek for inspiration, and seeing a stool, plumped down upon it for something to do. There he sat, playing with the guard of his rapier, and wishing himself dead a thousand times over, and buried in the nastiest kitchen-heap in France. His eyes wandered round the apartment, but found nothing to arrest them. There were such wide spaces between the furniture, the light fell so baldly and cheerlessly over all, the dark outside air looked in so coldly through the windows, that he thought he had never seen a church so vast nor a tomb so melancholy. The regular sobs of Blanche de Malétroit measured out the time like the ticking of a clock. He read the device upon the shield over and over again, until his eyes became obscured; he stared into shadowy corners until he imagined they were swarming with horrible animals; and every now and again he awoke with a start, to remember that his last two hours were running, and death was on the march.

Oftener and oftener, as the time went on, did his glance settle on the girl herself. Her face was bowed forward and covered with her hands, and she was shaken at intervals by the convulsive hiccup of grief. Even thus she was not an unpleasant object to dwell upon, so plump, and yet so fine, with a warm brown skin, and the most beautiful hair, Denis thought, in the whole world of womankind. Her hands were like her uncle's ; but they were more in place at the end of her young arms, and looked infinitely soft and caressing. He remembered how her blue eyes had shone upon him full of anger, pity, and innocence. And the more he dwelt on her perfections, the uglier death looked, and the more deeply was he smitten with penitence at her continued tears. Now he felt that no man could have the courage to leave a world which contained so beautiful a creature ; and now he would have given forty minutes of his last hour to have unsaid his cruel speech.

Suddenly a hoarse and ragged peal of cockcrow rose to their ears from the dark valley below the windows. And this shattering noise in the silence of all around was like a light in a dark place, and shook them both out of their reflections.

" Alas, can I do nothing to help you ? " she said, looking up.

" Madam," replied Denis, with a fine irrelevancy, " if I have said anything to wound you, believe me it was for your own sake and not for mine."

She thanked him with a tearful look.

" I feel your position cruelly," he went on. " The world has been bitter hard on you. Your uncle is a disgrace to mankind. Believe me, madam, there is no young gentleman in all France but would be glad of my opportunity, to die in doing you a momentary service."

" I know already that you can be very brave and

generous," she answered. "What I *want* to know is whether I can serve you—now or afterwards," she added, with a quaver.

"Most certainly," he answered, with a smile. "Let me sit beside you as if I were a friend, instead of a foolish intruder; try to forget how awkwardly we are placed to one another; make my last moments go pleasantly; and you will do me the chief service possible."

"You are very gallant," she added, with a yet deeper sadness; "very gallant—— and it somehow pains me. But draw nearer, if you please; and if you find anything to say to me, you will at least make certain of a very friendly listener. Ah! Monsieur de Beaulieu," she broke forth—"ah! Monsieur de Beaulieu, how can I look you in the face?" And she fell to weeping again with a renewed effusion.

"Madam," said Denis, taking her hand in both of his, "reflect on the little time I have before me, and the great bitterness into which I am cast by the sight of your distress. Spare me, in my last moments, the spectacle of what I cannot cure even with the sacrifice of my life."

"I am very selfish," answered Blanche. "I will be braver, Monsieur de Beaulieu, for your sake. But think if I can do you no kindness in the future—if you have no friends to whom I could carry your adieux. Charge me as heavily as you can: every burden will lighten, by so little, the invaluable gratitude I owe you. Put it in my power to do something more for you than weep."

"My mother is married again, and has a young family to care for. My brother Guichard will inherit my fiefs: and if I am not in error, that will content him amply for my death. Life is a little vapour that passeth away, as we are told by those in holy orders. When a man . is in a fair way and sees all life open in front of him, he seems to himself to make a very important figure in the world. His horse whinnies to him; the trumpets blow and the girls look out of window as he rides into town before his company; he receives many assurances of trust and regard—sometimes by express in a letter—sometimes face to face, with persons of great consequence falling on his neck. It is not wonderful if his head is turned for a time. But once he is dead, were he as brave as Hercules or as wise as Solomon, he is soon forgotten. It is not ten years since my father fell, with many other knights around him, in a very fierce encounter, and I do not think that any one of them, nor so much as the name of the fight, is now remembered. No, no, madam, the nearer you come to it, you see that death is a dark and dusty corner, where a man gets into his tomb and has the door shut after him till the judgment-day. I have few friends just now, and once I am dead I shall have none."

"Ah, Monsieur de Beaulieu!" she exclaimed, "you forget Blanche de Malétroit."

"You have a sweet nature, madam, and you are pleased to estimate a little service far beyond its worth."

"It is not that," she answered. "You mistake me if you think I am so easily touched by my own concerns. I say so, because you are the noblest man I have ever met; because I recognise in you a spirit that would have made even a common person famous in the land."

"And yet here I die in a mousetrap—with no more noise about it than my own squeaking," answered he.

A look of pain crossed her face, and she was silent for a little while. Then a light came into her eyes, and with a smile she spoke again.

"I cannot have my champion think meanly of himself. Any one who gives his life for another will be met in Paradise by all the heralds and angels of the Lord

God. And you have no such cause to hang your head. For—— Pray, do you think me beautiful ? " she asked, with a deep flush.

" Indeed, madam, I do," he said.

" I am glad of that," she answered heartily. " Do you think there are many men in France who have been asked in marriage by a beautiful maiden—with her own lips—and who have refused her to her face ? I know you men would half-despise such a triumph ; but believe me, we women know more of what is precious in love. There is nothing that should set a person higher in his own esteem ; and we women would prize nothing more dearly."

" You are very good," he said ; " but you cannot make me forget that I was asked in pity and not for love."

" I am not so sure of that," she replied, holding down her head. " Hear me to an end, Monsieur de Beaulieu. I know how you must despise me ; I feel you are right to do so ; I am too poor a creature to occupy one thought of your mind, although, alas ! you must die for me this morning. But when I asked you to marry me, indeed, and indeed, it was because I respected and admired you, and loved you with my whole soul, from the very moment that you took my part against my uncle. If you had seen yourself, and how noble you looked, you would pity rather than despise me. And now," she went on, hurriedly checking him with her hand, "although I have laid aside all reserve and told you so much, remember that I know your sentiments towards me already. I would not, believe me, being nobly born, weary you with importunities into consent. I too have a pride of my own : and I declare before the holy Mother of God, if you should now go back from your word already given, I would no more marry you than I would marry my uncle's groom."

Denis smiled a little bitterly.

" It is a small love," he said, "that shies at a little pride."

She made no answer, although she probably had her own thoughts.

" Come hither to the window," he said, with a sigh. " Here is the dawn."

And indeed the dawn was already beginning. The hollow of the sky was full of essential daylight, colourless and clean ; and the valley underneath was flooded with a grey reflection. A few thin vapours clung in the coves of the forest or lay along the winding course of the river. The scene disengaged a surprising effect of stillness, which was hardly interrupted when the cocks began once more to crow among the steadings. Perhaps the same fellow who had made so horrid a clangour in the darkness not half an hour before now sent up the merriest cheer to greet the coming day. A little wind went bustling and eddying among the tree-tops underneath the windows. And still the daylight kept flooding insensibly out of the east, which was soon to grow incandescent and cast up that red-hot cannon-ball, the rising sun.

Denis looked out over all this with a bit of a shiver. He had taken her hand, and retained it in his almost unconsciously.

" Has the day begun already ? " she said ; and then, illogically enough : " the night has been so long ! Alas ! what shall we say to my uncle when he returns ? "

" What you will," said Denis, and he pressed her fingers in his.

She was silent.

" Blanche," he said, with a swift, uncertain, passionate utterance, " you have seen whether I fear death. You must know well enough that I would

as gladly leap out of that window into the empty
air as lay a finger on you without your free and full
consent.   But if you care for me at all do not let
me lose my life in a misapprehension ; for I love
you better than the whole world ; and though I will
die for you blithely, it would be like all the joys
of Paradise to live on and spend my life in your
service."

As he stopped speaking, a bell began to ring
loudly in the interior of the house ; and a clatter of
armour in the corridor showed that the retainers were
returning to their post, and the two hours were at an
end.

" After all that you have heard ? " she whispered,
leaning towards him with her lips and eyes.

" I have heard nothing," he replied.

" The captain's name was Florimond de Champ-
divers," she said in his ear.

" I did not hear it," he answered, taking her
supple body in his arms and covered her wet face
with kisses.

A melodious chirping was audible behind, followed
by a beautiful chuckle, and the voice of Messire de
Malétroit wished his new nephew a good morning.

PROVIDENCE AND THE GUITAR

CHAPTER I

MONSIEUR LÉON BERTHELINI had a great care of his appearance, and sedulously suited his deportment to the costume of the hour. He affected something Spanish in his air, and something of the bandit, with a flavour of Rembrandt at home. In person he was decidedly small, and inclined to be stout; his face was the picture of good-humour; his dark eyes, which were very expressive, told of a kind heart, a brisk, merry nature, and the most indefatigable spirits. If he had worn the clothes of the period you would have set him down for a hitherto undiscovered hybrid between the barber, the innkeeper, and the affable dispensing chemist. But in the outrageous bravery of velvet jacket and flapped hat, with trousers that were more accurately described as fleshings, a white handkerchief cavalierly knotted at his neck, a shock of Olympian curls upon his brow, and his feet shod through all weathers in the slenderest of Molière shoes—you had but to look at him and you knew you were in the presence of a Great Creature. When he wore an overcoat he scorned to pass the sleeves; a single button held it round his shoulders; it was tossed backwards after the manner of a cloak, and carried with the gait and presence of an Almaviva. I am of opinion that M. Berthelini was nearing forty. But he had a boy's heart, gloried in his finery, and walked through life like a child in a perpetual dramatic performance. If he were not Almaviva after all, it was not for lack of making believe. And he enjoyed the

artist's compensation. If he were not really Almaviva,
he was sometimes just as happy as though he were.

I have seen him, at moments when he has fancied
himself alone with his Maker, adopt so gay and chivalrous
a bearing, and represent his own part with so much
warmth and conscience, that the illusion became catching,
and I believed implicitly in the Great Creature's pose.

But, alas! life cannot be entirely conducted on these
principles; man cannot live by Almavivery alone; and
the Great Creature, having failed upon several theatres,
was obliged to step down every evening from his heights,
and sing from half a dozen to a dozen comic songs, twang
a guitar, keep a country audience in good humour, and
preside finally over the mysteries of a tombola.

Madame Berthelini, who was art and part with him
in these undignified labours, had perhaps a higher position in the scale of beings, and enjoyed a natural dignity
of her own. But her heart was not any more rightly
placed, for that would have been impossible; and she
had acquired a little air of melancholy, attractive enough
in its way, but not good to see like the wholesome, sky-
scraping, boyish spirits of her lord.

He, indeed, swam like a kite on a fair wind, high
above earthly troubles. Detonations of temper were
not unfrequent in the zones he travelled; but sulky fogs
and tearful depressions were there alike unknown. A
well-delivered blow upon a table, or a noble attitude,
imitated from Mélingue or Frédéric, relieved his irrita-
tion like a vengeance. Though the heaven had fallen,
if he had played his part with propriety, Berthelini had
been content! And the man's atmosphere, if not his
example, reacted on his wife; for the couple doated on
each other, and although you would have thought they
walked in different worlds, yet continued to walk hand
in hand.

It chanced one day that Monsieur and Madame

Berthelini descended with two boxes and a guitar in a fat case at the station of the little town of Castel-le-Gâchis, and the omnibus carried them with their effects to the Hotel of the Black Head. This was a dismal, conventual building in a narrow street, capable of standing siege when once the gates were shut, and smelling strangely in the interior of straw and chocolate and old feminine apparel. Berthelini paused upon the threshold with a painful premonition. In some former state, it seemed to him, he had visited a hostelry that smelt not otherwise, and been ill received.

The landlord, a tragic person in a large felt hat, rose from a business-table under the key-rack, and came forward, removing his hat with both hands as he did so.

"Sir, I salute you. May I inquire what is your charge for artists?" inquired Berthelini, with a courtesy at once splendid and insinuating.

"For artists?" said the landlord. His countenance fell and the smile of welcome disappeared. "Oh, artists!" he added brutally; "four francs a day." And he turned his back upon these inconsiderable customers.

A commercial traveller is received, he also, upon a reduction—yet is he welcome, yet can he command the fatted calf; but an artist, had he the manners of an Almaviva, were he dressed like Solomon in all his glory, is received like a dog and served like a timid lady travelling alone.

Accustomed as he was to the rubs of his profession, Berthelini was unpleasantly affected by the landlord's manner.

"Elvira," said he to his wife, "mark my words: Castel-le-Gâchis is a tragic folly."

"Wait till we see what we take," replied Elvira.

"We shall take nothing," replied Berthelini; "we shall feed upon insults. I have an eye, Elvira; I have a spirit of divination; and this place is accursed. The landlord has been discourteous, the Commissary will be brutal, the audience will be sordid and uproarious, and you will take a cold upon your throat. We have been besotted enough to come ; the die is cast—it will be a second Sedan."

Sedan was a town hateful to the Berthelinis, not only from patriotism (for they were French, and answered after the flesh to the somewhat homely name of Duval), but because it had been the scene of their most sad reverses. In that place they had lain three weeks in pawn for their hotel bill, and had it not been for a surprising stroke of fortune they might have been lying there in pawn until this day. To mention the name of Sedan was for the Berthelinis to dip the brush in earthquake and eclipse. Count Almaviva slouched his hat with a gesture expressive of despair, and even Elvira felt as if ill-fortune had been personally evoked.

" Let us ask for breakfast," said she, with a woman's tact.

The Commissary of Police of Castel-le-Gâchis was a large red Commissary, pimpled, and subject to a strong cutaneous transpiration. I have repeated the name of his office because he was so very much more a Commissary than a man. The spirit of his dignity had entered into him. He carried his corporation as if it were something official. Whenever he insulted a common citizen it seemed to him as if he were adroitly flattering the Government by a side-wind ; in default of dignity he was brutal from an overweening sense of duty. His office was a den, whence passers-by could hear rude accents laying down, not the law, but the good pleasure of the Commissary.

Six several times in the course of the day did M. Berthelini hurry thither in quest of the requisite permission for his evening's entertainment ; six several times he found the official was abroad. Léon Berthelini began to grow quite a familiar figure in the streets of Castel-le-Gâchis; he became a local celebrity, and was pointed out as "the man who was looking for the Commissary." Idle children attached themselves to his footsteps, and trotted after him back and forward between the hotel and the office. Léon might try as he liked; he might roll cigarettes, he might straddle, he might cock his hat at a dozen different jaunty inclinations—the part of Almaviva was, under the circumstances, difficult to play.

As he passed the market-place upon the seventh excursion the Commissary was pointed out to him, where he stood, with his waistcoat unbuttoned and his hands behind his back, to superintend the sale and measurement of butter. Berthelini threaded his way through the market-stalls and baskets, and accosted the dignitary with a bow which was a triumph of the histrionic art.

"I have the honour," he asked, "of meeting M. le Commissaire?"

The Commissary was affected by the nobility of his address. He excelled Léon in the depth if not in the airy grace of his salutation.

"The honour," said he, "is mine!"

"I am," continued the strolling player, "I am, sir, an artist, and I have permitted myself to interrupt you on an affair of business. To-night I give a trifling musical entertainment at the Café of the Triumphs of the Plough—permit me to offer you this little programme—and I have come to ask you for the necessary authorisation."

At the word "artist," the Commissary had replaced his hat with the air of a person who, having condescended too far, should suddenly remember the duties of his rank.

"Go, go," said he, "I am busy; I am measuring butter."

"Heathen Jew!" thought Léon. "Permit me, sir," he resumed, aloud. "I have gone six times already——"

"Put up your bills if you choose," interrupted the Commissary. "In an hour or so I will examine your papers at the office. But now go ; I am busy."

"Measuring butter !" thought Berthelini. "O France, and it is for this that we made '93 !"

The preparations were soon made ; the bills posted, programmes laid on the dinner-table of every hotel in the town, and a stage erected at one end of the Café of the Triumphs of the Plough ; but when Léon returned to the office, the Commissary was once more abroad.

"He is like Madame Benoîton," thought Léon : "Fichu Commissaire !"

And just then he met the man face to face.

"Here, sir," said he, "are my papers. Will you be pleased to verify ?"

But the Commissary was now intent upon dinner.

"No use," he replied, "no use ; I am busy ; I am quite satisfied. Give your entertainment."

And he hurried on.

"Fichu Commissaire !" thought Léon.

CHAPTER II

THE audience was pretty large ; and the proprietor of the café made a good thing of it in beer. But the Berthelinis exerted themselves in vain.

Léon was radiant in velveteen ; he had a rakish way of smoking a cigarette between his songs that was worth money in itself ; he underlined his comic points so that the dullest numskull in Castel-le-Gâchis had a notion when to laugh ; and he handled his guitar in a manner worthy of himself. Indeed, his play with that instrument was as good as a whole romantic drama ; it was so dashing, so florid, and so cavalier.

Elvira, on the other hand, sang her patriotic and

romantic songs with more than usual expression ; her
voice had charm and plangency ; and as Léon looked
at her, in her low-bodied maroon dress, with her arms
bare to the shoulder, and a red flower set provocatively
in her corset, he repeated to himself for the many
hundredth time that she was one of the loveliest
creatures in the world of women.

Alas ! when she went round with the tambourine, the
golden youth of Castel-le-Gâchis turned from her coldly.
Here and there a single halfpenny was forthcoming ;
the net result of a collection never exceeded half a franc ;
and the Maire himself, after seven different applications,
had contributed exactly twopence. A certain chill
began to settle upon the artists themselves ; it seemed
as if they were singing to slugs ; Apollo himself might
have lost heart with such an audience. The Berthelinis
struggled against the impression ; they put their back
into their work, they sang louder and louder, the guitar
twanged like a living thing ; and at last Léon arose in
his might, and burst with inimitable conviction into his
great song, "Y a des honnêtes gens partout ! " Never
had he given more proof of his artistic mastery ; it
was his intimate, indefeasible conviction that Castel-le-
Gâchis formed an exception to the law he was now
lyrically proclaiming, and was peopled exclusively by
thieves and bullies ; and yet, as I say, he flung it down
like a challenge, he trolled it forth like an article of
faith ; and his face so beamed the while that you would
have thought he must make converts of the benches.

He was at the top of his register, with his head
thrown back and his mouth open, when the door was
thrown violently open, and a pair of new-comers marched
noisily into the café. It was the Commissary, followed
by the Garde Champêtre.

The undaunted Berthelini still continued to proclaim,
"Y a des honnêtes gens partout ! " But now the

4—U

sentiment produced an audible titter among the audience. Berthelini wondered why ; he did not know the ante-cedents of the Garde Champêtre ; he had never heard of a little story about postage-stamps. But the public knew all about the postage-stamps and enjoyed the coincidence hugely.

The Commissary planted himself upon a vacant chair with somewhat the air of Cromwell visiting the Rump, and spoke in occasional whispers to the Garde Champêtre, who remained respectfully standing at his back. The eyes of both were directed upon Berthelini, who per-sisted in his statement.

" Y a des honnêtes gens partout," he was just chanting for the twentieth time ; when up got the Commissary upon his feet and waved brutally to the singer with his cane.

" Is it me you want ? " inquired Léon, stopping in his song.

" It is you," replied the potentate.

" Fichu Commissaire ! " thought Léon, and he de-scended from the stage and made his way to the func-tionary.

" How does it happen, sir," said the Commissary, swelling in person, " that I find you mountebanking in a public café without my permission ? "

" Without ? " cried the indignant Léon. " Permit me to remind you——"

"Come, come, sir ! " said the Commissary, " I desire no explanations."

" I care nothing about what you desire," returned the singer. " I choose to give them, and I will not be gagged. I am an artist, sir, a distinction that you can-not comprehend. I received your permission and stand here upon the strength of it ; interfere with me who dare."

" You have not got my signature, I tell you," cried the Commissary. " Show me my signature ! Where is my signature ? "

That was just the question; where was his signature? Léon recognised that he was in a hole; but his spirit rose with the occasion, and he blustered nobly, tossing back his curls. The Commissary played up to him in the character of tyrant; and as the one leaned farther forward, the other leaned farther back — majesty confronting fury. The audience had transferred their attention to this new performance, and listened with that silent gravity common to all Frenchmen in the neighbourhood of the Police. Elvira had sat down, she was used to these distractions, and it was rather melancholy than fear that now oppressed her.

"Another word," cried the Commissary, "and I arrest you."

"Arrest me?" shouted Léon. "I defy you!"

"I am the Commissary of Police," said the official.

Léon commanded his feelings, and replied, with great delicacy of innuendo—

"So it would appear."

The point was too refined for Castel-le-Gâchis; it did not raise a smile; and as for the Commissary, he simply bade the singer follow him to his office, and directed his proud footsteps towards the door. There was nothing for it but to obey. Léon did so with a proper pantomime of indifference, but it was a leek to eat, and there was no denying it.

The Maire had slipped out and was already waiting at the Commissary's door. Now the Maire, in France, is the refuge of the oppressed. He stands between his people and the boisterous rigours of the Police. He can sometimes understand what is said to him; he is not always puffed up beyond measure by his dignity. 'Tis a thing worth the knowledge of travellers. When all seems over, and a man has made up his mind to injustice, he has still, like the heroes of romance, a little bugle at his belt whereon to blow; and the Maire, a

comfortable *deus ex machinâ,* may still descend to
deliver him from the minions of the law. The Maire
of Castel-le-Gâchis, although inaccessible to the charms
of music as retailed by the Berthelinis, had no hesitation
whatever as to the rights of the matter. He instantly
fell foul of the Commissary in very high terms, and
the Commissary, pricked by this humiliation, accepted
battle on the point of fact. The argument lasted some
little while with varying success, until at length victory
inclined so plainly to the Commissary's side that the
Maire was fain to re-assert himself by an exercise of
authority. He had been out-argued, but he was still
the Maire. And so, turning from his interlocutor, he
briefly but kindly recommended Léon to get back
instanter to his concert.

"It is already growing late," he added.

Léon did not wait to be told twice. He returned to
the Café of the Triumphs of the Plough with all expedition. Alas! the audience had melted away during his
absence ; Elvira was sitting in a very disconsolate attitude
on the guitar-box ; she had watched the company dispersing by twos and threes, and the prolonged spectacle
had somewhat overwhelmed her spirits. Each man, she
reflected, retired with a certain proportion of her earn-
ings in his pocket, and she saw to-night's board and
to-morrow's railway expenses, and finally even to-
morrow's dinner, walk one after another out of the
café-door and disappear into the night.

"What was it ?" she asked languidly.

But Léon did not answer. He was looking round
him on the scene of defeat. Scarce a score of listeners
remained, and these of the least promising sort. The
minute-hand of the clock was already climbing upward
towards eleven.

"It's a lost battle," said he, and then taking up the
money-box, he turned it out. "Three francs seventy-five!"

he cried, "as against four of board and six of railway fares ; and no time for the tombola ! Elvira, this is Waterloo !" And he sat down and passed both hands desperately among his curls. "O fichu Commissaire !" he cried, "fichu Commissaire !"

"Let us get the things together and be off," returned Elvira. "We might try another song, but there is not six halfpence in the room."

"Six halfpence ?" cried Léon, "six hundred thousand devils ! There is not a human creature in the town — nothing but pigs and dogs and commissaries ! Pray heaven we get safe to bed."

"Don't imagine things!" exclaimed Elvira, with a shudder.

And with that they set to work on their preparations. The tobacco-jar, the cigarette-holder, the three papers of shirt-studs, which were to have been the prizes of the tombola had the tombola come off, were made into a bundle with the music ; the guitar was stowed into the fat guitar-case ; and Elvira having thrown a thin shawl about her neck and shoulders, the pair issued from the café and set off for the Black Head.

As they crossed the market-place the church bell rang out eleven. It was a dark, mild night, and there was no one in the streets.

"It is all very fine," said Léon : "but I have a presentiment. The night is not yet done."

CHAPTER III

THE Black Head presented not a single chink of light upon the street, and the carriage gate was closed.

"This is unprecedented," observed Léon. "An inn closed by five minutes after eleven ! And there were several commercial travellers in the café up to a late

hour. Elvira, my heart misgives me. Let us ring the
bell."

The bell had a potent note ; and being swung under
the arch it filled the house from top to bottom with
surly, clanging reverberations. The sound accentuated
the conventual appearance of the building ; a wintry
sentiment, a thought of prayer and mortification, took
hold upon Elvira's mind ; and, as for Léon, he seemed to
be reading the stage directions for a lugubrious fifth act.

"This is your fault," said Elvira ; "this is what
comes of fancying things !"

Again Léon pulled the bell-rope ; again the solemn
tocsin awoke the echoes of the inn ; and ere they had
died away, a light glimmered in the carriage entrance,
and a powerful voice was heard upraised and tremulous
with wrath.

"What's all this ?" cried the tragic host through the
spars of the gate. "Hard upon twelve, and you come
clamouring like Prussians at the door of a respectable
hotel ? Oh !" he cried, "I know you now ! Common
singers ! People in trouble with the Police ! And you
present yourselves at midnight like lords and ladies ?
Be off with you !"

"You will permit me to remind you," replied Léon,
in thrilling tones, "that I am a guest in your house,
that I am properly inscribed, and that I have deposited
baggage to the value of four hundred francs."

"You cannot get in at this hour," returned the man.
"This is no thieves' tavern, for mohocks and night-rakes
and organ-grinders."

"Brute !" cried Elvira, for the organ-grinders touched
her home.

"Then I demand my baggage," said Léon, with un-
abated dignity.

"I know nothing of your baggage," replied the
landlord.

"You detain my baggage? You dare to detain my baggage?" cried the singer.

"Who are you?" returned the landlord. "It is dark—I cannot recognise you."

"Very well, then—you detain my baggage," concluded Léon. "You shall smart for this. I will weary out your life with persecutions; I will drag you from court to court; if there is justice to be had in France, it shall be rendered between you and me. And I will make you a by-word—I will put you in a song—a scurrilous song—an indecent song—a popular song—which the boys shall sing to you in the street, and come and howl through these spars at midnight!"

He had gone on raising his voice at every phrase, for all the while the landlord was very placidly retiring; and now, when the last glimmer of light had vanished from the arch, and the last footstep died away in the interior, Léon turned to his wife with a heroic countenance.

"Elvira," said he, "I have now a duty in life. I shall destroy that man as Eugène Sue destroyed the concierge. Let us come at once to the Gendarmerie and begin our vengeance."

He picked up the guitar-case, which had been propped against the wall, and they set forth through the silent and ill-lighted town with burning hearts.

The Gendarmerie was concealed beside the telegraph-office at the bottom of a vast court, which was partly laid out in gardens; and here all the shepherds of the public lay locked in grateful sleep. It took a deal of knocking to waken one; and he, when he came at last to the door, could find no other remark but that "it was none of his business." Léon reasoned with him, threatened him, besought him; "here," he said, "was Madame Berthelini in evening dress—a delicate woman—in an interesting condition"—the last was thrown in, I fancy, for effect; and to all this the man-at-arms made the same answer—

"It is none of my business," said he.

"Very well," said Léon, "then we shall go to the Commissary." Thither they went; the office was closed and dark; but the house was close by, and Léon was soon swinging the bell like a madman. The Commissary's wife appeared at a window. She was a thread-paper creature, and informed them that the Commissary had not yet come home.

"Is he at the Maire's?" demanded Léon.

She thought that was not unlikely.

"Where is the Maire's house?" he asked.

And she gave him some rather vague information on that point.

"Stay you here, Elvira," said Léon, "lest I should miss him by the way. If, when I return, I find you here no longer, I shall follow at once to the Black Head."

And he set out to find the Maire's. It took him some ten minutes' wandering among blind lanes, and when he arrived it was already half an hour past midnight. A long white garden wall overhung by some thick chestnuts, a door with a letter-box, and an iron bell-pull—that was all that could be seen of the Maire's domicile. Léon took the bell-pull in both hands, and danced furiously upon the side-walk. The bell itself was just upon the other side of the wall; it responded to his activity, and scattered an alarming clangour far and wide into the night.

A window was thrown open in a house across the street, and a voice inquired the cause of this untimely uproar.

"I wish the Maire," said Léon.

"He has been in bed this hour," returned the voice.

"He must get up again," retorted Léon, and he was for tackling the bell-pull once more.

"You will never make him hear," responded the voice. "The garden is of great extent, the house is at the farther end, and both the Maire and his house-keeper are deaf."

"Aha!" said Léon, pausing. "The Maire is deaf, is he? That explains." And he thought of the evening's concert with a momentary feeling of relief. "Ah!" he continued, "and so the Maire is deaf, and the garden vast, and the house at the far end?"

"And you might ring all night," added the voice, "and be none the better for it. You would only keep me awake."

"Thank you, neighbour," replied the singer. "You shall sleep."

And he made off again at his best pace for the Commissary's. Elvira was still walking to and fro before the door.

"He has not come?" asked Léon.

"Not he," she replied.

"Good," returned Léon. "I am sure our man's inside. Let me see the guitar-case. I shall lay this siege in form, Elvira; I am angry; I am indignant: I am truculently inclined; but I thank my Maker I have still a sense of fun. The unjust judge shall be importuned in a serenade, Elvira. Set him up—and set him up."

He had the case opened by this time, struck a few chords, and fell into an attitude which was irresistibly Spanish.

"Now," he continued, "feel your voice. Are you ready? Follow me!"

The guitar twanged, and the two voices upraised, in harmony and with a startling loudness, the chorus of a song of old Béranger's :—

"Commissaire! Commissaire!
Colin bat sa ménagère."

The stones of Castel-le-Gâchis thrilled at this audacious innovation. Hitherto had the night been sacred to repose and night-caps; and now what was this? Window after window was opened; matches scratched, and candles began to flicker; swollen, sleepy faces peered forth into the star-light. There were the two figures before the Commissary's house, each bolt upright, with head thrown back and eyes interrogating the starry heavens; the guitar wailed, shouted, and reverberated like half an orchestra; and the voices, with a crisp and spirited delivery, hurled the appropriate burden at the Commissary's window. All the echoes repeated the functionary's name. It was more like an entr'acte in a farce of Molière's than a passage of real life in Castel-le-Gâchis.

The Commissary, if he was not the first, was not the last of the neighbours to yield to the influence of music, and furiously threw open the window of his bedroom. He was beside himself with rage. He leaned far over the window-sill, raving and gesticulating; the tassel of his white night-cap danced like a thing of life: he opened his mouth to dimensions hitherto unprecedented, and yet his voice, instead of escaping from it in a roar, came forth shrill and choked and tottering. A little more serenading, and it was clear he would be better acquainted with the apoplexy.

I scorn to reproduce his language; he touched upon too many serious topics by the way for a quiet story-teller. Although he was known for a man who was prompt with his tongue, and had a power of strong expression at command, he excelled himself so remarkably this night that one maiden lady, who had got out of bed like the rest to hear the serenade, was obliged to shut her window at the second clause. Even what she had heard disquieted her conscience; and next day she said she scarcely reckoned as a maiden lady any longer.

Léon tried to explain his predicament, but he received nothing but threats of arrest by way of answer.

"If I come down to you!" cried the Commissary.

"Ay," said Léon, "do!"

"I will not!" cried the Commissary.

"You dare not!" answered Léon.

At that the Commissary closed his window.

"All is over," said the singer. "The serenade was perhaps ill-judged. These boors have no sense of humour."

"Let us get away from here," said Elvira, with a shiver. "All these people looking—it is so rude and so brutal." And then giving way once more to passion— "Brutes!" she cried aloud to the candle-lit spectators— "brutes! brutes! brutes!"

"Sauve qui peut," said Léon. "You have done it now!"

And taking the guitar in one hand and the case in the other, he led the way with something too precipitate to be merely called precipitation from the scene of this absurd adventure.

CHAPTER IV

To the west of Castel-le-Gâchis four rows of venerable lime-trees formed, in this starry night, a twilit avenue with two side aisles of pitch darkness. Here and there stone benches were disposed between the trunks. There was not a breath of wind ; a heavy atmosphere of perfume hung about the alleys ; and every leaf stood stockstill upon its twig. Hither, after vainly knocking at an inn or two, the Berthelinis came at length to pass the night. After an amiable contention, Léon insisted on giving his coat to Elvira, and they sat down together on the first bench in silence. Léon made a cigarette, which he smoked to an end, looking up into the trees, and beyond them at the constellations, of which he tried vainly to recall the names. The silence was broken by the church bell; it rang the four quarters on a light and tinkling measure; then followed a single deep stroke that died slowly away with a thrill; and stillness resumed its empire.

"One," said Léon. "Four hours till daylight. It is warm; it is starry; I have matches and tobacco. Do not let us exaggerate, Elvira—the experience is positively charming. I feel a glow within me; I am born again. This is the poetry of life. Think of Cooper's novels, my dear."

"Léon," she said fiercely, "how can you talk such wicked, infamous nonsense? To pass all night out of doors—it is like a nightmare! We shall die!"

"You suffer yourself to be led away," he replied soothingly. "It is not unpleasant here; only you brood. Come, now, let us repeat a scene. Shall we try Alceste and Célimène? No? Or a passage from the *Two Orphans*? Come, now, it will occupy your mind; I will play up to you as I never have played before; I feel art moving in my bones."

"Hold your tongue," she cried, "or you will drive me mad! Will nothing solemnise you—not even this hideous situation?"

"Oh, hideous!" objected Léon. "Hideous is not the word. Why, where would you be? '*Dites, la jeune belle, où voulez-vous aller?*'" he carolled. "Well, now," he went on, opening the guitar-case, "there's another idea for you—sing. Sing '*Dites, la jeune belle*'! It will compose your spirits, Elvira, I am sure."

And without waiting an answer he began to strum the symphony. The first chords awoke a young man who was lying asleep upon a neighbouring bench.

"Hullo!" cried the young man, "who are you?"

"Under which king, Bezonian?" declaimed the artist. "Speak or die!"

Or if it was not exactly that, it was something to much the same purpose from a French tragedy.

The young man drew near in the twilight. He was a tall, powerful, gentlemanly fellow, with a somewhat puffy face, dressed in a grey tweed suit, with a deer-stalker hat of the same material; and as he now came forward he carried a knapsack slung upon one arm.

"Are you camping out here too?" he asked, with a strong English accent. "I'm not sorry for company."

Léon explained their misadventure; and the other told them that he was a Cambridge undergraduate on a walking tour, that he had run short of money, could no longer pay for his night's lodging, had already been camping out for two nights, and feared he should require to continue the same manœuvre for at least two nights more.

"Luckily, it's jolly weather," he concluded.

"You hear that, Elvira," said Léon.—"Madame Berthelini," he went on, "is ridiculously affected by this trifling occurrence. For my part, I find it romantic and far from uncomfortable; or at least," he added, shifting on the stone bench, "not quite so uncomfortable as might have been expected. But pray be seated."

"Yes," returned the undergraduate, sitting down, "it's rather nice than otherwise when once you're used to it; only it's devilish difficult to get washed. I like the fresh air and these stars and things."

"Aha!" said Léon, "Monsieur is an artist."

"An artist?" returned the other, with a blank stare. "Not if I know it!"

"Pardon me," said the actor. "What you said this moment about the orbs of heaven——"

"Oh, nonsense!" cried the Englishman. "A fellow may admire the stars and be anything he likes."

"You have an artist's nature, however, Mr.—— I beg your pardon; may I, without indiscretion, inquire your name?" asked Léon.

"My name is Stubbs," replied the Englishman.

"I thank you," returned Léon. "Mine is Berthelini —Léon Berthelini, ex-artist of the theatres of Montrouge, Belleville, and Montmartre. Humble as you see me, I have created with applause more than one important *rôle*. The Press were unanimous in praise of my Howling Devil of the Mountains, in the piece of the same name. Madame, whom I now present to you, is herself an artist, and I must not omit to state, a better artist than her husband. She also is a creator; she created nearly twenty successful songs at one of the principal Parisian music-halls. But to continue: I was saying you had an artist's nature, Monsieur Stubbs, and you must permit me to be a judge in such a question. I trust you will not falsify your instincts; let me beseech you to follow the career of an artist."

"Thank you," returned Stubbs, with a chuckle. "I'm going to be a banker."

"No," said Léon, "do not say so. Not that. A man with such a nature as yours should not derogate so far. What are a few privations here and there, so long as you are working for a high and noble goal?"

"This fellow's mad," thought Stubbs: "but the woman's rather pretty, and he's not bad fun himself, if you come to that." What he said was different: "I thought you said you were an actor?"

"I certainly did so," replied Léon. "I am one, or, alas! I was."

"And so you want me to be an actor, do you?" continued the undergraduate. "Why, man, I could never so much as learn the stuff; my memory's like a sieve; and as for acting, I've no more idea than a cat."

"The stage is not the only course," said Léon. "Be a sculptor, be a dancer, be a poet or a novelist; follow your heart, in short, and do some thorough work before you die."

"And do you call all these things art?" inquired Stubbs.

"Why, certainly!" returned Léon. "Are they not all branches?"

"Oh! I didn't know," replied the Englishman. "I thought an artist meant a fellow who painted."

The singer stared at him in some surprise.

"It is the difference of language," he said at last. "This Tower of Babel, when shall we have paid for it? If I could speak English you would follow me more readily."

"Between you and me, I don't believe I should," replied the other. "You seem to have thought a devil of a lot about this business. For my part, I admire the stars, and like to have them shining—it's so cheery —but hang me if I had an idea it had anything to do with art! It's not in my line, you see. I'm not intellectual ; I have no end of trouble to scrape through my exams., I can tell you ! But I'm not a bad sort at bottom," he added, seeing his interlocutor looked distressed even in the dim star-shine, "and I rather like the play, and music, and guitars, and things."

Léon had a perception that the understanding was incomplete. He changed the subject.

"And so you travel on foot?" he continued. "How romantic ! How courageous ! And how are you pleased with my land ? How does the scenery affect you among these wild hills of ours ?"

"Well, the fact is," began Stubbs—he was about to say that he didn't care for scenery, which was not at all true, being, on the contrary, only an athletic under- graduate pretension ; but he had begun to suspect that Berthelini liked a different sort of meat, and substituted something else: "The fact is, I think it jolly. They told me it was no good up here ; even the guide-book said so ; but I don't know what they meant. I think it is deuced pretty—upon my word, I do."

At this moment, in the most unexpected manner, Elvira burst into tears.

"My voice!" she cried. "Léon, if I stay here longer I shall lose my voice!"

"You shall not stay another moment," cried the actor. "If I have to beat in a door, if I have to burn the town, I shall find you shelter."

With that, he replaced the guitar, and, comforting her with some caresses, drew her arm through his.

"Monsieur Stubbs," said he, taking off his hat, "the reception I offer you is rather problematical; but let me beseech you to give us the pleasure of your society. You are a little embarrassed for the moment; you must, indeed, permit me to advance what may be necessary. I ask it as a favour; we must not part so soon after having met so strangely."

"Oh, come, you know," said Stubbs, "I can't let a fellow like you——" And there he paused, feeling somehow or other on a wrong tack.

"I do not wish to employ menaces," continued Léon, with a smile; "but if you refuse, indeed I shall not take it kindly."

"I don't quite see my way out of it," thought the undergraduate; and then, after a pause, he said, aloud and ungraciously enough, "All right. I—I'm very much obliged, of course." And he proceeded to follow them, thinking in his heart, "But it's bad form, all the same, to force an obligation on a fellow."

CHAPTER V

LÉON strode ahead as if he knew exactly where he was going; the sobs of Madame were still faintly audible, and no one uttered a word. A dog barked furiously in a courtyard as they went by ; then the church clock struck two, and many domestic clocks followed or preceded it in piping tones. And just then Berthelini spied a light. It burned in a small house on the outskirts of the town, and thither the party now directed their steps.

"It is always a chance," said Léon.

The house in question stood back from the street behind an open space, part garden, part turnip-field ; and several outhouses stood forward from either wing at right angles to the front. One of these had recently undergone some change. An enormous window, looking towards the north, had been effected in the wall and roof, and Léon began to hope it was a studio.

"If it's only a painter," he said, with a chuckle, "ten to one we get as good a welcome as we want."

"I thought painters were principally poor," said Stubbs.

"Ah !" cried Léon, "you do not know the world as I do. The poorer the better for us ! "

And the trio advanced into the turnip-field.

The light was in the ground floor ; as one window was brightly illuminated and two others more faintly, it might be supposed that there was a single lamp in one corner of a large apartment ; and a certain tremulousness and temporary dwindling showed that a live fire contributed to the effect. The sound of a voice now became audible ; and the trespassers paused to listen. It was pitched in a high, angry key, but had still a good, full, and masculine note in it. The utterance was voluble, too voluble even to be quite distinct ; a stream of words, rising and falling, with ever and again a phrase thrown out by itself, as if the speaker reckoned on its virtue.

Suddenly another voice joined in. This time it was a woman's ; and if the man were angry, the woman

4—v

was incensed to the degree of fury. There was that
absolutely blank composure known to suffering males ;
that colourless unnatural speech which shows a spirit
accurately balanced between homicide and hysterics ;
the tone in which the best of women sometimes utter
words worse than death to those most dear to them.
If Abstract Bones-and-Sepulchre were to be endowed
with the gift of speech, thus, and not otherwise, would
it discourse. Léon was a brave man, and I fear he
was somewhat sceptically given (he had been educated
in a Papistical country), but the habit of childhood
prevailed, and he crossed himself devoutly. He had
met several women in his career. It was obvious that
his instinct had not deceived him, for the male voice
broke forth instantly in a towering passion.

The undergraduate, who had not understood the
significance of the woman's contribution, pricked up his
ears at the change upon the man.

"There's going to be a free fight," he opined.

There was another retort from the woman, still
calm, but a little higher.

"Hysterics ?" asked Léon of his wife. "Is that the
stage direction ?"

"How should I know ?" returned Elvira, somewhat
tartly.

"Oh, woman, woman !" said Léon, beginning to open
the guitar-case. "It is one of the burdens of my life,
Monsieur Stubbs ; they support each other ; they always
pretend there is no system ; they say it's nature. Even
Madame Berthelini, who is a dramatic artist ! "

"You are heartless, Léon," said Elvira ; "that woman
is in trouble."

"And the man, my angel ?" inquired Berthelini,
passing the ribbon of his guitar. "And the man,
m'amour ? "

"He is a man," she answered.

"You hear that?" said Léon to Stubbs. "It is not too late for you. Mark the intonation. And now," he continued, "what are we to give them?"

"Are you going to sing?" asked Stubbs.

"I am a troubadour," replied Léon. "I claim a welcome by and for my art. If I were a banker, could I do as much?"

"Well, you wouldn't need, you know," answered the undergraduate.

"Egad," said Léon, "but that's true. Elvira, that is true."

"Of course it is," she replied. "Did you not know it?"

"My dear," answered Léon impressively, "I know nothing but what is agreeable. Even my knowledge of life is a work of art superiorly composed. But what are we to give them? It should be something appropriate."

Visions of "Let dogs delight" passed through the undergraduate's mind; but it occurred to him that the poetry was English and that he did not know the air. Hence he contributed no suggestion.

"Something about our houselessness," said Elvira.

"I have it," cried Léon. And he broke forth into a song of Pierre Dupont's :—

> " Savez-vous où gîte
> Mai, ce joli mois ? "

Elvira joined in; so did Stubbs, with a good ear and voice, but an imperfect acquaintance with the music. Léon and the guitar were equal to the situation. The actor dispensed his throat-notes with prodigality and enthusiasm; and, as he looked up to heaven in his heroic way, tossing the black ringlets, it seemed to him that the very stars contributed a dumb applause to his efforts, and the universe lent him its silence for a chorus. That is one of the best features of the heavenly bodies, that they belong to everybody in particular; and a man like Léon, a chronic Endymion who managed to get along without encouragement, is always the world's centre for himself.

He alone—and it is to be noted, he was the worst singer of the three—took the music seriously to heart, and judged the serenade from a high artistic point of view. Elvira, on the other hand, was preoccupied about their reception; and as for Stubbs, he considered the whole affair in the light of a broad joke.

"Know you the lair of May, the lovely month?" went the three voices in the turnip-field.

The inhabitants were plainly fluttered; the light moved to and fro, strengthening in one window, paling in another; and then the door was thrown open, and a man in a blouse appeared on the threshold carrying a lamp. He was a powerful young fellow, with bewildered hair and beard, wearing his neck open; his blouse was stained with oil-colours in a harlequinesque disorder; and there was something rural in the droop and bagginess of his belted trousers.

From immediately behind him, and indeed over his shoulder, a woman's face looked out into the darkness; it was pale and a little weary, although still young; it wore a dwindling, disappearing prettiness, soon to be quite gone, and the expression was both gentle and sour, and reminded one faintly of the taste of certain drugs. For all that, it was not a face to dislike; when the prettiness had vanished, it seemed as if a certain pale beauty might step in to take its place; and as both the mildness and the asperity were characters of youth, it might be hoped that, with years, both would merge into a constant, brave, and not unkindly temper.

"What is all this?" cried the man.

CHAPTER VI

LÉON had his hat in his hand at once. He came forward with his customary grace ; it was a moment which would have earned him a round of cheering on the stage. Elvira and Stubbs advanced behind him, like a couple of Admetus's sheep following the god Apollo.

"Sir," said Léon, "the hour is unpardonably late, and our little serenade has the air of an impertinence. Believe me, sir, it is an appeal. Monsieur is an artist, I perceive. We are here three artists benighted and without shelter, one a woman—a delicate woman—in evening dress—in an interesting situation. This will not fail to touch the woman's heart of Madame, whom I perceive indistinctly behind Monsieur her husband, and whose face speaks eloquently of a well-regulated mind. Ah ! Monsieur, Madame—one generous movement, and you make three people happy ! Two or three hours beside your fire—I ask it of Monsieur in the name of Art—I ask it of Madame by the sanctity of womanhood."

The two, as by a tacit consent, drew back from the door.

"Come in," said the man.

"*Entrez*, Madame," said the woman.

The door opened directly upon the kitchen of the house, which was to all appearance the only sitting-room. The furniture was both plain and scanty ; but there were one or two landscapes on the wall, handsomely framed, as if they had already visited the committee-rooms of an exhibition and been thence extruded. Léon walked up to the pictures and represented the part of a connoisseur before each in turn, with his usual dramatic insight and force. The master of the house, as if irresistibly attracted, followed him from canvas to canvas with the lamp. Elvira was led directly to the fire, where she proceeded to warm herself, while Stubbs stood in

the middle of the floor and followed the proceedings of
Léon with mild astonishment in his eyes.

" You should see them by daylight," said the artist.

" I promise myself that pleasure," said Léon. " You
possess, sir, if you will permit me an observation, the
art of composition to a T."

" You are very good," returned the other. " But
should you not draw nearer to the fire ? "

" With all my heart," said Léon.

And the whole party was soon gathered at the table
over a hasty and not an elegant cold supper, washed
down with the least of small wines. Nobody liked the
meal, but nobody complained ; they put a good face
upon it, one and all, and made a great clattering of
knives and forks. To see Léon eating a single cold
sausage was to see a triumph ; by the time he had done
he had got through as much pantomime as would have
sufficed for a baron of beef, and he had the relaxed
expression of the over-eaten.

As Elvira had naturally taken a place by the side
of Léon, and Stubbs as naturally, although I believe
unconsciously, by the side of Elvira, the host and hostess were left together. Yet it was to be noted that
they never addressed a word to each other, nor so much
as suffered their eyes to meet. The interrupted skir-
mish still survived in ill-feeling ; and the instant the
guests departed it would break forth again as bitterly
as ever. The talk wandered from this to that subject
—for with one accord the party had declared it was
too late to go to bed ; but those two never relaxed
towards each other ; Goneril and Regan in a sisterly
tiff were not more bent on enmity.

It chanced that Elvira was so much tired by all the
little excitements of the night, that for once she laid
aside her company manners, which were both easy and
correct, and in the most natural manner in the world

leaned her head on Léon's shoulder. At the same time, fatigue suggesting tenderness, she locked the fingers of her right hand into those of her husband's left; and, half-closing her eyes, dozed off into a golden borderland between sleep and waking. But all the time she was not unaware of what was passing, and saw the painter's wife studying her with looks between contempt and envy.

It occurred to Léon that his constitution demanded the use of some tobacco; and he undid his fingers from Elvira's in order to roll a cigarette. It was gently done, and he took care that his indulgence should in no other way disturb his wife's position. But it seemed to catch the eye of the painter's wife with a special significancy. She looked straight before her for an instant, and then, with a swift and stealthy movement, took hold of her husband's hand below the table. Alas! she might have spared herself the dexterity. For the poor fellow was so overcome by this caress that he stopped with his mouth open in the middle of a word, and by the expression of his face plainly declared to all the company that his thoughts had been diverted into softer channels.

If it had not been rather amiable, it would have been absurdly droll. His wife at once withdrew her touch; but it was plain she had to exert some force. Thereupon the young man coloured and looked for a moment beautiful.

Léon and Elvira both observed the by-play, and a shock passed from one to the other; for they were inveterate match-makers, especially between those who were already married.

"I beg your pardon," said Léon suddenly. "I see no use in pretending. Before we came in here we heard sounds indicating—if I may so express myself—an imperfect harmony."

"Sir——" began the man.

But the woman was beforehand.

"It is quite true," she said. "I see no cause to be ashamed. If my husband is mad I shall at least do my utmost to prevent the consequences. Picture to yourself, Monsieur and Madame," she went on, for she passed Stubbs over, "that this wretched person—a dauber, an incompetent, not fit to be a sign-painter—receives this morning an admirable offer from an uncle—an uncle of my own, my mother's brother, and tenderly beloved—of a clerkship with nearly a hundred and fifty pounds a year, and that he—picture to yourself!—he refuses it! Why? For the sake of Art, he says. Look at his art, I say—look at it! Is it fit to be seen? Ask him—is it fit to be sold? And it is for this, Monsieur and Madame, that he condemns me to the most deplorable existence, without luxuries, without comforts, in a vile suburb of a country town. *O non!*" she cried, "*non—je ne me tairai pas—c'est plus fort que moi!* I take these gentlemen and this lady for judges—is this kind? is it decent? is it manly? Do I not deserve better at his hands after having married him and"—(a visible hitch)—"done everything in the world to please him?"

I doubt if there were ever a more embarrassed company at a table; every one looked like a fool; and the husband like the biggest.

"The art of Monsieur, however," said Elvira, breaking the silence, "is not wanting in distinction."

"It has this distinction," said the wife, "that nobody will buy it."

"I should have supposed a clerkship——" began Stubbs.

"Art is Art," swept in Léon. "I salute Art. It is the beautiful, the divine; it is the spirit of the world and the pride of life. But——" And the actor paused.

"A clerkship——" began Stubbs.

"I'll tell you what it is," said the painter. "I am

an artist, and as this gentleman says, Art is this and the other; but of course, if my wife is going to make my life a piece of perdition all day long, I prefer to go and drown myself out of hand."

"Go!" said his wife. "I should like to see you!"

"I was going to say," resumed Stubbs, "that a fellow may be a clerk and paint almost as much as he likes. I know a fellow in a bank who makes capital water-colour sketches; he even sold one for seven-and-six."

To both the women this seemed a plank of safety; each hopefully interrogated the countenance of her lord; even Elvira, an artist herself!—but indeed there must be something permanently mercantile in the female nature. The two men exchanged a glance; it was tragic; not otherwise might two philosophers salute, as at the end of a laborious life each recognised that he was still a mystery to his disciples.

Léon arose.

"Art is Art," he repeated sadly. "It is not water-colour sketches, nor practising on a piano. It is a life to be lived."

"And in the meantime people starve!" observed the woman of the house. "If that's a life, it is not one for me."

"I'll tell you what," burst forth Léon; "you, Madame, go into another room and talk it over with my wife; and I'll stay here and talk it over with your husband. It may come to nothing, but let's try."

"I am very willing," replied the young woman; and she proceeded to light a candle. "This way, if you please." And she led Elvira upstairs into a bedroom. "The fact is," said she, sitting down, "that my husband cannot paint."

"No more can mine act," replied Elvira.

"I should have thought he could," returned the other; "he seems clever."

"He is so, and the best of men besides," said Elvira; "but he cannot act."

"At least he is not a sheer humbug like mine; he can at least sing."

"You mistake Léon," returned his wife warmly. "He does not even pretend to sing; he has too fine a taste; he does so for a living. And, believe me, neither of the men are humbugs. They are people with a mission—which they cannot carry out."

"Humbug or not," replied the other, "you came very near passing the night in the fields; and, for my part, I live in terror of starvation. I should think it was a man's mission to think twice about his wife. But it appears not. Nothing is their mission but to play the fool. Oh!" she broke out, "is it not something dreary to think of that man of mine? If he could only do it, who would care? But no—not he —no more than I can!"

"Have you any children?" asked Elvira.

"No; but then I may."

"Children change so much," said Elvira, with a sigh.

And just then from the room below there flew up a sudden snapping chord on the guitar; one followed after another; then the voice of Léon joined in; and there was an air being played and sung that stopped the speech of the two women. The wife of the painter stood like a person transfixed; Elvira, looking into her eyes, could see all manner of beautiful memories and kind thoughts that were passing in and out of her soul with every note; it was a piece of her youth that went before her; a green French plain, the smell of apple-flowers, the far and shining ringlets of a river, and the words and presence of love.

"Léon has hit the nail," thought Elvira to herself. "I wonder how."

The how was plain enough. Léon had asked the painter if there were no air connected with courtship and pleasant times; and having learned what he wished, and allowed an interval to pass, he had soared forth into

> "O mon amante,
> O mon désir,
> Sachons cueillir
> L'heure charmante!"

"Pardon me, Madame," said the painter's wife, "your husband sings admirably well."

"He sings that with some feeling," replied Elvira critically, although she was a little moved herself, for the song cut both ways in the upper chamber; "but it is as an actor and not as a musician."

"Life is very sad," said the other; "it so wastes away under one's fingers."

"I have not found it so," replied Elvira. "I think the good parts of it last and grow greater every day."

"Frankly, how would you advise me?"

"Frankly, I would let my husband do what he wished. He is obviously a very loving painter; you have not yet tried him as a clerk. And you know—if it were only as the possible father of your children—it is as well to keep him at his best."

"He is an excellent fellow," said the wife.

They kept it up till sunrise with music and all manner of good-fellowship; and at sunrise, while the sky was still temperate and clear, they separated on the threshold with a thousand excellent wishes for each other's welfare. Castel-le-Gâchis was beginning to send up its smoke against the golden east; and the church bell was ringing six.

"My guitar is a familiar spirit," said Léon, as he and Elvira took the nearest way towards the inn; "it resuscitated a Commissary, created an English tourist, and reconciled a man and wife."

Stubbs, on his part, went off into the morning with reflections of his own.

"They are all mad," thought he, "all mad—but wonderfully decent."